CAN
YOU
SEE
HER?

BOOKS BY S.E. LYNES

Mother
The Pact
The Proposal
Valentina
The Women
The Lies We Hide

CAN YOU SEE HER?

S. E. LYNES

bookouture

Published by Bookouture in 2020

An imprint of Storyfire Ltd.
Carmelite House
50 Victoria Embankment
London EC4Y 0DZ

www.bookouture.com

ISBN: 978-1-83888-622-6
eBook ISBN: 978-1-83888-621-9

This book is a work of fiction. Names, characters, businesses,
organizations, places and events other than those clearly in the
public domain, are either the product of the author's imagination
or are used fictitiously. Any resemblance to actual persons, living or
dead, events or locales is entirely coincidental.

To my children, Alistair, Maddie and Franci, love from Mum xxx

She had the oddest sense of being herself invisible; unseen; unknown; there being no more marrying, no more having of children now, but only this astonishing and rather solemn progress with the rest of them, up Bond Street, this being Mrs Dalloway; not even Clarissa anymore; this being Mrs Richard Dalloway.

Virginia Woolf, *Mrs Dalloway*

CHAPTER 1

Rachel

'There are things I don't know. But I know people are dead, I know I killed them and I know it all started the day I realised I was invisible.'

'Mrs Edwards.' Her chair creaks. She must have shifted position. 'Do you think you could take us back to that? To realising you were invisible?'

'I can.'

Of course I can. Like most people, if my *Mastermind* specialist subject was myself, I'd win hands down. I look about me, try to settle. They've done their best to make this room look like an ordinary lounge in an ordinary house – impressionist landscape in a frame on the wall, me on a sofa, her in the armchair opposite. Neutral shades. But there's a recording device on the coffee table next to the box of tissues and the jug and two glasses of water, so I'm not fooled.

'When you're ready,' she says. 'Take your time.'

Her eyes are blue. The colour of sea on white sand. I want to run in but I'm not sure I won't drown in the cold water. I've forgotten her name. I know she's telling me to take my time so I'll give them what they want, but I'm here to give them what they want. It was me that made the call after all.

I glance up from fists clenched around a screwed-up tissue on my lap. 'No one wants to be invisible, do they?'

Blue Eyes doesn't answer. I obviously didn't say that out loud. So much is unclear. Words spoken, words thought. What we hear, what we pick up by instinct. How we achieve affinity with another human being.

'It was a Saturday night,' I say. 'I know that because it was our Katie's party. We usually get a takeaway on Saturdays. Chinese, normally…'

I tell her how I got home from work that day: sore-eyed, heavy-boned, dog tired; how I put the plates and dishes from the side of the sink into the dishwasher, switched it on and put a cloth round. How I emptied the washing machine and put the clothes over the drying rack. There's precious little chance of Mark spotting a load waiting to be hung out. Frankly, if he ever needed to find a saucepan, which is unlikely, you'd have to draw him a map.

'We had quarter crispy duck.' I look up at Blue Eyes, but only for a second. 'Sweet and sour pork, Szechuan king prawn, egg-fried rice and a bag of prawn crackers. We have the same every other week. Mark usually goes for it in the car. We didn't have crispy beef that week because Katie wasn't eating, what with it being her party.'

Blue Eyes jots something down. Maybe I've put her in the mood for chicken chow mein. Why these thoughts come to me at inappropriate moments, I don't know. Stress, I should imagine.

She looks up, tips her head back a bit. She has what I'd call natural authority. Regal, if you know what I mean. She did tell me her name, she did, but no, it's gone. 'Can you tell me when this was, Mrs Edwards?' That hushed, patient voice you hear them use in police dramas. She scans the report on her knee but I've got nothing to hide anymore. I've already told it all to the other two, in the other room. The ones in uniform.

'This is going back to June,' I say.

'That's Saturday the twenty-second?' She glances up from my statement and suddenly I'm not as sure as I was.

'Or was it the week before?' I say. 'Hang on, no. Sorry. Let me just… It was the week before… before the girl… Jo. Joanna. I know that because… Hang on, sorry. Sorry, just let me…'

The trickle of water. I look up. Blue Eyes is holding out a glass. 'Here.'

'Thank you.' I take the glass and drink. The water is cool in my throat.

'So, your daughter had a party?'

'Yes. We'd been banished from the kitchen, so we ate on trays while we watched a film.'

'And then?'

'And then the ad break came on.'

'And?'

'And Mark said, do you fancy a coffee? Which means, can you make us a cup of coffee? Twenty-seven years into a marriage, you get used to what your other half means when he says something, and it must be a year since Mark's made me a coffee. Or a tea, for that matter. So anyway, I said I'd make it and he said, you sure? And I said, course. The dance we do, like, you know.'

I raise my eyebrows at Blue Eyes, but her face stays the same: neutral, like the colours in this room. Warm beige with a hint of encouragement. Again, I'm not sure what I've said and what I haven't, what she can hear, what she's picking up by instinct or police training. Over sixty per cent of communication is non-verbal. I read that in… oh, somewhere or other.

'So, you made a cup of coffee for yourself and Mark, your husband?'

'Sorry, yes.'

I carry on. Carry on regardless, carry on camping, carry on up the Khyber. How Katie had asked if she could have a do and I'd said no more than ten because our house is small. I said I'd chip in for the booze – I'd already given her a cheque towards her holiday in Ibiza so I thought that was fair enough. We used to get the neighbours over for barbecues all the time, and our mates from the pub, and Lisa and Patrick, of course, before they split up. We used to put ice in this big plastic frog bucket we had for camping trips and put all the beers in there with a bottle opener tied to the handle with string. Funny the little details that come back to you, but my heart's not in anything like that anymore. And anyway, when I was growing up, you had your eighteenth and that was that. Katie's eighteenth cost me a month's wages. She wanted to hire out the cricket club off Moughland Lane so she could invite the best part of a hundred mates. She's very sociable, is Katie. Anyway, it was a good do; Kieron DJ'd for it. He played all the old tunes and every single one of us danced the night away, so I'm not saying I regret it. It's probably the last time I can remember feeling properly happy, although that could have been Kieron making me do a Jägerbomb. But even now I know Katie'll be angling for another big bash for her twenty-first, because they all do now and if you don't give them something decent, you're a tight-arse.

Blue Eyes is making a note. I have no idea how much of that lot made it out of my mouth.

'Mrs Edwards.' A warm but businesslike smile from dark red lips. 'If we could get to the moment you say started things… the moment you say you became invisible?'

Sounds like she's prompting me. Mark says I drift off topic or off altogether. Get on with it, woman, he's started saying lately, and I'll realise I'm either rattling on about something or I've stopped halfway through a sentence. He'll be there going, what? And I'll have literally no idea what I was talking about. Sorry, I'll say. It's gone. And he'll shake his head like I'm beyond hope. Which I am. I don't suppose he'll be shaking his head at me anymore. Not now.

'Sorry,' I say to Blue Eyes. 'I was in the hallway, wasn't I?'

I can picture it as if it were last week, so I don't forget *everything*, apparently: I can see Katie and her mates through the finger-smudged glass panel of our kitchen door. The music is throbbing against the walls. Clouds of cigarette smoke. There are about twenty kids in there, not ten as we agreed, but it's too late to make a fuss now, so I just stand there like a robot with dead batteries, one hand on the door handle. They're laughing and shrieking the way young people do. The French doors are open to the back garden.

Next thing, I'm panting away, both hands pushed to my knees. I'm burning hot. I feel sick, really sick. I get them, these... attacks, I suppose you'd call them. Raging heat and jitters that flush in from nowhere. I've been getting them more and more, along with the where-the-heck-am-I moments, what Lisa calls my fugues. One minute I'm all right; next thing I'm not sure if I can go through with even the smallest thing, in this instance, opening my own kitchen door. My chest is tight. I take deep breaths, in through the nose, out through the mouth like they tell you to, then reach for the door handle again and pull myself upright. With the hem of my T-shirt I wipe the sweat off my face. A few more seconds and the attack passes, dragging bits of me with it like the tide pulling loose pebbles from the shoreline.

Meanwhile, oblivious, the kids are looking beautiful by accident the way young people do, and there's me in my jogging bottoms and slippers having a sweaty little breakdown. I watch them, try to take them in without them becoming aware of me. I'm an intruder, an intruder in my own home. I don't want to go barging in there. I'm worried I'll break the spell. I don't want to make them all self-conscious. I don't want to ruin their fun.

But Mark is waiting for his coffee, so I suck in one last deep breath and open the door.

'So you went in?' Blue Eyes' head tips forward; her eyebrows shoot up. You're doing well, she says, without speaking. Keep going.

The interview room is hot. I take off my cardie and drink half a glass of water. Once I settle again on the sofa, it takes me a second to get back there, to my kitchen full of smoke, to the rushing roar of twenty-odd teenagers all talking at once. The bass thumps in my chest and the smell nearly floors me: sweet weed and fresh sweat, sticky drinks and the hair gels and body sprays young people favour. Fashion's on a loop, isn't it? Today's skinny jeans are just yesterday's drainpipes, Kopparberg is what we used to call cider and black, and often they're listening to the same tunes we did, except for them it's retro. Never thought I'd hear Luther Vandross again, let alone Bon Jovi. Kids think they're the first to discover everything, don't they? First to get drunk, first to be felt up in the dark, first to get their teenage kicks right through the night. They think they invented all of it.

In the corner, a semicircle of girls, faces blue in the light of a smartphone. Judging by their sly expressions, they're gossiping about whoever it is they're looking at. They wear so much make-up now. These slug eyebrows that are all the rage – what's that about? – and not one of them has her belly covered up. I suppose it's for their Instagrams and their Facebooks. They have to be supermodels now as well as everything else. When I was a kid, as long as you scrubbed up OK, you were all right. Quick squirt of Sun-In on the flick, strawberry lip gloss from Woolies and off you went. By the time I got to Katie's age, Doc Martens were in, so we could walk miles no bother. These kids know what they look like from every possible angle; we had about four tatty photos of ourselves in a drawer. You went to school on foot – that was exercise. No one went to a gym, no one.

'Mrs Edwards? Mrs Edwards?' Blue Eyes throws out her hands and fixes me with an earnest expression. 'You went into the kitchen…' *Get on with it, woman.*

'Sorry, yes. Yes, so I kept my head down like a soldier dodging bullets and made for the kettle…'

I wasn't allowed to talk to anyone, Katie had made that *very* clear. She'd still not forgiven me for saying 'the Antarctic Monkeys' in front of the boyf. I wouldn't mind – I'd got the right band, just the wrong pole, that's all, but Katie can get in a nark about absolutely anything, more so lately. Anyway, as I was waiting for the water to boil, a girl I recognised as an old school friend of Katie's slotted herself between her boyfriend's spread legs, and while he swigged from a bottle of cheap vodka, she turned her head and stared at me. I was about to wave and mouth hello, but she pulled the vodka out of his hand, closed her eyes and tipped the bottle to her lips.

And I realised she hadn't been staring at me; she'd been staring *through* me.

Blue Eyes leans forward. Against her pale skin, her ruby mouth twitches at the corners.

I hear you, Blue Eyes. I'm picking up your impatience even though you didn't say anything. but we'll get on to that later.

'I made the coffee,' I say. 'We always have decaf of an evening, though I don't suppose that's relevant anymore, and of course I suppose I wouldn't be allowed near a kettle now.' A quick glance at her tells me I'm not wrong… What we hear in words, what we pick up…

'I walked back down the hall into the living room and I… I sat down on the sofa.' My chest inflates, deflates. My eyes sting. 'I sat down on the sofa. On the television, a man dived out of shot against a backdrop of flames. That was the hero. The baddie was in the fire, finally got his comeuppance. Revenge equals a world put to rights, according to Hollywood, and then they lecture us on raising our kids not to be violent.'

'Mrs Edwards…'

'Sorry, yes, so I put our coffee cups on the table, on top of my *Prima* magazine so they wouldn't stain, and I said, "Coffee," and he might have grunted but he didn't look up.'

I make myself meet her eyes. Take a dive into that blue. She's hanging on my every word, as if what I have to say is important. She's looking at me, really looking at me. She reaches forward, tops up my glass of water and hands it to me. There is such kindness in the gesture that my own eyes fill.

I take a sip, wait for my breathing to slow down a bit.

'I think that's when it hit me,' I tell her after a moment or two, my voice so quiet I can barely hear it. 'That's what I'm trying to explain. All this, the terrible things I've done, why I'm here, started there. You see, I'd been worried about disturbing my daughter and her friends. I'd listened at the door like I do outside Katie's room sometimes, chin pressed to an armful of laundry... I'd crept into the kitchen. That's where I'd got to in life. Creeping about in my own house, cringing at my own footsteps like a maid from *Downton Abbey* or something. It was my house and there I was, scared of disturbing them.

'But the thing is, the thing I need you to understand, is that I *didn't* disturb them. The kids, I mean. They weren't rude to me. They didn't stop and stare. They didn't stop at all. They didn't ignore me either, because they'd have had to make a conscious effort of will to do that, wouldn't they? I hadn't spoiled their fun or made them self-conscious, no. The music carried on playing and they carried on kissing and fighting and gossiping and flirting and smoking and drinking and posing and preening the way of kids everywhere. They hadn't been embarrassed or inhibited by my presence. Not at all.

'The truth was, I'd had no effect on them whatsoever. They hadn't noticed me come in or go out. I had no presence. They hadn't *seen* me. And when I got back with the coffees, Mark didn't nod or say thanks or take any notice of me. He hadn't seen me either.

'I was invisible. I no longer existed. Like I'd vanished from my own life.'

CHAPTER 2

Rachel

It's all been a bit overwhelming. I expected to still have the hand-cuffs on but they took them off at some point, before they brought me here. Actually, I'm wearing fresh clothes. They're mine but I can't think when I... Hang on, no, I think I slept here. I did, of course I did. Did I bring an overnight bag, or what? No, of course not. They led me out of the house in handcuffs. Not like I could have said, hang on a minute while I grab my toothbrush, is it? They must have brought me these clothes at some point, brought me here. My jeans are too big for me now; they fall down when I walk. But that's not important. She seems happy to let me waffle on. I know she's thinking she'll get more out of me if she lets me take the road less travelled. It might take longer but there'll be less traffic, less risk of a standstill. We'll always be moving forward.

Blue Eyes coughs into her hand. 'Mrs Edwards—'

'Rachel. Call me Rachel. Can't be doing with Mrs, and to be honest, Edwards is Mark's name, isn't it? I was Ryder originally. Rachel Clarissa Ryder. Think my mother had delusions of grandeur, bless her.'

'All right. Rachel.' She smooths her hand across my notes, as if to flatten them, and presses her lips together. Same shade of lippy as yesterday – must be her favourite. 'You realised you were invisible. That came as a big shock, which is understandable. Then what happened?'

'Blood everywhere, that's what happened.'

'Blood?' The eyes widen, sparkle like crystals.

'First nosebleed in thirty years or more. Used to get them when I was a teenager in moments of stress. I can remember apologising to Mark as I dashed in front of the telly on my way out. Needn't have worried, when you think about it. He should have been able to see right through me.'

I meet her eyes again but my smile dies on my lips. She's right to look at me like that. There's nothing to joke about. And why I said sorry to Mark for having a nosebleed, I can't fathom, but as I keep saying, this is where I'd got to in life – apologising for myself while doing everyone else's bidding. It's no wonder I was invisible. I'd done that to myself. I didn't realise it then, obviously. But I do now. I'd done it to myself.

'So, you left the room?' The eyes flicker with… is that frustration? Was I talking out loud or have I been sitting here catching flies?

Actually, there's a fly in the room. I can't see it but I can hear it buzzing and tapping against the window pane. It's fallen quiet now. Must have given up. What did Blue Eyes say her name was? Angela. Andrea. Alison. Something that starts with an A.

I try and think what I last told her. I'd run out with my nose bleeding, hadn't I? Yes, yes, I had. I carry on from there, tell her how I sat on the edge of the bath and held a tissue to my nose. So far, so normal. I held up my hands one at a time and turned them over and over to check that I could see them – not so normal. They were definitely there, my hands. I was there too, in the bathroom mirror: straggly grey hair badly in need of a cut and colour, glasses in need of a clean, flab pooling over my elastic waistband and a face full of bloody tissues. I was shaking. I looked knackered, as in literally fit for the knacker's yard. Gaze off-focus, like an NHS poster for the devastating effects of… oh, something bad.

All of that, yes – but not invisible, surely? *I* could see me. I *existed*. I blew onto the palm of my hand. My breath was hot, which meant I was alive. Another trickle ran from my nose. I thought it had started bleeding again, but it hadn't – it was running clear. As were my eyes.

'At least I was in the bathroom,' I say to Blue Eyes, tears running in the then and the now. 'Plenty of loo roll and I wasn't bothering anyone.'

She passes me a tissue from the box on the table. 'It sounds like you were very sad.'

Her kindness is confusing under the circumstances.

'I'm sorry,' I say. 'I've not cried in front of another person in a very long time.'

That night, Mark switched the bedside lamp off, muttered good-night and rolled away from me as per. I lay there blinking, making stars. Can't remember what I was thinking about. Composing a shopping list, probably. A list of some sort, anyway. Actually, no, I was thinking about how Mark and me first got together. How he walked me home from the community centre disco one night because Lisa had gone home with another lad. We'd stopped at the end of my mum and dad's driveway, unable to say goodnight, and just stood there in the dark, talking and talking about our dreams, life, God, the universe and all that stuff you talk about when you're in those fragile years between youth and adulthood and you're figuring everything out: who you are, what you want, what you don't. Even though we'd known each other as kids, that night it was as if I saw him for the first time. It was the first time I realised that a proper conversation that runs true and deep is one of the most intimate things there is. We carried on talking like that through our first date, when I bought a can of Bass shandy from the Spar and we sat on a bench and ate Hula Hoops and it seemed like our conversation would never end. By the time there was anything physical between us, I thought I was going to pass out with excitement. It was just a kiss, that first time, his hand resting softly on my waist. And just like a conversation, when a kiss is deep and true, it can change the course of your whole life.

I must have dropped off eventually, because I woke at quarter to five, which you could attribute to stress but actually it wasn't unusual. I'd been waking up with the covers thrown off for a year or two, limbs like gravestones, legs and cleavage sticky-salty with dried sweat. But it wasn't the sweats that had woken me; it was a nightmare, which came back to me as I hauled my heavy bones out of the sour sheets.

I'm running down the high street. It's daytime. In front of the Co-op, five or six turquoise buses rattle in the depot. Shoppers crowd the pavement. And here comes me, naked, completely naked, running, trying to hold my hands over my bits while my stomach wobbles like raw bread in a gale. That's when I realise to my sweating horror that I know everyone, absolutely everyone.

But no one is taking any notice…

I can't catch my breath. Heat flares up in my chest and my forehead pricks with sweat. 'Sorry,' I say. 'Just let me…'

Blue Eyes is holding out my glass of water. 'It's OK, Rachel. Don't rush. Would you like a cup of tea? Should I open a window?'

I shake my head. The glass smells of dust but the water's wet and it soothes me. With my tissue I dab at my forehead, focus on breathing myself cooler.

'Sorry,' I say.

'It's OK. No need to apologise. Tell me what happened after that.'

'I went downstairs,' I say after a minute or two. 'I made a cup of tea and ran my usual checks on the iPad.'

A glance at her notes. 'Checks?'

'For violent crime. Regional and national news. I do that every day. Well, I did. I started it last year. I was building up evidence to take to my MP. I mean, it's an epidemic, isn't it, this knife crime? Who'd be a parent of young adults now? I tell you, it's terrifying.'

That has her scribbling with that lovely silver fountain pen of hers. Her nails are short and painted dark grey. I suppose I didn't mention my clip file in my statement. But they didn't ask. They'll have found it by now, I expect. That and the knife. And that poor lad's clothes would still have been in the washing machine.

My eyes fill. She hasn't replied, and for the umpteenth time I've no idea whether I said that last bit out loud or what. She's still writing me up, anyway. Writing me up before they lock me up. They've brought in the big guns with this one: Blue Eyes, big boss, top dog. Her hair is short. Trendy, you'd say. I thought it was white, but it's more of a pale lilac. Rainbow colours glint in it from time to time, like petrol caught in the sun. What must she make of me? I wonder.

She looks up, the merest twitch of the lips. 'Carry on.'

I tell her how the sun was coming up when I went downstairs that morning. How ghostly my reflection looked in the buttery windows. How the teaspoon clinked loudly against the side of the mug when I stirred in the sugar.

Armed robbery leaves two dead in Stockton Heath.

I skim-read. Both gunshot wounds, another seriously injured in Liverpool General.

House fire in Warrington. Suspected arson.

Suspected arson… but no casualties. Kids, I thought. Arson about. It's an old joke, one of my dad's, when he was compos mentis enough to make jokes.

I printed off the armed robbery, slid it into a plastic sleeve and clipped it into the file. The nationals had a stabbing. Croydon. Young lad, as per. Intensive care. The usual links: *Reform school exclusions to tackle knife crime*; *One in four teenage girls involved in violent crime*; *Hold schools accountable for expelled students, MPs urge*; *Third man arrested over double murder at Warrington house party.*

The Warrington house party had been the week before. I wondered if the Croydon lad would make it through the night.

The first twenty-four hours are crucial. I printed that off too and put it with the others.

'The clip file.' Blue Eyes' fore- and middle fingers make an L around her mouth, her thumb a chinrest. 'This is the same file you showed to your neighbour, Ingrid Taylor?'

'Ingrid? Why, did she say she'd seen it? I never showed anyone.'

The police must have spoken to Ingrid. I wonder what everyone's been saying about me. Who else the police have spoken to. Ingrid must have looked in the file when I went to the loo or something. I wouldn't have thought she'd be interested in anything to do with me, to be honest. She was so stressed about her own life. I felt sorry for her. I thought it was her with the problems. Turns out it was me.

Blue Eyes must think I'm getting agitated, because she asks if I want to take a break. I don't. I'm just getting started.

'Let's leave the file for now,' she says. 'Tell me about the morning after—'

'Invisiblegate?' One glance tells me she thinks I'm being flippant, which I'm not. 'Right you are,' I add. And I press on.

Once I'd done my clippings, then said a few words and observed a minute's silence for the victims, I cleaned up the kitchen after Katie's do. It was mostly bottles and cans to recycle, crushed crisps to hoover up, then a good mop. Someone had put their fag out in the plant pot and there was a smashed glass on the patio, but that was about it for damage. It only took an hour or two so, and by eight o'clock I was showered and dressed. But on precious little shut-eye, I was still jittery. Katie's mate kept staring right through me in my mind's eye. A pain had lodged itself in my chest. The panicky feeling wasn't as bad as it had been the night before, but I did catch myself staring at my reflection in the bathroom mirror, literally foaming at the mouth. I spat into the sink, splashed off the excess toothpaste and faced myself head on. Leaning in close,

I bloodshot-eyeballed myself, wondered how I'd got to be this woman no one saw.

'Who the hell are you?' I said. 'Who are you, Rachel Clarissa Edwards?'

I used to be Rachel Ryder, fittest girl in fifth year. It was my name scrawled on the lads' toilet walls, me that got to go out with Nick… Nick… oh, what was his second name? No, it's gone… Anyway, he was the best-looking lad in our school. God, he was boring. I used to panic whenever he started talking to me. Turned out to be gay in the end, but we were none the wiser back then, although the eyeliner should have been a clue. Suffice to say, when I was young, I'd walk into a room and heads would turn. I expected it. I dressed for it. I wanted it. Quite when I'd stopped expecting it or dressing for it or wanting it, I don't know. Now I could walk into a room and no one would even see me.

Bedford. Nick Bedford, that's it.

Anyway, somehow the years had worn it all away. Worn me away. I'd been so busy raising a family, working, looking after my mum at the end, getting my dad settled into the home up in Halton. I'd been looking one way and now I'd looked back and there I was: someone who used to be Rachel Ryder, a woman whose husband once told her she was out of his league, the same woman who now washed his pants and made his dinner, and he didn't even know she was there, let alone say thank you. Hadn't done recently, anyway.

I thought a long walk might help. I stuck Archie on the lead and headed down Boston Avenue to the town hall gardens.

'The town hall?' Blue Eyes glances at the statement, as well she might.

'Where they found two of the victims, yes. But it's also where Mark and me got married, back in the Jurassic age, when we were young and I was pretty and confident and he was funny and kind.'

When our friends said he was punching above his weight. No one would say that now, obviously. He still has a good head of hair, albeit silver, whereas I've let myself go – I hold my hands up to that. But I want you to know that I was trying so hard to get myself back, the old me, honestly I was, before all this happened.

'Why did you go to the town hall specifically?'

She's not daft. Hardly going to let that drift by, is she?

'I'd been going there a lot this last year,' I say, 'to the bench by the pond, even before the… attacks. I suppose it'll be taped off now, won't it, until they've gathered the forensics, if that's what they're called, or is that only America? I'm guessing they've taken the body to the morgue by now.'

Her mouth flattens. The slightest inclination of her head. 'So you walked there.'

'That was my first long walk. You might say it was the start of… everything. It was definitely when I started looking for someone who could see me, even though I don't think I knew that was what I was doing at first.'

Angela who might be Andrea or Alison is scribbling away. I look down before she looks up.

I walked and walked that morning. There were only about half a dozen people out and about. None of them looked in my direction. If they did, their eyes didn't register me, their mouths didn't curl into any kind of smile. And yes, I did wonder at that point if any of them could see me or whether all they saw was the dog walking on a floating lead like a cheap special effect from some low-budget film.

'So you went to the crime scene.' Blue Eyes taps her pen against the palm of her hand. 'Although it wasn't a crime scene as yet.'

The fly has started up again, buzzing, headbutting the pane as if sooner or later it'll fly out. I wonder if Blue Eyes can hear it, whether it's bugging her like it's bugging me, but she's as self-possessed as a sphinx.

'It was just my thinking place then,' I say. 'That's all it was. I suppose it'll have that yellow and black tape you see on the news, won't it? Will there be a white outline of a body taped out on the ground?'

Her mouth tightens. Disapproval, that's what I read anyway.

'I expect I'll be on the news, won't I?' I go on, like an idiot. 'One way to get seen, I suppose – *I'm a Celebrity, Don't Let Me Out of Here.*' A laugh escapes me but dies. 'It's where I took the girl as well, obviously. But she was found on the road, wasn't she?'

Blue Eyes gives me something on the smile/indigestion spectrum. She's saying nowt, giving me enough rope. I wish she would; I'd hang myself right away, save anyone else the bother. I take the customary deep breath. Once more unto the breach. What's a breach? No clue. *Get on with it, woman.*

I get on with it. There was a man in the town-hall gardens that morning. He was standing at the top of the rise, behind the kids' park where I used to take Kieron and Katie and push them on the swings. He had an Alsatian on the end of a long lead and he was looking out over the main road. Loneliness came off him. I could almost see it shimmering in the air. His trousers needed a good iron and he looked to be in his mid-fifties, but at the same time he looked older – as if, like a dodgy mechanic, life had added years to his clock. He didn't notice me looking. I wondered if he'd see me if I stood right in front of him. I didn't, obviously, that would've been nuts, but I knew, or felt I knew, instinctively, that he'd suffered. Lost someone – his wife, possibly. Don't ask me how. He seemed sort of... trapped in himself, unsure of how to get out. Something about the way he looked across to the houses beyond the railings, as if something might appear for him. Someone. He was yearning... just... yearning.

I grab two tissues from the box and wipe my eyes. 'I just had this overwhelming urge to ask if he was all right.'

'And did you?'

'I didn't. I mean, you don't, do you? We don't ask people we don't know if they're OK, do we? Not as a rule. I just said good morning but I don't think he heard me. He hadn't seen me, that's for sure, so I went and sat on my little bench, where I used to sit while Kieron and Katie fed the ducks. We used to take a picnic there when it was warm enough; they thought it was our secret place, bless them, and their eyes used to pop out of their heads with excitement when they heard the ice-cream van coming up the town-hall drive. An egg-mayonnaise bap, a few breadcrumbs for the ducks and one vanilla cone each, and honestly, you'd have thought I'd given them the world.

'I didn't sit there for long. I was too antsy. In the end, I thought I'd pop and see Lisa.'

'That's Lisa Baxter?'

'Yes. She's my best friend. Well, she was.'

CHAPTER 3

Ingrid

Transcript of recorded interview with Ingrid Taylor (excerpt)

Also present: DI Heather Scott, PC Marilyn Button

IT: I could tell there was something wrong with her the first time I saw her. Her appearance was… I mean, I'm not being mean, but I just thought she'd let herself go like a lot of women that age do. Then when I stepped inside her house that first time, she had this folder thing on the side by the hob, and when I asked her about it she was really quite shifty. She said it was bank statements or something, but she closed it quickly – too quickly, I thought – and put it on the shelf on the dresser, as if she didn't want me to steal her lasagne recipe or something.

HS: And you looked inside it?

IT: Look, I know you shouldn't go snooping in someone else's house, but the way she was acting made me curious. Anyone would be. She went to fetch an ashtray – I mean, I always smoke in the garden but she insisted I could smoke indoors – and when I heard her plod upstairs – she has a very heavy tread – I had a quick glance through, that's all. And I can tell you something: it wasn't recipes.

HS: Ms Taylor, can you tell us what you found?

IT: Well, the cuttings, obviously. All those deaths. Violent crimes. Related articles too – knife crime on the rise, how safe are our streets, campaigns, that sort of stuff.

HS: And what was your reaction?

IT: Shock. It was shocking. I couldn't believe what I was seeing, to be honest. Page after page of it. There must have been over a hundred articles in there – stabbings, shootings, armed robbery, you name it. Mark told me she wanted to organise some sort of campaign, but of course now it all makes perfect sense. I mean, this was before I got to know Mark, and I have to say, I almost ran out of the house screaming. I mean, hello? Talk about psychopathic, my God! *What's your hobby? Oh, I collect violent deaths and keep them under cellophane so they don't spoil.* I mean, who does that? You'd have to be… well, she was, wasn't she? In the guise of a mother figure. I mean, it's straight from Stephen King.

HS: Ms Taylor—

IT: I suppose there'll be more clippings in there now, won't there? Including the… the ones she did herself… Oh God, I don't even want to think about it, but it was the *organisation*, you know? The care. That was almost the most terrifying thing. Each one in its own clear sleeve like it was a precious document. And when I found out about… about what she'd done, I thought, why not keep a folder on the computer? Call it something random like, well, like *Recipes* or *Kids* or something. *Expenses.* Anything. Why keep paper, these days? But I guess you can't settle down on the sofa and leaf through a computer file quite the same, can you, if that's even what she spent her time doing. Who knows? Maybe she liked to flick through them on her days off. Perving over other people's murders while she sipped the rank instant coffee she served. That makes sense, I suppose. I mean, it's sick, isn't it? Morbid. Actually, this is making me stressed. Can I smoke in here?

CHAPTER 4

Rachel

'Bloody hell.' Lisa was still in her dressing gown. 'What's the matter, wet the bed?'

'Very funny. I was up early, that's all, so I thought I may as well walk the dog.'

She backed up, still holding the front door open. 'Come in then, if you're coming.'

I've known Lisa since we were kids – jigsaws and Sindy dolls, primary school, secondary, first boyfriends, first time getting drunk, borrowing each other's clothes, make-up, you name it. Even got pregnant at the same time – my first, her second. Kieron and Jodi. Both her girls are at uni now. Jodi went off to Leeds the year before Kieron to do modern languages and Kieron went to Goldsmiths to do fine art last year after his foundation. I thought Katie would leave home this year with her being so academic, but she said she wanted to do a gap year, which so far seems to mean seventy-two zillion hours alternating between Instagram, YouTube and Netflix. Oh, and getting bladdered with her mates twice a week. I'm not sure she'll ever go to uni now to be honest. What a waste.

Lisa brought us a coffee. It wasn't quite warm enough to sit out, so we went to sit in her conservatory, where Archie had a quick sniff before curling up for a doze. 'So, what's new?'

I dived straight in, told her about how I'd become the invisible woman.

'I was so shocked it gave me a nosebleed,' I said.

I'd expected her to tell me I was mad or to call an ambulance, but she didn't. She was nodding her agreement before I'd even finished.

'I know exactly what you mean,' she said. 'I was in a café the other day and the guy served the woman behind me in the queue. Behind me, can you believe that? He literally looked through me to her as if I was made of glass.'

'What did you do?'

She eyeballed me and raised her forefinger. 'I said, "Oi, ferret face! What am I then, chopped liver?"'

'You never did.' I laughed.

'I didn't, no, but when he took my order, I told him how kind he was to give me a complementary cappuccino, that I appreciated the gesture.'

'He gave you a free coffee?'

'He did then. He was too embarrassed not to.'

'Bloody hell, Lis.' I was full-on laughing by then. Lisa has this way of building her routines until you're helpless on the couch. She shows no mercy; won't stop even if you tell her to – especially if you tell her to.

A determined expression setting in on her face, she put her coffee down on the smallest of her nest of pine side tables.

'I was furious,' she started. 'Costs them ten pence to make a coffee – it's a bloody licence to print money – and I reckon after all I've already been through, with periods and pregnancy and torn lady bits from childbirth and spaniel's ears from breastfeeding and mopping up shit and sick and you name it I've cleaned it, and all the invisible woman-hours spent running a hotel cum counselling service single-handed for non-paying guests, and reduced job prospects and low pay and divorce from a randy dog man-child, if on top of that I'm now going to be having the sweats and the rages and the memory loss and this bloody extra tyre I seem to have acquired that seems to be made entirely from porridge, not to mention the face, oh, the face, the sodding eyebrows on it, disappearing as fast as the bloody beard seems to be growing, do you know, I now have to push down my facial hair with moisturiser every sodding morning, literally smear it down and hope to God it doesn't fluff back up…' She breathed, finally, eyebrows shooting up. 'So I reckon I deserve a free frigging coffee.'

She cracked a smile and we both chuckled.

'I mean,' she added. 'Backlit, I look like Robert Redford.'

I wiped my eyes, feeling better already. Five minutes with Lisa's like a shot in the arm. 'I can't get out of a chair without making a noise these days.'

'Just be thankful you can still get out of a chair. Woman down the road got stuck in the bath last week. She had to call 999. She's only fifty-eight and thank God she'd taken her phone in with her, but talk about embarrassing… Pass me a towel, officer, isn't in it.'

Hysterical. God, I miss her.

Once we'd stopped laughing, she had a good moan about her ex, Patrick, a headmaster, who, in a fit of originality, had left her for a young geography teacher with a pierced belly button called Caz – the woman, not the belly button – before we came back around to where we'd started, i.e. me moaning about Mark.

'He might not look at you like he used to,' Lisa said. 'But at least he's a decent bloke. Unlike Pat*dick*, he's actually there.'

'In body if not in spirit.' I regretted saying that straight away. Yes, you could be lonely in a marriage, but Lisa was lonely full stop and she'd always liked Mark, always had a soft spot for him. And before Patrick left, he made sure he drove in the final nail by telling her he didn't find her attractive anymore and that he only had one life. Talk about kicking her when she was down. It was as if he'd died, she said at the time. Except that he hadn't and she wanted to kill him. And all the jokes in the world couldn't hide the longing in her for someone to grow old with now that her girls were off living their own lives. All she had was the smoke and mirrors of gags and laughter to hide her pain, her fears, the yawning abyss of loneliness.

'Like most of us,' I say, and give Blue Eyes a smile.

She almost smiles back. 'And did you tell Lisa that you'd read or felt you'd read the man in the park? That you'd understood him by instinct?'

'I did, actually.'

'And how did she respond?'

I tell Blue Eyes that, again, Lisa didn't seem at all bothered.

'That's a skill you've been practising your whole life,' was all she said, as if telepathy were the most natural thing in the world.

'How d'you mean?' I said. 'Like mind-reading?'

'Not like Derren Brown, you nit. You're not a bloody Jedi. But we weren't born yesterday, were we? We've got to a stage in life where we can pick up on things, read people if not minds exactly. We don't see everything in black and white like kids do. At our age we know nothing and no one is simple. It comes with being older.'

I thought about the chap's crumpled trousers. When I was young, I would've assumed he was a slob. This morning, I'd had the compassion, I suppose you'd say, to think a bit more deeply about why he hadn't ironed them. Same when I saw an older woman all dolled up like mutton dressed as lamb – before, I would have said to myself, look at the state of her, still thinks she's twenty-one. Now, I know she doesn't think anything of the sort. She knows bloody well she's not twenty-one anymore. And it's killing her.

'Maybe you're right,' I said to Lisa.

'No one gets to our age without living through something that knocks them about a bit.' She met my eye and a flash of understanding passed between us, the one subject we never talked about. 'We lose our certainty about things, don't we? And that's no bad thing sometimes when you look at the state of the world, people thinking they're right all the time, that their way is better.

We've spent most of our lives putting others first, haven't we, you and me and a trillion other women? Meeting other people's needs while pushing our own to the side, forgetting what our own needs ever were sometimes, not to mention who we were when we last had them. A tough habit to break, but it must make us more in tune with what others are feeling. It has to, doesn't it? Stands to reason.'

I nodded. 'I got eighty-five per cent in *Grazia*'s "Are You an Empath?" quiz the other week.'

'There you go. And that's bloody science, is that.' She shot me a wicked grin. 'God knows, if I'd had to discuss my interior life all those years with Patrick instead of you, I'd have thrown myself off the nearest bridge. He'd probably have started talking to me about the football scores. In fact, there's no probably about it. He did. He used to. That or the mortgage.'

She pushed her once brown hair over one ear. She'd made that tricky transition to honey-toned blondey-grey without ever having the old caterpillar roots situation. Only reason I didn't have grey roots was because I hadn't bothered to dye mine at all this last year. My hair was pretty much salt and pepper these days, if you were being kind; geriatric mouse if you weren't, and if I went back to the original black now I'd end up looking like something from *The Addams Family*. Lisa wore trendy clothes too, and even though she'd complained of a spare tyre, I couldn't see one. Silently I vowed to get back on my hip and thigh diet the next day. My diets always start on Mondays. By Wednesday I think I can still turn it around. By Friday I've reached sod it I'll try again next week, pass the chocolate.

'Rach? Rachel?' Lisa was staring at me. 'Are you all right?'

'Yes, why?'

'Just… you were off somewhere else there for a second. Are you sure you're OK?'

'Of course I'm OK – why wouldn't I be OK? I'm just not sure I'm ready to be invisible, that's all.'

'Oh, I don't know.' She leaned forward and tapped me on the knee. 'If no one can see you, you can do anything you want, can't you? You can get away with murder.'

CHAPTER 5

Lisa

Transcript of recorded interview with Lisa Baxter (excerpt)
Also present: DI Heather Scott, PC Marilyn Button

LB: We were just chatting, that was all it was. I thought it was no more than our age, time of life type thing. I didn't realise she was so fragile until later on, and even then I thought it was the hormones, because I was in the same boat – hot flashes, tiredness and feeling cross about everything all the time. But I should have known it was more than that. I mean, I knew it was, obviously.

HS: It was more?

LB: (Pause) She'd been ill before. When her Kieron was born. Mark and I were frantic. In the end we called the hospital and they came and took her, and to be fair, she did get better. Postpartum psychosis she had, so I should have put two and two together, what with it being another hormonal time for a woman. But I'm only putting two and two together now. At the time, I didn't know she had anything to do with those attacks. It never occurred to me. Thing is, Rachel's kind to everyone, and I mean everyone, from the man in the street to her best friend. That's me. I'm her best friend, always have been.

I'd do anything for her, literally anything at all. She was a bloody rock to me when Patrick left. Both my girls call her Auntie Rach. She never forgets their birthdays, never. She even sends them both a Valentine's card every year with *love from guess who?* on it. I mean, they're in their twenties now so I suppose I should break it to them, like... Sorry, I make jokes when I'm nervous. I'm just so up to here with it all. I just wish I'd done more to help her. I kept asking her if she was OK, but she wouldn't let me in. She wouldn't talk to me about it. So in the end I had to respect that. She knew I was worried about her. She knows I love her to bits, like. We didn't need words to know that the other one wasn't right. You don't, do you, when you've known somebody that long?

HS: So you're saying that you had no concerns about Rachel's mental health back in June?

LB: Not then, no. No more than was normal. But as the weeks went on, she withdrew. I should've recognised the signs. But she'd just button up and that'd be it, change the subject, say she had to go. It was like a screen came down, one of them metal shutters like they have on shop doors, you know?

HS: Mrs Baxter, do you remember telling Rachel that she could get away with murder?

LB: What? I mean... I might have said something like that, but I was only joking. Come on, you can't take something like that and turn it into something else. That's twisting my words, that is. She was upset because she felt like Mark didn't notice her anymore. Or her Katie. I knew exactly how she felt – don't we all? I was just trying to cheer her up, that's all. I didn't for one moment suggest that she should go out and start killing people. Come on, that's completely mad. I still can't believe she'd attack anyone, let alone kill them. I mean, that young girl? No way. It's just not Rachel, do you know what I mean? She wouldn't hurt anyone. I can't believe it. I won't believe it. It's just not her. (Breaks down)

CHAPTER 6

Rachel

'Get away with murder.' Blue Eyes' head twitches to one side. 'That's a bold statement.'

I see what she did there. I'm not daft.

'I think it's fair to say it got under my skin,' I admit. 'But I didn't come over all "I Don't Like Mondays" and go on a shooting spree or anything. Things got weirder, yes. *I* got weirder, I mean, but weirdness is like ageing: you don't notice it as much day by day, do you? It creeps up on you and one day you catch your reflection and see your own mother staring back. Or father, in my case, beard and all unfortunately.'

She doesn't laugh, even though I'm trying to lighten the mood. But she's spot on when she suggests the words might have stuck. Most of what Lisa said stuck, to be honest. Why? Because she's my best friend, that's why, and at the time I thought she had only good intentions towards me. But that evening, maybe because I'd had a moan, I noticed more than usual that it was me that made the dinner, me that cleared up, me that put the washing on the rack after folding the dry clothes and sorting them into piles to iron, me that took them upstairs and put them away. I noticed how Mark went straight through to watch telly without saying thank you, how Katie disappeared to her room the moment her knife and fork clattered on china.

'Where are you off to?' I called after her. 'Your plate won't get clean if you put it next to the dishwasher, you know. Cake doesn't bake outside the oven, does it?'

'Oh my God,' she shouted back, already at the foot of the stairs. 'I'm doing my contouring tutorial.' *Bang bang bang* went her feet. 'I told you, like five thousand—' *Slam* went her bedroom door.

Contouring, I thought. Didn't that have to do with maps?

That night, my clothes stood up on their own like the Invisible Man. A kitchen knife floated in the air at the end of a sleeve, the steel blade glinting in the dark. Daggers pierced skin. Blood oozed. Sirens wailed. My own face came in and out of the fog: moonlit and pale and weeping.

In the early hours, I broke from those troubling dreams salt-crusted as a fat white slab of cod. I was shivering, exhausted, sweat running down my cleavage, bottom sheet soaked through. I hadn't sweated like that since I was breastfeeding Kieron, and that too had gone hand in hand with the visions. Except back then they happened in the day as well. I'd be chopping onions for tea and next thing I'd see myself throw the knife at Kieron as he lay sleeping in his Moses basket. It's not something I talk about to anyone. Only Mark and Lisa knew about it at the time, and I don't even talk to them about it anymore. Blue Eyes will have read it in my notes, if she's requested them from my GP, which she's bound to have done. It was Lisa who phoned Mark, Lisa who phoned for an ambulance. The NHS were amazing. The right diagnosis, the right drugs and the right person to talk to, and they got me back on track within the year. I can still remember the doctor, how kind she was when I cried into my hands and told her I was mad, mad, mad.

'I prefer not to call it madness,' she said. 'It's really just love. Love on steroids, if you like. The love we have for our children particularly can be terrifying.'

I'll never forget her saying that. It helped me so much at the time, and I still often think of it and her. Love on steroids. My first baby,

I was overwhelmed by love. Made mad by love for my little boy. I'd thought I loved Mark, and I did, but this! It was the most petrifying thing I'd ever experienced. It was beyond any kind of control. It took some strong meds and a kind psychiatrist to help me understand that my fears were manifesting themselves in frightening fantasies of my own making. The fear of anything bad happening to my baby was so deep in me it became a reality in those moments. My love was a knife sailing through the air. And it was me throwing it.

Downstairs, the pink pre-dawn filtered through the patio doors. I sat with a cup of tea and trawled through the local news sites.

One dead and several injured in knife attack outside McDonald's in Birkenhead.

Young lads, as per. One arrest. The usual statistics. At least they'd charged someone this time. The related links had an article about weapon checks in primary schools after a four-year-old was found carrying a knife. Police seized knuckledusters, swords and a meat cleaver. One child had adapted a fidget spinner with a spike and made it into a weapon.

I made another brew and cleaned the kitchen, put a wash on and made sandwiches for work for Mark and myself before I sent the story and the article to the printer, slid both into plastic sleeves and clipped them into my file. I was saying a few words for the victims, their families and friends when the doorbell went.

On the step, a lanky blonde stood shivering in a silk dressing gown. Seven o'clock in the morning. I was cold just looking at her.

'I'm Ingrid Taylor,' she said, as if she were apologising. 'I've just moved into the flats opposite and in all the upheaval I've mislaid the teabags. I wondered if you'd have a spare one. I'll find them eventually so I can pay you back.'

'You don't have to pay me back for a teabag, love,' I said. 'The Edwards family will still eat.'

Her forehead wrinkled. I smiled to show I was joking, and she opened her mouth in an O of relief.

'Oh my God, thanks. That's really kind of you.'

She struck me as quite posh for round here, from the way she spoke, the out-of-proportion gratitude posh people have when they talk to the hoi polloi and her silk dressing gown – which I didn't dream might be actual silk; she only told me that later. Shoulders hunched, she appeared fragile but glamorous. A bit Blanche DuBois, if you know what I mean. I felt sorry for her in the way normal people do for a certain kind of vulnerable but beautiful woman, do you know what I mean? Men, especially.

Blue Eyes is nodding, but I suspect she's humouring me. 'So, you gave her a teabag?' *Get on with it, woman.*

'I invited her in, actually. She looked like she was about to burst into tears.'

I can picture soppy Ingrid as if it were last week. The silk robe was olive green with flowers embroidered down the front, the ties knotted around an impossibly skinny waist. She was almost leaning backwards, as if waiting for a second invitation.

'Come in then if you're coming,' I said. 'It's chilly out. Kitchen's through the back.'

'Thank you.' In a whiff of perfume I didn't recognise, she scurried through to the kitchen and stood with her fingertips pressed together at her waist, shoulders still round her ears.

'Sit down,' I said. 'Don't stand on ceremony.'

'Thank you. It's kind of you to let me in.' She sat, looked around her as if doing a recce for a film shoot or something. 'You were filing?'

I followed her eyes to my clip file, which I quickly picked up and took over to the dresser. 'Just bank statements. A very exciting household is this.'

She forced a brief laugh.

Before Blue Eyes asks me anything about the file, I tell her that Ingrid was a funny mix. Obviously not a hugger or a smiler. Not a great sense of humour either, apparently.

'So how're you settling into the street?' I asked her once I'd got us some coffee.

'It's early days. I'm still unpacking.' She gave a sad smile, a half nod. She pushed her thumb to her mouth and tore off a strip of thumbnail, picked it out of her mouth and rolled it between her thumb and forefinger. She patted at her robe.

I recognised the gesture, saw the rectangular bulge in her silk pocket.

'I'll fetch an ashtray,' I said.

Neither me nor Mark smokes but Katie's boyfriend and a few of our friends do, or did when we used to have them round, so we do keep an ashtray in the house.

I dashed into the living room. The ashtray wasn't in the usual place on the sideboard, which wasn't unusual, if you know what I mean. I knew where it would be, even though I've told Katie a thousand times that we don't smoke in the house and that her boyfriend is not exempt. I dashed up to her room, pushed open the door, felt it snag against clothes on the floor.

'Mum!' One syllable, into which my daughter managed to muster a world of disdain, before she threw the duvet over her head, an action that muffled but failed to disguise the 'What the fuck?' that followed.

'Good morning to you too, darling.' I grabbed the ashtray – home to some shady-looking butts of the hand-rolled variety, if you know what I mean, and four mugs from her chest of drawers, kicking her pile of dirty clothes out of my way as I left, all the while trying not to breathe in a smell so rank I thought it might stick in scales to the back of my throat. The mugs were half full of a brownish liquid that might once have been coffee, mini flotillas of grey-green discs bobbing on the surface. I love Katie, don't get me wrong, but she's an absolute pig in knickers sometimes.

Ingrid seemed to be taking a tour of the kitchen when I got back. When she saw me, she returned to her chair and lit up, slid the lighter back into the packet and blew out a jet of smoke, obviously no intention of stepping into the garden like our friends do. Still, she could have been sitting on a spike for how uncomfortable she looked. She'd blagged her way into my home but it was as if she no longer wanted to be there. As if she wanted company like a vase with a hole in the bottom wants water: she seemed to want to be filled up, only to let it run out of the bottom. I wondered if her chewed-off piece of thumbnail was in her pocket or whether she'd chucked it on the lino or what.

'So where did you move from?' I asked her once I'd rinsed and dried the ashtray and sat down.

'Helsby way.' She flapped at the smoke. 'It's so hard coming to a new place.' She dropped her hand to her lap, the better to pick at her nails.

'It is,' I said, no clue really, as I've only ever lived here.

'Especially if you don't have kids or a job. I suppose I'm feeling a bit lost.' Her accent sounded like she was from the north-west, like me, but posher. The Wirral, maybe.

'Have you plans to get a job?'

She nodded sadly, as if employment were a personal tragedy. 'I'm afraid I'll have to. The joys of an addict for a husband.' She met my eye. Hers were filmed in tears. 'Ex-husband, I should say.'

'Sorry to hear that.' I didn't want to pry. I didn't want to know, to be honest. Addicts frighten me a bit, and I'm ashamed to say this, but I was shocked as well. To look at her, you'd never have thought. 'So, what kind of work are you looking for?"

She shrugged. 'Maybe a gallery assistant? Or a music tutor. I play the flute. I thought I'd ask at the Brindley – you know, the arts centre on the canal?'

'Yes.' I wondered why she'd think I wouldn't know the arts centre if I'd lived here all my life. Sorry, I mean I knew why and I bet she didn't think I read books either when actually I'm an avid reader. But it was fine; I'm used to people underestimating my intelligence.

We chatted for a bit. I told her I'd not been to uni – financial reasons. That I had two kids, one at uni, one still at home. She told me her ex was a businessman but not which business specifically. Small talk really, until the conversation stalled.

'Maybe I'll open a café,' she said after a moment. 'I'm quite a good cook.'

Maybe you need more than a flute and a flair for quiche, I almost said. Business smarts, for example, and capital, which had presumably disappeared up her ex-husband's nose, but who was I to say? She was a bit dolly-daydream, I thought. A bit dippy in the way you can afford to be when you've never had to work.

'I work in the old town.' Never being asked a question makes you good at volunteering information about yourself. 'The Barley Mow, you know? The pub on Church Street.'

She stared at me, her eyes wide and clear. I wondered if she was Swedish, taking in her blonde hair, the length of her limbs, her first name. I smiled. At least she was looking at me.

'I used to live in a house,' she said, apropos of nothing at all. 'Victorian. Detached. Now I have a one-bedroom flat.' She gave a half laugh, as if she found it funny, which I doubted she did. 'We had a garden twice the size of this. Three times, actually.' She looked out of the French windows at my garden, gave a wistful smile and stubbed out her cigarette. The butt had lipstick on it, even though she was still in her nightie. 'Now I have an equal share of a tiny lawn with two half-dead potted geraniums, whoop-de-do.'

The rattle of the kitchen door handle startled us both. It was Mark, dressed and ready for work. He saw Ingrid and pulled his mouth into a smile of sorts, which was more than he usually managed.

'Mark, this is Ingrid,' I said. 'She's moved into one of the flats across the way.'

Ingrid smiled, showing an even set of teeth. 'I was just admiring your beautiful garden. You must have very green fingers.' She wiggled her own fingers, in case he didn't know what fingers were.

Mark nodded and opened the fridge. He pulled out his packed lunch, held up the Tupperware, as if to show it to us. 'I'm off then.'

Ingrid pulled her robe around her and stood up. 'I should go too.' She smiled at me. 'You probably need to get on. It was nice meeting you.' Another second and she was following Mark out of the house. I went as far as the kitchen door, watched them leave.

'ICI,' I heard Mark say, and, 'Castner Kellner,' and, 'Chemical processing engineer,' and, 'Just in the labs, you know.'

It sounded like he was answering an interrogation.

'I'm actually looking for work,' I heard her say, scampering after him like a puppy, a feat for someone so tall and thin. 'Do you know if they have any vacancies?'

A warm jet of air shot through my nose. What, love? I nearly called out. Safety flautist? Piping the workers out of danger to a laid-on buffet? It's an industrial chemical plant, for God's sake, with 30,000 employees, not a cultural centre with walk-in café.

Still, Mark seemed happy to say he'd have a word with Pamela in personnel, that there might be something on the admin side.

It was the most I'd heard him say in a while. And it was only when they'd both gone that I realised I'd never given her any teabags.

CHAPTER 7

Katie

Transcript of recorded interview with Katie Edwards (excerpt)
Also present: DI Heather Scott, PC Marilyn Button

HS: Hi, Katie. Thanks for coming in to talk to us. I know this is a difficult time. We're just trying to build up a picture of everything that's happened over the past few months, all right? Does that sound OK?

KE: Yeah. No worries.

HS: Would you like a cup of tea or anything?

KE: I'm OK, ta.

HS: OK. All right. So, first of all, can you tell us anything about your mother's state of mind, going back to the end of June this year?

KE: She was depressed. That's why I took a year out.

HS: You took a year out because of your mother?

KE: Don't tell her. Don't tell her, will you?

HS: Of course not. Can you tell us why you wanted to keep that from your mum?

KE: (Pause) It was before June. She was bad last year – not as bad, but bad, like, you know? I was meant to be going in the October, a month after Kieron, but I just felt really heartless leaving her. But I didn't want her to know I knew how bad she was, like, so I said I wanted to do a gap year, and to be fair, I was meant to be doing psychology but I was thinking of changing and going into stage management or stage make-up or something on that side, so I wanted to be sure before I took out a big loan. So yeah, I was worried about her. But can I just say, she didn't kill those people. My mum'd never kill anyone.

HS: All right, Katie. Let us do our job. I promise we'll get to the truth for you. I'm going to ask you where you were on the following dates, is that OK?

KE: Of course. Ask me anything you like. It wasn't her, though. I'm telling you. It just wasn't.

CHAPTER 8

Rachel

As I said to Ingrid, I work behind the bar at the Barley Mow. I've been a barmaid for about three years, but I've done everything. You name it, I've had a go at it. More careers than Barbie, me. Mark used to tease me that I'd be an astronaut before I was done – when he used to tease me, that is. I've been a shop assistant, supermarket shelf stacker, restaurant receptionist, childminder, waitress. Before I had Kieron, I was a line manager over in a paper-ware factory on Astmoor Industrial Estate – party cups, napkins, tablecloths and the like. It had to be me that gave up work. I never suggested Mark be a stay-at-home dad in the same way I never suggested he wear a tiara to the pub, if you know what I mean.

Then, when the kids were little, I looked after some of the other kids along with mine. That way, I made a bit of cash on the side and I always had plenty of mum friends. We used to go to the park together and to the soft-play centre, where we could drink coffee and natter safe in the knowledge that the kids wouldn't hurt themselves on anything sharp. Kieron was mad for the coloured ball pit, used to cry when we left, bless him.

Once my own kids became more independent, I got a cashier job in the Co-op, but then I saw they were hiring in the Barley Mow. I love talking to people and you don't get decent conversation if someone's just paying for milk and a packet of sausages, so I went in and asked at the bar and got the job on the spot.

I suppose my favourite jobs have always involved dealing with people, which is maybe why I thought I could read them so well. University of Life type thing. You might find this hard to believe once I've finished, but I like people. I do. I really do. And I didn't mind Dave getting the manager position over me, even though he'd only been working there for a year, because he has a BTech in hotel management and I think for him it's more of a career.

'David King.'

Christ, I'd almost forgotten old Blue Eyes was there. My hand flies to my chest. I gasp. I must have been speaking out loud without realising.

'Mr King is your manager, is that right?'

'He was, yes.'

'Why *was*?'

'Because I don't work there anymore, do I? I mean, I'm guessing I won't be going to prison on a part-time basis. I'm guessing murder doesn't look good on a CV.'

She scribbles on her notepad and looks up, tips her head forward ever so slightly. 'And you say you weren't angry at Dave?'

'I don't think so, no. Why? Is this to do with the next weird thing?'

'No, not at all. It's just interesting.' She notes down something else, looks up. That smile/indigestion again. Which is it, Blue Eyes – are you pleased with the progress we're making, or is it nothing a good belch won't sort?

She doesn't answer. I guess I didn't say that last bit out loud.

'I mean, Dave got on my nerves, but I wouldn't say I was *angry* at him. I mean, I was angry all the time, but not with him specifically.'

She chews her cheek, presses her lips together to stop herself. After a moment she says, 'Why don't you talk us through the next weird thing?'

Oh, she's good. She's like that Kirsty Wark on *Newsnight*, leading me gently with that rope of hers until I've tied myself in knots. She doesn't need to. I'm busy tying my own hangman's hitch. As I said, it's me that turned myself in, me that gave my statement to the ones in uniform… yesterday, was it? Day before? Last week? Whatever, I tell Blue Eyes about the next weird thing.

It will have been the Monday. Katie was still in her pit as per and Mark had said his usual two words as we went about our morning routines, dodging each other like bumper cars, scared that one jolt would wake both of us up to reality. You wouldn't think we used to wake up and cuddle listening to the news on the radio alarm before we got out of bed. There was a time we couldn't bear to leave the warmth of ourselves. Getting up used to feel like breaking myself in two, half of me going wherever he went. And when the kids were babies – we had Kieron and Katie so close together they were nearly twins – when he went to work I used to miss him so much I'd often walk all the way to ICI just to meet him for half an hour in his lunch break. Used to take him the Scotch eggs that he liked, and cheese and onion crisps, and we'd eat them, delighted as teenagers having a midnight feast, Kieron and Katie asleep in the double buggy, Kieron, a year older, looking like the twin that had drunk all the milk. Lately, we'd been more like grumpy old geezers than teenagers. I called goodbye to him from the front door, not loud enough that he could hear but just so that I'd be able to say I'd said it if he asked me why I hadn't, which he would have done once upon a time, though he never would now.

I was on the early shift that day. I parked the car next to the arts centre by the canal. Mist rose from the brown water; there were a couple of brightly painted barges that hadn't been there the week before, an arrow of ducks gliding up towards the bridge. I walked down the path that runs past the GPs' surgery. It was a grey day, the air heavy. As I walked, I held my hands out in front of me and turned them this way and that. I touched my cheek, sort of patted it.

'I am here, I am here,' I muttered. 'Definitely here. In the sagging flesh.'

There was a chap coming up the path towards me. Mid-forties, thereabouts, grey suit and white shirt with no tie, grey hair pushed back from his forehead. Clean-looking, if you know what I mean. Silver fox type. Past me he came, head down.

'Good morning,' I said.

He jumped, blinked; his hand flew to his chest. 'Ah. Oh. Yes, good morning,' he blurted and carried on up towards the canal, but in those few seconds, I knew two things: one, he hadn't seen me until I'd spoken; and two, I knew him like I'd known that chap in the park the day before. I don't mean knew him as in knew him inside out and back to front sort of thing – I'm not psychic. I mean by instinct. That he was a GP, for a start. Well educated. And that he was lonely. I thought he might be divorced, although thinking about it, I could have noticed the pale band where his wedding ring used to be. There was something in the weary set of his shoulders, his face beaten and harassed at the same time.

He walked to his car and grabbed a file of documents from the passenger seat. I was still rooted to the spot, watching. I see now that maybe that was a strange thing to do, but I wasn't one hundred per cent aware of myself in that moment. It was only the fact of him coming back down the path that shook me out of one of what Katie calls my 'earth to Mother, come in, Mother' moments. When I blink out of them, she always says, 'Three, two, one... you're back in the room,' like the funny hypnotist off that comedy show.

I came back to myself. My breathing was ragged and I felt faint. A cloud of heat was expanding inside me but I wasn't sure exactly where it was, whether it was in my brain or my body or what.

A rivulet of sweat trickled down between my breasts. Knowing I should move but for some reason unable to, I watched the GP stride past. Off he went, rounding the corner clutching what I suspected were a patient's files. He was diligent. He'd taken some case notes home to read through.

I think about how that must sound, how *I* must sound. I don't want Blue Eyes to think I'm bonkers, even though it's a bit late for that now, and besides, what anyone thinks of me is irrelevant.

'I didn't know any of this for certain, obviously,' I qualify. 'But it's like Lisa said: when you get to a certain age, you get the hang of people. University of Life, as I said. But it was still weird. What I mean is, it felt weird.'

Blue Eyes frowns in a way that suggests she thinks everything I've said is reasonable. The fact that she's treating me with respect and warmth and kindness makes me think she might have kids, though younger than mine – she looks about thirty-five. Not that you need to have kids to show compassion to someone who has done terrible things, but just... something. It could be tactics, obviously. She's the good cop, not pinning me against a wall to force the cuffs on, more holding them out for me to willingly place my guilty wrists inside.

'So what are you saying?' Her mouth purses and she chews the inside of her cheek again, then presses her lips together, inflates them to stop herself. Ah. The cheek chewing is a nervous habit; she's trying to quit.

'I suppose I'm saying that I was noticing other people more than I had before. Or that I was noticing how much I noticed them, if you know what I mean. And I was starting to wonder if noticing people was connected to being invisible in some way.'

How it all connects to the bleeding bodies left for dead, I don't know. But she's told me to take my time, and time is what I'll take and maybe we'll find out together. For the moment, her guess is as good as mine, but it does feel good to lay it all down in this silent room in front of the woman with the neutral smile and the crystal-blue eyes that seem to see me in a way I can't remember being seen for a long, long while.

I admit that my imagination took over as I made my way through the bus station onto Church Street. I had this GP chap's marriage failing because his wife had left him for another man; now he was involved in a new relationship with a woman he really liked but who he worried would cheat on him in the end. His kids were both at university, and he feared he would lose touch with them one day because they visited his ex-wife more often than him. He was trying to get a bigger flat so that they would have a room each whenever they came. He'd even thought about getting a dog as an extra draw, but he couldn't look after it, what with the hours he did. His life was a mess, he was thinking. How had it all come to this?

'And how did imagining all that make you feel?' Blue Eyes says.

I think for a minute.

'Like I was connected to someone,' I say, 'even if he was a total stranger. My husband and my daughter took no notice of me. Lisa and I were still close at that point but it wasn't enough. I wish it had been enough.' My voice falters. 'But it wasn't. It wasn't enough.'

The interview room falls silent. Outside, I hear the traffic go by. We're next to the expressway, near the shopping centre and the big Asda and the library. Touchstones of my life before. I wonder how long it will be before I go shopping again, borrow a book; if I ever will. I wonder if there's a library in prison or if they'll let me take my Kindle in or what. How will I get on *inside*, as they call it? I've no airs and graces; that should count for something.

I realise I haven't said anything for several minutes, possibly more.

'Were you troubled by your imagination at that point?' Blue Eyes says. 'By how developed it was?'

I shake my head, even though I was; I was nothing but troubled.

'I love people,' I say instead. 'Always have. I love their complications and their faults as much as their qualities. I love what makes them *them*, if you know what I mean. And I suppose I've developed a way of flowing around people, keeping everyone afloat sort of thing.'

'Like water?'

'Exactly like water, yes.'

'So you use your instinct or your natural empathy to read people so as to accommodate them? Their needs?'

'I suppose so, yes.'

But how did this crone's insight relate to being invisible? To my own husband shuffling around me as if I wasn't there, no one smiling at me in the street anymore? To Katie's mate staring through me to the kitchen wall? These were the questions in my mind that morning as I took in with new attention all the people going about their business. Some of them I knew to say hello to, some not. No one really looked at each other, I realised. People got on with their lives. You could be having a quiet breakdown and people would just think you had heartburn or something. You'd have to drop to the ground clutching your head in your hands, crying *it's all too much*, or strip off and start telling people you're Jesus before anyone took much notice.

Don't get me wrong, I wasn't about to strip off and walk into work just so I could see how invisible I was, although to be honest, Dave would probably have just grunted and asked me to fill the ice bucket. But at the same time, there'd been that fleeting expression of shock on the GP's face when I'd said hello, the flashing understanding of the basics of him that had stuck my trainers to the tarmac like gum.

My appearance didn't attract attention, fine. But what did that have to do with instinct?

I stepped onto the zebra crossing. A car coming towards me didn't slow down. Another step and I realised it wasn't going to.

If I hadn't run across, it would have flattened me. I stood on the opposite pavement, gasping like a marathon runner after twenty Silk Cut, swearing under my breath. The car – it was only a Ford Focus, not even a sports car – turned right at the end of the high street and drove off. It had been a woman driving it, youngish, thirties tops. She hadn't slowed down not because she was mean or reckless, but because she hadn't seen me.

Perhaps I really was invisible.

And then it hit me, square on.

The link, not the car.

You can get away with murder, Lisa had said. What she meant, what I thought she meant, was that if no one could see me, it left me a kind of freedom, didn't it? With no one looking at me, I was free to see out. I was a birdwatcher in one of those hideaway things, a slot in the leaf-covered hut for my eyes. I was a Muslim woman in a burqa, hidden from the world under swathes of black cloth, watching the world without the world watching me.

'I can get away with anything,' I muttered to myself, there on the pavement. 'I'm free.'

And I was. Free of being observed, noticed, appraised, judged. With no one's gaze on me, I could put my gaze wherever the heck I wanted. I could observe by stealth.

I didn't feel too bad about being invisible then. I could hardly wait to bump into someone else to see if it would happen again: that instinctive knowing, that connection, that affinity. I wanted it to. I yearned for it. I think even then I wondered how far it would take me.

I just wish it hadn't taken me so far.

CHAPTER 9

Rachel

On the way into the pub, I said hello to the homeless lad who sometimes sleeps on the bench outside. He waved and said hello back – at least *he* saw me, I thought. I always get in at about quarter to, so I have time to open up properly before any punters arrive. I popped my coat into the office, took the cash out of the safe and put it in the till, and emptied the dishwasher. At five to, Bill the chef arrived, gave me a cursory wave and headed for the kitchen to start the lunch prep, and on the dot of eleven, Phil, a regular, took up residence on his stool.

'All right, Phil,' I said.

'Morning, Rachel.'

'All out?'

He nodded, as he always did, regardless of whether he'd won or lost.

'Usual?'

'Please. And a Jack Daniel's, thanks.'

Jack Daniel's meant a loss. I poured his pint and a measure of bourbon, took the ten-pound note and gave him his change before filling the ice bucket and putting out the bar towels. The smallest glance over my shoulder at Phil was enough to take in the silhouetted hunch of his back. And that was it. I felt his loneliness and pain as if it were my own. I mean, I'd seen him deteriorate these last few years. He used to be really quite a good-looking chap, did Phil. Smartly dressed, the occasional flutter. Now he was a shell with a gambling habit, which he indulged at the betting shop along the road. If he won, he drank to celebrate; if he lost, he drank to drown his sorrows – a little less, since he'd usually cleaned himself out to his last tenner. He'd told me once that his nan used to take him out with her on Saturdays after his parents split up, an acrimonious event that traumatised him as a kid. He didn't use those exact words; the bit about being traumatised was in what he didn't say.

'While she went to lay a fiver on the horses,' he'd told me, 'she'd give me a few coins for the one-armed bandit and I'd sit there with my legs dangling off the stool, slotting those coins in, waiting for that waterfall of cash.'

'And did you ever get it?' I'd asked him.

'Twice,' he'd replied. And then he'd said something really interesting: 'But that wasn't what kept me on the stool,' he'd said. 'It was the waiting. The stress of it made me feel calmer.'

I didn't say anything at the time, but I remember thinking it was probably because, in those moments, at least he knew what he was stressed about. He could name his unease, unlike so many other woollier sources of dread in his life. And that morning I realised something else as I watched him wander over to drop what little change he had left into the one slot machine we have in the bar area. I realised that sitting at the slots took him back to the safety of those Saturdays with his nan, waiting while she placed her bets, away from his troubled domestic life. And then I wondered whether fresh domestic trouble had brought him back to gambling, his childhood escape.

Something had.

My hand was at my chest. My eyes filled with tears. I almost bumped into Dave, stood there with his crusty red hands on his hips, bright copper locks sticking up in an unintentional quiff caused by putting a beanie hat on while his hair was still wet.

'All right, Dave?'

'Parched, actually.'

'Brew?'

'Go on, if you're making.' He handed me the dirty mugs from yesterday, and as he did so, the backs of our fingers touched, which made me go all shivery but not in a good way.

'Coming right up,' I said, almost breaking into a run.

I went upstairs to where there's a grotty little staff kitchen with a kettle, a microwave and a two-ring stove to heat stuff up. There's a bedroom up there too, where Dave sometimes sleeps when he closes up, a loo, a sink and a very basic shower, the cleaning of which is left to guess who. I put the kettle on and rested my hands on the counter top. My heart was battering in my chest; my brain felt like it was pressing against the inside of my skull.

I already knew quite a bit about Dave, having worked with him for a year or two. But now I saw the dirty fridge, the Xbox and the Domino's pizza boxes, crusts hardening on the crumby living-room floor of his flat in Duke Street. I saw the ring of dirt around his kitchen sink, saw him sniff a pair of underpants before putting them on in the yellow dawn light. I even saw the psoriasis on the backs of his knees and knew, completely without wanting to, that he never had sex with the light on because of it.

I make myself look straight at Blue Eyes, who remains as impassive as ever. 'Not right, is it, to know that about a colleague? You think I'm nuts, don't you?'

She coughs into her hand, shakes her head a fraction. 'That's not a term I would use. I'm wondering how much of Dave's personal life you actually knew. And, as with Phil, how much you tuned into what you already knew about him that day more than other days because of your trauma.'

'Trauma?' The hair stands up on the back of my neck. Where she's going with this, I don't like.

'The experience of invisibility. That was a trauma.'

I laugh. 'Come on, I hardly lost a limb.'

She shifts, crosses her long legs. She has the most fabulous shoes – silver, wedge heels. Not afraid of her height, obviously. 'Rachel, you don't need to lose a limb to experience trauma. Trauma is subjective. You might cope with a whole host of terrible things but it might be something relatively small that pushes you over the edge. Can you relate to that?'

'I can, yes. After Patrick walked out on Lisa, she seemed all right, but then one day she dropped red wine on her trousers and that was it. She wept like a professional mourner. I had to take her in my arms and calm her down, promise her I'd get them clean. I did. I soaked them in cold water and washed them on cool and they came out fine.'

But here I am again, going off topic.

The light alters. A cloud.

'So, Rachel, with a revised view of trauma and what it might have caused you to believe about your own abilities to know people by instinct, what do you believe when you say you *saw* the psoriasis on Dave's legs?'

'I mean in my mind's eye. But I'm guessing I'm not far off. I'd glimpsed his flat once when I dropped off a parcel he'd left at work. And I suppose he had red patches on his hands and in summer, when he wore short sleeves, the same thing on the inside of his elbows.'

'So you made a deduction?'

'I filled the kettle is what I did. But yes, I know what you're getting at.'

She's right. I suppose I was honing my detective skills, but instead of trying to crack cases, I was trying to crack people. I'd become hyper-aware. Woken. I was looking for connections where I shouldn't, having little affairs of the mind, I see that now. But that's all it was. It was all it was ever supposed to be.

I made the teas and took a mug out to the homeless lad, because I did that every day and I knew how he took it: white, two sugars. He gave me one of his lovely smiles and said thanks, and then I went back in to Dave.

'Here's your tea,' I said, handing him his Everton mug.

He put it on the counter behind the bar. 'Here, look at this.' He rolled up his sleeve to reveal a blue crest inked into still blazing red skin: *Nil Satis Nisi Optimum*, a turret and two laurel wreaths. I recognised it, of course. It was the same crest as the one on his mug.

'New tattoo,' I said.

'Come on the Blues!' He beamed. 'What do you think? *Nil Satis Nisi Optimum*. That's my message to you today and every day, Rachel. Nothing but the best is good enough, eh? Nothing but the best.'

He'd enjoyed the pain of having that tattoo. A bit like Phil, I thought – it comforted Dave to know what was hurting for once. It was all about putting it somewhere. The pain, I mean. You have to put pain somewhere, whether it's into a slot machine or into your skin or into your veins. I could add that Dave's a bit of a knob, but I think that's self-evident from what he said, isn't it? Nothing but the best? Sod off, Dave. It's a boozer, not the ruddy Hilton. I didn't say any of that, obviously.

'Oh, Dave, that's smashing is that,' was what I did say and set about cutting up some lemons.

For the rest of the day, I kept my head down, but customers don't serve themselves, do they? Our pub is what you'd call a community pub. Our clientele are a little older and we never get any trouble, not even at the weekend, as the younger crowd tend to go elsewhere. Most of our punters are regulars: Sid, who comes in at quarter past four every single day, overalls covered in paint splashes – pint of mild, always one, never more, never less; the couple that show up every Monday lunchtime for the buy one get the second one half price steak and chips offer, pint of lager for him, half for her, and never say a word to one another; and Lena, who generally gets in at about five, half five for her first gin and tonic, always in the high heels, the tight clothes, and always alone. If I do a late shift, I generally see her leave at around ten o'clock, though where she goes I've never asked. It's not my job to know their business; my job is to create a friendly atmosphere for them, and that's what I did that day like any other. Only that day, as the punters came and went, my head filled with their fears and boredom, their money worries and tiredness levels, their petty bitterness and secret longings, and most of all their howling, fathomless black wells of loneliness. Not that any of them said any of that aloud. By five, my head was aching with it: all that angst, all that anger. All that damn despair.

I'm not asking for sympathy, by the way; I'm asking you to understand what I did to that poor girl, that's all. It was unnerving, all this intuition. I felt like a radio tuned to several different channels at once. But I was trying to take Lisa's advice and see it as a gift. Human beings need to connect with each other. What else are we in this life for, if not? I was water. I'd always been water, flowing around those I loved and, quite often, those I didn't. But now I was waiting for fresh drops to swell the depleted puddle I'd become.

For that week, all I did was go to work and come home again. That was enough. By the time I got in at night, I was too exhausted to do more than walk Archie round the close for his wee.

'Did you see anyone at that time? Anyone you knew?'

I think for a minute. 'I only saw a couple of neighbours. Mostly I was looking at the lights coming from the windows, the families sitting round the table or watching television together. Mrs Lang from number twenty-four was putting a bag of rubbish into her dustbin. I tell you what, she is a very unhappily married woman indeed. Oh, and I waved to Ingrid, who was closing her curtains.'

'So you weren't going any further than your own crescent?'

'No. Well, I did go as far as the Spar, which is at the end of the estate before you get to the bus stop on the main road, and I suppose I should tell you that I tied Archie up outside, went in and… I nicked a packet of biscuits. Just to see if I could get away with it. Which I did. But the following Saturday was my first really long evening walk. And I swear to God, when I met that young girl, the one in the paper, all I wanted to do was talk to her. Jo. Well, you know her name. But that was the start of things stepping up – I can see that now. That was when I started to feel afraid.'

CHAPTER 10

Mark

Transcript of recorded interview with Mark Edwards (excerpt)
Also present: DI Heather Scott, PC Marilyn Button

HS: Mr Edwards, can you tell us anything about your wife's behaviour? Had she changed in any way recently, perhaps around the end of June? Was there anything specific you might have noticed or which might seem relevant in the light of what's happened?

ME: I suppose she was a bit funny after our Katie's nineteenth. She had a nosebleed that night and she seemed upset, I suppose. And the next morning she'd gone into herself, further than usual.

HS: Can you tell us anything about the folder containing the crime reports?

ME: (Pause)

HS: For the benefit of the tape, Mr Edwards is clearing his throat.

ME: She'd started with the file the year before. I asked her not to, but she was determined to get enough articles together to take to our MP. She wanted him to take it to Parliament and get something done about all the knife crime. She was very committed to it. I'd hear the printer going sometimes and I'd check the alarm clock and it'd be like five, six, half six in the morning. But it was only after Katie's do that she started going out in the evenings. Only round our way at first. Took the dog, like. I didn't think too much about it. But then... then she started going further.

HS: Did you ask her where she was going?

ME: She said she was walking the dog. But our Archie doesn't need much walking. He's eight. That's middle-aged, in dog years. She just seemed to need to get out of the house. She'd be out for hours. And I couldn't think of a reason to stop her. I mean, I had no idea. So... so I didn't. Stop her, I mean.

CHAPTER 11

Rachel

I met Jo about forty minutes' walk from our house. It was further than I'd walked in years.

On the Wednesday, I think it was, and this is embarrassing, I'd nicked some chewing gum from the Spar to stop me stuffing my face of an evening. I can't believe I did that, but I did, and I've nicked other stuff since, so maybe that should be added to the charges. But the chewing gum was because I'd put on weight over the last year or so and I suppose I was hoping the evening strolls would pay off eventually, especially as they meant that I was laying off the Hobnobs and the Cadbury's in front of the telly, and whatever white wine was on offer in the Co-op that week.

'And you took the dog?' Blue Eyes uncrosses her legs, recrosses them the other way. She's wearing a black tunic thing today with a big necklace of coloured glass beads, what Katie would call a statement piece. I'm wearing jogging pants and a T-shirt. I'm not in a prison, which makes sense because there's no prison overlooking the Shopping City. I'm in a psychiatric unit.

They still lock us up at night, though, which is a relief.

'Rachel?' Oops. Earth to Rachel, come in, Rachel. 'You took your dog with you when you walked?'

'The dog was my alibi.'

'What do you mean by that?'

Good question. I have a think before I tell her I was trying to pull myself out of the hole I was in, get fit, take my mind off things. But I can see that if I was thinking of the dog that way, I must have known deep down that what I was doing wasn't strictly speaking a simple leg-stretch.

The girl, Jo, the one in the news, was wandering around in front of the station. I mean, I didn't know her name then, obviously. She was wearing a too-big tweedy overcoat, skinny jeans and monkey boots and she looked to be about Katie's age. She looked lost and a bit frazzled so I asked her if she was all right and, as was becoming depressingly familiar, she almost jumped out of her skin. Really, I thought, I should buy a sheet and some chains to rattle just to wring some drops of amusement out of the situation.

'I've lost my satchel,' she said, fingers bunched at her forehead 'I thought it was in my rucksack but it's not. It's got my purse and my phone in it. I think someone must have taken it while I was asleep. Or I might have left it on the train, I don't know.'

'You poor lamb,' I said, with the lightest touch to her sleeve. 'Can I help?'

She transferred her fingertips to her teeth, *tap tap tap*, eyes darting about. 'Er... oh God, my mum'll kill me.'

Tobacco had yellowed the knuckles of her fore- and middle fingers. Probably started smoking at school in order to shake off the goody-two-shoes image her parents had drilled into her, and now she couldn't stop. Her eyes were big, too big, and her collarbone jutted like the handlebars of a bike. She smoked to stay thin and I guessed it was only her alcohol consumption that kept her weight from plummeting to dangerous levels. She drank to cope, to relax. She didn't tell me any of this. I caught the vapours on her breath. And I don't know what it was about her particularly, but something drew me to her – her vulnerability, perhaps, and the ever-present loneliness I was beginning to realise was all around me.

'Have you told the stationmaster?' I asked her.

She shook her head. 'There was no one there. I don't suppose you have a phone I could use, do you?'

I shook my head. 'I'm sorry, love, I've left it at home. You can come back to mine if you like and ring from there?' I rummaged in my bag, found some tissues and offered her one.

She accepted the tissue but took a step back. I'd been too forward. Dammit. She still saw me as harmless, but she didn't think she should come to my home just like that. And she was right. Stranger danger. I'd have told Katie the same. Usually, the ones with strict parents are lacking in street smarts, but this girl had seen enough television to be wary. I wanted to reassure her, tell her that she wouldn't end up in a Netflix documentary, but I knew that would sound wrong.

'I'm here to see a friend,' she said. 'I was meant to ring her from the train but I fell asleep and I only woke up at the stop. I nearly ended up in Liverpool, so I suppose in the rush I must've left the bag behind.'

'Do you know where she lives, your mate?'

'Erm, Festival Way, I think.'

I smiled. 'I live up that way. It's quite a walk from here, but I was on my way back. You can walk along with me if you like. Safety in numbers. Or you can walk a little behind me if you're not sure. I won't be offended. I'd call you a cab but we've neither of us got a phone, have we? It's like my mum used to say: we could've had bacon and eggs if we had any bacon, except we haven't got any eggs.' I gave a little laugh.

'Erm…' She met my eye, still not a hundred per cent. Fred and Rosemary West have a lot to answer for.

'Or I can give you directions, but they're a lot to remember.' Archie sniffed at her crotch. Time of the month most probably, but again, not something to say out loud.

'Your dog's cute,' she said.

'My daughter's dog. Not that she ever walks him.'

'Aw, what's his name?' She bent and tickled Archie's ears.

I thought for a second. 'Fido.' I cursed myself. Really, Rachel, is that the best you can do?

But she half laughed. 'Good name.'

'Our Polly thought it was hilarious, and it was for about a day.' Two name changes. The second was better by a country mile. I'd wanted the name Polly, but Mark had preferred Katie.

The girl smiled and stood up. The murderous Wests and other assorted famous predators scuttled away, left her brow clear. Meanwhile I tried to remember the last time Katie had smiled at me the way this young girl was doing, as if I'd said something amusing, as if she liked me.

'My daughter's about your age,' I said. 'A couple of years younger, but round about.'

The old woman has a daughter, she was thinking, judging by her eyes. She won't do me any harm. God bless the young. They have such black-and-white ideas about things.

'We'll be safe as houses,' I said. 'We've got our guard dog now, haven't we?'

'My name's Jo,' she said.

'Pleased to meet you, Jo.'

She didn't ask my name, which I was quite used to; I didn't feel any need to give it. Together we walked up Shaw Street towards Greenway Road. To the left, behind the houses, was the off-licence; to the right, the cemetery and St Michael's church. It started to spit so I pulled up the hood of my anorak.

'How do you know your friend if you're not from here?' I asked. The young need more questions; they don't just chat on like older folk do, and they rarely ask anything back.

'From university,' she said.

'So you're at uni?'

'Not anymore. But I haven't really got a proper job and neither has she. We're both living with our parents at the moment, on zero-hours contracts.'

I nodded. 'My daughter's on a zero-hours. Except with her, it's literally zero; she spends most of her time in bed.'

And then Jo did something. She laughed. And my God, it felt so good to have someone laugh at something I'd said on purpose to be funny and not at something I'd got wrong. It felt so good to have someone *hear*.

'I don't like to be too hard on her,' I said. 'The world's a tough place for you young ones, what with Instagram lifestyles and all that. Our K— Polly can't go out the door until she's got her eyebrows on. Honest to God, full make-up when she goes for milk.' I thought I'd managed a light-hearted mickey-take. I didn't feel too guilty sending Katie up like that, because Katie's a pain in the neck.

Jo laughed again. She was thinking I was a nice lady. She was starting to trust me. It's easy to trust a nondescript middle-aged woman in a cagoule in a way it isn't to trust a middle-aged man in a dirty mackintosh rooting for something in his pockets, if you know what I mean. As for me, I was finding my sense of humour again. All I'd needed was a little encouragement to get it out of the box and dust it off. A bit of connection.

'Do you go in for those lifestyle accounts?' I said. 'YouTube and Twitface and all that? An influencer, that's what our Polly wants to be, whatever that is. Do you do that? You know, take a photo of some mushed-up avocado on toast and say hashtag healthy eating hashtag avocado?'

Jo giggled. 'Sometimes. My friends all do it, so...'

'Oh, I remember that. When I was younger, if my mates wore wellies on their heads, I'd be up that shed looking for mine before you could say *Last of the Summer Wine*.'

Jo laughed a lot at that. She shook her head. 'You're hilarious.'

She'd never heard of *Last of the Summer Wine*, couldn't have done, she was way too young. It was the way I spoke that tickled her, my funny local accent, but I didn't care. I have quite good delivery. Deadpan is something you earn the right to once you've been around the block a few times, another scarce advantage in the shitstorm of the cruel ravages of time.

By the time we reached the end of Norman Road, we were chatting like best friends. It was the first time in years I'd felt confident talking to someone new. I think it was because she was so much younger. And of course, by the way she reacted I could tell she thought I was the bee's knees. She rattled on and on and on, the way shy people often do once you've pressed the right buttons. Wealthy family, judging by the voice, the casual references to holidays in France, the way she said Mummy and Daddy not Mum and Dad, and the village in Hampshire she called home.

We headed down Heath Road to the mini-roundabout, where the town hall stands white and proud in its gardens. We'd been walking for about twenty minutes by then. From the town-hall walls, soft floods bathed the gardens in vanilla light.

'That's where I got married,' I said, pointing to it.

'Aw,' she said. 'Are you still married?'

'Can't you tell? Look at the state of me – of course I'm bloody still married.'

Well, she laughed so much I thought she was going to stop breathing or start crying or both. Must be dry as parchment in your house, I wanted to say but didn't obviously. That would have stopped the connection we were feeling, the connection I'd set out to find. She was hungry, was Jo. I felt the pit of her starvation in my own stomach, the nasty taste of it in my mouth. We were conjoining like those twins you see on the news sometimes; I could feel it.

'You could feel her hunger?' Blue Eyes, popping up on me again. Honest to God, I get so lost in what I'm saying, I forget she's there.

'Yes,' I say.

'And do you believe that's possible? To feel someone else's hunger in your own belly?'

I think for a second. 'I thought I could feel it, but yes, I might have been over-empathising, what with her being so thin. And all I'd had since my tea was some chewing gum, which I suppose had set my gastric juices off, hadn't it?'

Mouth twitch. I think that's a good sign. 'I think you're probably right. But you mentioned your magazine quiz telling you that you were highly empathic, and if you're too empathic, that can be a problem. You're not differentiating sufficiently between yourself and others. You're suffering on everyone else's behalf, which can leave you exhausted, as you've described. So it could well be that the young girl's thinness upset you, as a mother or as an empath, or both. Do you have experience of being hungry? Very hungry, I mean.'

I almost snort. 'I tell you what, I've been on more diets than Gwyneth Paltrow's had colonic irrigations. I'm always on some diet or other, starving myself, and of course by late afternoon I'm snatching chocolate bars from passing toddlers. So yes.'

She raises her eyebrows and presses her mouth tight, a slight nod: there you go, then – it was your association of the vivid experience of hunger after all. We read so much in the expressions of others, don't we? Like that, just now, actual words in the simple realignment of a few facial muscles. It can be less, much less – the smallest twitch of the ears, an all-too-hasty nod, and you still understand, you still hear the words that were never said. Jo communicated her hunger to me in the high set of her shoulders, the way she held her arm across her belly, her hand a soft fist. It's possible I smelled hunger on her breath along with the wine. That halitosis models get from starving themselves, I read about it in… oh, some magazine or other. What a world we live in. And there we were, Jo and I, stopped at the perimeter fence to the town hall.

'My secret place is in there,' I said, nodding towards the dark gardens.

'Up there?' Jo pointed to the trees that hide my special bench. Her sleeve fell back to reveal a criss-cross of thin pink scars. A cutter. Suicidal thoughts sometimes, I bet.

'I go there when I'm stressed or angry or whatever. When I feel like the world doesn't understand me.' World doesn't understand me? World doesn't bloody see me, I thought. It has no interest in understanding me what-so-bloody-ever.

She peered into the darkness. She was thinking about how the world didn't understand her either but that I did. There was a longing in her. You could feel it in the air. She was pining for connection too. She was so lonely inside the walls she'd built around herself. She needed a mother, but not the one she had. She needed a mother like me.

'I can't see anything,' she said.

'It's up at the top of that grass verge,' I said. 'Behind the trees. You can't see it from here.'

'What is it?'

'It's just a bench beside a little pond. In the summer, it's very pretty, and you can feed the ducks. I used to take our Polly and our Kie… vin there. But in the evenings no one ever goes there. Well, except me, of course. And the dog.'

She peered in again, her head craning forward. Something deep within her, some restless core, yearned to see the secluded place even though she knew she should be getting to her friend's house.

'I just climb over,' I said. 'Or you can go around. No one bothers. I climb over and walk up and sit on the bench. I call it my bench and I have a little smoke, sometimes a little cry if I'm upset, and I just step off the world for five minutes. I'd go now only I've left my ciggies at home.'

Ciggies my foot. I don't smoke, as you know.

'I've got some,' she almost cried, her developing crush on me taking full flight. I was so much calmer, so much kinder than her own skinny, Lycra-clad, neurotic mother who wanted only academic success from her so she could bathe in that reflected glory and somehow make up for her own failed promise. I was soft and warm, my promise had never failed because it had never been made, and I didn't give a monkey's about her degree, only about her, what made her heart ache, her soul sing. Meanwhile she wanted to stand beneath the spread of my arms and shelter there and be loved.

And there was me with all this love going spare.

I gave her a sideways glance. 'What're you thinking, missy?'

She smirked. 'We could go and see your secret place,' she said, her voice thin. 'And I'll roll you one of mine.'

I smiled at her. 'Well, I don't normally share my secret place with anyone. But as it's you…'

She was excited; I felt the burn of it in my chest, although now, like the hunger, I'm wondering if the excitement was my own. She also really did need a fag but hadn't wanted to make me stop and wait while she rolled one. I put one hand on the railing. She hesitated.

'I can only stop for a minute, by the way,' I said. 'Literally a couple of minutes. My husband's expecting me back before half nine.'

Before I could say anything else, she'd climbed over. That put me in a spot. I never climb over the railings; I follow the hedge to the end, where you can just walk into the gardens. But I was here now, caught in my own lie. I had to pick up the dog and hand him to her. She didn't question how I usually did this on my own; she was too busy laughing at me stuck with one leg one either side of the fence.

'Can I help you?' She took my hand and pulled me towards her.

I almost fell onto her and we both laughed.

'What are we like?' I said, leading the way up the grass verge to where the trees huddled, whispering in a dark amorphous clump. I was panting a bit by now, because the lawns are on a slope and the walking hadn't yet got my fitness up.

We reached the trees and I led the way to the pond. It was dark in there, but the moon bleached the tiny path, yellowed the edge of the pond where the water sliced the reeds. And the bench.

'Shame you lost your phone,' I said. 'We could have used it for a torch. Still, we've got the moon.'

She pulled a tin from her jacket pocket and sat down. She'd gone quiet. Now we were here, I sensed that she'd begun to ask herself what the heck she was doing, and to feel afraid. But beneath her apprehension she was enjoying herself, enjoying the pull of the fear, the danger. There was some nugget of rebellion in there for her. Oh, I remembered my own youth as if it were the week before. That urge to do something reckless. I remembered a lad with a motorbike offering me a ride one night after we'd been clubbing at Mr Smith's. No, I'd said, when what I'd wanted but not dared to say was yes. I remembered summer nights roaming the streets with Lisa and our other mates in drunken noisy packs. I remembered a stranger's face blurring on the dance floor late at night in some seedy dive as it loomed in for a thick-tongued kiss. Wanting to do things we shouldn't is as old as time.

We sat together on the bench. I waited while she rolled me a cigarette. She handed it to me, rolled one for herself. She lit first mine, then hers. I didn't inhale, but even so, I coughed.

'Not used to roll-ups,' I said.

'I prefer them.'

Oh, Jo, you funny little soul, with your millennial worries and your self-sabotaging ways. Nothing matters, I wanted to tell her. But it'll take you until you're my age to realise that, and then you'll be free to not give a—

'It's nice here,' she said. 'Peaceful.'

I took another puff and coughed again. I was enjoying her cigarette more than mine, if that makes sense. She pulled hard; the nicotine relaxed her shoulders a fraction, down from her ears, lowering my stress levels with them. I almost understood smoking in that moment.

I moulded into the bench, stretched out across the back. I wanted her to relax against my arm so that I could comfort her little bird-like frame, but at the same time I feared the connection might be too strong. It might electrocute me. It was exactly like a bond between mother and daughter. That closeness. Affinity. It's what I'd had once with Katie.

Jo stood and wandered over to the pond. The orange glow of her cigarette tip pulsed in the dimness. I was thinking about what it would be like to drown myself in that pond, how cold the water would feel on my face. Except *I* wasn't thinking that; she was. Christ on a bike, the way she stared. The longing was written into her body as sure as ink on a page. I tied Archie to the leg of the bench and went to join her. I stood close, felt the pull towards that black mirror. If I pushed her in now, I could drown her – I knew that. I was bigger than her, stronger, and I had the advantage of surprise. All these years I'd existed as water flowing around my loved ones, fluid around their needs, keeping them afloat; now I was water once again and she was a drop, a drop ready to lose its meniscus, to become part of the whole, part of me. That was the ultimate connection: drops together with other drops lost all boundaries, became water. Cohesion, that was the word I wanted. In her death, it was possible I'd experience cohesion. Or at least something real, something important. I didn't know how that would be, only that I wanted it.

I placed my hand on her back, between her shoulder blades. I could just—

She turned to look at me, stepped back.

'What do you do with your fag butt?' she asked, throwing hers down but crouching to pick it up once she'd ground it out with her boot.

I staggered backwards, almost fell. 'I just put it out like you're doing.' I wondered if she could hear the change in my voice. I barely had the breath to say the words. 'I pick it up and either find a bin or take it home. Doesn't do to litter, does it? I can't stand people who litter.'

'I'd better get to my friend's,' she said.

'Yes. Let's get going.'

I look up to find Blue Eyes studying me. Intent is how you'd describe her expression.

'And that's the last you remember?' she asks. 'She left you in the gardens?'

'No, we walked back down. I helped her over the railings. Passed her the dog. I asked her if she wanted me to walk her the rest of the way and she said no. We parted company on Boston Avenue, just along from… from where she was found.'

CHAPTER 12

Rachel

'So you remember nothing after saying goodbye?'

'No. Next thing I was back home, hanging up the dog lead and my coat. I remember having a shower and getting into bed and I remember how cold I was, which was weird because I'm always so hot these days. I had to get up and put my dressing gown on. Trembling from head to toe I was, flipping like one of those fortune-telling fish you put on the palm of your hand. I remember Mark climbing into bed later. He was warm, always is. I used to call him my hot-water bottle. I can remember spooning against him, trying to get some warmth. That's the last I remember.'

I'm lying, but the rest is none of her beeswax. I was in the mood, to put it bluntly. That conversation with Jo had lit something inside me. Obviously I had no idea what had already happened to her by then; all I knew was that the connection between us had made me feel alive in a way I hadn't for a long time. I circled my arm around Mark's waist, thinking how a year ago he'd had too much of a belly for me to reach round him but how now, despite him drinking more, I could almost touch my fingers to the mattress on the other side. I kissed the warm hollow between his shoulders, smelled his skin, stroked him, pushed my hands through the hair on his chest. But nothing stirred. After a minute, he grumbled, lifting my hand away as if it were an object he needed to put to one side. A moment later he was snoring and

I was lying on my back closing my eyes tight against the sting of rejection, opening them again, making kaleidoscopes. Another moment and heat was climbing the walls of me, shortening my breath. Sweat ran in trickles into my hair. I kicked the covers off and wrestled myself out of my dressing gown. I was boiling, literally, boiling like a kettle.

And more. I can't explain it; it was like I was carrying all the anger of the world in that moment. All the anger of women. You see, they talk about hormones and they talk about the change, but sometimes I think we're angry for a reason. I was full of rage, full of it. I couldn't separate what was my body and what was my mind. Because reasons, real reasons, kept coming and coming at me in the darkness, the man I'd married and loved snoring next to me. I was stuck in this thankless no-woman's-land between kids and parents. I had put and put and put into this land: blood and tears and scars and milk and flesh and love and the unacknowledged woman-hours that didn't count, never counted, like man-hours did, and love, and love again – measureless, infinite quantities of it. I had volunteered my body to give us our two children. I had given the very bones and skin of myself in service as gladly as you'd give a cardigan to a friend when the evening turns chilly – *here, have this* – only for them to take it home and wash it on the wrong setting, return it misshapen, no longer fitting. Ruined. I had donated my body and my life to love. My body and my life had repaid me with nothing, frankly. After all the bleeding and the baring and beating of my mother's heart on the sidelines of the football pitch and the ballet classes and the nativity plays and the broccoli on the fork, *come on, eat it, love, it's good for you, it's a tree, pretend it's a tree and you're the giant come to eat a whole tree...* For what? For what? Ashes. Ashes from a tree left black and standing after a forest fire, a tree that's dead but doesn't know it yet.

And now, when my body had tried to reclaim some interest on all that love, there was none. Mark did not see his body as something of service, certainly not to me. He had never had to give it whether he wanted to or not. There were no wars on; he'd never had to volunteer to fight. Maybe women don't make wars because we've already got a war going on every single day of our lives: our own bodies, fighting against us. The world telling us that we're beautiful as we are while it sells us diets and clothes that would only ever look good on a twig, telling us that it's fair, that it's equal, when it isn't, like one big gaslighting god.

Whatever, thoughts like that rolled in as I tried to get the boiling water inside me under control, mop up rivers of sweat with the tissues from the box beside the bed, fetch a towel from the bathroom to lie on. There were more thoughts but I've forgotten them; more rage but it burned itself out eventually. The bottom line was that Mark and I hadn't done anything in getting on for a year. He didn't see me that way anymore. He didn't see me at all.

We ground through Sunday. I didn't check the news sites that day. I was a zombie, living in a zombie state. Roast chicken dinner I spent two hours preparing eaten in near silence. *Pass the gravy.* I walked out with Archie but headed up Halton Brow, so I didn't see the flickering black and yellow tape on the corner of Boston Avenue, the police van, the officer with his clipboard asking passers-by if they'd seen anything. It was only when I was trawling through the online local news at five thirty on the Monday morning that I saw the article.

Girl critical after random knife attack.

I sipped my tea and read on, a pain building in my gut.

A young woman was found bleeding and unconscious at the corner of Boston Avenue and Festival Way late on Saturday night.

Boston Avenue. The pain tightened. My throat closed. I put my mug down on the table.

Customers of the Red Admiral pub were on their way home from an evening out when they saw the girl lying on the pavement.

'We thought someone had been fly-tipping,' said Mr Simon Kitchener, a resident of Festival Way. 'But when we saw it was a girl, we called 999 straight away.'

The woman was taken by ambulance to Halton General Hospital, where she was given an emergency splenectomy and a blood transfusion. She had sustained two knife wounds to the ribs and a contusion to the back of the head. A spokesperson for the hospital described her condition this morning as critical. The woman was carrying no identification on her person but was later identified by a friend who had reported her missing as Joanna Weatherall, from Hampshire. Police are appealing for anyone who might know the victim or think they saw anything suspicious to come forward.

My heart was battering by now. Hands to my knees, I made myself breathe.

'Oh God,' I whispered to no one. 'Oh my God oh my God oh my God.'

A flash: a knife tip pressed against skin. Breakthrough, the sudden pooling of red blood, the soft plunge of blade into warm flesh.

I knew it was her. Jo. Joanna. She hadn't told me her last name, but I knew. My leg shook. I planted my foot down flat to stop it. Read the whole article again before sending it to the printer. I tried to sip my tea, but I hadn't the strength in my hands to lift the mug. After a few minutes, I walked at the speed of a pall-bearer into the living room and pulled the article from the printer tray. I didn't read it again. Only the headline. Back in the kitchen, I fetched my clip file from the dresser, slid the article into a clear plastic sleeve and clipped Jo inside with the other stories before sitting down again. My head was in my hands but I had no memory of putting it there. I was shaking from head to toe, crying, but it seemed to me that I'd been crying for a while. It was her. Who else could it be?

'I'm so sorry, Jo,' I whimpered. 'I'm so, so sorry, love.'

CHAPTER 13

Ingrid

Transcript of recorded interview with Ingrid Taylor (excerpt)
Also present: DI Heather Scott, PC Marilyn Button

HS: Ms Taylor, can you tell us how you first came to be in Rachel Edwards' house?

IT: I'd just moved into the close. I couldn't find the teabags so I asked if she had any spare. She invited me in.

HS: Is there any reason why you asked Rachel Edwards specifically?

IT: It was early. I could see that her lights were on. That she was up. Awake, I mean.

HS: And what about Mr Edwards?

IT: Mark? He was there that morning. (Pause) Look, can I just say that the only reason I've ended up getting involved in this stuff is because my ex left me practically penniless. Without that, I'd never have had to move and I'd never have asked Mark about a job. Honestly, apart from him, I wish I'd never met that family.

HS: So you have no income other than your salary from your clerical job at ICI?

IT: A pittance. Yes. What's that got to do with anything?

HS: Nothing, just building up a picture. And that's the job that you get a lift with Mr Edwards to each day, is that right?

IT: Yes.

HS: How would you describe your relationship with Mr Edwards now?

IT: Mark and I are... well, we're close. You know, we get on really well. We make each other laugh. We just... clicked, I suppose. But that's it. He was really kind to me, he's so sweet. He practically got me that job and I guess on our car trips together I realised he needed someone to talk to, you know with Rachel being as she was. I could have driven in my own car obviously but that would have been a waste with us going to the same place every day, and I suppose I felt like I could pay him back by offering a sympathetic ear. I mean, I think he wanted more. You get a sixth sense for these things as a woman, but we were just friends. We are friends still, I hope. I mean, I'm not a husband stealer or anything. I'm not some sort of Jezebel home wrecker. I'm a feminist.

HS: Ms Taylor, if we could go back to the evening of Saturday the twenty-ninth of June this year, the night Joanna Weatherall was attacked. Did you have any suspicions with regard to your neighbour, Mrs Edwards?

IT: Well, obviously I'd seen Rachel's weird file by then, but I didn't leap to any conclusions other than perhaps having doubts about her mental health. I knew she went out every night. I would see her sometimes from my front window, either with the dog or coming home with a takeaway of some sort. So many takeaways. I used to wonder why people got them. I mean, why not go out for a meal? Be civilised instead of troughing down luminous MSG in your jogging pants? Sorry, I don't mean to sound flippant; I'm not like that, and since my change in circumstances, I understand it. It's cheaper, basically. I hadn't thought about that. So, to answer your question, I might have seen her go out that night, I might not have – I couldn't possibly pin down the date.

HS: So you had no suspicions?

IT: Not then. Obviously with hindsight I realise that Rachel must have taken the knife with her. I mean, to me, that's premeditated, isn't it? That's like putting a silencer on a gun or something. She *knew* she was going to stab that girl and that's a pretty chilling thought, to be honest. I mean, we used to have coffee together, chat over the fence when I was watering the neighbour's plants. So no, no suspicions at the time other than her general spaced-outness, but it all makes sense now. Mark was worried about her. When I mentioned her nightly walkabouts to him, he said she'd started doing that quite recently. After their daughter's birthday party, I think he said. Said she'd gone a bit strange suddenly, although he didn't put it like that. He wouldn't talk about her that way, he's too nice.

HS: So you were worried enough to express concern to Mr Edwards?

IT: I did say to Mark that she didn't seem well. I tried to get him to see that, but only because I was worried about her. If I happened to see her out talking to strangers, I would mention it to Mark because it felt like the right thing to do. At first I was only trying to alert him to the fact that she might need help. He did eventually tell me she'd suffered with her nerves, as he put it, after their son was born and he knew she'd been a bit down lately. I guess he really needed someone to talk to. It was the least I could do.

HS: So you saw yourself as his confidante, would you say? A shoulder to cry on?

IT: I'm a good listener. At least, men find me easy to talk to. So yes, sometimes when Rachel went off on her little walkies, I'd either call in to see if he was OK or text to see if he wanted to pop over for a glass of wine and a chat. As friends, obviously.

CHAPTER 14

Mark

Transcript of recorded interview with Mark Edwards (excerpt)
Also present: DI Heather Scott, PC Marilyn Button

ME: She wasn't well. She wasn't well before, years before. When Kieron was born, she kept thinking she was going to kill him. We were worried sick.

HS: We?

ME: I mean her mum, her dad. And Lisa.

HS: That's Lisa Baxter? For the benefit of the tape, Mr Edwards is nodding.

ME: It was diagnosed quickly, once we'd called the hospital. Well, we ended up calling the emergency services because she went missing and no one could get hold of her. Then Lisa spotted her at the edge of the estate, looking… dishevelled, like, and distressed. So actually it was Lisa who rang and they sent an ambulance. I can't believe I didn't recognise the signs, to be honest.

HS: What signs?

ME: Well, she was very down. She'd been down even before Kieron went to uni…

HS: For the benefit of the tape, Mr Edwards is taking a moment.

ME: Then this last year, she and Katie were always rowing, sniping at each other, you know? And they never used to do that. They used to make each other laugh. In hysterics, they'd be, over one of those pictures with the captions or a silly video clip Katie had found on her phone. Used to get on my nerves sometimes, but obviously it's better than doors slamming, the shouting and the swearing and that. I'd give anything to hear them mucking about now, obviously. And then… and then the walking. And when she was at home, she was vacant, you know? I'm supposed to be her husband and I didn't even see her. I was too… I couldn't look at her… and now she's… I can't believe what she's… She never laid a hand on the kids. She was a lovely mum. The kids adored her. She'd never hurt anyone. She was gentle. My Rachel… (Breaks down)

HS: For the benefit of the tape, I am pausing the recording.

HS: Mr Edwards. Mark. Can you tell us your where-abouts on Saturday the twenty-ninth of June?

ME: There's nothing on the calendar. We don't really go out anymore, but I think I was at the Norton Arms with Roy, just for one or two, like. I'll have gone out after she did. You can check with him but he might not remember. I was going out a lot. I've been drinking too much lately, I know that, and Roy didn't expect me to talk about anything apart from football and crap like that. I didn't know what to say to Rach. Just looking at her broke my heart. I couldn't fix her... I couldn't... (Breaks down)

HS: (Pause) Mr Edwards, I know this is difficult, but can you tell us what time your wife returned home that night?

ME: I think it was about ten o'clock. Maybe a bit earlier. I was back watching the telly by then and she pushed the dog in and said she was going up. I didn't take my eyes off the television. I heard the shower go and then she must have gone to bed, like. That was it.

HS: And how would you describe her state of mind the following day, Sunday?

ME: Like she was there but not there. I played a round of golf with Roy. Rachel did a roast chicken – she generally does a roast on Sundays – but she was spaced out, for sure. It was the next day, the Monday, that she started banging on about the knife.

CHAPTER 15

Rachel

I'd assumed that I couldn't remember anything about my walk home on Saturday night because there was nothing memorable about it – no, that's not right, I hadn't assumed anything, I hadn't even *thought* about my walk home. It was only then, reading that report, that I realised I simply couldn't remember a single thing. The houses on our estate are as familiar to me as my own corns, so there was no reason to notice anything unless it was something out of the ordinary. And there was nothing out of the ordinary. There was no one about. Two lads vaping in the Cherry Tree pub car park came to me eventually, but that was it. Hardly *hold the front page*, was it?

I tried and failed to eat a bowl of cereal while I flicked through my file, mentally adding up all the knife crimes I'd collected since the previous September. I put the radio on, but they were playing a sad song so I switched it off. That poor, poor girl. Her poor parents. Her poor friend. Mindless, absolutely mindless.

Mark's feet came clumping down the stairs. I jumped up and put the file back on the dresser shelf. My breathing was beginning to settle but I was still shaky. I wiped my cheeks with the back of my hand.

'Coffee?' I just about trusted myself to say.

'If you're making.'

He knew I wasn't, but as I've said, it's the dance we do. I put the kettle on and tried to act normal, which is more difficult than you think. I felt like a puppet trying to pull my own strings, all my movements jerky, my head at the wrong angle somehow.

'Sleep OK?' I asked.

'Not bad. You?'

'Fine.'

'You were out a long time.'

'Went for a long walk. Needed some head space.'

Mark poured his cereal and some milk into a bowl, flicked on the iPad and brought up the BBC sports page. If he noticed that I'd been crying, he didn't say anything. It was a pretty regular occurrence, to be honest, and we all run out of comfort eventually. I would have managed to keep calm, I think, if I hadn't taken my sandwiches for work out of the fridge, made to put them in my bag and seen the knife.

My bag was on a hook in the cupboard under the stairs. I fetched it and plonked it on the kitchen table so I could put my sandwiches and my flask in. None the wiser, I opened the zip that goes across the top.

The air made this big sucking sound.

'It was me,' I say, meeting Blue Eyes' gaze briefly. 'Gasping.'

'And why was that?' She has her pen poised. She knows what's coming next, I know she does, because I've told this bit to the others.

I tell her anyway. I tell her that there was a knife in my bag. It was on the top, on top of the cloth bags I keep in there for the supermarket, my purse, my glasses case, my brolly, my tissues. I took it out but almost immediately threw it back. The blade was folded into the wooden handle, but even so I recognised it straight away. It was Mark's. He'd bought it on holiday in Spain a couple of years before.

'Oh God.' I backed away. My Tupperware box with my sandwich in it was still in my hand.

Mark didn't look up from the iPad.

'There's a knife in my bag,' I said.

'What?' Eyes still glued to screen.

'There's a knife. In my bag.'

'A knife in your bag how?' He swiped his forefinger across the screen. Still he didn't look at me.

'In my bag,' I said. 'There's a knife in my bag. I think it's yours.'

His brow furrowed, but I couldn't tell if it was in response to me or something he'd read. The lack of reaction made me wonder whether I'd spoken out loud, whether I'd imagined seeing the knife. Between the hot flushes and the fugues and the nightmares and the rages, I wasn't myself – I knew that much.

I stepped back and peered into the bag. The knife was still there. It looked peaceful, as if it were sleeping.

'Mark,' I said, louder this time. 'Will you listen to me? Your hunting knife's in my bag.'

Finally he looked up, not quite at me, and his eyes were screwed up in a cynical expression. 'My *hunting* knife? Since when did I go hunting? What're you on about?'

'It's your knife. From Spain. The one you bought as a souvenir but we realised afterwards how sharp it was? Look, I might be menopausal, but I'm not mental. That knife you bought on holiday the year before last. The fancy one with the blade that pops out when you push the little button.'

Still he didn't move from his chair. More than half an eye on the iPad, he said, 'Did you read about this girl getting attacked Saturday night near the town hall?'

'Mark,' I said. 'Mark, didn't you hear me? The hunting knife from Spain. What's it doing in my bag?'

He moved. Stood. Took a step towards me. Like an ocean liner inching out of a harbour or a glacier creeping down a hill, you needed time-lapse photography to see the progress. 'A knife?'

'Look.'

He dragged his limbs over to where I was standing and peered at the knife, lifted it carefully out by the handle. Can't rush these things. 'Mine, you say?'

'It's that one you bought in Spain. Don't you recognise it?'

He was inspecting it as if he'd never seen it before, turning it in his hands like he was on that *CSI* show. He's not the most observant, Mark. Not with material things. Wouldn't recognise our crockery in a line-up, and you could give him another man's shirt to wear and he'd never know. When Kieron was at home, Mark would only realise he had the wrong trousers once he couldn't get them past his knees, and even then he'd swear blind they'd shrunk in the wash.

'Don't you remember?' I prompted. 'Malaga, the year before last.' Christ, it was like playing charades, except you're allowed to speak plain English and still no one can guess what you mean. I wouldn't mind, but we've only been abroad once. 'Don't you remember buying it in that little tourist shop? It had a brown leather sheath with beige patterns on, wherever that is. You had to pack it in your hold luggage because of airport checks. No? Don't you remember you cut yourself within seconds of buying it? You didn't even notice until your hand started gushing.'

He opened his hand and stared at it as if he expected to find it bleeding all over again. Light appeared to dawn. His mouth opened. His brow furrowed. 'What's it doing in your bag?'

'Oh my God, that's what I've been saying for the past half hour, love. That's what I'm asking you. What's your hunting knife doing in my bag?'

'How should I know? What are you getting all het up about?'

I took a moment, made myself breathe.

'I'm not getting het up,' I said with as much calm as I could muster. 'I'm just asking.' Honest to God. Marriage is a spiral into madness sometimes. It's like *Alice in Wonderland*, except with a lot more chores.

I took the knife out and pressed the button on the side. The blade flicked out, flashed under the kitchen lights. It was clean. Why wouldn't it be clean? I thought. What had I expected?

I didn't say any of this out loud. I felt Jo's shoulder against the palm of my hand, remembered my urge to shove her, push her face under the water. A knife tip pressed against skin. Breakthrough. The warm plunge into bloody insides. My chest tightened, as if someone had put a weight on it. I was getting hotter. I think I was scared, somewhere deep down, that I might have done something very bad.

'We keep it in the garage,' I said. 'In the old chest of drawers.'

'Did you lock the garage?' He meant the door that leads out from our kitchen.

'Why the hell would I lock the garage? What kind of weird question is that? I never go in there.'

And then I remembered that I'd been into the garage to fetch dog food the day before yesterday. I remembered seeing the knife in a drawer but I couldn't remember why I was looking in that drawer or whether I had taken the knife out. But it had definitely had its leather sleeve on it then. So where was that now?

'The case is here.' Mark was standing by the open cutlery drawer, the ornate leather sheath in his hand. 'Are you sure you didn't bring it in from the garage, use it for something?'

'I went in for dog food, that's all.'

'Maybe you used it to open the dog food bag or something? Maybe it was already in the kitchen drawer?' His eyes drifted towards the dresser, rested a moment on my file. It was only a second, but I saw it.

'It's got nothing to do with that,' I said.

'With what?'

'You know what I mean. It's got nothing to do with my clippings.'

He sighed. Shook his head. 'You've got to stop with that, I've told you. I told you it'd make you paranoid and it obviously has.

Carrying knives around. This is Halton, not *Grand Theft Auto*. You can get arrested for carrying a knife, you know.'

'I'm not paranoid. And I'm not carrying knives around. It's just…'

But he was walking away. Out of the kitchen, shaking his head. His sandwich box was in his hand even though I had no memory of him taking it from the fridge. He walked up the hall, disappeared for a moment into the cupboard under the stairs and appeared a minute later threading one arm into his coat. At the front door he stopped, shrugged the rest of his coat on and leaned on the door frame a second before turning to look at me. I wasn't enjoying him never looking at me, obviously, but the way he looked at me then… well, I'd rather he hadn't bothered. His eyes were dark and puckered and tiny as raisins. They were the eyes of someone who thinks that what they're looking at is too exasperating for words.

Except he wasn't looking at me, not really, not into my eyes. He was looking at some point near my collarbone. 'Might you have been having one of your… you know, your hormonal whatsits.'

Hormonal whatsits. I nearly snorted, made a mental note to tell Lisa. She'd love that one.

'Rachel,' he said. 'Are you listening to me? It's not funny.'

'I know.' I hadn't even realised I'd been giggling.

'Are you sure you didn't bring the knife in from the garage?'

'No.' I stopped laughing then. 'I'm not.'

The latch clicked shut. At the sound of a woman's voice coming from outside, I wandered into the hallway, opened the front door.

Ingrid. Hands clasped girlishly at her waist, in her nightie and a fluffy coral-pink cardie this time, and I was sure her lips couldn't be the exact same shade of pink naturally. It seemed to me that she'd brushed her hair. And she was smiling at Mark like he used to be in Take That or something.

'I applied to Pam like you suggested.' Her words reached me in snatches. 'And guess what? She rang… come in… interview.' Jeez, Louise, the squeaky tone of voice on it. You'd have thought she'd won the pools. I wouldn't mind, but I knew from talking to her that she wasn't keen on anything resembling hard work, so why she was so excited was anyone's guess.

Mark had stopped on our drive – well, he had no choice, did he; he'd been ambushed. He was smiling, actually smiling at her, teeth and everything. His ears had gone red.

'That's great news,' he said.

'It's next Wednesday,' Ingrid said. I could hear her better now. 'So-o-o-o, I need to ask you a few things, maybe later when you're not busy, like about dress code and parking and…'

My head spun. I steadied myself against the wall and closed my eyes. I saw Jo, little anxious Jo, laid out on a hospital bed. Intensive care. Critical. Her bony little shoulders, her yellow fingers. Bags of blood. Bags of saline. Bags of urine. Needles, tubes, my God.

'I'm so grateful,' Ingrid was simpering on. 'You must let me buy you a drink!'

I should go to the hospital. Say I'm Jo's aunt or something. Ask her what she remembers. What do *I* remember? Please God, let her live.

The click of Mark's car lock, his voice, different from the one he used for me; this one had a smile in it. 'It's nothing. Don't worry about it. Glad to help, like.'

'It's not nothing at all, don't be silly! It was really sweet of you. I'm so-o-o-o grateful, you can't imagine.'

Mark ducked into the driving seat. He was blushing. 'It's fine,' he said. 'Honestly, don't worry about it.' The car door slammed; the engine growled into life. He backed out of the driveway and off he went. A fat plop of rain, then another, spotted the driveway.

Drops. Drops on drops become puddles. Puddles become streams. Streams become rivers. Rivers become seas.

Things that were separate become whole.

I watched Ingrid watching him, waving like a child. But she wasn't a child.

'Congratulations,' I called out to her from the porch and couldn't help but smirk when she jumped out of her skin. Didn't see me standing here, did you, love? Remember me, do you? Mark's wife? 'Great news on the interview.'

She turned to me, head to one side, all coy. 'Thanks,' she said, beaming. Shamelessly, I thought. 'It was so nice of Mark to pull a few strings for me.'

How easily she said his name.

'He's a nice man,' I said. 'He's nice to everyone – it's just what he's like.' I knew that my smile reached nowhere near my eyes.

'Don't suppose you fancy a coffee?' Ingrid squinted into the low sun, put her hand up to shield her eyes. The rain thickened.

'Sorry, love.' I looked up, wondered if there'd be a rainbow in a bit. Or a storm. 'I've got to get to work.'

'Another time then.'

'Sure. Good luck with your interview.'

'Thanks, Rachel.' Her smiled faltered. Hers hadn't reached her eyes either. 'Are you all right? You look a bit...'

'I'm fine, love. Just need to crack on, that's all.' I turned away. The sight of her all thin and wan and not moving a muscle despite the thickening rain was getting on my nerves. What was she, waterproof?

Two minutes later, cagoule on, I dashed for the car. Ingrid was gone. As was the sun. The sky had committed and the decision was rain, no rainbow today. The clouds were smudged charcoal, like one of Kieron's sketches. I made a mental note to take some to the framers, sent him a quick text to say I'd be doing that this week before setting off, eyes focused on the road, wipers going nineteen to the dozen. I was breathing funny, my head throbbing. Jo in her too-big coat, her fingertips pinched at her forehead; Jo laughing as she pulled me over the railings; Jo bleeding out on the pavement, mistaken for a heap of rubbish in the night. She was still alive, thank God. But she had been stabbed. There was a sharp knife in my bag. But where was the blood? I pulled into the car park by the canal, a full-on wave of panic rolling into my chest. A buzzing of bees, a terrible static. I switched off the engine, pushed my forehead against the steering wheel. I was shaking, crying, everything cold and in flames. I gripped the steering wheel with both hands, tried to get my breathing under control.

'Poor sweet girl,' I whispered. 'Poor, poor sweet girl.'

I knew I should call the police and tell them what I knew. But I didn't.

CHAPTER 16

Lisa

Transcript of recorded interview with Lisa Baxter (excerpt)
Also present: DI Heather Scott, PC Marilyn Button

HS: Ms Baxter, can you remember where you were on the night of the attack on Joanna Weatherall? The evening of Saturday the twenty-ninth of June?

LB: I've looked at my calendar and I haven't got anything marked down. My life is pretty empty just at the minute. My girls are at uni and my husband left me. I mean, it was almost two years ago now, but I'm not really the dating type. Patrick, my ex, always said I was too gobby. He said I put men off, said they didn't like women to be funnier than them. Mark was never bothered. He used to laugh at my jokes almost more than Rachel. But then Mark's a great bloke. They were such a close family. They always had a good time together, do you know what I mean? Always throwing barbecues in their back garden, Sunday roasts, what have you. And they were great with Kieron when he came out, just great. Him and Rachel were always up in Liverpool shopping or seeing films or down the library – book nuts the pair of them. They used to lie top to tail on the couch reading and you couldn't get a word out of either of them.

HS: Ms Baxter. So you can't remember where you were that night?

LB: Sorry, no. But I'd remember if I'd tried to stab someone, wouldn't I? And I'd tell you now if Rachel had turned up at ours with blood all over her. I can't protect her, can I? She's turned herself in.

HS: Did you have any contact with Rachel Edwards that Saturday?

LB: I think I saw her a couple of days before. She turned up quite early in the morning with the dog. Actually, it was the Sunday, the previous Sunday. We've talked about that, haven't we?

HS: And how would you describe her state of mind?

LB: She was… she was unsettled, I suppose, but I don't know if I saw it at the time or whether I'm seeing it now, with hindsight.

HS: Unsettled in what way?

LB: I think she thought something weird was happening to her, but as I say, I just thought we were talking about the change. She used to be a real looker back in the day, so maybe it was harder for her. I was always the mate, do you know what I mean? In her shadow sort of thing. But she'd let herself go this last year, which, I mean, I'm not judging, I'm not criticising at all – it's completely understandable.

HS: Was she unhappy in her marriage?

LB: (Pause) It was a bad patch. Mark's not the type to send flowers or whisk a girl off her feet, but he's a good bloke, do you know what I mean? We used to tease him when he first got together with Rach because all the lads were after her. But she chose him because he wasn't after her for the same reasons. He saw her, if you know what I mean. Didn't just see the face and the figure and all that. He saw who she was and that's what she wanted, to be seen like that. But any sign of emotional turmoil and he's like most men, rabbit in the headlights. Back when she was ill, it was me that told him she needed to go to hospital. He was a bit hopeless, like.

HS: And would you have said he was equally perturbed in recent months, given her behaviour?

LB: We were both worried. But I didn't know she was printing off all these knife crimes until he told me. We should have acted sooner. I never thought... never imagined... well, you don't, do you? How can anyone imagine anything like this?

CHAPTER 17

Rachel

How I got through work that day I will never know. Nothing was solid, if you know what I mean. I felt like I wasn't tethered to the earth, like I might float away and never be able to get back down. That young lass. Stabbed, left for dead. She was just a girl, on the cusp of womanhood, lying on the pavement alone, a crumpled heap of clothes. And so near to her friend's house. So near to where I'd said goodbye, my God. It didn't bear thinking about, but think about it was all I could do. I did nothing but imagine that knife, how hard you'd have to push to break the skin. How easy it would be after crossing that precious boundary to drive the blade in, how much blood, how soon she'd lose consciousness. I saw it. I felt it, over and over – the pressure in my hand, the sudden lurch forward once the skin broke.

Had she tried to crawl to her friend's house or had she just dropped where she'd been attacked and passed out?

Around lunchtime, the *Weekly News* website was updated. *Doctors fear for knife-attack girl.* I caught it later, towards two, on my lunch.

> The woman found unconscious near Runcorn Town
> Hall late on Saturday evening, Joanna Weatherall from
> Farnborough, Hampshire, is said to be in a critical
> condition.

'She's lucky to be alive,' said Helen Parkin, a spokesperson for Halton Hospital. 'But it's too early to predict her chances of survival at this stage.'

Nicky Andrews, a friend of Ms Weatherall's, was at the hospital.

'Jo was coming to visit,' Ms Andrews told the *Weekly News*. 'We started to get worried when she didn't answer her phone. I drove to the station to find her, and when she wasn't there, I drove round all the roads, thinking she must have walked. She walked everywhere, did Jo. She loved her fitness. But there was no sign of her, so in the end I called her parents and then I called the police.'

One eyewitness said he saw a young woman matching Joanna's description talking to a middle-aged woman near the town-hall park earlier in the evening. He thought they might be mother and daughter. He described the young woman as thin and pale, with dark hair, but couldn't give any details on the older.

Police are appealing for information.

'We're keen to establish the identity of both these women,' said police spokesperson Keith Woodhead. 'If anyone has any information they believe to be relevant in any way, they are encouraged to call the following number...

There was the number followed by the usual links: *Knife crime on the rise*; *How safe are our streets?*; *Knife crime at record high*; *How to talk to your kids about knives.*

I sent the link for Jo's story to my home email to print off later. The witness either hadn't seen or hadn't remembered the dog, which was lucky. I was glad we'd gone for a small black Cockapoo, though why these thoughts were coming to me I didn't know. I hadn't touched Jo apart from laying my hand on her back. I hadn't harmed her in any way, and I certainly hadn't driven a blade through her ribs. Twice. I was pretty sure the middle-aged woman in the article was me. That would have been when we stopped, before we climbed over the fence. Or after. If it was me, that would explain why the witness couldn't remember anything. Not easy, is it, describing someone invisible?

But Jo would wake up sooner or later. Surely she'd remember something about me, something more than *middle-aged*? And for all that being The Woman No One Saw was bothering me, I wasn't sure if I wanted Jo to remember me at all.

That week I kept my head down, checked the news for updates. Tuesday, another appeal for information, a report that the CCTV camera had been out of order, police keen to speak to the woman who might have been talking to Joanna Weatherall shortly before she was attacked; Wednesday, another appeal, Joanna still critical; Thursday, nothing. Forecast: rain again – it was all right in the morning but bucketing it down when I came out of work. I'd put my cagoule in my bag, thank heavens, but even so, I hadn't expected it to be so heavy. I didn't have my umbrella with me and I knew I'd be soaked by the time I'd crossed town. I hovered in the doorway even though I was running late because there'd been a bit of argy-bargy with a customer, as there sometimes is when they've had one too many. It wasn't about the wrong change, which was what he was claiming I'd given him; I was just taking the flak for his shitty day. He'd probably fallen out with his missus or something. Constipation, whatever. Piles.

Outside the pub, people scurried past the Devonshire Bakery, the indoor market, shoulders hunched, faces pinched, eyes thrown upwards in disgust. Pulling a face, the great British defence against the weather. There was no sign of the homeless lad and I hoped he'd found shelter somewhere; couldn't stand the thought of him getting wet through with no way of drying off. I really didn't fancy getting wet either, but with the downpour showing no sign of abating, in the end I grabbed the dog-eared *Racing Post* that Phil had left on the bar, shoved it over my head and legged it.

I ran all the way up Church Street and past the Co-op. Katie and Mark would be chomping at the bit for their tea, as would the boyf if he was there, as he often was, sitting on the kitchen table, legs swinging, shovelling my stash of digestive biscuits down his cakehole like there was no tomorrow. I was supposed to be doing cottage pie, and I knew that if I didn't get a shift on we wouldn't be eating much before seven. Katie says I'm a weirdo for thinking everyone needs at least one hot meal a day, and I suppose it is old-fashioned, but that's me. I've never been into food fads, and how sushi is classed as a meal I will never know. Raw fish, what's that about?

There I go again, veering off topic. Rushing past the Co-op, wasn't I, betting paper on my head, odds of staying dry very low indeed. I ran across the high street and hit the path that leads past the doctors' surgery, where I'd seen the GP, to the car park beside the canal. At the near end of the path, raindrops splashed into a puddle. I stopped a moment, transfixed by how quickly the drops lost their edges and became one with the murky water, but then a great trickle ran into my collar, down my back and became one with my pants.

By the time I got to the car park, I was wetter than a haddock's bathing costume, the *Post* all but reduced to papier mâché on my head. I fumbled for my keys, got myself into the car and sighed massively. The windscreen and all the windows were fogged up. I turned the key for the ignition. The engine coughed and fell silent.

'No,' I said through my teeth. 'No, no, no, no, no.'

It doesn't rain, does it? I thought. It bloody pours. And it really was chucking it down, so the expression fitted doubly. If I hadn't been so hacked off, I might even have laughed at the irony. I tried again with the ignition, but there wasn't even a cough this time, just a last asthmatic gasp. And then I noticed the switch for the headlights was turned to on.

'For crying out loud,' I said to no one. And then I had a good old swear, but that kind of language doesn't need repeating here, does it? Suffice to say that what little air there was in my rusty Renault was a filthy shade of blue.

I dug around in my bag for my mobile, found it, switched it on. I was about to call Mark, but I didn't. He'd be just in the door from work and I couldn't face the sulky voice on the other end of the line when I told him I'd left the headlights on, which in that moment I decided not to tell him at all.

I would try and flag someone down on the high street and see if they'd give me a lift home. I knew where the jump leads were – in the dresser in the garage. Yes, jump leads. Sisters are doing it for themselves.

Of course, at that moment I didn't have a clue how the evening would go, did I? I had no clue what terrible significance those jump leads would come to have.

CHAPTER 18

Ingrid

Transcript of recorded interview with Ingrid Taylor (excerpt)
Also present: DI Heather Scott, PC Marilyn Button

HS: So, to clarify, your relationship with Mark Edwards was purely platonic?

IT: (Laughs) Look, the worst thing Mark ever did was have one or two of my cigarettes. I suspect he's the kind of man who has no idea when a woman wants him and wouldn't dare do anything about it if he did. Not that I wanted him. I had no interest in him, not in that way, but I can't help whatever feelings he had for me. As I've said, it was friendship, nothing more. I'm not even looking for a relationship at the moment, I'm still getting over my divorce. A man is literally the last thing on my mind.

HS: So you wouldn't say you were close?

IT: We became close, yes. I've said that. He could talk to me in a way he couldn't talk to her. She was never there, and even when she was there, it's like she wasn't really, you know? You'd be talking to her and you could tell she wasn't listening. And then she'd kind of twitch her head and stare at you as if she'd just woken up and was shocked to see you. It gave me the creeps, to be honest. But I told Mark I'd keep an eye on her, pop in, that sort of thing. I'm not a snob, far from it. It didn't bother me that they were more working class; I'm not like that, I was genuinely trying to fit in. I wasn't used to the whole community thing, but I have to say it bugged me that she didn't appreciate him. He's such a good man. Decent, you know? And, not to be bitchy, but he's aged a lot better than her. I mean, it must've been like living with a robot. Walking dead. At some point you've got to get on with your life and she still had her daughter to look after, not that I could see much evidence of that going on, honestly, coming home at all hours, drunk by the looks at her. The daughter, I mean. For all her superficial kindness, Rachel was quite a selfish woman, I think.

HS: And the evening of Thursday the fourth of July? The following week?

IT: What about it?

HS: Can you tell us where you were?

IT: At home.

HS: You sound very sure.

IT: I'm always at home.

HS: That night, Rachel Edwards' car broke down and they had a chip supper. Does that jog your memory at all?

IT: Chip supper, well, I'm sorry, that doesn't really narrow it down. But yes, that must have been the night I heard their front door open and the daughter shouting 'Large scampi and fries!' so loudly I heard it from over the road.

I felt like shouting back, 'Are you sure you should be eating that, darling? At your age?' I wonder sometimes if these people actually read any freely available dietary information. Not to be unkind, but they're literally storing up trouble for later life.

HS: So you're saying you saw Rachel Edwards leave the house?

IT: No, it was Mark. I thought it was Mark, I mean, getting into his car and driving away.

HS: And then you went out?

IT: I think so. I might have done. I'm really not a hundred per cent sure. Look, I can't keep track of my every move from months ago. It's not as if I knew these dates would turn out to be relevant at the time, is it? Why? What's this got to do with the stabbings? Did she murder someone else that night? Oh my God, did she?

CHAPTER 19

Rachel

I glance up at Blue Eyes.

'I suppose you've seized them, haven't you?' I say. 'The jump leads? Exhibit A sort of thing?'

The merest inclination of her head, as if she's bidding for a painting and knows the auctioneer well. I take that as a yes.

I'd seen the jump leads the other day when I'd gone in for the dog food, when I'd seen Mark's knife. Sitting in the car, I came up with a plan:

Thumb lift home.

Get dinner in oven.

Say I was going out to walk the dog.

Sort car out for myself.

I couldn't face the withering looks, to be honest. The head shakes, the sighs. But then maybe once they'd been fed, Mark or Katie would give me a lift back and help me jump-start my car. Maybe. Yes, this was where I'd got to. Status: doormat. Unable to admit to a mistake for fear of ridicule. Unable to ask for a kindness for fear of refusal.

So that was why I was on the high street opposite the surgery at quarter to six, trying to hitch a lift from random cars ploughing through the sheeting downpour like Mad Max machines. You'd think someone would have recognised me, wouldn't you? Stopped and said, *hop in, love, you'll catch your death*. You'll be ahead of me,

I'm sure. If I was invisible before, try adding dark cloud and thick rain to the mix. I must have stood on that flooded pavement for over thirty minutes in what passes for rush hour in my northern industrial town, but could I get any bugger to stop? Could I thump. By the time I gave up, I was soaked to the skin and, I have to say, close to tears.

I trudged back to the car and called Mark from there, but he didn't pick up. I called Katie, but despite the fact that her phone could be mistaken for a bionic extension grafted onto her right hand, she didn't pick up either. We didn't have a landline because Mark said it was a waste of money if we were all paying for expensive iPhone contracts, so I couldn't ring the house either. Ironic, I know: all three of us with our own phones and we couldn't even communicate with one another. I didn't have cash for a cab, let alone one of them Uber apps, so in the end I thought, sod it, I'll walk.

It stopped raining just as I was passing the town hall. Even though I knew Mark and Katie would be wondering where I was, I stopped at the fence to have a look in. There was nothing to see, obviously. I don't know what I was expecting. I stared into the gardens, picturing my hand white against Jo's back. The smallness of her. How safe she'd felt in my maternal embrace. How near to death she'd been in my care. The corner near where we'd parted ways had been taped off. There were two bunches of flowers propped against the wall. I gave a deep, sad sigh – for Jo, for myself, for the knife I'd found in my bag and what it might or might not mean. And when I saw what I took to be the remnants of a bloodstain on the pale grey paving stones, I sank to my knees and wept.

That was when I got the first proper flash. The first one that frightened me. I'd been imagining the knife, but this felt more like a memory. The knife slicing through cloth, pushing into firm young skin. A slick across my knuckles, fingers covered in thick wet blood. A form collapsing onto the pavement, collapsing like a bag of jumble.

'Oh, Jo.' I sobbed for her there on the pavement. 'Jo, my love, what happened to you?'

I must have got up eventually. It took me forty-five minutes to reach home, so I was probably on my knees for ten, fifteen. I can remember running, the horrible thought that Jo might have died making me race back. Once I was in the door, I peeled off my cagoule in the hallway and carried it carefully into the downstairs loo, where I hung it over the tap so it would drip into the sink. There didn't seem to be anyone home. The iPad was on the worktop, so I checked the *Weekly News* straight away. There were no updates. My breath left me in a long, heavy blast of relief. If she were dead, they would have reported it. If she'd woken up, they would have reported that too.

'Hello?' I called out, wandering back into the hall. No answer. 'Hello?' I shouted, leaning my head into the stairwell. 'Katie? Mark? Anybody in?'

'In here.' Mark. Lounge.

I put my head around the door. I must have looked a state, hair plastered to my head with a mixture of sweat and rain, and flushed from exertion. But he didn't look at me so I don't suppose it mattered. He was reading the paper. The telly was on. *The One Show*, I think it was, not that I could swear under oath or anything – one grinning idiot presenter is much the same as another in my book.

'Sorry I'm late,' I said. I checked my watch and saw it was after seven. No way we could have cottage pie now, not if we wanted to eat before nine.

'Have you had any tea?' I asked him, even though I knew he wouldn't have.

He cleared his throat. 'I was waiting for you. Didn't know what you'd want.'

Didn't know what you'd want. As if I'd say, *Pasta bake, are you joking?* As if someone cooking a meal and setting it before me without me asking wouldn't be enough to send me into tears of gratitude.

'Our Katie in?'

He raised his eyebrows, but I couldn't tell if it was a response or whether he'd read something that had mildly surprised him. Or whether his gall bladder was playing up again.

'Watching something on her laptop, I think.'

I hesitated. 'Mark?'

'Hmm?'

I wondered if he'd even noticed I was late. 'My car wouldn't start, love. That's why I'm so late. It's the battery. I think the rain flattened it. I couldn't get hold of you or Katie. I've had to walk home.'

And then, hallelujah, he looked at me. I watched him take in my bedraggled appearance, my grey work trousers black with water from mid-thigh down, the expression of defeat I felt sure I was wearing. His eyes creased at the edges in dismay or disbelief or something. He was staring at me, really staring, as if I'd materialised from the plug-in air freshener.

'You're joking?' he said.

I think it was at that point that I realised something else. I'd already got as far as knowing that I wasn't invisible like air is invisible. Or carbon monoxide or whatever. I knew that if you looked at me you couldn't see through me or anything like that. I was invisible the way that household objects are invisible, like the hoover or the dishwasher or the kettle, in the sense that yes, they're solid objects, but you don't really see them, do you? Or notice them or whatever. But now it dawned on me that the one time you do notice the hoover or the dishwasher or the kettle is when they go wrong. My husband was looking right at me. I knew he could see me, could feel his eyes on my face. He wasn't gazing at me with love, obviously; he was looking at me because it was nearly seven and there was no dinner. I had malfunctioned. I was a hoover that had stopped picking up, a dishwasher that didn't get the plates clean, a kettle with a dodgy element.

And actually, I started to feel exactly like a kettle in that moment. I was full of water, the liquid insides of me heating around a red-hot element at the core of my being, tiny bubbles rising.

'I'm just…' I muttered.

I left Mark in the lounge and went to sit in the kitchen with my head in my hands. Sweat ran down my back, prickled on my forehead. I felt like I was going to be sick, had the impression I was going to slide off my chair. My head throbbed and I closed my eyes to try and calm everything down. Another second and I was wrestling myself out of my cardie. I pulled my work T-shirt over my head. I was down to my bra with a vest on top, knew I should get out of my wet trousers, but I couldn't move. I was panting, trying to suck in air in small swallowed breaths, trying to get oxygen into my lungs. My eyelids were sweating, for crying out loud; my armpits sent more perspiration trickling down my sides, into my waistband. I kept my eyes closed, focused on bringing my temperature down, and all the while I was thinking, I'm a kettle, I'm a kettle, I'm a kettle. I'm a kettle with a dodgy element. I'm going to explode. And when I do, I will rain boiling water down on everyone.

The kitchen door squeaked. I opened one eye a crack and saw the tip of Mark's slippers.

'What's the matter?'

'Nothing. Just hot, that's all.'

A heavy sigh. 'I suppose we'd better go and get the bloody car then.'

We drove there in Mark's Astra. It only took ten minutes or so, but from the vice-like set of his jaw, you'd think I'd asked him to drive me to France. At least he let me have his cagoule, which was dry and, being menswear, actually covered my bottom, and it's got the big hood and the big pockets – which was where I put the jump leads.

I close my eyes and I'm there. It's cold despite it being early July. The rain has started again and it's heavy: glass javelins spearing the canal. Mark is grunting like an old fella, propping open both bonnets while I hold his golfing umbrella over his head. I know how to attach jump leads to batteries and it was my car, but he's done it, mood filthy as the night, before I have a chance to open my mouth. He gets into my car to start it, which I also know how to do, obviously. But I let him get on with it; I'm grateful for the help.

The heat inside me has died down. I'm clammy and washed out, but nothing more.

The Twingo starts more or less straight off.

'May as well drive this one now I've got it going,' he shouts through the window. 'No sense both of us getting wet. You take mine.'

'OK.'

I still have my hood up. The rain is going off but there's mizzle in the air. I shove the jump leads back into Mark's cagoule pocket. By the time I've got into the driving seat and readjusted it to my short legs, he's gone. I turn on the ignition, almost die of a heart attack at the deafening blast of Radio 5. I turn it off. I get enough of ill-informed men pontificating on things they know nothing about at work.

It's quarter to eight when I finally get home. But at least I don't feel like I'm going to erupt anymore, start spouting boiling water all over the kitchen floor. I should get changed. Only I'm halfway up the stairs when Mark says: 'Where are you going?'

What he means is: *Where's my tea?*

'I was just going to get some dry clothes on. I might even change into my PJs.'

His face is the original bulldog chewing a wasp. He's hungry and it's my fault. I feel the irritation, the hunger in my stomach like I did with Jo, but then I think that I'm probably hungry too and I don't really know if I'm hungry or Mark is or we both are or what. And as for the irritation, well, obviously I know Mark inside out and back to front and I can tell what mood he's in by the back of his head, so I suppose it isn't clear what's normal and what has to do with the finely tuned instincts of the perimenopausal woman.

'What were you thinking for tea?' He's still standing in the hallway.

'I was going to do cottage pie. But it's too late now.'

'Shall we have fish and chips?'

'Do you want me to go?'

'Are you sure?'

The dance we do. I trudge back down and put his cagoule on again.

'What do you want then?' I shove a twenty into my damp trouser pocket.

'Large fish and chips. And curry sauce. I'm starving.' He isn't looking at me anymore. He's walking away.

The *tsh* of a ring pull reaches me from the kitchen. I'm on the lip of the front door when I hear, 'Are you going to the chippy?' Katie, shouting from the top of the stairs. Didn't even know she was in. 'Can you get us large scampi and chips and mushy peas?'

'All right. Set the table.'

I close the door, thinking how funny it is that when I call out hello in the hope of a friendly hello back, no one hears me. But one muttered conversation about fish and chips and Katie develops the hearing of a bloody bat.

CHAPTER 20

Katie

Transcript of recorded interview with Katie Edwards (excerpt)
Also present: DI Heather Scott, PC Marilyn Button

KE: On the Saturday I was with Liam and that Thursday I was at home because I was learning how to do acrylic nails in my room – you can check with Thea 'cause I was on FaceTime with her – and then Mum came home with the chips. I had scampi.

HS: Great, that's great, thanks. And did you see your mother on the Saturday?

KE: I don't think so.

HS: And the Thursday? How did your mum seem that night?

KE: She was in a right mood. My dad should've gone for the chips but she just went in quite a pass-agg way. She does that. She, like, wants you to do something but then she does it before you've had time to do it. She was ages getting the chips and by the time she got back she reckoned she was so cold she had to go for a bath, but that was just a guilt trip. Me and dad ate ours in the kitchen.

HS: So your mother was angry? How angry would you say?

KE: She was just in a mood. She wasn't, like, screaming for murder or anything. I'm telling you she didn't do anything – she just wouldn't do anything like that.

HS: Was there anything else about that night you can remember?

KE: Erm. (Pause) I heard the doorbell go and I could smell fags.

HS: When would that have been?

KE: Erm. About twenty minutes or so before my mum got back.

HS: So someone came into your house? Do you know who it was?

KE: It was probably our neighbour. She was always popping in. Ingrid.

HS: So Ingrid Taylor came to your house that night?

KE: I'm just saying that the doorbell went and I could smell fags. Ingrid was always coming round when Mum was out. Why do you want to know about that night anyway? I thought there were only three attacks?

CHAPTER 21

Rachel

The chip shop was rammed, queue coming out the door. Impossible to park anywhere near. I found a space eventually on the other side of St Michael's church. That's why I cut through the graveyard, in case you were wondering. And can I just say, I did think twice, of course I did, I'm not daft. It was dark, and though I might be a bit past it, I'm still a woman and like every other woman have spent my whole life avoiding shady corners and empty streets, scurried along many a road late at night listening behind me for footsteps. But I was starving, my kecks – sorry, my trousers – were sticky and I just wanted to get the chips and get home. Anyway, talking to Phil every day, I'd started seeing the world in terms of odds, and I reckoned the odds of me getting through the shortcut without being seen were in my favour, what with me being invisible.

The iron gate whistled on its hinges like something out of a gothic horror. I had a good grin to myself about that, even whispered *woo* sarcastically under my breath as I set off down the path. I walked slowly at first, but after no more than two or three paces, I heard a heavy scraping noise behind me. That wiped the grin right off my face. I walked faster. When the noise got faster too, I stopped. The noise stopped. Hulking graves crouched all around. My heart was hammering by now and my forehead was drenched. I was an idiot. I'd cut through a graveyard in the mizzling dark, to gain, what, five minutes? Madness, bloody madness. I took three quick strides – heard three dragging scratches behind me. A whimper escaped me. I half walked, half ran. *Sht sht sht* came from behind, *sht sht sht*, faster and faster, in time with me. My breathing came shallow and fast. I had at least another fifty paces to get to the other side.

I stopped. The noise stopped. With all my courage, all my strength of will, I made myself turn around.

Nothing. No one.

'Hello?' I squinted down the dark path. The cemetery was as silent as, well, a graveyard. On the far side, the street was deserted. I peered into the gloom. 'Who's there?' I called out. 'If you think this is funny, well, it's not.'

Nothing. The whisper of leaves. Night's cut-out shapes. My throat thickened. I turned back. Took one step.

Sht.

'Oh for God's—' I spun around on my heel, furious now, looked behind me, up, down. And then I saw it.

I glance up. Blue Eyes is on the edge of her seat.

'It?' she says.

'There was a big twig,' I say, 'caught on the hem of my trousers, one end on the path. It had been dragging behind me.'

And for the first time in all these hours we've spent together, she laughs.

'What did you do?'

I tell her I pulled the twig off, tutting and swearing, my heart not slowing, not yet, the sweat on my forehead going cold. I tell her I called myself names: bloody idiot woman, daft bat, loony tune.

It was funny, I knew that even then. Would be funny in a bit, anyway. It would be a story to tell Lisa. Lisa would do a whole routine on it, take the mickey until neither of us could breathe. But still, I was shaking and, for the second time that day, nearly crying. I ploughed on, a sick feeling in my stomach. Kept up a brisk pace. My mother had a plaque here; she'd been cremated.

The plaque was on the far wall but I didn't have time to visit it now. Not like she was there. She never bothered much with me when she was, to be honest, too wrapped up in my dad, as he was in her. My dad, now him I did need to visit. I hadn't been to see him for a week or so.

The church loomed. In its shadow, the ground darkened. I could see the arch of the sandstone doorway up ahead, the recess of the porch black as all hell. I was walking silly fast by now, like one of those race walkers in the Commonwealth Games, all elbows and wiggling bottom. I told myself not to be so stupid. It wasn't far now to the other side. There was no one here, no one at all. It was all in my mind. It had been a twig, just a twig, and now I was spooked, that was all. The chill on my legs got colder. I was about two or three metres from the church when I heard a grunting sound. I stopped. It was coming from the doorway. A noise I recognised and didn't all at the same time, if you know what I mean. The grunting was regular, rhythmical. I knew exactly what it was but no part of me wanted to admit that that was what it could be. I screwed up my eyes and stared towards the doorway. A man's back, shoulders hunched forward, head tipped down. His arm chugged back and forth in a rhythm that meant I could no longer deny what I was hearing, seeing.

'Oh for goodness' sake,' I whispered to myself. 'In the doorway of the church, for Pete's sake.'

I had half a mind to shout at him, call him a pervert, tell him to sling his hook. I didn't, but I must have whispered louder than I'd thought, or gasped in shock or something, because he turned quite suddenly to look behind him. Turned and stared right at me. I swear to God, he peered into my face as if he were trying to make out if I had a nose or not. Apparently seeing nothing at all, he looked past me then, over my shoulder, into the silent darkness. A second or two later, he turned back and carried on. *Carried on*, would you believe? Animal.

I took a step nearer, another. My hands sank into my pockets – well, into Mark's pockets. The jump leads were still in there. I dug them out and stopped walking, teased them apart and returned one to the pocket. Alligator clip in one hand, I wound the lead around my other hand, pulled the smooth, thick cord tight, testing it. It was very strong.

I ducked behind a gravestone so he wouldn't see me. He was engaging in this indecent activity to shock, that much was obvious. To shock himself mostly. The noise I'd made had excited him, for crying out loud. He was getting off on being seen, on being observed in a holy place doing an unholy thing. 'Dirty bastard,' I whispered. 'Have you no shame?'

The cord was wrapped double around my hand. It slid about on my knuckles. Teeth gritted, I pulled tighter. Echoes of images took shadowy shape in my mind's eye. In them he became a child, a child abused by, oh, guess what, by a ruddy priest. Not in this church, not in any church in this town. How original, though. How depressing. It started to make sense. Poor chap. *Have you no shame?* I'd wanted to spit in his ear. But he was riddled with shame; I felt the queasy roll of it in my guts, the cold heat of it burning through my body, head to toe. All his life, this shame for something that had been done to him when he was a nipper, a shame that was not, was never his. And my God, the loneliness, loneliness to make a grown man howl at the moon. He'd been lonely all his sodding life.

Blackness. The rustle of leaves above me. A pain throbbing on the left side of my head. I coughed, once, twice. I was on my knees, coming to my senses. I had the impression that time had moved on, but I couldn't say how far. The jump lead was loose around my hands but my knuckles were sore. I had dropped to my knees, here, behind a gravestone. I was still here, behind the gravestone. Had I passed out, hit my head?

Quick footsteps. Panting. I peered over the top of the stone to see the chap running as if startled across the dark cemetery, away, away, towards the road. His wheezing receded into the night. I stared down at my hands, which were dark with what looked like blood. I rubbed at it, wiped the backs of my hands against my legs and set off for the chippy.

The queue had died down. The clock on the wall said it was twenty-five to nine. I'd lost half an hour, I reckoned. Round about that. The jump leads were in my pocket but my hands were pinky-brown where my knuckles had bled and were filthy with soil. I'd rubbed them clean as best I could, but I'd done no more than smear the remaining blood into my skin. One knuckle was still bleeding a bit. My mouth was full of a metallic taste. I felt sordid, grimy. I was sure I must stink of mud and oil, wet clothes. Maybe sweat, too.

The line moved forward, the lush hiss and waft of salty battered cod; sausages on the warmer plate; thick, soft chips. The ring and clink of the till, the slam of the cash drawer, the sing-song of the northern pleasantries I'd heard all my life: *Y'all right, love? Usual, yeah? Hiya, love, large and chips? How's your Debbie? She's not still in hospital, is she? I thought it was only mumps.*

'Love? Love? D'you want serving, love?'

I shook my head. Yvonne, the woman who owned the chippy, was staring at me.

'Sorry, love,' I said. 'Miles away.'

CHAPTER 22

Rachel

The house smelled weird when I got back. Cigarettes, I thought, but couldn't be sure; it was more of a top note than a whiff, if you know what I mean. I shouted Mark from the lounge and called up to Katie on my way past the stairs.

'Katie! Your scampi and chips!'

The big light was off in the kitchen and the house was chilly. The smell of ciggies was stronger in here, if that was what it was.

'You've been ages,' Katie said, swinging in through the door. Again, she'd heard me this time, the promise of chips apparently cutting through noise-cancelling headphones in a way that *can you clean the bathroom?* couldn't.

'There was a queue.'

'It's freezing in this house.'

'Put the heating on then.'

She made a face. 'What's the matter with you?'

'Nothing's the matter. I'm just cold and tired, that's all. Has Liam been over?'

'No, why?'

'Smells like someone's been smoking.'

She shrugged. 'The doorbell went about half an hour ago.'

I took my order out, handed her the bag and flicked the heating on. 'Did anyone answer the door?'

'I dunno.'

The words *blood* and *stone* came to mind. I literally hadn't the strength to ask anything else. My stomach was hollow and the skin on my legs was starting to itch.

'Shame no one put any plates on to warm,' I said. 'And the table's not set. Wouldn't have been too much, would it, to set the table?'

She threw up her hands. 'Whoa. Pass-agg or what?'

At that moment, Mark came in. 'I was about to send out a search party. We're starving here.'

Rage. Flashing heat all through me. A glimmer, a tiny fraction of what I'd felt in the graveyard, but still – strong enough. As I often said to Lisa, I could strangle Mark sometimes. Which, now I think about it, is probably not the best wording.

'Well, I'm sorry the delivery service isn't to your satisfaction.' I put my chips into the oven and turned it on low, slammed the door. 'Next time you can get your own.'

'Mum!' Katie said, shoving her nose in. 'Calm down, will you?'

Because saying that always works.

'Katie, can you set the table please?' I said through gritted teeth. 'Ketchup and that.' I didn't look at her. I didn't look at either of them.

'Oh my God why are you in such a mood?'

'I'm going for a bath.' I left them to it, made a point of closing the door quietly.

To the muffled sound of Katie's outrage at her mother's appalling rudeness, I climbed the stairs on aching legs. Lazy pair, I thought. Couldn't be bothered to answer the sodding door, waited for me to come home to flick one small switch to put the heating on, couldn't be arsed to fetch three plates from the cupboard and put them in the oven to warm or get the ketchup out of the sodding fridge, and I bet, I flipping well bet, the washing was still in the machine, setting in its creases so that it would be an absolute nightmare to iron. And meanwhile, tired out, wet through and fed up to the back teeth, I was the one who'd gone to get their pigging dinner. Meals on wheels, me, and all I'd got was a *where've you been?*

'Where're you going now?' Mark was calling up through the banister at me as if I'd gone mad. 'I thought we were eating.'

'I said I'm going for a bath. I'll catch my death in these wet clothes. Eat without me.'

Just because I didn't wait for the heavy sigh didn't mean I couldn't hear it. Didn't mean I didn't know he was shaking his head at me either. I put a bath on to run, pictured Mark glued to the television like he'd lost the use of his limbs, Katie upstairs stuck seething in front of some Netflix drama with umpteen series – or *seasons* as she called them now – probably in her onesie, sticking diamonds to her toenails or staring at herself in the mirror or taking her fiftieth selfie of the day or scrolling endlessly through bloody Instagram or whatever the hell it was that took all her time between her one shift a week at Lee's bakery and the next, and neither of them answering the door. Although if the house stank of fags, one of them must have. Maybe it was a canvassing politician who'd called round. The Avon lady. Jehovah's Witnesses.

The water wasn't too scalding hot so I lowered myself in and let it carry on running. Soap bubbles like blown glass, the smell of my rose bath foam. My head hurt, as if I'd bashed it. When I put my hands into the shining suds, my knuckles stung. The rage still coursed around my system. I felt the hot power of it. Perhaps that was what was giving me these bursts of strength. They made up for the sudden attacks of tiredness that made me think I must have been hit round the head by a tree. I didn't know much, but I knew something – if Katie and Mark had seen me half an hour ago, they wouldn't be talking to me like I was nothing. There'd be at least a bit of recognition.

I pushed my head under the water. I missed Kieron.

CHAPTER 23

Rachel

They hadn't set a place for me, obviously. They hadn't cleared their plates into the dishwasher or wiped away the crumbs from the bread and butter. The washing was still in the drum, starting to smell. A hot thumb of irritation burned somewhere around my sternum. But it was an ember of an hour ago.

'Mark?' I called out.

No answer. I can remember thinking he must be back in front of the idiot box, but actually it turned out later that he'd gone to the pub. I was so preoccupied that I didn't even realise until he crawled into bed around midnight, stinking of beer and cigarettes.

'Have you been smoking?' I asked him, but he was already snoring, one hand on my boob. I knew he wasn't making a pass so much as passing out; that if I reciprocated, he wouldn't respond. Like an overtired toddler, he was clutching a comforter to help him get to sleep.

But that hadn't happened yet, and when it did, it was the least of my worries, to be honest. As it was, as I ate my cod, chips and mushy peas (peas a bit crusty on the top), what floated to the top of my mind wasn't Mark, Katie, Kieron or even poor Jo, but the chap in the cemetery. I don't know if it was a delayed reaction or what, but it was only then, after I'd had my bath and got warm to my bones and got some dinner down my neck, that I started to remember in vivid detail how I'd pulled on that jump lead with the strength of a lion, enough to make my own knuckles bleed. And how I had woken as if from a dream, on my knees, with a pain in my head and no clue as to what had just gone on, or why.

Thinking about it there in the kitchen was like coming up from under anaesthetic. It was the same feeling as when I'd read about Jo a few days earlier, found out she'd been stabbed and left for dead moments after we'd gone our separate ways. The knife in my bag… I must have put it in there for self-protection, but I couldn't remember doing it. And now the jump leads in my hands, my skinned knuckles. He had run away, seemingly unharmed, but still, an unsettled, preoccupied feeling persisted in my guts. Maybe Mark was right when he said that collecting violent crimes in a file was making me paranoid. But the clip file was something I had to do. I had to build a body of evidence. I couldn't talk to him or anyone about that and I couldn't talk about the memory losses either. Maybe I should confide in Lisa. But I'd have to leave out the part about worrying whether or not I was attacking people. There's a limit to how many sandwiches short of a picnic you can admit to being before you're no longer welcome on the day out, if you know what I mean.

But I *hadn't* murdered young Jo and I hadn't attacked that chap, of that I was almost certain. And I certainly hadn't had violence or the intention to commit violence on my mind. To commit murder, to attack someone, you have to really want to, don't you? You have to be so full of anger, rage, hate that you get to a point of not caring. And whether a victim dies or not only depends on how good you are at the murdering, doesn't it? What your skill set is, whether your luck is in that night, whether you get the right weather conditions, privacy, lighting, tools, protective clothing, what have you. Whether you wanted to do it badly enough.

I hadn't wanted to kill Jo and I hadn't wanted to kill or harm that man. I had been disgusted by him, that was all – a revulsion that had soon given way to pity. If I was avoiding my reflection in the black French windows of my kitchen, it was only because I didn't want to bear witness to my own beaten appearance, my slack-shouldered confusion now that my rage had subsided. If it was true that no one saw me, it was equally true that I didn't see myself.

'Mum?'

Katie was staring at me as if I was sitting there naked belting out a one-woman chorus of 'My Bonnie Lies Over the Ocean'. She was wearing her Dalmatian onesie, her hair was in rollers and she had one eye done out in green eyeshadow, the other in blue. She filled the kettle at the sink without looking at it, only broke her stare to put it back on its electrical pad and flick it on.

You'd only see that kettle if it broke, I thought but didn't say. But she was looking right at me again, so then I thought: maybe *I'm* broke.

'What's the matter?' I said.

'Nothing's the matter with *me*. I was talking to you. I was trying to tell you something actually, and you were just staring into space. As usual.'

Ah, so I *was* broken. I wasn't giving her my full attention. *Beep beep*, malfunction, malfunction. Request error report.

'Sorry, love,' I said. 'Just a bit tired, that's all.'

She rolled her eyes and muttered what sounded like *no change there then*, turned back to the cupboard and pulled down a mug. Just the one.

'I'll have a tea if you're making,' I said.

She sighed – she can be quite the luvvie when she wants to be, can Katie – and fetched another mug down.

'Can you pass the milk then?' she said, like it was the principle of the thing.

'I haven't finished my chips.' I sat firm. You'd have been proud of me. Literally, I didn't budge.

Mouth half open, the merest shake of her head, the faintest mutter of an oh-my-God she didn't believe in, she crossed the kitchen on the world's heaviest legs and heaved, yes, heaved the milk out of the fridge door. Back the same way, oh, the effort, plastic flagon dangling from her forefinger like a dirty pair of pants no one would own up to.

'You should get one of them apps,' I said. 'A Fitbit, is it? One of them things that measures how many steps you've done. You must have done at least thirty today.'

Her eyes widened to the size of flying saucers. Her mouth dropped all the way open. Honestly, I thought her chin might land smack on the kitchen table. I kept my face straight, but it was a struggle. You might not think I'm funny anymore, I wanted to say. But Jo did. She thought I was hilarious.

'What's the matter with you?' she said. 'What's that supposed to mean?'

'Nothing,' I said. 'Put us a sugar in, will you? I need a bit of something sweet.'

Heavens above, the eyebrows on it. The gob.

'Unbelievable,' she said, shaking her head. Poor put-upon slave. Someone call social services.

When she'd gone – my tea left next to the kettle, door slammed, don't worry you've made your point, love – I ran my fingers over my knuckles. My left hand was the worst, but it had started to scab up now. I'd just have to be careful I didn't knock it, perhaps not use the jump lead again.

Perhaps not use the jump lead again.

Yes, I had that thought, I can remember having it. Which makes me think I thought there was a chance I'd done something for real.

I would have worried about Katie or Mark noticing the grazes but for the fact that neither of them could see me at all unless I was failing to do something for them. So I stopped worrying. As long as I got the dinner on and the shopping in and their laundry done and delivered to their wardrobes, I'd be fine, knuckle-wise. Kieron would have noticed, but he wasn't here, was he, so there was no point dwelling on that. I sent him a quick text: *Thinking of you. Hope you're not going too mad. Send us some piccies of your latest work, I'm curious.*

I scrolled back to his last one:

All good. Got a date tonight! Love ya.

I'd replied: *Get you. Be good. Love Mum xx*

My head was still sore, under my hair, and I could still feel the slide of the jump lead, the smear of the muck and blood. The roots of my teeth. The gasping, grunting sound that poor grubby article had made. I didn't think I'd gone anywhere near him. But that didn't mean I hadn't. And it didn't explain why I'd woken up with bleeding knuckles, as if I'd done something violent. The way he had run away... had he been running from me? Had we fought? Was that why my head hurt – from a fall?

He could call the police, I thought then, as I washed down my last mouthful of chips with the cup of tea. He might have already called them. He might have legged it straight to the cop shop and be giving a statement right now. I wondered what he'd say. Actually, that was a point, what *would* he say?

I was indulging in a bit of self-abuse, Officer, when some middle-aged woman jumped me from behind and tried to strangle me...

No. Impossible. I ran my finger around my plate and sucked the salty grease off my fingertip. My nerves died down a bit. Odds on he wouldn't go to the police after all, would he? He was a lowlife, a flasher. He was an abused child carrying a shame not his and making it his every day, poor sod. Even if he did report it, whatever it was, I doubted he could give a description. He'd stared at me without seeing me in the dark, and then for the rest of it, I'd been behind him like a chubby Nosferatu. If I'd even been behind him, that is. And then in the chippy, no one had looked at me funny. No one had looked at me at all. If anyone had noticed me, they'd have seen some grey-haired middle-aged woman in her husband's raincoat, forgotten me seconds later. No bugger would have noticed that one of my hands was bleeding, that my eyes were glittering with the electric thrill of what had just happened. Most of them had been on their phones.

I put the plates into the dishwasher, switched it on and swabbed the decks. I'd keep an eye on the *Weekly News* website as usual, I thought.

Except this time I'd be looking out for myself.

CHAPTER 24

Mark

Transcript of recorded interview with Mark Edwards (excerpt)

Also present: DI Heather Scott, PC Marilyn Button

HS: Mr Edwards, can you tell us where you were on the night of Thursday the fourth of July?

ME: Thursday? Thursday I generally… let's see…

HS: It was the Thursday following the Saturday that Joanna Weatherall was attacked.

ME: Oh. Oh, OK.

HS: Your wife says her car broke down?

ME: Oh, right, yes. Right you are. She was late home. I was watching the telly when she came in. She was soaking wet, said could I give her a lift and help her start the car, so I did. It was just the battery.

HS: And how would you describe your manner that evening? With your wife?

ME: My manner? Erm… I suppose I might have been a bit off with her, yes, I think I was, but you know what it's like, long day, getting near the end of the week, last thing I needed, like.

HS: (Pause) So you helped her start the car?

ME: Like I said.

HS: And then?

ME: And then nothing. There was nothing in for tea so she said she'd go to the chippy. (Pause) I should've gone. I should've gone but I didn't. I let her go.

HS: Can you remember which car she used?

ME: Which car? (Pause) She'd have taken mine, yes, she would have done, because she drove mine back after we started hers, so she'd have parked it behind hers and I definitely didn't go out and swap them or anything because it was bucketing down. (Pause) I should've gone for the chips, though. She never seemed like she minded, Rachel. But I knew that about her and I let her do it anyway. Just because someone's willing to do anything for you doesn't mean you should let them, does it? I suppose my mum did everything around the house when I was growing up, but that's no excuse, I don't even know why I said that, sorry. I... I know the change is a difficult time. I could hear her up and about in the night, and I did see her having one of them hot flush things, but she didn't really talk about it. I should've thought of ways to make life a bit easier, tried to cheer her up, like. But I couldn't take her out for a meal or anything. I couldn't take her out full stop, to be honest. What would we have said to each other? I had nothing to say to her. (Breaks down)

HS: For the benefit of the tape, PC Button is handing Mr Edwards a tissue. Mr Edwards, if we can just reach for the facts, as you see them. Where were you that evening?

ME: (Pause) At home. Ask our Katie. Ingrid called round to ask about something. Some pretext or other. But she only stepped in for a few minutes. Actually, she could tell you I was home. Then about half an hour later, Rachel got back from the chippy.

HS: And can you describe her state of mind?

ME: She was… she was angry. She seemed really angry. She was slamming around, making snippy comments. I tried to ask her if she was OK, but she didn't even eat her tea with us, which is unheard of. She went up for a bath, said she needed to chill out. So I let her. I didn't know what she wanted half the time. She just seemed furious. I told myself it was hormones, but it was more. I knew it was more. What is this anyway? Why are you asking about that Thursday? Was there another attack I don't know about?

HS: Did you notice any injuries on your wife?

ME: No. Why? What's this about?

HS: Did you notice that her knuckles were bleeding?

ME: What? No!

HS: Did you go out later that night?

ME: No.

HS: Are you sure?

ME: Yes. No. Hang on. I might have done. I don't keep a diary. Why?

HS: Can you tell us where you went?

ME: Why? Why do you need to know?

CHAPTER 25

Rachel

The next day, there was nothing for me to print off, not even in the nationals. But the day after, it took me only two seconds to find my chap. It was the Saturday, 6 July, and for the second time that week, my blood froze in my veins.

Homeless man found unconscious outside cemetery gates

A homeless man was found fighting for his life near St Michael's church on Thursday evening at approximately 10 p.m. Police have told the *Weekly News* that the man was found collapsed near the cemetery. He had vomited and was struggling to breathe. No further details have been released at this time. A spokesman for Merseyside Constabulary has appealed for witnesses to come forward.

'Oh my God,' I whispered. Because I think that up until then, I'd held on to the remote possibility that nothing had happened.

I sent the article to the printer, ran to the cupboard under the stairs and grabbed my bag off the hook. The knife was still in it – in its sheath. My heart lurched into my mouth, but honestly? I couldn't remember whether I'd taken it out after I'd seen it the first time. I remembered finding the sheath in the cutlery drawer, but it looked like I'd slipped the knife into it and put the whole kit and caboodle in my bag. But that was OK, I told myself, making myself think it through calmly. I hadn't taken my bag out with me to the chippy, just shoved some cash in my pocket. I was sure of that.

Besides all of which, the man hadn't been stabbed, had he? Unless that was a detail yet to come out.

I took out the knife and pushed the button on the handle. The kitchen light bounced off the blade. It was clean. I closed my eyes and let out a strange sob. It was clean it was clean it was clean, and anyway, I'd only imagined myself as the jump-lead strangler for a few brief minutes of madness, hadn't I? And I was now putting that down to a hot flash with major side effects.

The police were calling for witnesses. There was a number. I wondered if it was the same one as for Jo. That was two calls I should make. Two calls I wouldn't make because, really, I had nothing to say. No one had come forward. There had been no one about. If anyone had seen me, they'd have seen no one at all.

The man was discharged the following day. The article was no more than a paragraph in Monday's update: *The homeless man found in a state of semi-asphyxiation near St Michael's church on Thursday evening was discharged from hospital yesterday. Police are not treating this incident as suspicious.* Not suspicious? Were they serious? How suspicious did it need to be? A flaming axe sticking out of his head?

Oh God. I dry-heaved into the sweating palm of my hand. There was a pressure in my forehead, right across the front. Strangled. Almost to death. I ran my thumb softly over the tiny burgundy scuffs on my knuckles. I closed my eyes and willed myself to remember, but… no. Nothing.

A few more details followed. The cemetery strangler victim (my phrase, not theirs) had a name: Henry Parker. No fixed abode, history of mental illness. A footnote even in the local weekly news of a northern industrial town. That made me feel even worse: for his ruined, wasted life, for the crimes I felt sure had been committed against him when he was a child, for those I may or may not have committed myself.

For the invisibility we shared.

I printed the article out on a sheet of plain A4 in the usual way before sliding it into a clear sleeve and clipping it into my file with Jo and the others. It wasn't knife crime, but violence was violence. I closed the file. It felt like I was shutting him out. Out of sight, out of mind. My eyes filled with tears.

'I'm so sorry,' I whispered to him. 'I'm sorry for what I think happened to you when you were little and what I'm scared I might have done to you the other night. I'm sorry I said what I said to you even though I don't think you heard me. I wish you peace, I really do, but I know you can't find it and I doubt you ever will. I wish I could give you some comfort, but I have none to offer, I'm afraid.'

'Mum?'

Katie was standing at the door looking at me like I'd completely lost my marbles, which it's possible that by then I had. 'Who were you talking to?' She glanced at the dresser, at the clip file, at me. Her eyes filled.

'No one, love,' I said, wiping my eyes with the back of my hand. 'Well, to myself.' I smiled as best I could. 'Only way I get a decent answer, isn't it? Anyway, what're you up to?'

Her face hardened. She held up a wad of tissues covered in blood. When she spoke, it was with barely concealed fury. 'I'm moving these. They were freaking Liam out. So disgusting.'

'Liam.' Blue Eyes says, making me jump. 'That's Katie's boyfriend?'

'Yes.'

'And Katie was holding bloody tissues?'

'Yes.'

She jots that down. 'And what was your reaction to that?'

I think back, trying at the same time to breathe my way out of a hot flash I can feel coming at me. My forehead and armpits go from dry to wet in a split second. Focus, Rachel. What was my reaction? I stared at my daughter, that was my reaction. I stared at the bloody mess she was holding up like an accusation or a victory trophy or something, the mess she was now putting in the kitchen bin with a gob like she'd bitten into a lemon. A blunt pain pushed into my sternum.

'Where did you find those?' I asked her, although I thought I knew.

'In the bathroom. On the windowsill.'

'When?'

'Now. I mean, they've been there for ages but I didn't think I should have to clear them up as they're not mine. It's a bit gross, to be honest.'

'God forbid you should have to tidy up after someone else,' I muttered, turning away from her. I had to. I was shaking, but it wasn't anger. I was worried she'd see guilt in my face. I was thinking about seeing the knife in my bag and thinking it was clean. I hadn't even noticed those tissues on the windowsill. When had I put them there? *Had* I put them there? Why not flush them down the loo? And whose was that blood?

I pressed my hands to the dresser top, glanced at my file, away, out into the back garden. I thought I caught a glimpse of the top of a blonde head over next door's fence. Looked like Ingrid, but that didn't make sense; she didn't even know next door so far as I knew, and anyway, I thought, I was pretty sure they were away on a six-month cruise. There was a thrush on the fence warbling its territorial cry, I seem to remember, and remembering that, it strikes me now that it was dusk, not dawn.

'Sorry, love,' I managed, still not looking at Katie, keeping my voice as level as I could.

'Are you OK, Mum?' Her voice had softened, which was worse, somehow.

'I'm fine. I'm just tired, but I'm fine. Might go and read for a bit.' Avoiding her eye, grabbing the worktop for support, I struggled out of the kitchen one handhold, one foothold at a time.

'Me and Thea are going into Liverpool tomorrow,' she called after me as I headed upstairs. 'We're going to get some stage make-up for a shoot.'

'OK, love!' I closed my bedroom door behind me. Sat on my bed, quivering, crying, trying to shake off the way she'd looked at me. Holding up tissues like a Medusa's head, turning me to stone. My tissues. Covered in blood. Been there for… how long? Days, presumably. The knife had been clean. I had seen it in my bag and I had had that thought. I had had that thought then wondered why, *why* notice the blade being clean? Why wouldn't it be?

Who are you talking to? Katie had asked me.

I don't know, I thought. I don't know.

It only struck me later that if Katie could curb her disgust enough to pick up my bloody tissues, then she could easily have disposed of them without comment. That if she or Mark had seen them days or even weeks ago, then either of them could have done that without a fuss, the way I'd cleared away countless things for them, not to mention flushing the loo, which both Kieron and Katie seemed allergic to doing even when the contents were fit for the bomb-disposal unit. But no, she'd had to score petty revenge for all the times I'd told her that her room stank or was a tip, asked her how she could live like an animal.

Later still, when I heard her go out, presumably to Liam's, I ran downstairs, dug the tissues out of the kitchen bin and flushed them down the loo myself. I washed the knife with hot soapy water, dried it on loo roll and flushed that away too. I put the knife back in the cutlery drawer, in its leather case. If I'd taken it out with me for protection, now I was putting it back for the same reason. I needed protection from myself.

Lisa texted: *Drink this week?*

I texted back: *I'll call you later.*

Later came. I didn't call.

That night I went walkabout again. I had to; it was the only way I could breathe. I called at the Spar and nicked a large bag of Jelly Babies, literally walked out with them while the assistant was serving a group of kids without anyone even glancing in my direction. A chap called Simon was walking his dog, a blonde Cockapoo called Carl. He was getting out of the house – Simon, not Carl – to escape his fifteen-year-old daughter and her friends. He was going to kill an hour in the pub was what he didn't say. Tuesday night was the same: young woman called Karen, all dressed up nice and in a rush. She asked me if I knew where the Red Admiral pub was, so I directed her to it before telling her she looked great, to boost her confidence. She was obviously meeting someone for the first time, possibly a colleague or perhaps one of those Tinder arrangements, and she was feeling a bit nervous about it. I didn't persuade either of them into any dark corners. Didn't feel anything even near a murderous or violent tendency. The knife was at home. It was in the cutlery drawer, where I had put it.

Mark went to the pub both nights, no surprise there. To meet his mate Roy, he said, although Roy doesn't smoke so far as I know, and yet again I smelled tobacco on him when he got into bed. Wednesday, I don't know what he did because I was out again, walking, walking, walking. It was a habit I didn't seem to be able to break. I limited myself to the odd greeting, a polite two minutes passing the time of day: the weather, the unreliability of public transport, the country going down the pan.

But on the Thursday, nearly two weeks after Jo had been attacked, came the worst possible news.

Parents' grief as knife-crime girl dies.

I scanned the iPad screen with frantic eyes.

Complications… did everything they could… Joanne Weatherall lost her fight for life in the early hours of this morning.

Two lines further down, my blood slowed in my veins.

The police are still keen to speak to the woman who was seen talking to Joanna Weatherall earlier that evening. She is believed to be in her fifties and was walking a small black dog.

'Oh God in heaven,' I whispered.

I sent the article to the printer, carried it back to the kitchen as carefully as if it were a pot of funeral ashes. I read it again and again, hands shaking. I slipped her into her plastic sleeve. I clipped the file shut, trapped my finger in the ring binders and drew blood. Sucking the blood so it wouldn't go all over, I closed my eyes. Closed my mind to my own terror.

'I did not hurt that girl,' I whispered to no one. 'I did not hurt her.'

She never asked for my name. I never gave it.

The witness had remembered almost nothing about my appearance, but someone must have come forward and told them about the dog. I tried to slow my breathing, which was coming quick and shallow. There was no mention of my height, my weight, the colour of my eyes, not even the colour of my hair. A raincoat wouldn't give me away, not when half the population had a nondescript cagoule that could be black or navy or dark grey in the night. If no one can see you, you can get away with murder. But someone had remembered the colour of the dog. Black.

All morning I was a robot. At lunchtime, I was polishing wine glasses because there were only two punters in when the bar phone rang.

'Barley Mow, Church Street, Runcorn, can I help you?'

'Rachel?'

It was Mark. My chest filled with heat. 'Mark? Everything all right?'

'I've been ringing you all morning. Have you left your phone at home?'

'I might have. It might be off, why?'

He sighed. I heard exasperation with a dash of weariness. 'Have you seen the article in the *Weekly News*, that lass that was stabbed?'

'No. Why?' Phone hooked in the crook of my neck, I dug around in my bag.

He gave another sigh, longer. Disbelief this time, with an undercurrent of depression. He knew I was lying. Knew I would have read it, printed it off. I made myself wait out the pause he was trying to get me to fill. My mobile wasn't in my bag.

'She's died,' he said eventually. 'They're saying they want to speak to a woman with a small black dog,'

'Are they?' I could barely keep my voice steady. My head felt thick, creaking, like it was full of lagging.

'Here, I'll read it to you.'

'You don't need to—'

'It says the police are keen to speak to a woman believed to be in her fifties with a small black dog.'

'Mark, I heard you the first time. You don't need to read it to me – I'm not deaf. It's not... it won't be me, will it?'

'But...' I could hear him searching for words. 'But you were out, weren't you? With the dog? Near the town hall, they found her. And our dog is small and black. I mean, you walk down that way... you might've seen something.'

I hadn't said where I'd been. I never did. He didn't care, wouldn't have heard and certainly wouldn't have remembered even if I had told him. 'But I'm always out with the dog. And there's loads of small black dogs – they're ten a penny. I mean, I spoke to a girl briefly. But I didn't know it was the same girl, did I? How could I have known that?'

'So you *did* speak to her?'

Bugger.

'Only in passing, like.'

'But… don't you think you should speak to the police?'

I tried to pick up whether or not he was thinking of the knife in my bag, about my distress at finding it there, but it was difficult over the phone. It occurred to me then that while he didn't look at me often, when he did look at me lately it was like Katie did sometimes: eyes screwed up, the way you look at someone who's behaving weirdly. Maybe they both thought I was mad. Maybe he actually thought I had something to do with this Jo but couldn't come out and say it. But surely he didn't think I was capable of—

'Rachel? Are you still there?'

'I'm not going to speak to the police. That's like turning yourself in for going into a shop in the morning that gets robbed in the afternoon. It's got nothing to do with me. What would I say? Well, Officer, she definitely didn't have any stab wounds when I spoke to her? She's not saying the woman with the dog attacked her, is she?'

'Well, she can't, can she? She's dead.'

'You know what I mean. I didn't see anything, or anyone for that matter. I just spoke to her for five minutes and gave her directions, that's literally it.' My breath caught in my throat, sending the last few words up an octave. I grasped the edge of the bar and lowered myself, shaking, onto a stool, thanking God that Dave was upstairs doing whatever it was managers did, or vaping thick clouds of vanilla through the back window into the alley. 'I didn't even realise it was the same girl. Why would I? Did they give a description of the woman?'

No, they didn't.

'Just says in her fifties. Black dog. I think you should give them a ring, Rach. It says they're keen to speak to you.'

Rach. He hadn't called me that for a long time. Hadn't called me anything at all, if I'm honest.

'Well I'm not keen to speak to them. I'm not going to waste their time – they've got enough to do. I've got to go anyway; I've got punters.' I looked up at the *Mary Celeste* that was the lounge bar. 'See you at home.' I put the phone down before he could say anything else and ran upstairs and into the staff toilet. I sat with my head between my knees. Heat flared up in my stomach, my chest, boiling through me, prickling in sweaty beads on my forehead. My cheeks blazed; more sweat ran from my armpits down my sides, from the back of my neck down my spine, trickled between my buttocks, for crying out loud, the indignity of it all.

I made myself breathe, and one, and two. And one, and two. Breathe, Rachel. Breathe.

I did not hurt that girl. I did not. I did not hurt that girl. I did not hurt that man. I did not hurt anyone. I did not kill that girl I did not I did not.

CHAPTER 26

Rachel

I didn't call the crime line. Mark dropped it. But at least he was looking at me now. Looking at me funny, I mean. Me? I was scared stiff. Of what had happened, of who might have done it, of myself.

I kept up my daily newspaper cuttings. I needed to do it more than I needed to stop. The police urged people to be vigilant, to come forward with any information, no matter how insignificant. That meant they were stuck, I thought, pushing Lisa's words from my mind but unable to stop asking myself if there was a deeper truth to them now. Had I got away with murder? Had I?

The following week, I saw Ingrid three times in as many days. Three times! Once for a coffee when I was trying to get on, one evening when I didn't go walking and ended up feeding her, and one afternoon when I chatted to her in the close.

Over coffee, Ingrid told me that the week before, she'd been to see Pamela Bain, the HR manager Mark had put her onto.

'She said I can do a week's paid work experience and they'll take it from there.' She sighed, pulled out her second Marlboro. 'Starting next week.'

'But that's good, isn't it?'

She nodded, but the expression on her face told a different story. 'I won't have any time for my flute,' she said, circling her fingertip sadly round and round on the table. 'That's what I hate him for most of all. More than losing the house, the holidays I'll never get to go on now, the clothes I'll never wear. I played for my health. For us, actually. I gave up work to focus on my health and all the while he pretended to care while pissing our life savings away with his fucking filthy habit.'

She was so well-spoken that she sounded even posher when she swore, if that makes sense.

I smiled at her, trying to show sympathy while finding it hard to see a tragedy of the gravity she seemed to think it was. 'Oh, Ingrid, I am sorry.'

'Why would you be sorry?' she almost snapped before rearranging her features into the slightly pathetic expression she usually wore: head a little to one side, shoulder raised an inch. 'It's not your fault, is it?'

'Of course not,' I said. 'That's not what I meant. I'm sorry, I didn't mean anything by it.'

'No, I'm sorry.' She shaded her face with her hand. 'I'm still a little raw with it all.'

'Of course you are, love. You've had a lot to cope with.'

There was a short silence.

'Do you have kids?' I asked, to try and change the subject.

'Absolutely not!' She shook her head. 'All those shitty nappies, the mushed-up food and brain-dead baby talk. Enough to drive anyone mad.' She shuddered. I waited for her mouth to drop open when she realised she'd put her foot in it, for the apology, but it didn't come.

'They do grow up, you know,' I said. 'And I know their conversation's a bit limited in the early days, but it does develop. Especially if you stick with the brain-dead baby talk.' I'll admit, I put it in silent air quotes, if you know what I mean. 'And if you read to them and that. Me and Kieron used to talk about books all the time. We'd get a stack each from the library and we'd read our own and each other's and then we'd talk about them. I had better conversations with him than I do with my husband. I miss him now he's away.'

It was good to see her crack a smile for once. I wasn't smiling but she had no idea why I wouldn't. You think Mark's all sweetness and light, love, I wanted to add. But he isn't. Neither of us are.

The following night, Ingrid stayed for dinner. She'd only called round to tell us her car had broken down and did we know a mechanic, but of course Mark went and had a tinker and soon got it going – probably by trying the key in the ignition, if you know what I mean – and by that time I'd made us a cup of tea so then Mark had to have one, and she was still making a big fuss of him for nothing much when the timer went off for the hotpot. It smelled so good and she'd just told me she'd been feeding next door's cats and watering their plants while they were away, which I thought was kind of her and it also explained my sighting of her over the fence the other evening or morning or whenever it was.

'Why don't you stay for tea?' I said. 'It's only hotpot but at least it's hot. And in a pot.'

'Oh no, don't be silly.' She waved her hand, put on a show of not wanting, not being desperate, actually, to eat with other people instead of on her own for a change, even if it was only us.

'There's plenty,' I insisted. 'I've done too much as usual. Can't seem to get into the habit of making less with our Kieron off at uni!' I chuckled, to show her it was no big deal, and busied myself putting the broccoli and spring cabbage on to boil.

'Well, if you're sure…'

Mark went to wash his hands – he'd splashed his face too by the looks of it when he came back. Didn't normally spruce himself up for dinner.

Ingrid helped him set the table while I shouted Katie down from her pit. She was only just in the kitchen door when she eyed up the table with suspicion, then glared at me. 'Whose is that place setting?'

'Ingrid's going to eat with us,' I said.

Eyes like coals, she looked at Ingrid, then at her dad. Then again at me.

'Sit down, then, love,' I said, a bit embarrassed at her rudeness.

Katie did as she was told, but not before asking if she could have a can of Coke. I wouldn't usually say yes during the week, but I suppose she was claiming her bribe – I'll stop throwing daggers Ingrid's way if you make it worth my while sort of thing. And she did lose the hostility, to be fair, once we'd sat down together. After that sticky moment, having a guest put us all on better behaviour, I have to say; even if Katie didn't address Ingrid directly, she was halfway to cheerful.

'Me and Thea took such cool photos today.' She passed her phone round to show us her horror-movie shoot: her and Thea in scary make-up and fright wigs, looking like they were having a great time.

'These are incredible,' cooed Ingrid. 'You're so imaginative.'

'Thea's dad let us use his garage,' Katie said, really only to her dad, smiling more than I'd seen her smile in months. 'It was so cool. It had these rusty paint tins and massive spider webs, actual real ones.'

'Thought kids were only interested in the World Wide Web,' Mark said, and Ingrid laughed so much I thought she was going to have an embolism. In a rare moment of solidarity, Katie rolled her eyes at me. Ingrid didn't see, thank God, and Mark made another joke, which she also wet herself at, though I've forgotten now what he said. He was on witty form rather than strictly speaking hilarious, but he was better company than he had been in ages, and I almost felt as if we were a family who knew how to eat together, how to talk and laugh with one another. How to be.

On the Friday, I had the day off. This must have been mid-July. On my days off I generally catch up on housework. I know. It's like something out of *Hello!* magazine. *Here's Rachel, pegging out the clothes on her bijou lawn to the rear of her sumptuous semi-detached abode. Jogging pants by Primark, slouch T-shirt by vintage M&S menswear, plastic laundry basket by Argos.*

I was hanging out Katie's bed sheets first thing when I saw Ingrid sitting in next door's garden having a fag, in shorts, a camisole top and a thin cream-coloured bomber jacket. At first I thought it was weird, her sitting there like an out-of-work rock star, then I remembered she was feeding their cats.

She was reading *Vogue*, although how she could afford it, I'll never know – not the clothes, the actual magazine, I mean. She had a cup of coffee on the go – a cappuccino by the looks of it in a white cup and saucer, like in a café, and I have to say I did think that might be taking a liberty, using next door's crockery and coffee machine; somehow more of a liberty that she'd brought her own milk over, if you know what I mean. Anyway, she looked… what's the word? Languorous, is it? Old Hollywood – Marlene Dietrich, Barbara Stanwyck type thing. Statuesque. Some women just have the knack, don't they? She'd fallen fast from her position, that much was true. But round our way, no one would notice anything. She was the type that would be bothered by wearing last season's fashions, but no one here would know last season from next, and it would be years before her clothes became as shabby as everyone else's, so she still stood out. Her blonde hair was tied back, but even the brown roots looked like they were there on purpose – Katie told me that you can pay to have that done, have roots actually put in, that it costs a fortune, which made me laugh at the time, but looking at Ingrid, I could see she had a look that I must have spotted on celebrities in *Grazia* and not thought twice about it until now.

I said hello and gave her a wave and she waved back.

'Aren't you at work?'

She shook her head. 'Woke up with a headache, so…' She shrugged by way of completing the explanation.

So bloody what? I thought but didn't say.

'Are you feeding the cats?' was what I did say.

She nodded, lifted her eyes to my washing line. 'Your sheets'll dry in no time in this summer breeze.'

'They will that.'

'They'll smell so fresh too.'

'They will.' I nodded to the cappuccino on her lap. 'May as well enjoy a coffee in the garden, eh?'

She raised her chin, her eyelids lowered. 'Not like I can do this on my grotty patio. And they have a Gaggia.'

I carried on pegging out. I was trying to see what I could pick up from her. I'd never seen any friends visit her, but then I wasn't at home much. Maybe she was like me, couldn't face her old mates. Maybe she was ashamed of her reduced circumstances. Maybe slumming it with me and my family made her feel better by comparison, who knows? Maybe… maybe… maybe nothing. Dread was all I could feel coming off her, an *oh God oh God oh God* feeling. That would be the ex. Probably some memory of finding him comatose with a needle in his arm or something – not that she'd ever said anything like that – or him getting violent from time to time – not that she'd said that either – or the moment it dawned on her that the bank account was empty and the house repossessed. That she had said, in so many words. The rest was me guessing.

She pulled on her cigarette – she'd lit another with the first. I supposed at least she wasn't smoking in next door's house. But she was edgy. Yes, definitely edgy, but whatever else was going on, she was shutting me out.

I stood at the fence, laundry basket under one arm. From here I could see her long, slim legs, which were that perfect honey colour some women manage but I never have, and which disappeared into cowboy boots. Not a look I could ever imagine pulling off.

'Are you all right, Ingrid?' I asked her.

'Gives you a lift, doesn't it?' she said, as if I hadn't spoken, pulling the jacket from her perfectly square shoulders and closing her eyes to the sun.

'Mark says that whatever the weather, fresh air is good for the soul. The ozone, he says. You never regret getting out.' I wondered to myself when was the last time that Mark had taken any ozone apart from in the pub car park on his way in for four pints of Greenall's.

But at the mention of his name, it was as if someone had yanked an invisible thread attached to her shoulders. She sat up and opened her eyes, shielded them with her hand. 'Mark's so nice. He's such a good bloke.'

Like the swearing, in her mouth the word *bloke* sounded posh.

'Yes, he's a good bloke.' I shifted my laundry basket to the other hip. 'If I had a pound for every time someone had said that,' I muttered, 'I'd be bloody rolling in it.'

The words didn't reach her. They flew off, swallowed by the bitter wind.

CHAPTER 27

Katie

Transcript of recorded interview with Katie Edwards (excerpt)
Also present: DI Heather Scott, PC Marilyn Button

HS: Would you say that things were good at home? Were you a happy family, would you say?

KE: (Pause) We were getting better.

HS: You mentioned that your neighbour, Ingrid Taylor, came over to see your dad sometimes when your mum wasn't there? For the benefit of the tape, Miss Edwards is nodding.

KE: She was always coming over. She pretended to be friendly and that, but I didn't trust her, to be honest. She made up excuses to come over while my mum was out and she knew Mum was out because she was always looking out of her window. I saw her. I saw her follow my mum as well.

HS: She followed your mother?

KE: I saw her do it a few times, when I was watching or doing a video tutorial or whatever, and then I'd hear her at the door or in the kitchen talking to my dad. I think she only offered to feed next door's cats so she could accidentally-on-purpose bump into my dad in the back garden. She was a bit sad, to be honest. She's, like, one of those women who thinks they're a teenager? Like, giggly and stuff. But Dad wasn't interested in her. He'd never do something like that to my mum.

HS: And what about your mother's friend Lisa?

KE: What d'you mean, what about her?

HS: Were her and your dad close?

KE: Well, yeah, but Auntie Lisa's sound. She's not my real auntie but, like, she wouldn't do anything. Her and my dad are solid.

CHAPTER 28

Rachel

My clip file expanded; I could barely close the rings. I would soon need a new one.

Mass stabbing in Croydon, gang-related, police suspect.
Double knife death in Manchester club.
Nottingham reels after girl-gang knife death.

A fuzzy CCTV capture of a violent crowd; a picture of the Manchester club during the daytime; a photograph of a boy, no more than seven, at his mother's grave. Girls were carrying knives now; that wasn't the first I'd seen, and if it didn't strengthen my case, I didn't know what would. How much longer would the government turn a blind eye? Couldn't they see that it wasn't just hoodlums now? These were normal kids, kids who thought they were arming themselves for protection when all they were doing was making sure an argument had every chance of turning into a tragedy.

I printed them out, these victims, slid them under cellophane and took a moment for every single one. I said a few words and closed the file for another day.

You'd think all that crime on the streets alongside Jo's death and the attempted strangling of that Henry Parker chap would have put me off walking out altogether, but, like a cigarette that leaves you feeling sick, no sooner had the nausea cleared than I craved another drag.

I was frightened, very frightened, of myself as much as anyone, but a passing greeting just wasn't enough anymore. I was talking to strangers more than I knew I should. But I didn't take anyone anywhere secluded, I swear – strictly public places only, Mark's knife safe in the cutlery drawer. I didn't trust my jinxed timing, my bad luck, myself. All I did was listen to problems, share recipes and housekeeping tips, commiserate about the daily news, how full of anger and hate the world seemed. I stopped to talk to a chap sleeping rough in the doorway of the Co-op, gave him twenty quid, which I couldn't really afford but which I hoped would buy him something hot or get him halfway to oblivion. Whatever helped him make it through the night; it wasn't my place to judge. But there were no grimy encounters in graveyards, no near-suicides in town-hall ponds, nothing to report.

Days became weeks. Joanna Weatherall faded like a memory. The man in the cemetery? Well, in the eyes of the public, he'd been little more than nothing to begin with. He was like me: invisible.

I scanned the *Weekly News* each day as usual.

Knife attack in Warrington nightspot, two teen boys in critical condition.

Armed robbery in Toxteth bank.

Fatal shooting in Manchester – three dead.

A spate of house burglaries. The knife attack in Warrington turned out to be gang-related, no surprise there. I wondered if any of them would be able to say why, where it had all started, the hate.

Tragedy of scholarship boy in drugs-row death.

I pored over that one: two Liverpool schoolboys, high as kites, a drugged-up altercation in a kebab shop that proved final. Why? Because earlier that evening they'd thought it a great idea to arm themselves with knives like proper gangsters. Not even for protection; just for the thrill. Fifteen years old, both from good homes, starring in their own bad-lad fantasy – one dead, one facing murder charges. The waste. Very few kids carry knives with the intention of using them, I genuinely believe that. But when you throw drugs and alcohol into the mix, the extreme passions of the young, their rage and their hormones, their insecurities and their prejudices, their violent films, violent computer games, the prejudices of the parents, the news, those who are in power who should know better spouting the rhetoric of hate willy-nilly, you name it – you throw all that into the mix and what should only ever have been kids having a scrap leaves the ground flooded with too much blood to ever clean up, no going back, families left with nothing to do but wring their hands over holiday snaps, Facebook pages become memorials, bedrooms become shrines.

I checked the nationals too, of course, every day. Some days it seemed to me that we'd become a country, a world hooked on hate, the origins of which had been lost in a fog of pre-World War Two-style propaganda, anger-mongering that was OK or not OK depending on what colour you were, which school you went to: the enemy is anything other than yourself, beware the other, hate the other, kill the other. Anger is a leak in the bathroom. Hate is its outlet in the kitchen wall. Anger. Hate. Rage. Ramped up, misdirected, always misdirected.

Liverpool boy charged with manslaughter. An outrage, victim's parents say.

Those two Liverpool lads. The follow-up report. The deceased's family baying for blood. Blood and more blood. Anger and more anger. Hate on a loop, round and round. Eye for an eye. You did this to me, so I'll do that to you or someone else, anyone else, who looks at me wrong, who wears clothes I don't like, worships a god I don't know about, has sex with people I don't think they should, whatever, repeat ad infinitum. Terrorists, gangs, religious maniacs, racists, ageists, misogynists, homophobes, transphobes, anyphobes… people just wanted somewhere to put the fury they were carrying inside themselves. They just wanted someone, anyone to pay the price to help them make sense of it. Ramped up, misdirected: a leak in the kitchen wall that has nothing to do with the kitchen.

The sadness and rage of the world took up lodging in my chest. It camped on my back. It lived in my heart.

And so I carried on with my walkabouts – waged my one-woman campaign, as I saw it, against hate. Love and understanding, that was what I thought I was promoting, honestly I did – you have to believe me on that. One chap's stress over the J62 bus making him late for his hospital appointment? A warm smile from me, a friendly ear and suddenly his day isn't so bad. Some other dog-walker's daughter a dreadful worry with her recent withdrawn behaviour? Feels better for having got it off her chest, if only to a stranger with a stolen bag of sweets to share and a little black dog called Archie. An old man fretting about the state of the world – *Where are we all headed? Hell in a handcart!* Laughing because I say I'll be driving it, shake my head and tell him: *You've got to laugh, haven't you?*

I walked out and I walked out and I walked out.

I listened and I listened and I listened.

Sometimes I learned their names, sometimes I didn't. Sometimes we walked together a little way, sometimes a longer way, parting with a cheery *goodbye then, nice to meet you, you too, ta-ta.* Sometimes I bumped into the same people, talked some more – *goodbye* turned to *see you later, love, take care, mind how you go.*

Mark didn't bother asking me where I was going anymore, never bothered saying goodbye. Katie? Who knows, you tell me.

Meanwhile, the visions still came, less often but still troubling. I'd be in the Co-op picking up a few bits for tea and I'd see the back of Jo's shoulders in that old man's coat, her face frozen in shock and disbelief as she fell away onto the pavement. Or I'd be slicing up chicken breasts for a curry and just the resistance of flesh against blade would have me shaking and crying in horror. It was almost as bad for Henry Parker. My knuckles had healed but I couldn't rid my mind of the image of him turning to peer at me from the dark doorway of the church, the screwing-up of his eyes, the eventual looking beyond.

Lisa texted me regularly: *How's things?*

I would text back: *Same old! Keeping on keeping on.*

She'd write something like: *Fancy getting together for a drink/ that new quiz night/the Prosecco offer at Bank Chambers?*

I could see, or thought I could see, that she was trying to get me out of myself.

Definitely! I would thumb.

She'd come back with heartbreaking speed: *How about next week?*

And I'd think, bless her, she's trying her best, and reply with a version of: *Sounds good, I'll let you know.*

I wouldn't get back to her, hoping the trail would go cold. Which it did. Until, on one of my days off in lieu, she texted: *Have you emigrated? Haven't seen you in months!*

I can remember staring at the words on my phone, thinking, *Months?* Surely it's only been weeks? I couldn't hold her off any longer.

Undercover operations, I texted. *Secret government business. You in later? Will pop in 4ish.*

Once again the speediness of her reply tore me up: *Great! Will have kettle on!*

I set about the rest of the chores. Katie's room was a bombsite of mouldy mugs and crumby plates; the hoover actually made a stripe when I pushed it over her carpet. When Kieron had gone to uni, I'd just closed the door to his room and hadn't opened it since, and our room was nothing that fresh sheets, an open window and a squirt of Febreze wouldn't sort.

When I'd finished, I sat down on the sofa for a quick cuppa.

I woke up to cold tea and a headache. My watch told me I'd been out of it for two hours. Two hours! I had no memory of falling asleep, only of how heavy my limbs had felt when I'd sat down, then lain down, telling myself it was just for a minute, how my bones had felt like they were being sucked deep into the cushions as if being pulled into the underworld by Hades himself. If you're shocked by the Greek reference, don't be. I know I haven't had a classical education, but I did watch the Hercules cartoon with Kieron and Katie when they were little.

I digress, as per. Sorry.

It was late afternoon by then. If I didn't get a shift on, I'd be late for Lisa. I popped up to the bathroom and put a comb through my hair. In the mirror, fine wrinkles magnified under the hard, white daylight. It was the first time I'd looked at myself close up for ages, and it was a bit of a shock, to be honest. There were four thick whiskers on my upper lip, which I plucked with Katie's tweezers. On either side of my chin, pouches had started to develop, as if the apple-blossom cheeks of my youth had slid down from the tree and were now hanging onto the lower branches for dear life.

I groaned but tried to keep in mind George Burns or whoever it was who, when asked how he felt on the occasion of his ninetieth birthday, apparently said something like: *compared to the alternative, pretty good.*

'You're alive,' I said to my reflection, though I can't say the fact made me particularly happy.

A swipe of Katie's mascara, a quick brush of my hair and a hasty scrunchy, and I decided I didn't look too bad, for me. That small attention to myself had made me feel better than I had in months.

'I'm fine,' I practised. 'Honestly, yeah, I'm great, actually. How's things with you?' I smiled to see if I could get my eyes to go with it.

Almost.

CHAPTER 29

Rachel

'I was wondering about calling Missing Persons.' With a flourish, Lisa stood back to let me in. She looked at me; her brow furrowed and her head fell to one side. 'Have you had your hair cut?'

'Just brushed it and put it in a scrunchy, that's all.'

'It looks nice off your face. You've got make-up on as well.' Her smile was one of encouragement, for God's sake.

'Not sure a paint job is enough these days.' Already flustered, I stared at the floor, heat climbing up my neck. I'd thought I could face her, but now I wasn't sure. 'Not when the brickwork is crumbling.'

'Don't be like that.' She laughed. 'Come in.'

Lisa didn't pick up her feet as she usually did, and her shoulders were rounder. On the kitchen table there was a dead cigarette butt in a saucer.

'Don't tell the girls,' she said, sliding it into the bin and running the saucer under the tap.

'Don't beat yourself up. It's not a crack pipe.' Her girls were both away. They'd been on holiday with their dad and now they were off on their own travels. 'You missing them then?'

'You're joking, aren't you?' She flicked the kettle on, busied about the kitchen, fetching mugs and milk and the tin off the high shelf where she hid her decent biscuits. 'They're never off FaceTime, and if it's not FaceTime it's WhatsApp. Jodi was WhatsApping her entire friendship crisis last night. *Ping, ping, ping* every five minutes, honest to God. Long-distance counselling service, really, I should start charging.'

'Fifty pounds an hour, apparently. Money for old rope.' I envied her having a close bond like that with her daughters. I'd had that not so long ago with both my kids. I'd been proud of it, proud of the hours it had taken, the baking, the picnics, the days out, the conversations lying on their beds in the late evening if they had a problem they needed to share. When they were little, there was never anything I couldn't fix. I used to love my ability to shrink their worries to nothing, feel their fraught little bodies loosen with relief. But now I couldn't figure out what the heck Katie was cross about all the time, what she was going to do with her life, unless you counted YouTube and getting hammered with her mates. I looked up to find Lisa poised to seize the kettle the moment it boiled.

'It's still empty nest syndrome,' I said.

'Nest shouldn't be empty, though, should it?' She poured on the hot water. 'Knob-end should still be here. We should be looking forward to long walks and drinking at lunchtime and whatever else you're supposed to do when you get your freedom back. Anyway, sod him, what've you been up to? I've not seen you for ages.'

'Oh, nothing much.'

She stopped stirring the tea and looked at me. I was not invisible to Lisa, never had been. She loved me, or so I thought then, and her gaze was like a bloody tractor beam. 'Are you OK, Rach?'

'Been a bit under the weather, I suppose. One thing and another, like, you know.' My eyes filled. Traitors.

Lisa's expression was full of sympathy and her eyes weren't dry either. But how could I tell her what I'd been up to? Not like I could say, actually, remember you said I could get away with murder? Funny that, because I'm terrified I might have stabbed a young girl to death in the midst of a menopausal fugue and throttled a man while he was having a you-know-what in the church doorway, although I can think of no reason why I would do something like that. PS, I found a knife in my handbag that I may or may not have put there, bloody tissues in the bathroom that I have no memory of either and on top of that I spend every single night on the street talking to people who aren't my friends. How about you?

'The girls down the Prospect have been asking about you,' Lisa said. 'Have you not seen anyone at all?'

'Not apart from sexy Dave at work,' I said. 'And the punters, obviously. I'm turning into a hermit. Borderline narcoleptic as well, I think.'

'Is that something to do with drugs?'

'I wish. No, it's the one where you fall asleep all the time.'

'Bloody hell, me too. I can't even read a magazine anymore without finding myself half an hour later flat out on the couch, dribbling into the cushions.'

'Thank God it's not just me!' I seized the comic turn in the conversation like it was a life raft. 'I think I might go on a Buddhist retreat. Find myself. Although I'm probably better off looking down the back of the sofa. At least that way I might find a pound coin.'

She laughed, as did I. But I felt like we were performing a double-act like we used to do when we were out with our other friends. Only there was no one watching. It was because of all that I couldn't say, couldn't expect her to understand, I knew that. If you can't talk to someone about what hurts, all that's left is what you watched on telly, what you had for your tea, the weather. The close friendship we'd always had, the friendship that had seen both of us through the toughest times, was fading, I could feel it. But with Mark and Katie lost to me, she was all I had left.

'Are you sure you're OK, Rach?' she said. 'Really, like? You've not… I've not seen you.' Her eyes were wary. That's the trouble with the people who love us most, isn't it? They know we're not right without us having to say. Those eyes were asking me to let her in. They were wondering why she was even standing outside in the first place.

'I'm fine.'

'Rach? Tell me.'

'I've been going on these walks,' I spluttered. 'At night, like, you know.'

'With the dog.'

'With Archie, yes. But it's not about the dog. It's this… this invisible thing. I know you said it's normal, but I think it's getting me down. No one looks at me at home, no one sees me except when I shout or mess up. When there's no food in or the clothes have been left to rot in the washing machine because I've forgotten to take them out again. As if no one else could possibly do that. As if no one else wears the clothes, walks on the floor, eats off the plates.'

'So you've been roaming the streets?'

'Only to get some conversation,' I said. 'To engage with other human beings.'

'I'm a human being,' she said softly.

'I know, love. I know, I do, but I can't be coming round here every five minutes, can I? You've got your own life.'

'But I've always got time for you, Rach – you know that. I'm your friend, remember? That's what the word means. I just don't want to badger you every five minutes asking if you're OK because I can see that might be a bit wearing.'

I nodded, a gasp of a laugh that might have been a sob.

'I've only been talking to people,' I said once I'd got it together enough to speak. 'That's all I've done.'

'What d'you mean? What else would you have done?'

'Nothing.' I took a moment, steadied my breathing. 'Only there was that girl the other month, stabbed near the Red Admiral. Killed, like, you know. And then that homeless man strangled outside St Michael's church just a few days later. And I was near both places both times.'

She frowned. 'I didn't hear about the homeless man. But what's any of that got to do with you anyway?' I heard her shift. Next thing, she was at my side, her arm around my shoulders. 'Hey, hey. Come on, Rach. Don't cry. Or do cry, actually. Cry all you want – a few tears never bothered me. But you can't be worrying about those things. You can't be taking on the weight of the entire world. You've got enough on your plate, love. It's a tough time, the toughest. Even without the hormones and the bits going south quicker than a swallow on a world cruise.' She rubbed my back. 'You have to stop reading the news the way you do. Keeping those stories… it's only going to make you feel worse, isn't it? You're hurting yourself, love.'

'I know. I know I am, but I can't help it. It's something I need to do. I can't explain it.' I could; I could explain it perfectly. 'It's just… that man, I saw him… on the way to the chippy, and the girl… Joanna, Jo, I spoke to her. I spoke to her that night, Lis. And then later she was stabbed and left for… she… she died. And I have these memory losses. I'll be on my way home and I'll get home and I'll have literally no idea how I got there.'

'But that's normal, Rach. Autopilot, that's all that is. Remember I went to see that hypnotist for stress when Patrick left? That's the state they put you in. That's how he explained it – they get you to that disconnected place like when you're driving your car home, or to somewhere you've been a thousand times. You do the gears and all that and you get home but you can't really remember the actual journey unless you saw something unusual or something happened. Like a road accident. Or a streaker that's the dead spit of Ryan Gosling.' She held me tighter to her. 'That's all it is, Rach. It happens to everyone.'

'But what if I've done something terrible and I can't remember? I mean, the blanks… and then there's these nightmares that wake me up at all hours, and the thinking… imagining I can read people I don't know.'

'You *can* read people. I told you that. You've always known what's going on with me – before I know it myself sometimes. That's just listening to the world, Rach. Seeing people.' She leaned her head into mine. I could smell her soap, her perfume, her. 'There is no way you'll have assaulted some homeless man—'

'Henry Parker.'

'Whatever his name is, and even less way you could've harmed that young girl.' She kissed my hair and sat up. A moment later and she was handing me a tissue. 'Here. Nutjob.'

I blew my nose. 'Thanks.'

'I do FaceTime sessions as well, if you're interested. Fifty quid an hour. And I'm not going anywhere, me, unless I bump into Patrick Swayze in Tesco.'

'Patrick Swayze's dead.'

'Oh aye.' She wrinkled her nose.

The two of us sat there in silence. There was something she wasn't saying. I could feel it. When I looked at her finally, I saw it, but what *it* was, I couldn't tell you in words.

'What?' I said.

She bit her bottom lip. 'Rach. I mean, do you… do you think you might… I don't know, maybe you need some help, like. Hormones can play havoc – you know that better than anyone.' She was staring at me. For a second I didn't know what she was getting at. But then it dawned.

'But that was years ago,' I said. 'And it was a post-natal thing.'

'I know, but… the change of life is another hormonal thing, isn't it? It's a tough one. I mean, we talk about it between us but I don't know many other women who do. It's like this big taboo. I mean, when you're pregnant, you tell your GP and you get put in some sort of system. Healthcare. Check-ups, leaflets, weigh-ins, support groups, what have you. You get a midwife who tells you off for eating too many bacon butties, makes you put your feet higher than your head when your ankles balloon. With the menopause, it's do you want HRT or don't you? And if that doesn't work, it's just tough, you're on your own to somehow figure out how to cope with it all.

'And some women cope better than others. No, that's not what I mean; I mean some women have it tougher than others and then you've got empty nest syndrome combined with kids that still need you and ageing parents or dying parents and you can barely hear yourself think for the sound of the new jowls no one told you you'd get slapping on the laminate floor… and I don't know about you, but…' She took a breath, but as funny as she was trying to be, when she spoke again the words came out ragged and her eyes filmed all over again. 'I'm not sure I know who I am without my girls, you know, and… I can't even put the radio on in case one of our songs comes on because I know that would finish me, so God only knows how you're feeling, that's all I'm saying.'

I shifted away from her, couldn't meet her eyes. My insides were burning, an all too familiar rage bubbling up in my lungs. 'Are you saying I'm madder than most people? Because of what happened twenty years ago? That's what you're really saying, isn't it?'

'Of course not.' She moved away from me, only an inch, but still.

'Maybe this is why I'm walking the streets at night. Maybe I'm looking for someone who understands rather than someone who's ready to ship me off to the nuthouse.'

'I didn't say that. Come on, I would never do that. For God's sake, Rachel, this is me, Lisa.' She laid her hand on my arm, ducked her head to try and meet my eye. I looked away. 'Remember Lisa?' she insisted. 'Can down a pint in less than ten seconds and fit a whole small pork pie in her mouth for a bet? Come on, I'm only asking if you're OK. Really OK, I mean. If I don't ask it, who will? I know you. I know you, Rach. Rach?'

I gave in, looked at her. 'What?'

'Don't be like this. Just tell me, are you OK?'

'Course I'm bloody not.' I sighed. 'I'm a murdering lunatic, our Katie's a grumpy cow and Mark's still breathing.'

Half an hour later, Lisa saw me out. It had taken us every minute of that half hour to recover.

'Don't worry about Katie,' she said, leaning on the door frame. 'Jodi was a beast before she left home. Now that she's had to wash her own pants for a year and pay for her own food, she sighs when she opens the fridge and says *oh my God, you've got sliced ham.* Honestly, she's almost human. And as for Mark, he's just... he's tired and feels just as crap as you do.'

I zipped my coat up and tried to smile. 'Not sure why. He doesn't even know where I keep the pans, and if I ask Katie to put a wash on, she's on to Childline.'

I waved goodbye and walked home, trying to convince myself that I was lucky to still have Mark in my life and that Katie would pass through the almost permanently belligerent ball of rage she seemed to be. Lisa wasn't short on rage either, to be honest. She'd done nothing but rant about Patrick, how he wasn't contributing to the girls' uni expenses, claiming not to have any money. 'Which doesn't quite explain the holiday photos on his Insta-friggin'-gram, does it?' she'd said, fury pinking her cheeks. 'Which he blocks me out of, by the way, but the girls show me everything. I mean, Tene-friggin'-rife, if you please, cocktails on the balcony, who wants to see a shot of the pool... Argh, he's a loser; I hate him.'

I look up at Blue Eyes, hanging on in there with her silver pen and her trendy nails and her lovely clothes.

'Love and hate,' I say.

She nods. 'They're close.'

I look directly at her, the sympathetic expression on her face. It doesn't make sense, her kindness, her understanding.

'Are you a police officer?' I ask.

She frowns. 'Is… is that what you think?'

'I don't know. I can't remember what you said.'

'I'm a forensic psychiatrist.'

'A psychiatrist?' My mouth drops open. I have no idea how I missed that. 'So are you building one of them criminal profiles? For the court?'

She takes a deep breath. 'Rachel. It would be better for both of us if you saw me as here to achieve some clarity on the events of the last few months. I suppose it would help if you trusted me.'

'Oh, I trusted you from day one. Even when I thought you were police. I've no secrets, love. It's me that turned myself in, don't forget.'

'All right,' Blue Eyes says.

'I've forgotten your name, I'm sorry.'

She smiles. 'Amanda.'

'Amanda.' I smile back. 'Knew it started with an A.'

She nods. 'So you recovered from your moment of tension with Lisa?'

'Yes. Yes, I did. Only when I got home, there was something playing on my mind.'

'Which was?'

'Well, I couldn't remember ever telling her about my clip file.'

CHAPTER 30

Lisa

Transcript of recorded interview with Lisa Baxter (excerpt)
Also present: DI Heather Scott, PC Marilyn Button

HS: You last saw Rachel back in August, is that right?

LB: Well, I saw her last Friday, but yes, in person it would have been August.

HS: And how would you describe her state of mind back then?

LB: Pent up, I suppose you'd say. I kept asking her if she was OK and she got upset and said she was worried she'd had something to do with the stabbing of that girl – the first murder, I suppose you'd call it now, that Joanna – and some homeless fella, which I knew nothing about obviously. I just told her not to be so daft. Why would I say anything else? I mean, there was no way, no *way* I would have thought she'd have had anything to do with that. It makes sense now. But then, no. No way.

HS: How did she seem to you?

LB: She seemed... down. It was understandable, totally. But then I tried to suggest, gently, like, that she might be imagining things. I was trying to be sympathetic. I mean, it's not like her postpartum psychosis was a secret between us. I'd been very involved in that, in getting Mark to see she needed help, you know? So it's not like it was a taboo, only we never spoke about it. Never. (Pause) So I suppose it was a taboo then, wasn't it? But then Rachel wouldn't talk to me about anything anymore. As if getting upset would be the end of the world, like there'd be so many tears she'd drown us both, do you know what I mean? She was like a balloon full of water. One jab and it would all come out. And I think she was afraid of that. But when I said about getting help, she got offended, which was horrible. I mean, we joked our way out of it, but she left soon after that and I didn't see her again, not to speak to. She replied to texts but I could tell she'd gone further into herself. I hadn't meant to upset her. I just keep thinking I could have helped her more… been a better friend… If I had been, she might never have killed anyone. (Breaks down)

CHAPTER 31

Ingrid

Transcript of recorded interview with Ingrid Taylor (excerpt)
Also present: DI Heather Scott, PC Marilyn Button

HS: For the benefit of the tape, PC Button is showing Ms Taylor a CCTV image. Ms Taylor, if we can go back a little. This CCTV capture was taken in Victoria Road on Thursday the fourth of July this year at approximately quarter to eight in the evening. Can you describe what's in the picture?

IT: Of course I can. I went for a drive. I think I said that, didn't I? So what?

HS: Ms Taylor, can you tell us what you were doing in the area of St Michael's church on the night that Mr Henry Parker was found collapsed on Langdale Road?

IT: Who?

HS: Henry Parker. He was a homeless man found in a state of asphyxiation near St Michael's church later that evening, five nights after the attack on Joanna Weatherall.

IT: What's that got to do anything? I thought he was just some drunk tramp?

HS: If you could answer the question, Ms Taylor.

IT: Has Rachel confessed to attacking him as well? Was he stabbed? I didn't think he'd been attacked. I can't remember anything about that in the news.

HS: Ms Taylor, Victoria Road is in the immediate vicinity of St Michael's church. Can you shed any light on what you were doing there that evening?

IT: Power of suggestion. Mark had gone out for some chips – at least I thought he had. I fancied some chips too. Is that so hard to believe? I know which chip shop the Edwardses use because she… Rachel had told me which one was the best, which I'm sure she did in the interests of being neighbourly. I suppose she'd filtered useful local info through her own priorities, and in her case that information was the chippy, the Co-op and the pub. I mean, (laughs) do I look like I eat chips?

HS: Ms Taylor, a moment ago you said you were out in your car because you were going for chips.

IT: Well, yes. Occasionally, yes. Once every six months. But not every *week*. My point was, what, looking at me, would give her the impression that I'd go anywhere near a fast-food outlet, or a cheap supermarket, or a working men's pub? (Laughs) She told me where the library was too. Even the bus stop! I mean, I suppose she assumed… I told her I'd won the Prius in a competition on daytime TV, but I only said that because at many points in my life I've struggled with other people's jealousy. I've been the victim of it, I mean. That's why I got out of Helsby. No one spoke to me after my divorce. I was barred from the Ladies' Circle. They said it was because my ex had dropped out of the Round Table, but that was a cover. I wasn't invited to drinks anymore, the annual charity raft race, nothing. It was just bullying. Basically, someone, and I know exactly who it was, spread a rumour that I'd had some sort of fling with her husband. It was all malicious gossip, not a word of truth – these women are toxic. Jealousy, as I said. Not my fault she couldn't keep her husband interested, is it? He used to text me all the time, stood outside my house sometimes begging me to come and meet him… How is that my fault?

HS: Ms Taylor, did you see Rachel Edwards that evening?

IT: Only when I was trying to park. At that point I realised it wasn't Mark, obviously. She was wearing his jacket and driving his car, though I didn't find out why until later.

HS: Did you say hello to her?

IT: What? No. She didn't see me. I saw her lock the car and glance about her. She looked quite shifty. Sort of watchful, you know? And now you're saying this man's collapse is suspicious, I'm wondering whether she was casing the joint. She headed towards the church, anyway, and when she pushed the cemetery gate open, I thought, whoa, surely not. More death-obsessed weirdness. It was like a scene from a film where there's an abandoned warehouse and instead of even trying the lights they're all, oh no, let's just go in with our tiny flashing torches just in case the murderer has sensitive eyes. So naturally that's the last I saw of her, and I certainly didn't see him. Dirty old man.

HS: You didn't follow her in?

IT: What?

HS: For the benefit of the tape, PC Button is showing Ms Taylor a CCTV image. Ms Taylor, can you tell me what you see on this image?

IT: That's Rachel Edwards, going into the churchyard. In Mark's raincoat. He let me borrow it once to run from the car into the office. He got soaked, poor man. So sweet.

HS: What about this image?

IT: It's a… I… I mean, it's very grainy, isn't it? It's a… is it a woman? Really, I can't make it out…

HS: Notice the time recorded on the images – 19:48 on the first and 19:51 on the second. The person entering the churchyard on the second image is tall, with blonde hair, and is dressed in women's clothes. You said you followed Mrs Edwards to the gate but you didn't go in. And yet here you are going in.

IT: That's ridiculous. This could be anybody.

HS: You recognised Mrs Edwards without hesitation from the same-quality photograph. (Pause) For the benefit of the tape, Ms Taylor is shrugging. Ms Taylor, you described the homeless man, Mr Parker, as a 'dirty old man'. Can you explain what you mean by that?

IT: Well, a pervert, obviously. In a public place.

HS: For the benefit of the tape, Ms Taylor has made a masturbating gesture with her hand. Ms Taylor, that aspect of Mr Parker's evening… activities was never reported. The only person to have witnessed it, by her own admission, is Mrs Edwards. Mrs Edwards has stated that she never told a soul. Given your casual acquaintanceship with Rachel Edwards, it's unlikely that she told you about it, don't you think? So how do you know what he was doing if you never went into the cemetery?

IT: I... I mean I... I mean, she must have told me. Or perhaps I saw him from the path. I did look over the fence so I must have seen him, I must have. That's right, and it quite put me off my supper, so in the end I decided to go home.

(Pause)

HS: Mrs Edwards describes waking up with a pain in her head, as if she had passed out and perhaps hit her head. Or as if she had been knocked out by a blow to the head. Can you tell us anything about that?

IT: Of course I can't. Are you accusing me of something? What, do you think I'd cosh her and make a run for it? (Laughs) Who do you think I am? Look, I'm her neighbour and I've come here to help you of my own free will. She handed herself in. I didn't have anything against her; she was kind to me. She was just weird, that's all. Why the hell would I attack her? (Pause) OK, so I followed her in. I did. I should have said that, but I was worried I'd sound as weird as her. I was curious, that's all. I suppose I was imagining satanic rituals or something. Sacrifice of a small rodent on a stone slab. She was walking slowly, as if she was scared. At one point she stopped. My heart was in my mouth, to be honest. And when she turned around, I nearly screamed. Thank God there was a large headstone right there and I was able to hide behind it quite easily, being petite. And then of course she ducked behind a grave herself.

It was then that I saw the Central Casting pervert in the doorway. I mean, do these people have no originality? I was going to walk away there and then. The grubbiness of it all reminded me too much of my ex. But Rachel! Oh no, she was transfixed. Could not take her eyes off him. And that made me realise that there really was no end to her weirdness. As I said to Mark, it was as if she wasn't there in her own head, or at all. I mean, I just thought he should know. But I didn't knock her out. Or bang her head on the gravestone. No way. I would never do something like that.

CHAPTER 32

Mark

Transcript of recorded interview with Mark Edwards (excerpt)
Also present: DI Heather Scott, PC Marilyn Button

ME: A couple of times I heard her talking to herself. To the file, I mean. And Katie walked in on her doing it. I did try and talk to her, to Rach, about it. When she started it, she said she'd already written to our MP, said she wanted to go to Parliament to protest about the terrible knife-crime statistics and what were they going to do about it. We're neither of us very confident about that sort of thing – public speaking, like – but I think she thought that the ones who are good at public speaking, the ones in charge who were bred and educated for it, like, weren't speaking the kind of language she thought they should be. She wanted to try and bring the numbers down. Make the government clamp down sort of thing. Or do something. I thought it was a pipe dream, something she needed to do until she didn't, if you know what I mean. I thought it was hopeless, to be honest. I don't trust politicians. They're all as bad as each other. Posh hate-mongering's the same as any old hate-mongering in my book, and I know Rach felt the same. The blame game, going round and round. It's always someone else's fault.

But she didn't take any notice of me so I stopped saying anything and she kept printing off the reports and I think they were affecting her health. I've thought about it since she turned herself in, obviously, about her having that episode all those years before. I've put two and two together. I don't know why I didn't think about that; it was Lisa who made me think about it, Lisa who said I should get her some help. I've been a bloody idiot. We were lost, me and Rach. Katie was lost as well. And Kieron, obviously.

When she went down, I should have stepped up. I should have saved her, saved all of us. When I think where she must have been up to, you know, mentally, to get to a place where she could have done those things, and me not even *noticing*... I mean, what kind of husband does that make me? What kind of husband doesn't notice his own wife, for God's sake?

CHAPTER 33

Rachel

I think Amanda is tired. She looks a bit pale and there are dark circles under her eyes, which the concealer can't quite hide. Maybe her kids kept her awake last night. Maybe she had a row with her husband. Maybe she went out on the lash. Who knows? As for me, I'm not tired. I'm like a boxer going in for round one, punching my big gloves together: *come on, let's do this*. I just want it all off my chest and no one, no one has ever listened to me like she does. Funny – quirky, you might say – but both times when the other woman, the one in uniform, has accompanied me to the loo, when I've come back Blue Eyes has reapplied her lipstick. That tickles me, that she would bother. It's a strong red-wine colour against her alabaster complexion. Harsh, almost, but it works. A face that hints that the smile, when it comes, will be worth the wait. She's tall and striking in the way a Greek statue is striking: soft curves chiselled from hard marble. Grace and power combined. She makes me think she can tell me it's going to be all right – that she has the authority to say this and make it so. And that makes me want to tell her everything, even though all is lost.

So I do. Because when you've held it all in for so long, once you start letting it out, you can't stop. And maybe that's what I've been afraid of all along. And maybe it's only now, talking to Amanda, that I realise that when there's too much inside, it creates this big pressure. The pressure comes from the very act of holding it all in. It's no wonder the walls of me were cracking.

I didn't see Lisa after that. Well, I saw her but she didn't see me and now I'm in here.

Even saying that feels surreal. That I wouldn't see Lisa every week would have been unthinkable once. But she went off to Majorca with some of the girls we used to meet up with – she invited me but I said no, obviously. Our lives had forked, I suppose. She was a single woman now and I was still married, to all intents and purposes, and that had changed things. When Patrick left her, he'd also left our little gang of four: me and Mark, Lisa and Pat, two couples happy as anyone doing happy things together. His scandalous dumping of her for a younger model had left us all reeling at the time, and that was before I had bigger things to worry about.

Meanwhile, somewhere in all of this, Katie went to Ibiza with her friend Thea and to Portugal with the boyf's family, who are quite wealthy and had rented a villa with a pool. They say you lose your sons but keep your daughters, but I could see she was drifting away from me. She'd made no moves to apply for uni and I couldn't broach the subject without her getting cross. She barely seemed to have time to chat or to want to spend time with me anymore, but that was understandable, I suppose.

I didn't want to spend time with me either.

Mark and I didn't go away. We hadn't booked anything and we didn't say it out loud but neither of us, I knew, saw the point. Instead, we drifted like shadows in the walls of our house. He went to the pub, or wherever he went, came back stinking of fags and beer; I went on my walkabouts. We ate our tea watching television: together but not together, looking anywhere but at each other.

I walked. I printed off the news. I went to work. I walked. I printed off the news. I went to work. Repeat to fade.

Dave continued to be a pain in the neck. Phil opened up a bit more, told me he'd got divorced the year before, which went some way to explaining the deterioration in his appearance.

'I lost everything,' he said, sitting on his regular stool after one of his gambling losses, ironically, though that's not what he meant. 'House, furniture, you name it.' He shook his head sadly. 'She used to shout at me, call me names.'

'Oh, Phil, I am sorry.'

He shrugged, gave a bitter half laugh. 'She cheated on me. I knew she was doing it. Used to leave little clues, and then when I asked her about them, she'd say I was controlling. Said she was innocent but everyone knew. Everyone. I thought I was losing my mind.'

'Oh dear. That's a bad do.' Poor chap. It was no wonder he sought comfort in the betting shop – and here.

'She made me feel about that big,' He made an inch with his thumb and forefinger. I knew without him telling me that he'd repeated a pattern learned during his childhood, but he told me anyway. 'My mum was what they used to call a scold.'

'Now that's an old word.' By this time, I'd sat down on the stool I keep behind the bar for the rare moments when I'm not serving, cleaning, refilling, what have you. Phil seemed to want to chat and there was only one other punter in, so I didn't see the harm.

'My nan,' he said. 'The one who used to take me along with her while she bet on the horses? She'd been the same, I think, although I never saw that side of her. A shrew – I heard her called that more than once. I suppose those were different times and to me she was wicked and fun. But she finished her husband off, that was the family rumour. Drove him to a heart attack with the stress of living with her. He smoked like a chimney, drank like a fish and ate like a pig, but that was how he coped, then *boom!* He made an explosion with his hands. 'Then my dad the same. Spent as much time out of the house as he could. I remember my mum shouting at him, him standing there with his shoulders slumped and his head down. He was a gambler too, but what's funny is I didn't know that till later, and by then I'd already run up a two-grand overdraft on top of my student loan.'

'Funny what we pick up without words, isn't it?' I said as he drained his glass. 'You must have known it somehow, somewhere in you, like, that he was a gambler, without anyone saying anything.' I stood, picked up his glass. 'Another one?'

He shook his head. 'Better not.'

I knew he'd run out of money. He'd paid his last quid in coppers. I'd have given him a free pint while no one was looking, but that wasn't the way to help him; it would only make things worse.

'I'd better get on,' I said.

'Yeah. No problem. Thanks, Rachel.'

Meanwhile I'd got to know some of the dog walkers by name. Pete only walked his chihuahua as far as the lamp post of an evening before he went to bed. His wife had dementia and was there one minute, gone the next. Marj, whose daughter had become withdrawn when I first met her, was happier now because said daughter had finished with her misery-guts of a boyfriend and was back to her old self. Claire's dog had died, actually, but Claire, bless her, a lovely woman with a bright white-blonde crop and never without her fabulous red lipstick, couldn't break the habit of her evening constitutional and was now thinking about getting a poodle because she'd always had poodles as a child. She was on her own, for the moment, having not found the right person. She worked a lot from home, copywriting, and came to the conclusion, talking it out, that she needed to find an office-based job at least part-time. She was a book nut too, like me. And like me, she was walking out for other reasons than the pooch.

'But one thing was bugging me,' I say.

Amanda raises her perfectly shaped eyebrows. 'What was that?'

'Something that was impossible to get around.' My chest swells, sinks.

'Which was?'

'Well, just as I stopped going anywhere secluded with the people I met…' I reach for the glass of water and cradle it in my hands, 'so the attacks stopped. There were no attacks locally that summer. Not one.'

I realise I can't hear that fly anymore. It must have escaped. Or died.

'Which brings us to September,' Amanda says, very slowly. 'To the next… to the next murder.' She narrows her eyes; her mouth flattens. 'Do you think you can talk about that?'

I drink the rest of my water in one go, feel it run cold down my gullet. I place the glass back on the table and make myself take a deep breath. Even now, I'm not sure what I can say; all I can do is tell her what I think I know.

'September came, like you say,' I begin. 'I mean, September follows summer, doesn't it? Like dessert follows a main course in one of those fixed menu things. Even if you don't want any pudding, it will still arrive. And you'll still eat it. Even if you know it'll make you feel sick.'

I look up. I look up at her a lot now that we've been here together so long. I feel like I need to see her, like she's my point on the horizon.

'I was desperate,' I say. 'I see that now. I was desperate to put everything behind me and somehow find my way out of the hole.'

'So you were starting to come out of this difficult period of your life?'

'Well, I did something I'd been meaning to do for a long time, so that's a sign, isn't it?'

'Breaking the inertia, yes. Usually, that's an indicator of positive energy returning. What did you do?'

'I put my name down for a spinning class.'

Not the great revolution, I know, if you'll pardon the pun, but it felt big at the time. In TK Maxx I found some cheap sports leggings with super-strength elastic that held everything in and which looked OK with one of Mark's old T-shirts over the top. As for not looking like Elle Macpherson, something Katie had read to me once from one of the body-positive accounts she follows popped into my mind: *the girl in the photo doesn't even look like the girl in the photo*. God help the middle-aged woman – you barely see a photo of her at all, let alone an airbrushed one. So I kept that in mind and resolved to see what my body could do, not judge how it looked.

Amanda's blue eyes are still there, a constant in all my zigzagging about. I wipe more endless tears from the bottom of my chin.

'Sorry,' I say. 'It's just that telling you this makes me feel so sad.'

'Do you feel sad for yourself?'

'Yes, but mainly for her. For Anne-Marie.'

'All right.'

'If only I hadn't gone to that class.' A huge sob catches in my chest.

'But you did. And we need to talk about that.'

CHAPTER 34

Lisa

Transcript of recorded interview with Lisa Baxter (excerpt)
Also present: DI Heather Scott, PC Marilyn Button

LB: Rach asked me if I wanted to go to this exercise class thing at Brookvale Leisure Centre. I said no, which I obviously regret now. It was by text, not a call; we hadn't spoken even over the phone for weeks. She replied OK, words to that effect. But I should've gone. She was reaching out, I can see that now, but I didn't think about it that way at the time.

HS: For the benefit of the tape, I'm pausing while Ms Baxter composes herself.

HS: Taped session restarting now. Ms Baxter, going back to last Thursday, Thursday the twenty-sixth of September, you're saying Mrs Edwards appeared calm?

LB: I don't know what she was like that evening. As I say, I didn't see her. I think she wanted us to do something together that maybe didn't involve too much talking. I mean, that's with hindsight, I don't know that for sure, obviously. I'm not a psychiatrist.

HS: Do you have any witnesses as to your whereabouts that evening?

LB: Not as such, but our Jodi FaceTimed me from her friend's house at about ten o'clock so she'd be able to tell you I was in my PJs and halfway through the new *Line of Duty*. Not to mention a bottle of Pinot Grigio.

HS: We have two witnesses who say they saw a woman with fair hair spotted near the driveway leading to Brookvale Leisure Centre at around eight forty-five on the evening of Thursday the twenty-sixth. Do you have any thoughts as to who that might have been?

LB: Not a clue. By which I mean it wasn't me, obviously. I've blonded my hair since it went grey, yes, but as I said, I was at home.

HS: You were at home at 10 p.m., but this woman was sighted at eight forty-five.

LB: It wasn't me. I don't know what else to tell you.

HS: Did you have any further contact with Rachel Edwards?

LB: Yes. She called me on the Friday afternoon. This Friday just gone. The day after.

HS: And how did she seem then?

LB: She sounded… she sounded bad. I didn't answer when she rang but I called her back from the car and asked if she wanted to meet for a drink. She'd been to see her dad that afternoon. But yeah, she sounded terrible.

HS: What did you talk about?

LB: I told her I'd been in the supermarket buying pizza for the girls.

HS: And had you? For the benefit of the tape, Ms Baxter is shaking her head.

LB: No. Well I had. But that's not where I was when she rang.

HS: Where had you been, Ms Baxter?

LB: I'd been... I... I was with Mark.

CHAPTER 35

Rachel

I'd texted Lisa on the Monday to see if she wanted to come spinning, but as expected, she texted back: *On yer bike. I'd rather eat my own ear wax!*

To which I replied: *Very witty, bon appétit!*

So the banter was still there, if nothing else. She asked if I fancied a cuppa on Friday afternoon or a drink later on, but I texted back that I was going to see my dad and that I'd probably stay with him all evening. That last bit was a lie, but I couldn't face seeing anyone, even her.

Are you OK? she wrote.

Yes, fine.

I wasn't fine, obviously; I was lonely. I was lonely because I couldn't talk to a single human being about what I was feeling. Not one. Not even by text. I was so lonely that I even stooped to asking poor-me Ingrid to come to spinning. I wasn't going to but she was out in next door's garden on the Sunday afternoon, sitting in their swing seat with a fag on the go, and a gin and tonic by the looks of it. I wondered whose gin she'd used, whose tonic.

As for me, I was bringing in the washing, nothing new there.

'I don't like exercise,' she said when I asked her – typically tactless. I almost suggested she might need to stretch her legs given that she was getting a lift to work most days with my husband.

'Me neither,' I said instead, humouring her. 'Endorphins, that's what I'm after.'

She took a long drag of her cigarette. 'I would, but working full-time is tiring me out.'

'Sorry to hear that.'

The sarcasm was lost on her.

I parked up and was on my way in, but just outside the leisure centre I had to stop due to an eruption of heat inside me. I leaned my hand against the wall and did some deep breathing, and slowly it passed.

At reception, I had to cough theatrically to be seen. Obviously. Even when the girl – and she was a girl – did look at me, it was with the kind of unfocused stare you see in ruminating cows. After following the world's most lacklustre directions, I reached the gym and performed an amoeba-like progression around the perimeter wall before clambering onto one of the bikes at the back, just about managing not to fall off the other side. Once aboard, so to speak, I spotted a woman two bikes down, about my age, hair the colour of a pomegranate. I smiled doubtfully, the way we women do, and was grateful when she threw her eyes heavenwards and blew at her fringe as if to say, *well, here we are*. Here we are indeed, I thought. Fighting off deterioration.

Her hair was so cheery, I thought, bracing myself against the handlebars for what lay ahead. I wasn't keen on the actual shade, but it was, as I say, bright, and I made the decision there and then to go to Shapers in town the following week and get a decent cut and colour, even if it meant going without the Saturday takeaway. Sod it, maybe I'd dye it pink! That'd put the cat among the pigeons!

I'm only telling you this because I want you to know I was getting better. I was. I had no idea I was on any kind of edge, certainly not one so sharp with such a deep, deep drop.

The teacher was a shouty lady of about thirty with one of those bodies you can bounce coins off. Seriously, not a scrap on her. Neck veins like cables, deep folds round her mouth. To lose weight she'd have to dig out an eyeball… you get the picture.

'Faster,' she kept saying. 'Let me see those legs pumping.'

I'll pump you in a minute, I thought, but I kept my head down, avoided eye contact at all costs. The rest of the women were younger by at least ten years, and I noticed that the woman who'd smiled was keeping her head down too.

Sometimes we want to be invisible.

When the first drop spotted the gym floor, I thought the roof was leaking, until I realised it was me – me, dripping sweat in great fat drops. I'd got my fitness up with my evening walks, but this was proper aerobic exercise. What had I been thinking, seeking out something that would make me even hotter? Honestly, I was sweating like a drug smuggler going through customs by the end. I didn't dare look in the mirrors. I knew I'd be redder than a cranberry at Christmas.

As everyone filed out, there was a mass move towards the showers – but one step at a time, sweet Jesus. Rome wasn't built in a day. I'd face the women's changing room when I was good and ready and not before.

I clambered off my bike, and my God, the pain. My undercarriage felt like it had been kicked by a goat.

'Ow,' I whispered to my own knees and grabbed my towel.

'Are you OK?' the teacher called after me. 'Lady with the red towel, are you OK?'

I ignored her and hobbled for the exit. I had to get into the cold air. Outside, it was dark. The woman who'd smiled at me was standing in front of the main entrance, drinking water from a proper sports bottle, one hand on her hip. She too was still in her kit and looked as red as I imagined I must be. Nearer purple, if I'm honest, and that made me warm to her even more.

'Jan's tough,' she said. 'But it's a great workout.'

'Wear-out, more like. I feel like I've been kicked in the hoo-hoo.'

She laughed. 'It does hurt at first. I've been coming for six weeks. Should have seen me week one – I was crimson.'

I wondered what colour she thought she was now, but she prattled on as if she'd read my mind.

'I mean, I'm crimson now obviously, but it'll go down quicker. Six weeks ago I looked like an aubergine and I was still red the next day. Seemed like it anyway. Was it Bette Davis that said ageing's not for wimps?'

'I don't know. Sounds about right, though.'

She held out her water to me. 'Do you want some of this? If you don't mind germs.'

I accepted it gratefully and took a sip, even though I could've downed the whole lot. 'Ta. I'll remember water for next week.'

She smiled. 'You did really well, though.'

Kind of her to lie.

'Thanks,' I said. 'I really want to get fit.'

'Me too. Important, isn't it, as we get older?'

We stood there chatting. And what can I say about that, other than it was lovely, really lovely? My God.

Blue Eyes is looking at me with concern, and I realise I'm in floods. 'Do you want to take a break?'

I shake my head, take the tissues she's holding out to me.

'I just can't believe what happened to her, you know? I mean, I can. I know I have to face it, but she was just so nice… no edge to her, y'know?'

Blue Eyes waits while I compose myself enough to carry on. I sip some of the water, wipe my eyes and take a few deep breaths.

Once I'm calm enough to speak, I tell her things I know she knows already, like the fact that the woman's name was Anne-Marie Golightly. Most people round our way will know that; it was in the *Weekly News* and the nationals. It will have been on the television, though I never watch the news on telly anymore. She was from Liverpool. To me, she was... she was just, you know, a lovely person. She had two kids, both grown up now, and referred to her husband as his lordship, which she said with real affection and it made me smile.

And she asked me questions too, which felt new, somehow. I told her Kieron was at art college and I didn't moan about Katie and her strops, just said she wanted to be a make-up artist and that she was currently a YouTuber and left it at that.

At a certain point, we both sighed.

She looked around her. 'Bloody hell, there's only three cars left. We must have been here an hour!'

I laughed, followed her eyes to the sky-blue Mondeo, my rusty red Twingo and a bright yellow, very expensive-looking sports car. 'I've lost all track of time. Too busy gassing.'

I shake my head and smile at the memory.

Amanda is looking at me like she's trying to solve a puzzle. 'That must have felt good,' is all she says.

'It did,' I reply. 'Have you ever done that? Met someone and just chatted away like you've known them for years? It's such a good feeling, isn't it?'

'It is. *Simpatico* is the term. I think it's from the Spanish but I'd have to check. It describes the feeling of mutual understanding, getting along with another person. Do you think it felt particularly good just then?'

'How d'you mean?'

'Well, you were feeling distant from Lisa.'

'Oh, yes, I suppose so.'

'Do you think you can tell me what happened after that?'

I nod, even though I can't, not really. I can only tell her what I remember. I remember that the leisure centre lights flashed and went out. I remember that a second later, the manager came out, locked the main doors and strolled over to the sky-blue Mondeo, whistling. I wondered if he'd seen us, whether the lesser-spotted menopausal woman is more visible in a pair. Apparently not.

'His lordship will be wondering where I am,' Anne-Marie said.

I wondered if Mark had even noticed I wasn't back yet.

She looked over at the car park and pointed her key, and to my surprise, the yellow sports car cheeped and flashed, at which point she returned her eyes to mine and gave me an enormous grin, really cheeky, like a kid's.

'Bloody hell,' I said. 'I'd never have put you in that! I thought you were on the bus.'

'That's my husband's menopause you're looking at. Daffodil-yellow Audi TT. Takes me ten minutes to get out of the bucket seat. Do you want a lift?'

'No, love. I mean, I'd love one, just to get a ride in one of them things, but that's my rustbucket over the other side. Ta, though. See you next week for some more torture.'

'Torture, aye. You're not wrong. Night, then.'

'Night. Nice to meet you.'

'You too,' she called over her shoulder, one arm up in the air by way of a last wave.

I watched her walk over to her car. For some reason, there was a tight sensation under my skin. Mind how you go, I almost called after her but didn't. I felt weird, really weird. I walked over to my own car and got in. I drove off before she'd even started the engine. I know now why she didn't, obviously.

Blue Eyes scrutinises me. 'And that's all you remember?'

'Honestly,' I say, 'I'm telling the truth. I don't remember getting into the car. Hers, I mean. I think I'd remember if I'd got into another woman's car, especially a sporty one like that, but at the same time, I know I could have forgotten. I know I could have said yes to that lift, got into that car and…' I shudder. 'I forget things all the time, walk into a room with no idea what I've come in for. I know that the mind is capable of anything so if there's my DNA

in her car, I don't know how it got there but I'll accept that it did.
It's as if someone else did it, do you know what I mean? Like it's
me, but another me, someone I can see as separate to myself. The
woman that used to be Rachel Ryder. Or that other woman, the
one who doesn't know who she is anymore.'

I think therefore I am. I'm pink therefore I'm Spam. I think I
must have got into her car. Therefore I did get in it. I did. I got
in that car and I… Oh God. God help me.

CHAPTER 36

Rachel

Blue Eyes hands me the umpteenth tissue. That's her job, I suppose, to wring these tearful confessions from criminals. Criminals like me. I will have a profile, I imagine, like any serial killer. Serial killer. How ridiculous it sounds, even in my head. It isn't something from life, from any life I can identify with, least of all my own. My life is almost defined by how normal it is. And that was all I wanted: to be normal, to be boring, two kids, a house, enough money to afford what I need, some of what I want, friends. Love. If you've got love, you're rich, that's what I think.

'So you believe you left Anne-Marie at the door of the leisure centre?' Amanda asks me again, and once I've got myself under control, I tell her yes, and that I can't remember anything about the drive home, but that when I did get back, the kitchen smelled of stale cigarettes yet again. I could hear the television blaring from the lounge, but as usual no one had shouted hello at the sound of the front door.

'And how did you feel?'

'I felt good,' I say. 'I felt pretty happy apart from the smell.'

It's the truth. That's all that bothered me. I popped my rucksack on the stairs. I went into the kitchen. I wasn't crying, I wasn't shaking, I wasn't upset in any way. At the sink, I drank a tall glass of cold water and it felt good, better than any bar of chocolate, better than wine, as if the taste of it was clearer somehow, like I was alive, or more alive, or something. But then yes, the smell of stale smoke got to me. I looked over the worktops for signs of an ashtray. Nothing. I looked in the kitchen bin. I did more than look. I dug around in the rubbish. And sure enough, hidden inside a yoghurt pot under a crisp packet that had been stuffed inside, were two fag butts. The bugger. That'd be him and bloody weeping willow Ingrid, I thought. And then I wondered if it was her when Mark's clothes smelled too, if what I'd thought was just the pub was in fact him going to meet her rather than Roy. The idea didn't bother me as much as it should have done. I was numb to it.

And don't ask me why I did this next thing – maybe because I was thinking I would confront him later – but I took the dog ends out, put them in one of the bread bags I keep back to save on using new plastic bags, went through the side door to the garage and stuffed it in the drawer where I'd found Mark's knife months earlier. I couldn't face asking him about them now. I was tired. I'd had my first good day in a long time.

'So that was it?' Amanda asks. 'Your only concern was the cigarette ends?'

I think back, really think. 'No. There was something else. I rummaged to the back of the drawer. There were some charger cables, an adaptor plug, a packet of paper napkins, but the knife wasn't in there – and now I think about that, I'm thinking, why would I check? What was in my subconscious that would make me do that? I tried to think when I'd last seen it. I thought I remembered putting it back in its sleeve and into the cutlery drawer... ages ago. I hadn't taken it with me on my walkabouts. I hadn't dared. I was sure I'd seen it in there the other day. Almost sure. I went back into the kitchen and straight to the drawer.'

'And did you find it?'

'No. There was only the potato peeler, serving spoons, salad tongs. A chopping knife, a meat knife, a cheese knife with the curly end, you know? The hunting knife wasn't there.'

'And how did you feel?'

'Nothing. Other than a bit bamboozled. I should have worried. I mean, I should have panicked. But at that point, don't forget, I had no idea what had happened to poor Anne-Marie, I only knew that meeting her had, for a few precious minutes, made me almost happy.'

On the Friday morning, I didn't check the iPad. I didn't know why at the time, but now I think that maybe a tiny chink of light had entered my world and that tiny chink had been enough to let me almost forget my routine. I even shared a joke with Katie, something about Dave and what an arse he is, how I'd put rat poison in his tea one day, and it seems to me, remembering, that Mark even smiled at me that morning, and I at him.

By the time I set off to see Dad, I felt almost cheerful. The September sun was on my face and I'm sure I caught the first fresh smells of autumn. It had been a couple of weeks since I'd last stolen a packet of sweets or a can of pop or anything at all. I walked. I breathed the air, took it into my lungs. I didn't know if I could see a future, but maybe I could sense one, just out of reach. Whatever, for that brief period, I felt more all right than I had in a long while.

At the home, Dad was agitated, as per. The weather was warm that day and he couldn't be doing with the heat.

'Linda, love,' he wheezed at me no sooner than my foot was in the door of his room. 'Where the bloody hell have you been?' Linda was my mother. Who's dead, as I think I said. And I know I was used to him saying it, but whatever fleeting good mood I'd felt on the way here evaporated.

'It's not...' I began, but then I thought, what's the point? I wasn't his daughter, not anymore. I hadn't been his daughter for a year or two. I was his wife, my mother. Linda. I was standing in front of him like an old photograph of the woman he used to love, the woman he loved so much that as a child I used to wonder sometimes whether he even saw me. For crying out loud, I thought. Even now, when he does see me, it isn't even me. He was like Katie, full of false logic. Lunacy of age, lunacy of youth – in both cases you had to humour their nonsense while looking after them as best you could. I was middle-aged, in the middle of ages, stuck between the demands of both as many women were – like Lisa was, between her girls and her own very difficult mother. So many women were on this train, trying their best to keep steaming forward, too many passengers, engines failing.

Dad fidgeted in his chair. 'They're stealing all my stuff, Linda, and you're off gallivanting.'

'Sorry,' I said. 'I wasn't gone long, though, was I, and I'm here now.' I opened the little cupboard by his bed, had a quick shufti inside and shut it again, for show. 'It's all right, whoever took your stuff has put it back. Nothing to worry about.'

That seemed to appease him. I sat down beside him on the visiting chair next to the commode. 'How are you feeling?'

'Rubbish,' he said. 'Absolutely rubbish.'

'Oh dear, I'm sorry to hear that.' And I was. Desperately. But what could I do besides sit with him and listen? 'What's the matter?'

And off he went. A litany of misdemeanours, funny looks and petty theft. The whole place run by witches and harridans, whatever a harridan is, the TV lounge a gangsters' hall of fame, if you were to believe half of it, which I didn't. I let him get it out of his system, made soothing noises as best I could. The care assistant brought him a cup of pond water by the looks of it and some flaccid Rich Tea biscuits, which seemed to calm him down a bit. Don't mind me spitting feathers in the corner, I thought but didn't say.

'All right, love?' she said to Dad, and, 'Let it cool, love, yeah?' and, 'I'll pop your biccies here for you, love, all right?'

I didn't like the way she spoke to him, as if he was stupid as well as deaf when he's neither. I could see she was near the end of her shift, probably thinking she still had to get to the supermarket before she went home, that she'd do spaghetti bolognese for tea or something like that and how she couldn't wait to change into her jogging bottoms and take her bra off. I felt her tiredness in my bones as if it were mine and, mostly, I forgave her.

'Soft in the head, her,' Dad said when she'd gone.

I chuckled to myself. Must save that one for Lisa, I thought. It would give her a right laugh.

And then I thought about suffocating him with a pillow and how I might go about it, whether my empathy was so strong that it was telling me that this was what he wanted now, and that if I did it, I'd feel that blessed relief too. I could get away with it. Not like the nurse had taken any notice of me, was it? Had she even registered my presence in the room? If I smothered him, would she remember I'd been here? Was my name even now fading from the visitors' book as if written in invisible ink?

On the way home, just approaching our road, I summoned up the courage and called Lisa. She didn't answer, but a minute later she called back.

'Sorry.' She sounded breathless. 'I was just in the supermarket getting supplies. Our Jodi goes back tomorrow.'

'Of course.' My throat closed. I ducked into a space between two houses and pressed my forehead to the brick wall.

'We're getting pizza and I've got a couple of bottles in.' She faltered. 'Nothing too grand, like.'

'Has it got to September already?' I knew very well it had. I had counted every hour, every day, every week, every month; the year nearly upon me.

She hesitated. 'Why, when did you think it was? I thought you'd…'

'No, I… I mean I've just lost track of time, that's all, you know what it's like.' I attempted a laugh but it choked on the way up. 'That's lovely anyway,' I managed, my voice wobbling all over. 'Pizza with your girls. They'll love that.' The tears were rolling by then but I put my hand over the phone so she wouldn't hear me.

Lisa was silent for a minute. 'Are you OK, Rach?' Her voice was quiet down the line. 'Where are you?'

'I'm just walking back from seeing Dad.'

'I thought you were staying there for the evening?'

'Well, I changed my mind.'

Another painful silence while she dug around for something to say. 'Are you sure you're OK? I've got loads of pizza. The girls'd love to see you – it's been ages. Why don't you come?'

'Don't be daft,' I managed. 'You enjoy your girls while they're here. I'm fine, honestly.'

'You sure? Please come. I've hardly seen you all summer, and Mark said…' She tailed off.

'Mark said what? When did you speak to Mark?'

'No, I… I mean, I saw him… in Church Street. Only in passing, like. He said you're barely at home anymore. Just want you to be careful that's all.'

She'd hesitated over where she'd seen Mark. Had he told her I'd spoken to that Jo and that I wouldn't call the police number a couple of months back? It sounded like she'd seen him recently. I wondered if I'd get home to find an ambulance waiting, a swift needle, kind men with soft voices asking me to come with them. Mark had promised he'd never do that again.

'Don't you worry about me,' I said, deliberately misinterpreting her concern. 'I'm the invisible woman, remember?'

She didn't laugh.

'Rach,' she said with a sigh. 'Mark's worried about you. I'm worried about you. Your Katie's worried about you. Seriously, if not tonight, how about tomorrow night? Come on, why don't—'

'I'm working tomorrow. Double shift, I'll be knackered. Listen, I'll leave you to it, love. Got to go. We'll catch up good and proper next week, all right?'

'All right, love.' She sounded defeated. I knew I was putting up a wall but I couldn't help it. 'I'll be here twiddling my thumbs, day or night, here or not here as you need. You'd be doing me a favour, to be honest.'

'Must dash. Give my love to the girls.' I couldn't stand it a second longer. I rang off without waiting for her to say goodbye and tried unsuccessfully to suppress the long wail that left me. I dug in my bag, found the tissues I'd started carrying in case of nosebleeds. I took one out, unfolded it and pressed it against my face. On the road, traffic hummed, close, closer, fading, gone. Footsteps sounded on the pavement. I hunched myself over, small as I could. The steps amplified, snatches of conversation got louder along with them… *but I was thinking if I got the red one then it'd go with them sandals…* quieter… *you know them ones I got in the sale with the gold buckles…* The footsteps ebbed. A moment, two, the yawn-like sigh of another passing car.

No one saw me there. I was a shadow, less than a shadow, against the cold wall.

CHAPTER 37

Rachel

The woman who takes me to the loo and stands outside the lockless cubicle has come in with a tray. There are two cups of tea and some Nice biscuits. The sugar granules glitter as they pass through a shaft of sunlight. They brought me some orange squash yesterday. It's amazing how nice squash tastes when someone else makes it and when you've not had it since you were about ten. It's all oddly civilised. *Here's some light refreshments while you give us all we need to lock you away for a very long time.* There's something a bit *Titanic* about it, the string quartet playing on the deck while the ship sinks. If it was a string quartet. Might have been a full orchestra. I forget, forget if I ever even knew.

'You refer to Lisa in the past tense,' Blue Eyes says, readjusting her bottom on the chair and pulling her long black wrap skirt over her crossed leg. Her shoes today are soft black leather ankle boots with studs going up one side and a wedge heel. 'You're no longer friends?'

'I've not told her we're not. But we're not.'

'Why not?'

Why not indeed. Because minutes after I'd spoken to her on the phone, she drove past me. I was on the corner of our road and it was definitely her. She has a silver-grey Ford Focus and the passenger side had been keyed a year or two before and still had the scratch. She was driving quite fast, it seemed to me, and if she saw me, she didn't let on. I only noticed her at the last moment, but her face was stern, her shoulders high, the whole position of her body at the wheel tense. She can't have been on her way from anywhere other than my house. We live on a cul-de-sac; the only people she knows on our road are us. To come out any other way she'd have to fly.

A hard pain, like a punch, landed in my gut. My face was burning. She'd said on the phone that she'd seen Mark on Church Street. She hadn't mentioned that she was at my house, but here she was in our road. I'd sensed that she hadn't been telling me the truth but I had no idea why not. I knew for certain then that she hadn't seen Mark on Church Street at all. She hadn't seen him in passing. You don't see someone in passing in their own home.

I hadn't got as far as why she might have been at my house while I wasn't there, why she hadn't said that was where she'd been. Across the road, Ingrid's blinds were closed on the upper floor. Her car was parked nearby on the close. Mark's car was on our driveway. Funny, both their cars here in the afternoon. My stomach churned. I felt like you do when you've eaten a dodgy meal but you're still trying to figure out whether it's just indigestion or full-blown food poisoning.

I opened the front door as quietly as I could and hung up my jacket. I didn't want any questions from Mark. I didn't want any questions from anyone. I didn't want anyone to ask me if I was OK or if I was sure I was OK, because I no longer knew what that meant.

I didn't want to ask Mark if he was OK, or ask him what he'd been up to and hear the lie.

I'd been wondering how I was going to get through the next thirty-six hours, and now I wasn't sure I could get through the next few minutes.

The clock in the kitchen said just after six. It was hours later than I'd thought. That was why Mark's car was there. And Ingrid's, although hers was usually there anyway due to her travelling in with Mark. Mark was home from work. As he would be, would've been since half past five or so. I couldn't fathom how I could have lost so much time, having left my dad at four, but then I remembered that I'd gone up to the town hall pond and sat quietly, tried to gather up the frayed strands of myself and somehow knit them back together. I had no memory of actually sitting there, only a vague sensation of the cold of the bench against my backside. I didn't remember leaving.

The kitchen smelled of cigarettes. Not stale, as such. Recently smoked.

The back door clattered against the frame.

'Mark?' I called out and headed to the lip of the back door.

He was standing on the lawn, his back to me. His hands were on his hips and he was looking down at the grass as if he'd spotted a pound coin and was building up to picking it up. He was so still, like cats are still, or pigeons, and you watch them wondering if they're a very realistic ornament until they twitch and, with a little shock, you realise they're alive after all.

I turned away. On the table were two cigarette butts on a saucer. I'd thought it was Ingrid here smoking when my back was turned, possibly making a play for my husband. I think I admitted that to myself fully only then. Wasn't that why I'd kept those cigarette butts and hidden them in the garage? To not face it or to put off facing it until I felt strong enough, lucid enough? Saying something out loud had felt too much like opening a gate to a field of stampeding cattle.

But now I knew even less. It wasn't Ingrid who had told me she was in the supermarket. It wasn't Ingrid who had just driven past me on her way out of our road. And it wasn't Ingrid who was sharing illicit cigarettes with my husband.

It was Lisa. Lisa, who liked the odd puff, more so since Patrick had left, more again since the girls went to uni. I'd even thought that Mark had taken up having the odd crafty fag at the pub, but actually, come to think of it, Roy didn't smoke. So where had Mark been? Mark the saint. Mark the good man. Unremarkable when he was younger, of no interest to the girls who lusted after the likes of Nick whatsisname with the eyeliner or any of the other boys who passed for heart-throbs back in the day. Mark never went in for fashion, preening, posing or pretension of any kind. He never saw the point in being anything other than himself. And this ordinary bloke had, without my realising it, suddenly come into his own now that certain women were ready to move on from the slick big spenders who had impressed them in their twenties, ready for someone who might not know how to be flash with the cash and the compliments but knew how to be truly kind.

I saw it. I saw it clearly in a way I hadn't before. Ingrid's husband had shot it all up his nose and left her penniless. Lisa's had smooth-talked her into bed, into marriage, into kids, only to leave her when he fancied falling in love all over again with the one thing she couldn't be: a woman he didn't yet know, whose faults were yet to be revealed. I saw how my unremarkable husband might appeal in a way he always had to me. I had never wanted the flash treatment. I had never wanted moonlight and roses. I had only ever wanted to be seen for who I was, not just for my looks. These days I wanted to be seen despite them.

But these are all thoughts that have come to me since. Then – and I think, though I'm not sure, it was only last week – in those last moments of trust, I didn't have an idea as formulated or as clichéd as him cheating on me with my best friend, not in a million years. The thought that came to me was: he hasn't even fetched the ashtray.

I stepped out onto the greening paving stones that pass for a patio. 'Mark?'

He turned around, his eyes creasing at the edges. 'Where've you been? It's gone six.'

'I've been to see my dad. I told you this morning I was going today.'

His eyebrows went almost high enough to be interest before pushing together into a frown, as if it all made sense now. 'Are we getting a Chinese?'

'It's Friday. So no.'

He looked towards next door's back garden before looking back to me – as far as my chin, anyway. Ingrid. She was why he'd been in the garden. A lift home hadn't been enough – he'd needed another chat in the garden. Or she had.

'Have you been smoking?' I said.

He spread his hands and made a funny rectangle with his mouth, the same one he did when Liverpool missed a goal opportunity. A look that said *yes, you caught me, but don't say anything.*

So I didn't.

'Ingrid wanted me to sign her passport form,' he said, apropos of bugger all.

I looked towards the fence, to where he'd just slid his shifty eyes. 'Is that who you were talking to just now? Ingrid?'

Now he was looking there too. Both of us staring at the dividing fence like we were waiting for a close encounter of the third kind. And as I'm remembering all this, I can't stop thinking that by this time, Anne-Marie was dead and I didn't even know it in any conscious way.

'I don't know where Ingrid went,' he said. 'I'd forgotten to put the date on the form. I filled in the photos on the back but I forgot to sign the form.'

'Which was it?'

'Eh?' Raisin eyes, screwed up at me.

'Which was it, the date or the signature? Which did you forget?'

'Eh? What? Both. She was feeding next door's cat. She passed it over the fence.'

'The cat?'

'No, the form.' He put his hands back on his hips and surveyed the garden like it was about to give up the secrets of the earth. 'I was thinking of getting the lawnmower out.'

Look at me, I wanted to say to him. Please look at me. I'm your wife and I've loved you for twenty-five years and I still do and I'm still here.

But I didn't. Obviously.

What I said was, 'I've got mince in. I'll do a spag bol.'

'Sounds good.'

He was already walking up to the shed; I was already back indoors. I picked up the saucer as I passed the kitchen table – no woman with kids ever walks through her own house without accumulating assorted random items, most often arriving at the top of the stairs loaded up like a kid on *Crackerjack*.

I glance up, and sure enough Blue Eyes looks perplexed.

'You're too young to remember *Crackerjack*,' I say. 'It was a kids' show in the seventies. They used to give two kids stuff to hold, pile it on until one of them dropped the lot or it all slid off. You couldn't see the kids for stuff. Whoever kept hold of it all the longest won.'

She smiles. It's not a smile of satisfaction, it's indulgence. *Get on with it, woman.*

I tell her how I put the cigarette ends into a piece of cling film. How I went into the garage and hid them in the drawer beside the others. Why I did this, I don't really know, and I'm quite surprised Amanda doesn't pick me up on it, but she doesn't – she just lets me carry on. If I had to answer my own question, I'd say I wanted a confrontation at some point, but not then. The world was bearing down on me. The world was a great big globe made of glass. It was heavy and I couldn't remember anyone giving it me to carry, but I could feel it and it was taking all my strength not to let it drop from my shoulders and fall in splinters at my feet. I was bent double with it. I was breaking in two. It was only a matter of time now.

The lawnmower sputtered, roared.

I got the chopping board out, the big knife, an onion, a carrot. When Kieron was a baby, I would throw that knife at him as he lay in his crib, over and over again, in my sleep, too. That knife sailing through the air. Me throwing it, screaming at my own violence. Love on steroids.

Katie was at the kitchen door, frowning through a full face of make-up, hair done in tiny plaits all over her head like cornrows. She looked like a Premier League footballer in drag. Three A levels: art, English literature and psychology. All As. For this.

'You're back,' she said.

'No, I'm still out,' I replied to the back of her head as she rummaged in the cupboard. Not a twitch. Hardly comedy gold, I know, but when had she stopped finding me amusing? What was the exact date?

'What's for tea?' A hard stare, a dead-eye special.

'Spag bol.' I nodded at the packet of crisps in her hand. 'Don't spoil your appetite.'

'Oh my God.' She waltzed out in her cloud of fury, stopped at the kitchen door and turned around, appearing to see me for the first time. And maybe I saw her then for the first time in a while because I remember thinking how beautiful she looked, how young, how fresh – as I had once been.

Her brow knitted. 'Mum, are you crying?'

I sniffed, tried to smile. 'No, love. It's these ruddy onions.'

And when I think back to it now, later that evening actually counted for as good as it got in the life I was living then. I know that sounds strange, but when I remember myself, it's as if there'd been a knife sawing away at whatever cord had tethered me to the ground, and now that cord was holding me by one thin, final filament.

We sat down together and ate the spaghetti bolognese. I was looking down at the three of us, from the ceiling or something, that's how it felt. Like I was at the table and at the same time I was floating above. Katie was telling us about a stage-make-up shoot that she'd done in Sefton Park, how she'd learned to do the plaits this afternoon and that she'd done some on Thea as well. She seemed less angry, less ready to roll her eyes or say something cutting. Mark was quiet but he did smile a couple of times, he did ask Katie about her YouTube channel. Did I speak? I don't know. Katie was up to 3,000 subscribers and had over 2,000 followers on Instagram, a separate account she'd set up under @KatieMakeUp. I didn't really get it but I supposed the point was that she did.

And I watched us: my husband and my daughter and myself, eating the meal that I'd made, wearing the clothes that I'd washed in the kitchen that I'd cleaned more times than I can bear to calculate. I wasn't part of them anymore. But at the same time, I was still attached, if that makes sense, by a long cord or something. Floating away. But tethered – just, only just.

'And afterwards?' Blue Eyes looks up from her notepad.

'Afterwards, nothing. I tidied up. I filled the dishwasher. I hung up the laundry load that I'd put on to wash before I'd gone to my dad's. The glass world I was carrying was heavy but I was still carrying it, yes, I was still carrying it then. Until the next morning. The next morning I dropped everything, of course.'

CHAPTER 38

Mark

Transcript of recorded interview with Mark Edwards (excerpt)
Also present: DI Heather Scott, PC Marilyn Button

HS: Can you tell us where you were on Thursday the twenty-sixth of September, the night of Anne-Marie Golightly's murder?

ME: I went to the pub for a couple then I came home. That's it. You can ask Roy Briars. He was with me.

HS: And can you tell me what time you returned?

ME: It would have been about half past nine.

HS: Can anyone corroborate that?

ME: Don't know. I'm not sure if Katie was in or out. She's usually in her room.

HS: And your wife returned later that evening?

ME: Later, yes. She said the aerobics class or whatever it was finished at nine, but she didn't get back till after ten. I was surprised she wasn't back, to be honest. I was watching telly but I heard the front door, heard her feet on the stairs. Then the boiler fired up so she must have had a shower, then she must have got into bed because I didn't hear her come down.

HS: So you didn't see her that evening?

ME: No.

HS: And what about the next morning? Did you notice anything unusual?

ME: She seemed happier. I suppose that was unusual. She was a bit more like her old self. Chatty, like. She said she'd met this woman and that they'd got on like a house on fire and she was looking forward to the next week. It seemed to have given her a lift, like. I didn't know who she meant, obviously, but I suppose that was that Golightly woman, wasn't it? The one she...

HS: (Pause) Mr Edwards, I know this is hard, but can you tell us what happened on the Friday evening, how she seemed?

ME: She went to see her dad. She got back later than she said she would. She looked tired. But we ate with Katie and she seemed... OK. A bit spaced out, but OK.

HS: And you had spent the afternoon with Lisa Baxter, is that correct?

ME: Not the afternoon, no. She'd called round to see me for half an hour after work.

HS: And why was that?

ME: We were worried about Rach. Lisa thought we should call the emergency services but I said I'd talk to her. I was planning to talk to her that weekend about getting help.

HS: And the next day? Saturday?

ME: On the Saturday, I could hear her getting ready to go to work but I stayed in bed. I suppose we were avoiding each other.

HS: And did you have any contact with your wife that day?

ME: I spoke to her briefly that morning when she was on her way out. I called her later but she didn't pick up. She often left her mobile at home. I called her work phone but no one answered. I should have kept calling. She said she was doing the double shift – she was set on it. I should have stopped her. I was giving up, I know that. On her, on both of us, like. I should've fought for her. For us. I didn't know how to talk to her. We couldn't talk to each other. It was like a bomb had gone off and we both had this ringing in our ears that blocked everything out. That's what it was like for me, anyway. Like I was blind, deaf and dumb. And even though when Kieron went to uni she told me she was struggling, that she felt unsettled, like it was all coming to an end, I didn't listen, not really. They were a pair together, heads in books, always laughing at some joke only they got. I used to feel a bit on the outside, to be honest, so when he left – and I feel terrible about this – I thought, good, I'll have more time with Rach. I had that thought.

HS: For the benefit of the tape, Mr Edwards is composing himself.

ME: Our first date was sharing a bag of Hula Hoops on a park bench, do you know that? Of course you don't, sorry. But that's all we needed, do you see what I'm getting at? There's too much materialism in the world now, too much stuff… and it all gets in the way of everything and there's all this hate. Hate, hate, hate, everywhere you look, everything you read. No wonder people are stabbing each other. I see it at work, people jumping to conclusions, never seeing the best in people, never giving the benefit of the doubt. And they want all this stuff, the young ones. They want film-star weddings and cars and designer clothes and the latest iPhone and the latest laptop and all this stuff they haven't earned the right to yet and it's really really important to them and when they don't get it, they're raging, you know? They're furious, as if it's their right to have it all, as if they really believe it'll make them happy. And where does all that rage go? I mean, I can understand why some people don't understand someone else's lifestyle; I had difficulty understanding it myself, at first, with Kieron, thought it was something I'd done, but Rachel helped me get my head round it, showed me that being gay wasn't anything wrong in the first place. But hate? I never hated. Hate doesn't solve anything, does it? Never has, never will. Love solves things and that's my biggest failure of all. I… I should've picked her up from work that day. I should've… and now it's all…

HS: For the tape, I am pausing the recording.

HS: Mr Edwards, when you're ready, and I know this is difficult… we have CCTV of a Vauxhall Astra, registration DM11 VCP, on Barnfield Avenue at eight thirty-five on Thursday evening. Barnfield Avenue runs adjacent to Brookvale Leisure Centre, where your wife went to her spinning class. She says she went there in her own car. You say that you were in the Norton Arms, which is at the top of Halton Brow, as I'm sure you're aware, nowhere near Barnfield Avenue. Can you explain what your car might have been doing in the vicinity of Brookvale Leisure Centre at that time?

CHAPTER 39

Rachel

Saturday, 28 September. My first memory of that morning is sitting at the kitchen table, iPad open, weeping into my hands. It was half past six in the morning. I'd been awake since three, had lain there trying to keep my eyelids shut over my stinging eyeballs, but in the end I'd come downstairs, made myself a hot milk with honey and sat on the sofa in my dressing gown crying through *The King's Speech* on DVD. I'd drifted off until six or so, but then I'd needed a wee so I'd given up and decided to start the second-worst day of my life. Sooner it started, the sooner it would end.

And now I was sitting in the kitchen in the bright light of an early autumn morning, staring at a headline with tears rolling down my face.

'Is this the article?' From her notes, Amanda pulls out a sheet and hands it to me. I scan it briefly. There is a black smudge on it, which tells me it's been photocopied.

'Yes,' I say, and take a moment to reread it.

Local mum fatally stabbed in car

Mrs Anne-Marie Golightly was found fatally wounded in her car outside Brookvale Leisure Centre in Halton in the early hours of this morning. Police were alerted to the incident late on Thursday night.

'Leisure centre manager Mr Timothy Dyer called the emergency services at approximately five minutes to midnight after spotting Mrs Golightly slumped at the wheel of her sports vehicle in the car park,' said police spokesperson Paul Gowers. 'An ambulance arrived a little after midnight but the attending paramedics had difficulty accessing the victim as the car had been locked from the outside. After breaking into the car, they pronounced Mrs Golightly dead at the scene. She had been stabbed in the ribs and died of her injuries.'

'I only went back because I'd forgotten to set the alarm,' said Mr Dyer. 'Thought she'd fainted after a gym session or something. I only noticed the car after I'd locked up for the second time, as it was over on the far side, by the trees. It's a nice motor, not the kind anyone would leave, but I thought maybe someone had had a few drinks at the bar and decided to come back for their wheels tomorrow. When I saw her inside, I couldn't believe it, to be honest. Not here. I can't take it in – it's just an absolute tragedy. I hope the police catch whoever did this and put him away for a very long time.'

Mrs Golightly's family are asking for privacy at this time. The police are urging anyone who might have any information, no matter how insignificant, to call them immediately on the number below.

'Rachel,' Amanda says. 'Are you OK?'

I nod, yes. But I'm not. I'm not OK.

The report had been posted the evening before. I'd not looked at the news at all. I'd been distracted, eating spaghetti and listening to Katie, thinking how passionate she was, actually, about what she was doing. All thoughts of Lisa and Mark together had been hovering somewhere else, somewhere I had to push them to until

I no longer had the strength to hold them there. And strangely, we'd almost been a family in that moment. I'd been almost happy.

I printed Anne-Marie off.

'I enjoyed meeting you,' I told her as the letters washed across the page. 'You were such a nice person.' I carried her carefully to the kitchen and laid her to rest in my file. 'I'm sorry we'll never be friends now. May you rest in peace.'

I looked at the police contact details at the end. I dialled the number, wiping my eyes with my hands. The dial tone sounded once, twice. I hung up. What to say? What *was* there to say?

I'd had nothing to do with it. I'd chatted to her, that was all. I'd chatted to her and then I'd come home and had a shower. I remembered the cigarettes, putting them with the others… Had I looked for the knife? I could remember checking the cutlery drawer and feeling a bit confused that it wasn't there. I had no memory of checking my handbag. But even if the knife were in my handbag, I hadn't taken my handbag to the leisure centre, only my rucksack with my towel and my hoody. I'd left the rucksack on the bedroom floor, forgotten it until now. The hoody and the towel would still be in there. But where was the knife?

I stood up, crossed the kitchen, opened the cutlery drawer. The knives and forks crashed as the drawer hit my stomach. I scrambled through the serving spoons, the knives, the salad tongs, the corkscrew… Mark's knife had to be in there, even if I hadn't seen it last night. I'd seen it recently, I was sure, and it had been in this drawer. I'd taken it out and closed my fingers around its leather handle, pushed the button, and now, remembering, it seemed to me that I'd seen the blade glint under the kitchen light. But had I? A different memory surfaced. Me, rummaging in the drawer, finding nothing. The two memories sat side by side, each as clear as the other.

Had I after all returned it to the garage? Perhaps when I stashed the dog ends?

I slammed the drawer shut, ran through to the garage. In the old dresser, in the top-left drawer, were the two cigarette ends balled up in cling film next to the other two in the bread bag. But no knife. No knife in the right-hand drawer, on the top of the unit, in the cupboards, on the shelves. A missing knife. A woman stabbed in her own car, children left without their mother, a man widowed in the blink of an eye. My eyes clouded. I wiped at them with the backs of my hands.

I am wiping my eyes with the backs of my hands now. There will never be enough tears and yet they will never stop.

'Do you need another break?' Blue Eyes sounds like she's calling to me from another room, but when I look up, she is there in front of me. 'Rachel? Do you need another break?'

I shake my head. 'No. No thank you. I want to get it over with. There's not much more and then you'll know everything there is to know and you can send me where I belong.'

Outside, a bus rumbles past. After a moment, I tell her the rest. About how I got through that awful day, about how I killed that poor lad and how I eventually made the call.

CHAPTER 40

Rachel

I'm at home. Saturday night. Silence and darkness. It's late. After midnight. The back door blows open and clatters against the wall of the house. I pull it shut and lock it. I make myself a hot drink and sit in the dark watching grey clouds float over the moon, and all I can think is that the day has ended. It's over. Now, hopefully, sleep will take me at least until the small hours. I am so tired. In the morning, I'll call the police and tell them everything I know about Anne-Marie, about Jo and about Henry Parker. But first I will rest.

On heavy legs, I climb the stairs to bed.

Mark is asleep, snoring softly. The room smells of stale beer, clothes thick with cigarette smoke. He said he was meeting Roy at the golf club Saturday night, tonight. Golf club, my arse. Look at him, sleeping the sleep of the righteous. Exhausted after an evening at Lisa's. Nothing stopping them now her girls have gone, is there? I'm out of their way, as I have been for some time.

I pull my shirt over my head and am about to drop it on the chair in the corner when I see my rucksack on the floor beneath. I never emptied it from Thursday night. I pull it out from under the chair and creep into the bathroom. I switch on the light and lock the door, close the loo lid and sit down. All day I've been shaking from head to toe whenever I sit down, but that's just shock. All day I've done nothing but run through what has happened since

Katie's party. The girl I made a meaningful connection with in a secluded place was brutally murdered. The man I saw hidden in the shadows of shame was strangled. The woman I spoke to as the light fell and the surroundings became deserted was stabbed to death. It is still unbelievable, even now, after having a whole day to process it.

Whoever killed Anne-Marie is the same person who attacked Jo, I know that. Maybe not the fella in the churchyard, but Jo, definitely. A knife in the ribs. The same… what d'you call it? Modus operandi. I hope that it was sharp like Mark's, the knife. I hope Anne-Marie didn't feel it, didn't know too much about it. She should have had someone with her. She should have had someone by her side in her last moments. She died alone and afraid. Alone and afraid, poor woman. Her poor family. Her kids, oh, her kids.

I pull sheets of loo roll from the holder and wipe my face. My throat aches with tears for Jo, for Anne-Marie, stolen from their loved ones in the cruellest possible way. They'll never get over it, never. You can't get over something like that.

With shaking hands, I unzip my sports bag and pull out my crumpled hooded top. I was too hot to put it back on. The towel that I used to wipe the sweat from my face and neck has dried. There's nothing else in the bag. The knife isn't there, thank goodness. Although why am I reassuring myself? Why would it be?

I'm about to drop the rucksack to the floor when I spot the front pocket is half undone.

I wipe my eyes, sniff hard, pull it fully open. I see and don't see what's inside. A balled-up wad of tissues. Bright white, bright red. Tissue. Blood.

'Oh God,' I whimper into my hands. 'Oh heaven help me.'

I am crying into my hands then and now. I don't expect you or Blue Eyes to feel sorry for me. I just want you to know that I'm sorry. I'm sorry for not being clearer, but this is all I know. I'm sorry for not getting to it in a straight path, but this zigzag was how it went. I didn't remember killing her then and I don't remember it now, but I know that I did it and for that I'm more sorry than I can say. And for Jo and for Henry. I'm sorry; I'll be sorry for the rest of my days. I'm a danger to myself and to others. I don't deserve to be free. I don't deserve to live.

Blue Eyes pulls the last tissue from the box and hands it to me. 'So was that the moment you became convinced you were responsible for the attacks?'

'Yes. No. I don't know. I'd already decided to call the police. I didn't know where the knife was but I knew they were my tissues and I knew it was her blood. Anne-Marie's.'

'How did you know that?'

'I don't know, I just did.' I look up at her. 'Well, it was, wasn't it?'

She frowns. 'You tell me.'

'There you go. It was.'

'But you didn't call the police?'

'I can't remember much more than numbness, all over, like your face after the dentist has injected your gums, you know? It was only the next morning that I rang them, the police. Only after I read about the lad. About Ian.'

'So that night you didn't call anyone or tell anyone?'

'No. Ian Brown was already dead by then, obviously. I'd already killed him, but that was nowhere, nowhere at all in my mind that night, honestly it wasn't. I've nothing to hide anymore and I swear to God I'd tell you if I'd had any idea, any ghost of an idea as I sat on the loo with those bloody tissues in my hand, I would. But honestly, it was only when I read about him the next morning that it really came back to me, not before. The whole of Saturday came back to me. The day. The evening. The night. I remembered all of it. And then there was no doubt, no doubt left at all.'

'I think we need to talk about that,' she says softly. 'Don't you? Don't you, Rachel? Do you think you can talk about it?'

Why are you so kind?

She doesn't answer. I haven't said it out loud, that's why. I wipe my eyes. My face is chapped. Sore.

Blue Eyes knows what's coming. She's read the statement, seen those terrible photos. But she needs to hear me say it, in a different way to the others. I know she's not police. I know she's a psychiatrist building a forensic case history of a criminally insane murderer. I don't care. I care only about how kind she is in this moment, the way she listens with that hidden, waiting smile, about the fact that she sees me. That's all any of us want, isn't it? To be seen, to be listened to with compassion and attention while we unload our troubled hearts.

'Rachel? Do you think you can tell me? Can you tell me what happened?'

She slides another sheet of paper towards me.

CHAPTER 41

Rachel

Teenager found injured in town-hall gardens in third knife attack

A boy was found stabbed in Runcorn Town Hall gardens late last night and is now fighting for his life. He has been named as sixteen-year-old Ian Brown, from Widnes. Police have not ruled out a link with the murder of Joanna Weatherall a little under three months ago and that of Anne-Marie Golightly on Thursday night. This latest attack is now being treated as attempted murder.

'The method would appear to be the same,' said police spokesperson Keith Woodhead. 'Two stab wounds to the ribs using a sharp hunting-style knife. Mr Brown had a high alcohol content in his blood, and this and the cold temperature may have complicated matters and prevented him from seeking help. We believe the person who did this is an opportunist, and that they are armed and dangerous, and would advise against going out alone at this time. We would urge anyone walking at night to be vigilant.'

The police are keen to speak to the woman who made the emergency call. Anyone with any information should call the following number.

After the number, the usual links: *Knife-crime epidemic sweeps UK*; *Have we become a nation of haters?*; *How to talk to your child about knives.*

I know this piece off by heart. It is the first news article I saw on Sunday morning. My eyes took it in but it was as if the electrical current relaying the information to my brain had short-circuited. Over and over I read it and slowly the realisation of what the words meant dawned. A boy I'd seen and spoken to less than twelve hours earlier was fighting for his life. He had been full of promise. I was going to help him make a future. And now he'd been stabbed, almost to death. He could still die. And I'd seen him less than… Oh God, they must have rushed the news out. Matter of urgency. Public safety warning.

'My God,' I whispered into the hot, damp palm of my hand. 'Ian.'

I printed it out, read it again, the paper shaking in my hands. Ian: an article in a news bulletin, reduced to facts, encapsulated in words to be glossed over in favour of a gossip column or the sports section. Soon to be a statistic.

He wasn't a statistic to me. He was a beautiful soul. I took him over to my clip file and gently sheathed him in plastic.

'I'm so sorry,' I whispered.

I brought him to my lips, felt the odourless touch of the soft cellophane, heard the dull crackle.

I laid him to rest with the others, the unremembered that I remembered. At the kitchen table, I sat down, opened the file at the beginning and read my first-ever entry. My head fell into my hands. I was crying so much I couldn't see, couldn't get my breath. I laid my forehead on the kitchen table and cried for that boy, for his mother, for his father, for his family, his friends, for everyone who knew him, who loved or had loved him.

Sometime later, I must have stopped. Morning climbed over the back fence. Light washed the kitchen a pale vanilla yellow. My breath shuddered and stalled. The previous day rushed at me. Frame by frame, it rushed. I couldn't stop it; all I could do was watch.

Saturday morning, twenty-four hours earlier, and I'm crying for Anne-Marie. I watched myself as if from above. Rachel. Rachel Edwards.

'I enjoyed meeting you,' I'm telling Anne-Marie as I print her off. 'You were such a nice person.' I carry her to the kitchen and lay her carefully to rest in my file. 'I'm sorry we'll never be friends now.'

I'm taking the dog round the block. I can see myself against the pink sky: tartan pyjama bottoms blown flat to my shins, flapping about beneath my big black Puffa coat. Mark's red woolly hat pulled low, thick hiking socks and Mark's Crocs, a few sizes too big. I'm still crying. I'm muttering to myself. The milkman's truck fizzes by and I see him glance in my direction. I see myself through his eyes. I look insane, shuffling along in shoes too big. To myself, remembering, I look insane.

By the time I get back I've stopped crying but I can hear myself moaning inside my own head. I sound close but distant, muffled. In the bathroom I stay quiet. I mustn't wake Mark. If he wakes up, I'll have to face him. I have no idea what to say to him, can't think I ever will. I want to wave the cigarette ends in his face. I want to ask which one of those whores he is shagging – my neighbour or my childhood friend. Or both. I want to pour boiling water over his head. I want to walk away with nothing but a suitcase and the shredded remnants of my dignity.

I know what's happened to poor Anne-Marie and to Jo and to Henry Parker. The knowledge is inside me. But I can't reach it.

I'm watching myself. There is something in my gut, something rotten. In the darkest, lowest corner of me a little voice is whispering, but I can't hear the words. The whisper is getting louder with every passing minute. Louder and louder it gets, and then I hear it, I hear the words: *You're a murderer, Rachel Edwards*, it says. *You're a murderer now.*

I'm standing naked under the shower, turning the dial to hot. The water runs over my head. It feels warm, warm and thick as raw egg. I push my face into the heat of the water, try to drown out the voices, close my eyes to visions of a round white moon flashing on a silver blade. To Jo, her face set in shock, falling away from me. My hands are clenched and bloody. But is this memory inside a memory of me holding Mark's knife in the kitchen, staring at it in shock and wonder, or is that from the dark, deserted car park at the leisure centre? The moon, was it out on Thursday night? And the knife, I didn't take it with me. So where is it? And what now? What now? What now?

'I don't know,' I sob into the water. 'I don't know I don't know.'

In the bedroom, Mark is pretending to be asleep. He doesn't want to look at me, not naked, not clothed, not at all. I don't want to look at him.

The kitchen clock chimes eight o'clock. I watch myself put on my coat and I put on my coat. I watch myself open the front door and I open the front door. Weeks ago, Dave rostered me on the Saturday late shift but I told him I'd do the early one too. He asked if I was sure. Yes, I said. I am sure. I want to. Please let me.

So.

I go to work.

I go to work.

I go to work.

Get on with it, woman. Sorry.

I am halfway out the door when Mark calls to me from the stairs.

'I'm meeting Roy later,' he says to his own shoes. He is standing in the hall now. The kitchen door is open; it lets in the day now truly dawned, the undeniable, unstoppable day, the hours I must get through. 'Golf club. Did my trousers come through the wash?'

'They're hung up in the wardrobe.' My hand is on the catch. My eyes are nowhere near his. He's there. He's not there. He's on the earth. He's floating in space. 'Your sandwich is in the fridge.'

'I'll probably have something with Roy, to be honest.'

I step out, shut the door behind me.

'I don't care what you have,' I mutter, pounding down the driveway. 'I don't care if you're really meeting Roy at his fancy-pants golf club or if you're going round to my best friend's house to stick your nine iron in her eighteenth hole.'

I do care. I care very much. I can see that now, watching myself. I can see that I am shaking, too furious to admit to my own rage. My latent trembling fury. I can see Mark's fury too, in everywhere he doesn't look, everything he doesn't see. Me. He doesn't see me. I can see, watching us from here, that we are trapped. We are trapped in silent rage. I can travel in my mind's eye and I can open Katie's door and step across the minefield of trampled clothes and I can see that even in sleep she is furious too. We are all furious. We are carrying the rage of the world, of this great glass globe that presses on my shoulders, too heavy to carry, too fragile to drop. I can see Anne-Marie. She is laughing at something I said when she was still alive, still a mother, still a wife, still a friend. She is a memory of herself, words on a page, photos in an album – that is all she is now.

I am a memory of myself. My husband is a memory of my husband. My daughter is a memory. My son is a memory. I can't reach them. They are lost. I am lost.

'Rachel. Rachel?' Amanda's blue eyes have filled with tears. Are they mine or are they hers?

'You need to stop,' she says. 'Let's take a break.'

Mark's a good man. Lisa loved to say that. That's the first thing I tell Amanda when we resume and that's what was on my mind as I walked to work. She'd always said it, ever since Mark and I had first got together. I thought she meant that he was a good man for me. For *me.* He made me feel like everything I did was clever and good. He made me want to try to be the person he thought I was – kind, funny, decent. When I got pregnant with Kieron, it was as if I alone had performed some sort of miracle.

How could I have forgotten that?

How had I lost my way to him?

Because I had. I saw it so clearly then I couldn't fathom how I'd not seen it all these long months. He'd believed in me, always, and now I was shuffling around the streets in my pyjamas, snivelling and fretting to myself, not to mention accosting strangers in the night, while Lisa, Lisa who'd been holding a candle all these years, had taken her chance. When Patrick left, she'd not been able to help herself. The concern she'd had for me this last year fell into a different place. Kindness, concern and love reframed themselves, showed me another picture altogether.

Are you OK, Rach?

Are you sure?

Hormones can play havoc – you know that better than anyone.

Bringing up an episode that happened twenty years ago so that I would think I was cracking up all over again when all the time she was urging me to do just that… lose my mind. Mark is a very passive man. Maybe Lisa thought it was time to get Rachel shipped off to the funny farm, take care of Mark in his darkest hour, a romance born of tragedy. *She was beyond help, poor thing. We tried to talk to her but she started this walking thing… We clung to each other with the worry of it all. We couldn't help it. We've always loved each other. And Rachel, well, Rachel had lost her mind. She was talking to strangers, taking them to dark and lonely places, she was… she was, oh God, we had no idea…*

Yes, yes, thinking about it, all those years ago, when Kieron was only weeks old, it was Lisa who had spoken to Mark, Lisa who had called an ambulance. And yes, I was ill then, I was very ill, but… was that the whole story? Had they plotted against me? Were they plotting against me now?

I look up, find Blue Eyes.

'I know I'm not well,' I say. 'Now, I mean. I do know.'

She nods. 'You're not, but—'

'But just because you're losing your mind,' I interrupt, 'doesn't mean you're losing *all* of it, does it?'

'No, it doesn't. Hold on to that, Rachel.'

There is delusion and there is instinct. There are visions and there are invisible things we're absolutely correct in picking up from the very air. All those years ago, my mind had told me that I was throwing knives at my baby and it was mistaken. These last months, my gut had told me things were not right and my gut had been correct. It was this, this unnamed wrongness that had made me feel unstable and alone, without knowing exactly why. Mark not looking at me was not because he didn't see me; it was because he was too ashamed. Lisa asking if I was OK all the time made me feel uncomfortable because I knew on some level that it was not because she cared. If you ask someone enough times if they're OK, if they're sure they're OK, of course they're going to start wondering if they're not. Katie's unrelenting angry tone, now that was more difficult to fathom. Was it because she knew about her dad and Lisa? Knew and couldn't find the words to tell me.

And in all of this, what about me attacking innocent people? Killing innocent strangers? Here, to my absolute sorrow, my mind and my gut agreed: it was not delusion. It was not. It was a truth too terrible to think or swallow, but it was a truth all the same.

'Over sixty per cent of communication is non-verbal,' I say to Blue Eyes. She doesn't write anything down, just looks, and listens. 'But words *seal* things, don't they? They let you hold those things tight. They live on the lines, where we're safe. But there's always what's in between. The white space. That's where we're not safe. In the terrifying white space of all that isn't said, all that isn't sealed up in words. That's why I called the police. That's why I want to tell you everything. I need to seal what I've done in words. I need to put it on the lines.'

Amanda nods. There is no shush of traffic. No one rattling the handle to bring in cups of tea. There is not even a fly to break the silence.

'So, Rachel. You went to work?'

'Yes.'

'Can you tell me about that?'

I can and I do.

The homeless lad wasn't on his bench; he was on the pub doorstep in a sleeping bag. I said the cheeriest good morning I could manage. The top of the sleeping bag unfolded. He was wearing a woolly hat.

'Morning,' he said and gave me the most generous, most beautiful smile I'd seen in a long time. His eyes were blue, like Kieron's; I think I saw that for the first time.

'Are you not cold?' I asked him.

He shrugged. 'A bit.'

'I'll bring you your tea, won't be a tick. Or coffee, if you prefer?'

'Coffee, please. Thank you.'

I returned his smile, unlocked the door and switched on the lights, which flickered and flashed. I stood in the lounge bar, my back pressed against the door. Empty chairs sat upturned on empty tables, the slot machine stood lifeless in the corner, spirits of amber and brown, yellow and clear, waited in their optics, upside down and doubled up in the mirror. Behind me, the latch clicked shut.

'Please God,' I said. 'Please let me not be responsible for Anne-Marie. Please let it turn out to be someone else.'

Blue Eyes narrows her eyes, recrosses her legs and leans forward. 'So, as late as Saturday morning, you still believed you hadn't attacked or killed anyone?'

'Yes, at that moment. Or hoped. Belief, hope – not much between them, is there? Both a question of faith, I suppose.'

'Why do you think that was?'

'Because my memory offered me nothing, not one shred, to make me believe that I'd done anything so terrible. Not then.'

'What about the flashbacks?'

'That's all they were. Flashbacks. Images. As I say, nothing concrete. I suppose I still had hope, so that's what I clung to.'

Hope. Hope that Mark's knife would not match the wounds on poor Anne-Marie, hope that the blood on my tissues was my own. Hope that my proximity to every single attack could be explained away by coincidence even though one coincidence is believable, three not so much. Hope that the police would discover some incriminating piece of evidence that pointed to a local madman.

My phone buzzed. A text. Lisa. *Are you OK? Thinking of you. Call me any time. I'm here, you know that. Xx*

I switched my phone off, felt my mouth contort. Anger had turned, as anger will, to hate.

I don't know what's worse, being betrayed by your husband or your best friend. A love triangle straight from one of the Trollope books I used to borrow from the library. There was something old-fashioned about it, a bit seventies – like sexism, or racism or homophobia: *Take my missus, I wish somebody would*; *Hey up, Chalky*; *I'm free, what a gay day.* Laughter from a can. Sunburn. Sideburns. Sheepskin coats.

In the staff kitchen of the pub, I pressed my fists to my temples and roared. So much for my dear ones not seeing me. Turns out I hadn't seen *them* at all, was blind to all but strangers.

The kettle rumbled. I took the young chap his coffee.

'What's your name, love?' I said. 'I'm so sorry I haven't asked you before.'

'Ian,' he said. 'What's yours?'

'Rachel,' I said.

'Pleased to meet you.' That lovely smile again. All the warmth of the sun in it.

'You too.'

I told him I'd be back in a minute. I had to get away, away from the bar, from everything. I locked the pub door and walked away, to the canal, to where I'd seen that GP, and carried on, left, towards the arts centre. The day was up, thick white cloud above me, the black water of the canal below. A man had been strangled and dumped in the water here in the eighties, under the bridge, they said. I remembered it from when I was a kid. I stood on tiptoe, caught the reflection of the top of my head. Water is a mirror. Life is a mirror. Mark never looked at me. But if you want someone to look at you, really look at you and see, chances are you have to look at them. You have to see them too. And I hadn't looked at him. Not for a year.

I walked back into town, past the swimming baths, round the corner into Church Street, past the betting shop and back to work. I didn't care about being late opening up but I didn't know what to do other than this. I had nowhere else to go, no one left, no one at all. All I had were the seconds, the minutes, the hours of this horrific day, of every day after this one, hours upon hours, chiming on a great cosmic clock. I had the town, the Co-op, the Barley Mow pub.

I had Dave, who, when he popped in to see if I was OK – checking up, more like – at around midday, in a newsworthy act, made me a cup of tea.

'Are you all right, Rachel?' he asked. 'Sure you're OK?'

Stop asking me that, I didn't say, of course.

'I'm fine, love. Don't be worrying about me – I like to be busy.'

I had the punters to make small talk with, pints to pull, meal orders to pass through to the kitchen and take to the tables. I had Phil to say hello to, sad and hunched over the slot machine with the last of his coins, ghost of a man. I got through those seconds and minutes and hours like you'd get through pushing your forehead up a tarmac road. Phil's suit was hanging off him, poor thing.

'Here,' I said, handing him my sandwiches.

'What's that for?' He looked shocked, like kindness was a surprise to him.

'Your suit's falling off you,' I said. 'And I'm not hungry.'

He smiled, then laughed.

'I'm not losing weight,' he said. 'The ex cut up all my suits. This one's from Oxfam. It's too big, that's all.'

'You're joking.' I shook my head. 'Bloody hell, Phil,' I said. 'I think that deserves a cup of tea an' all.'

I made him a cup of tea even though I'm not supposed to give anyone anything for free. But whenever conversation stopped or I was between punters, Anne-Marie fell into my mind's eye; she wouldn't stop falling, falling forward, slumping over the steering wheel over and over again. I'd met and spoken to tens of people in the last few months. Only two, three, tops, had become victims like the ones in my clip file.

But only three had provided an opportunity, hidden away from watchful eyes. And three was enough. Three was three too many.

Seconds ticked, minutes passed, hours struck. At half past two, I told Dave to go – there was no point in him being there, sad get.

'Are you going to be OK?' He was already shrugging on his jacket.

'Of course. Off you go.' *Stop asking me if I'm OK, because if you knew the real answer, you'd be horrified.*

Bill the chef left as usual at ten. Late on, there was no one in so I closed up at quarter to eleven. I turned all the lights off and sat behind the bar in the dark. I was thinking about Katie and how I'd not seen her in days.

I dug my phone out of my bag, switched it on and called her.

'Mum?' She sounded like she was in a disco or something, judging by the noise.

'Katie, love, is that you?'

'Course it's me, Mum. It's my phone.' She laughed. 'Mum? Are you all right?'

'Course I am. Not seen you, that's all.'

'I've been at Liam's.' The background noise became suddenly quieter, though I could hear what sounded like a road. 'Are you sure you're all right?'

'I'm fine. It's me asking if you're all right, remember?'

'I know, I just thought… Are you sure you're OK?'

Jeez, don't you start. 'I'm fine. About to set off home. Your dad's out, so shall I call and get us a bottle of wine in? I'm going past the off-licence. I could order a pizza, too. I know it's late, but we could watch a film, stay up past midnight, eh, be wild, what d'you reckon?'

She hesitated. Quite right, I supposed. It'd been over a year since we'd shared a bottle and made ourselves cry laughing looking at memes and silly videos on her phone. Over a year since we'd shared anything at all.

'I thought you were… I'm in Warrington.' The background noise died. 'There's a few of us. I've just stepped out of the club.'

I swallowed hard. Somehow this cut me to the bone in a way her rudeness never had. 'That sounds like fun.'

'I can come home. I… I thought you'd be doing something with Dad. Or Lisa.'

Dad and Lisa are doing something with each other, I didn't say. Perhaps she didn't know, then.

'Will you heck come home,' is what I did say. 'Go on. Have a Jägerbomb for me, will you? For… old times.'

She gave a little laugh. And it's pathetic, but I was so grateful for it, I started crying.

'Let's do pizza and wine next Friday, eh?' There was a catch in her voice.

'You're on,' I managed, but only just.

I was about to ring off when I heard her voice, small and trembling, from the speaker. 'Mum? Mum, are you still there?'

I don't know. I don't know if I'm still here.

'Did you need something?'

'No, I… Mum? I just… love you.'

I closed my eyes, covered the phone with my hand and took a great gulp of air. When I thought I could last the seconds, I took my hand away. 'Love you too, love,' I whispered. 'Have a good night.'

I rang off. My hands were on my knees. My hair had come out of its clip and was stuck to my forehead. The bottom of my nose was raw. I pushed at my face with my hands. I didn't bother with a tissue or even the hem of my T-shirt. Tears were an inconvenience but I knew there'd be no stopping them, not today. Katie was off out. Mark would be making small talk with boring Roy surrounded by men in cashmere jumpers, or over at my best friend's house stroking her hair and telling her he didn't know what he'd do without her. There was no rush for me to get back. To anywhere. Ever. I wanted out. I wanted to press the ejector seat on life but didn't know how to do it. It was like murder, a question of practicalities. Timing. Nerve. Opportunity.

Was that what I'd been doing these last months? Was that what I'd done? Tried to kill myself by proxy? See how far my high-scoring empathy could take me in someone else's death? Had I been trying to remove the last possible boundary? Skin dissolving. Drops. Water. Cohesion.

I was water. They were drops. A man was drowned in the canal. Cells from him would have floated into the water, become part of the water, indistinguishable from the water.

I tested the flex of the office phone. I wrapped it round my neck and pulled, making myself choke. The flex loosened. I couldn't. It wasn't fair on my family. I was trapped, buried alive.

I dug out my tissues and cleaned myself up, ran my fingers through my hair and put my clip back in because… because what else was I going to do?

I walked through the pitch-black lounge of the pub. One foot in front of the other, out of the front door. It was all I could think of doing.

'Hiya,' said a voice.

I looked down to see that beautiful smile. A young person who saw me.

'Ian. What are you doing still here?'

'My film premiere was cancelled.'

A laugh escaped me. My heart hurt just to look at him, to see him smile and joke. Seconds passed, became a minute.

'You look pissed off,' he said and shivered.

I looked at him, really looked at him. His face was pale, his hair matted, and his sleeping bag looked dirty. He looked no more than twenty years old, twenty-five tops.

'You're cold,' I said. 'You're hungry. There's a stack of food in the kitchen. How about I microwave something for you?'

He smiled. 'That'd be really great, ta.'

I rolled up the shutter and unlocked the pub again. 'Let's get you fed and warm at least.'

He followed me through to the kitchen carrying his sleeping bag and a holdall, thanking me all the way.

No sooner were we both inside than I noticed how badly he smelled. Poor lad. I wondered if he realised.

'There's a shower upstairs,' I said. 'It runs nice and hot – it'll warm you up. How does that sound?'

Now that we were indoors, his teeth looked whiter against his grubby face.

'That sounds amazing.'

'Come on then, I'll take you up.' I led the way up to the staff quarters. I think even then I was thinking I could let him sleep in the bed up there, even if it was for just one night. No one need ever know.

'You'll have to manage with the hand towel,' I said, showing him into the little staff shower room. 'But if you look in the cupboard there, you'll find some men's clothes. They belong to Dave but he only keeps them for emergencies. Give me the clothes you have on when you come down and I'll wash them for you tomorrow, then we'll swap back on Monday. How does that sound? Dave won't know a thing.'

He was standing there in the doorway, hands clasped in front of him. His hair was dirty blonde, thick, with a natural wave. He didn't look like Kieron but he reminded me of him. Same build, perhaps. Same gentle way about him. Trusting.

'I can't take someone else's clothes,' he said.

'You can. I said you can. I can handle Dave, don't worry. I'll wash the towel an' all. Dave won't know a thing – he's not in till Monday afternoon.' I smiled to show I meant it, but he still faltered. 'Go on. I'll warm us up a couple of steak pies, how does that sound? There's some frozen oven chips knocking about and I'm sure Bill the chef left a baguette out and some cheese.'

Finally, smiling all the while, he went through and closed the door. As I made my way back down the stairs, I heard the shower run and imagined how good that must feel, to have the lovely clean warm water run over you when you were filthy and cold.

At the foot of the stairs, I stopped. He was singing a song I recognised though I couldn't remember the words. He sang in tune; his voice was sweet. I had no idea where all this was leading. I'd acted on instinct and now here I was with a homeless boy in my work bathroom.

I put a steak pie in the microwave and shoved a tray of chips in the oven, which was still warm from a late order. While I waited, I cut a big chunk of baguette and made up a cheese and pickle sandwich, plenty of butter. I thought I could maybe put together a bag of supplies to tide him over. Until when, I didn't know, although Kieron's room was hovering at the edges of my mind.

The door upstairs opened – I heard the squeak of the hinge. Footsteps on the stairs and then Ian appeared in the doorway looking – and, I was sure, feeling – cleaner than anyone had ever felt. He looked a lot younger too. I'd put him in his twenties, but now he looked like a kid, possibly late teens. His face was pinker, his hair thinner, lighter with the dirt washed out.

'I used a bit of that deodorant spray,' he said, apology in his tone. 'I hope that's OK.'

'I tell you what,' I said, laughing a bit, 'those clothes look a damned sight better on you than on Dave. Dave's got a right gut on him.'

He looked down, patted his non-existent stomach. 'Not much danger of a gut at the moment.'

I told him to go and sit at the bar and followed him out into the main lounge.

'Drink?'

'Are you sure?'

I raised my eyebrows at him. 'You're eighteen, yes?'

'Nineteen actually,' he said. 'Would it be OK to get a pint of Stella?'

'Coming up. What's your full name, by the way?'

'Ian Brown. You know, like the singer from the Stone Roses? My parents were massive Stone Roses fans.'

'Oh, I used to love them. I went to see them at Spike Island back in the day.'

'No way! My parents went to that gig!'

'So if you're our Katie's age, you must have been born, what, 2000?'

A nod and another smile – how generous he was with them, like he knew they cost nothing to give. I put his pie and chips in front of him and he ate greedily, closing his eyes to the first mouthful of food. While he wolfed it down, he told me his tale. There wasn't much in the way of surprises, to be honest. It certainly came as no surprise to learn that after his parents had split up, he'd run into problems with what sounded like a string of boyfriends his mother had welcomed a bit hastily into the family home. The last one had proved final.

'I had to get out of there,' he said. 'Slept on a mate's sofa for a bit but I couldn't stay there forever. Things went OK, did a bit of building work cash in hand, found a room in a house, but I got into weed and next thing I couldn't afford the rent. It all went tits up basically. My own fault.'

'How will you turn yourself around?'

He shrugged. 'Not everyone's as kind as you. People don't see me. It's like I'm—'

'Invisible.'

He looked right at me. Something passed between us.

'Exactly,' he said.

He should be out with his friends, I thought, watching him eat first his meal, then the rest of mine. He was all alone, half dead from hunger, cold, loneliness. I thought back to Katie's party, and to the last time I'd been in a pub with Kieron, the night we dropped him at uni. I remembered the deafening noise, how the kids had all stood in groups, how they'd all been checking their phones every five minutes. I could remember thinking that no one really spent time with one another anymore. I said as much to Kieron. These kids were talking to friends who weren't there while the ones that *were* there were talking to other friends who weren't there either. They were living in a to-be-confirmed future and a photo-captioned past while the present and all it offered eluded them entirely. Now, I thought about those kids and realised they were all just like me: looking for connection elsewhere. Misplacing their love. If anger turned to misplaced hate, I thought then, so loneliness turned to this, this misplaced love.

I stood up to clear the plates. 'Tell you what we're going to do.'

'What?'

'We're going to go for a walk. I'm going to take you to where I go when it all gets too much. And we're going to work out a plan, a life plan. How does that sound?'

'Sounds good,' he said.

He helped me wash up and then together we locked the bar.

'Just let me stash this,' he said and jogged round to the back of the pub with his sleeping bag, returning a couple of minutes later without it.

'That took a while,' I said.

He sniffed and brushed his hands together. 'Just so no one nicks it. Right, let's go.'

Chatting non-stop, we walked through town, over the bridge that crosses the canal, and towards the bottom of Heath Road. This will have been getting on for half eleven, quarter to midnight.

'What is it you think you might want to do when you get yourself back on your feet?' I asked him.

'Plumber,' he replied straight away. 'The money's good and I like people. I get on with them, like. I did go to college but it was hard to stay clean and warm and fed, so in the end I… I dropped out.'

'I understand. Sounds like you got yourself into a bit of a mess, but you just need a new start. A base, food, routine, that type of thing.'

'I do, yeah. That's what I need, but it's so hard.'

I wondered if I could give that to him, that start. What Mark would say if I suggested it. It might be exactly what we needed. But at the same time, I could feel a tension building up in me, and when I pressed my arm against my bag, it came as no surprise, none whatsoever, to feel the solid shape of the knife against my wrist. I couldn't remember putting it in my bag and yet there was no surprise in it being there. My veins were rods running through me. It's a wonder I could bend my limbs at all. Yes, the knife was there, where I had known in some dark part of me it would be. But whether it was for protection or destruction, I didn't know.

We reached the town hall. Behind the railings, the grass verge stretched away, darkening by degrees into a deep jet void. In the upper branches of the oaks, the wind rustled the leaves. The town hall itself stood white and toy-like at the top of the rise. I thought about my wedding day, a day full of joy, of love.

On the other side of the road, the Red Admiral stood proud in its car park. The lights were still on; there were still people talking outside. It was a young person's venue, I thought. Probably had a late licence.

'Come on,' I said, nodding towards it. 'This used to be my local when I was your age.'

'So you took him into the pub?' Blue Eyes asks.

'I did, yes.'

Did it feel weird, taking a homeless lad for a drink?

Blue Eyes didn't ask that; that was me, asking myself.

And the answer would be no, not really. I'd flowed around this boy like water. I'd understood what he needed, what would make him feel better, and as no one else wanted my kindness, my love, I suppose you'd say, I'd offered it to him. Our feelings have to go somewhere, don't they? None of us are above that, and lately I'd effectively been practising my... I suppose, with hindsight, you'd call them my grooming skills: engaging strangers in conversation by using insights I'd spent a lifetime learning – how to read faces, how to read bodies, how to listen, how to adapt, what they were really asking me for beneath the words they said or didn't say. If someone was shy, I knew to chat so that they didn't feel any responsibility for maintaining the conversation, but at the same time, if there was something they were struggling to say, I could give them space to reach it. With the extroverts, I knew I could tease more quickly, establish something affectionate, almost intimate, from the off. And I could adapt to every human need in between.

I'd rehearsed. I was prepared.

They were drops. I was water.

At the door of the pub, I hesitated. I hadn't been inside since it was all crème de menthe and lemonade, cider and black, the crafty sighting of a Fourth Division footballer if you were lucky. The previous time I'd gone in, I'd not known it was the last time I'd go in as a young person, otherwise I might have made more of a fuss of it. We never know when it's the last time, do we? For anything. The last time I ever breastfed Katie, I would have savoured the moment instead of wishing she would hurry up so I could hang the washing out. The last time Kieron let me hug him before he went off to uni, I would have held on tighter.

There on the steps of the pub, I texted him: *Thinking of you. Hope you're behaving yourself. Love Mum xxx*

'Is there a problem?' Ian asked.

'No, love. Just texting my son.'

I knew I wasn't right. But I could never have known it was the last day I would spend as a free member of society.

CHAPTER 42

Rachel

'Last orders is half midnight,' the bouncer said, opening the door with a self-important tip of his chin.

I let Ian go in first, followed in his wake. Back in the day, I would have pushed first through these doors like a cowboy into a saloon. Drenched in Limara or Impulse or one of those other cheap body sprays, face smeared in foundation and blusher, hair quiffed up with sticky mousse, elasticated black miniskirt and my trusty Docs: the bee's knees, the dog's bollocks, the cream. A walking fire hazard, more like. We all were. And how smoky it would have been then. Our clothes used to reek when we got back to whoever's house we were staying at that night.

But now, walking in, it smelled only of bodies, the ammoniac whiff of badly dried clothes, trailing vapours of long-ago-applied aftershave. I kept my head down. The carpet had changed – purple and reds nowadays, though I couldn't have said what it used to be. There'd been fake books on fake shelves, I remembered, back in the day, and a kind of fenced-off raised podium, which was still there, tables and chairs on it just the same. I pushed through warm, sticky limbs, the dull rarararara, the ack-ack-ack of tipsy laughter.

There was a tiny space where the fag machine had been a million years ago, next to the ladies'.

'Wait there,' I said. 'What's your poison?'

'My poison?'

I chuckled, feeling older than Aristotle. 'I mean, what do you want to drink?'

'Oh, sure. Peroni? Is that OK?'

'Righto.'

Getting served would be tricky. I was invisible on a good day and this place was full of better-looking people half my age. Maybe I'd stand out on that basis. The bearded lady at the carnival type thing, a Zimmer frame thrown onto a dance floor. I'm exaggerating for laughs, I know, old habits die hard, but still. I queued at the bar. When I reached the front, I took a twenty out of my purse and held it up. Money is visible at least was my thinking. The barman with the goatee served first the bloke with a cantaloupe melon stuffed up each T-shirt sleeve and a neck thicker than a tree, then the woman next to him, arms thinner than toothpicks, but when he raised his eyebrows at the woman who replaced that woman, she nodded at me and said: 'I think it's this lady next.'

I thanked her, even though the look on her face said she was wondering why the bloody hell I was here when I'd be more at home in the Wilsons or the Prospect or, well, at home.

'A pint of snakebite and black, please,' I said, surprising myself – I hadn't had it for decades. 'And a pint of Peroni.'

'What's snakebite?' the barman asked. Bless him, he was no more than twenty.

'Half cider, half lager in the same glass, dash of blackcurrant.'

On the way back to Ian, one sip of snakebite was a time capsule to long ago, when I'd been fighting lads off with a shitty stick. They would skulk outside the ladies', fall over themselves to light me up in the days when I held a lit cigarette at arm's length for effect. As it was, no one was bothering me anymore. The #metoo movement was not a worry; more like #notme, to be honest.

As I handed Ian his pint, our eyes met. And there, as ever, at the howling core of him, was loneliness. Loneliness connects all of us, I thought. We are all so terribly lonely. The full weight of the sadness that had grown into my soul a year ago, that was now part of it, was now having its cover pulled away inch by slow inch. Until last night I'd had Lisa, but now she was gone, taking Mark with her from a place already lost to me: my heart.

'Cheers,' I said, and we chinked glasses.

'This is really kind of you.'

His eyelids drooped. I thought I caught spirits on his breath – whisky or brandy – but I couldn't be sure.

'I was supposed to be going out with my daughter.' I had to shout into his ear, it was so loud in there. 'But she stood me up.'

He cupped his mouth with one hand and shouted back, 'Is she at uni?'

I noticed he'd already drunk two thirds of his pint. 'No. Not as such. She's taken a year out.'

His head rolled a little. I realised he might have taken something but couldn't be sure. Picking someone up off the street wasn't straightforward – something I ought to have known. But he'd seemed so helpless, so innocent, and he'd reminded me so much of Kieron.

'I got stood up in here once,' he said, his shoulder grazing mine.

'What was her name?'

'Darren.'

Our eyes met. We laughed.

'Another thing that didn't play out well with my mum's last muscle man.'

'I wonder why that was.' I raised an eyebrow and we shared another grin. 'Had you been drinking before I let you into the pub?'

He bowed his head. From his jacket pocket he pulled out a quart of brandy, half empty. 'Soz,' he muttered to his tatty trainers.

'You don't need to say sorry to me.'

He shrugged. 'It's for the warmth, really.'

He looked so damn sad it was all I could do not to cry.

'I tell you what,' I said. 'I could do with some fresh air. Trouble with the no-smoking rule, you can smell the actual pub, can't you?'

'It's stuffy. I'm not used to being indoors anymore.' He swayed, leaned one tentative hand on the wall.

I helped him on with Dave's fleece jacket and picked up my bag and the cloth bag with Ian's dirty clothes inside. He seemed to have gone ever so quickly from tipsy to plastered.

'My nephew needs a bit of fresh air,' I said, winking at the bouncer on the door – again, advantage of age: no one thinks you're coming on to them. People assume you're winking the way their favourite auntie might when agreeing to a cheeky extra slice of Viennetta. Either that or you've got a lash on your eyeball. 'Don't mind if I bring my glass out, do you? Promise I won't drop it.' Twenty years ago, that would have been a saucy come-on. As it was, it barely registered.

'Sorry, love, no glasses outside.' He smiled at me, all indulgence and respect-your-elders. Cheeky get, he was no spring chicken himself. He couldn't have been more than five years younger than me – receding hairline, belly straining the buttons on his shirt. And his front teeth were capped. But he was a man. And as in most things, when it comes to signs of wear and tear, men are forgiven.

I turned to apologise to Ian, but he was downing the rest of his pint.

'There,' he said, wiping his mouth with the back of his hand. 'Let's get some air.'

I sat him down on the little wall outside. The tables there were still packed, and that worried me slightly, although no one was taking any notice of us.

A bus rumbled up Boston Avenue. Beyond, the calling darkness of the town-hall park. The shape of the knife pressed against my ribs. I had to get him over that road.

Ian said nothing. Sadness came off him in waves, as if he was wondering what the hell his life had come to, hanging out with a middle-aged woman on a Saturday night. It was lower than sleeping rough.

'I really liked Darren,' he slurred. 'Didn't love me, though, unfortch… unforshh…'

'Unfortunately.' I sat down next to him on the wall. 'Not easy, is it? Loving someone who doesn't know you love them. Especially if they're the same sex.'

He shook his head. 'S'hard.'

'You want to tell them, don't you? You want to tell them so badly but at the same time you're afraid to. Then you're scared they might be able to tell just by looking at you, that everyone can see it written all over you and there's nothing you can do to hide it.'

Basically, I was just reeling off what Kieron had told me the night he came out. He was fourteen, in tears. I hugged him to me while he told me what I'd known since he was three. When he'd finished, I told him I loved him exactly the same and always would; why on earth would that make any difference? It had felt good to hear his sobbing stop, to feel him go still in my arms. We sat in silence for ages afterwards, and when I asked him if he was all right, I realised he'd fallen asleep against me. He had his ups and downs after that, but he always had me and his dad on his side, and I think that counted a lot for him growing up.

'S'fine,' Ian slurred.

'Ah. The F word. Yes, we're all fine, aren't we? Spend your life pretending it's all fine, but it's not really. It hurts. Love hurts – that's why there are so many books and poems and songs about it. Oh sweetheart, I don't envy you, I really don't.'

'You're so nice.' A weight fell against me. It was him, his head. This young boy, this lonely, vulnerable young boy. I knew he was fighting back tears because I was too.

I put my arm around him. 'Come on, love. Everything will be all right, I promise. I know you don't think it will be now, but it will, trust me. And one day you'll be old like me and someone will say, oh, don't you wish you were young, and you'll think, no, no I bloody don't. Because it's hard, being young. You can't get forward for tripping over your own stupid mistakes. You don't know who you are, and even if you do, you don't know that it's OK to be who you are and that people love you for all the things you're busy trying to change. Happiness takes practice, but I'm here to tell you it's OK to be who you are – do you understand what I'm saying, love? That's where happiness starts. And it's OK to love someone even if they don't or can't love you back, though it's the hardest thing in the world. But I tell you what, one day you'll love someone and I promise they will love you right back. They'll love you like you deserve to be loved and you'll feel taller than a bloody skyscraper.'

The weight left my side. He wiped his eyes. 'Need to get back on my feet.'

'I know you do, love. And you will, I promise.'

It was time for a walk.

'Come on,' I said, jumping down from the wall. 'I want to show you something.'

His eyes opened, closed, opened. He took my hands, stood, staggered to one side. I knew then that he'd had more to drink than what he'd shown me. 'Where we goin'?'

'A place. A special place where I go when things are looking bleak. Come on.' I held out my hand. He took it.

CHAPTER 43

Rachel

We followed the hedge up to where it ends and walked across the grassland. We were coming at the pond a different way.

'Where are we going?' he asked again.

'To my special thinking spot.' I had a horrible sense of déjà vu: my hand on Jo's shoulder in the dark. Did I know what I was doing? Now, looking back, I think I was putting my own guilt to the test. Seeing if I could catch myself in the act. Which means I probably did know exactly what I was doing.

'In the park?' he said, knocking into me. 'Sorry.'

'That's OK. It's the little pond – have you ever been?' I turned to look at him, saw a smile brighten his face.

'My nan used to take us there when we were little. We used to feed the ducks.'

'That's the place. I used to take my kids, Kieron and Katie, when they were little. I got married in the town hall.'

We stopped at the pathway that leads to the pond. I followed his skinny frame into the black recess.

'Is this the place?' he asked.

'Yep. This bench. I just sit on it from time to time when I need to organise my mind. This last year I've come here a lot.'

We sat down. It was almost silent. Almost; the road was no more than an occasional dull rush. The water lay flat, the reeds sunk into its black mirror surface as if into pre-made holes.

I felt the living heat of him next to me. 'Peaceful as anything, isn't it?'

He nodded. A silence fell.

'My mum doesn't even know I'm gay,' he said.

God love him, I thought. Poor sweet boy.

'You'll find your way back to her one day,' I said. 'Everything will come right.'

'How do you know?'

I shrugged and sighed. 'I know things. Age. Experience. This fella she's got on the go will move on and you'll get your ducks in a row and make something of yourself. This is a bad time but you'll pull yourself up because you're a good person, Ian. You're polite and kind and you want to work. And one day you'll knock on her door and you'll be a man of substance and she'll see you and she'll be proud. I'm going to help you get back on track. I don't know how yet, but I will, I promise. And one day you'll be with your mum again and you'll tell her who you really are and she'll understand.' I could tell he was listening by the twitch of his head. 'And trust me, she'll love you just the same.'

'How do you know?'

'Because I do. Because when our Kieron told me he was gay, I couldn't have loved him more.' I put my arm around the boy and pulled him to me, rocked him gently, slowly. 'And in my darkest moments, the fact that I was there and that I was what he needed me to be that day is the only thing that keeps me tethered to this earth.'

His head had fallen onto my shoulder. I kissed his hair, felt the full weight of him in my arms. I felt his jacket fall open, the pressure of his borrowed T-shirt against the tip of the knife. I felt the skin yield, felt the blade slice through. The sickening shock when it sank between his ribs. The warm slick of his lifeblood on my hand. He didn't move. His brain had not yet caught on to what his body knew. I pulled the knife out and pressed it in again – it was easier this time, holding him to me, holding him tight.

'Shh,' I whispered. 'You're all right, my love. I've got you.'

His warmth infused me. Our skin dissolved. He was of me and I was of him. Drops into water. One body, one whole. His pulse beat like a timepiece, counting down seconds. Seconds, minutes, hours that chime. All the hours, all the never-ending hours. I felt myself go as he went. My vision clouded, blackened. Tiredness rolled in, unfathomable, unstoppable. We were sinking. We were part of the same. We were one, one body of water.

'Shh now, my darling boy.' I cradled his soft head in my hand. 'My darling, darling boy. I'm here with you. Be still now, my love. Everything will be all right. I'm here; I'll always be here with you. Let go now, I've got you. I've got you, my love, my darling boy.'

He was silent. He was still. He was heavy. The white moon flashed in the black pond. I held him to me. I felt him go.

I lowered my lips to his ear and whispered, 'Sleep now, my angel.'

CHAPTER 44

Rachel

Blue Eyes is looking at me, and it seems to me she's been looking at me for months.

'He died in your arms?' she says. 'You're saying you killed Ian Brown and he died in your arms?'

I nod. 'I comforted him in his last moments.'

'And you didn't remember any of that when you got home?'

'None of it. I've no memory of walking home. I know that when I got there, Anne-Marie had already returned to the forefront of my mind because I didn't know about Ian yet, do you see? I was thinking of Kieron too, maybe because of Ian. Kieron was with me very strongly, not that he ever leaves me. But no, everything I've just told you came to me the next day, when I read the news.'

'So what did you do when you got home?'

'I put Ian's clothes in the washing machine ready to put on to wash the next morning. I made myself a hot drink. Just hot water, actually – it was all I could face. The cider and lager had made me feel queasy; I couldn't handle it like I used to. I... checked Kieron's Facebook page, had a trawl through some of his photos. It was too late to message him, so I went upstairs, and that's when I checked my rucksack.'

'And found the bloodstained tissues.'

'It's a loop, don't you see? Bloody tissues found and found again. A knife in a bag. Memory and life. Life and memory. Loneliness to love, anger to hate to death, to anger to hate and so on. Round and round, never stopping, the world was filling up with it.'

'That's what you were thinking?'

'I was thinking... I was thinking that no matter how much love I had to give, it wasn't enough. It would never be enough.' I wipe at my eyes. The box says extra-soft but the tissue doesn't feel soft; it scratches. 'I was thinking that hate is turned on people who don't deserve it, who aren't responsible for the anger, who have nothing to do with the hate, not really, do you see?'

'Yes. I see. And the next morning?'

'The next morning, I stared at the second hand on the kitchen clock and tried to put myself under, like, to dive down, down, down and remember something.'

'You tried to hypnotise yourself?'

I nod. 'But I couldn't do it. I couldn't feel Anne-Marie's car door handle in my grip, couldn't get any sense of my leggings sliding over the leather seat of her posh sports car. I couldn't smell the sweat of our sports kits in the small tinny space, couldn't hear the car radio burst into life as she switched on the ignition. Maybe she never did. Maybe the seats weren't leather – that could be my imagination trying to get my memory to take a dictation so that I'll have a script to read from. I couldn't see our breath as condensation on the windows, the curve of my own arm as I held her fast with one hand. I couldn't feel the controlled jab of the knife in her ribs. I listened and I listened but I couldn't... I couldn't hear her scream.

'So you called the police?'

'No. I read about Ian on the iPad. And that's when it all came back: the whole of Saturday, day and night, the day I'd been dreading, the second worst day of my life.

'And then I called them. Because I remembered, you see? I remembered all of it. And I knew I'd killed Anne-Marie too. And tried to strangle that chap. And Jo, lovely Jo. I knew that any

violent flashbacks I'd had weren't my mind playing tricks at all.
They were memories.'

'So you called.'

'I dialled the crime number and a lady answered and I told her.
I told her I'd been killing people.'

CHAPTER 45

Lisa

Transcript of recorded interview with Lisa Baxter (excerpt)
Also present: DI Heather Scott, PC Marilyn Button

HS: Ms Baxter, how would you describe your relationship with Mr Edwards?

LB: Mark? What do you mean? As in friends? We were friends, good friends; – I'd have thought that was obvious.

HS: Do you often meet Mark without Rachel being present?

LB: No. Well, not like regularly, for coffee or a drink or whatever, no. That would've been, well, it would've been all wrong. But recently I'd been round to their house a few times when I knew she was on shift or out but that was only because I was worried. He was worried too. All the walking at night and the way she'd go sort of absent sometimes. And the file, of course. We were scared she was going... you know, down, like she did before. I've said all this.

HS: And last Friday afternoon, when you told her you were in the supermarket, you were with Mark?

LB: Yes. I'd gone round to see him when I knew she'd be out because she seemed more fragile than ever. She wasn't taking me on at all. She was going under. I knew she was seeing her dad that day and I thought I should have a word with Mark, as in a stronger word, and I did – I said to Mark, 'You need to call someone. She's not right. She's not well.' I did say that.

HS: And did Mr Edwards call anyone?

LB: He was going to talk to her about it first. He didn't want an ambulance just turning up like the first time, but they just weren't communicating. He'd tried to tell her not to do the file, but they'd lost their way to each other and it was so sad to see. They wouldn't come out for a drink or a meal or anything. And with Patrick gone, that's my ex, it wasn't the same without us being two couples. I think they were both trapped. They couldn't talk. And Katie had dropped out and I suppose she'd disappeared into YouTube, all that make-up, literally plastering on a brave face for the world. She was looking for followers, looking for a party, looking for anything... well, like Rachel was, wasn't she? Looking for love in the wrong places, I suppose, or at least someone to talk to. We all need it, don't we? To have someone who cares and who'll listen? And I suppose if you can't find it at home... It was heartbreaking to see them unable to talk to each other like they used to, but they just couldn't get on with each other anymore. Everything Rachel said was wrong, everything Katie did was wrong. And Mark was just standing on the sidelines bleeding.

HS: Ms Baxter—

LB: Sorry, can I just say something? I… I mean… none of us knew what Rach was getting herself into. I just want to say that. How could we have known? It was bad enough to think of her wandering the streets and obsessing over her press cuttings, but we didn't know she was talking to strangers let alone attacking them. She must have been so bloody lonely, poor thing. So miserable. Not that it makes it right. I'm not making excuses. I just wish she'd talked to me. It doesn't excuse what she's done, but she must've been in such a bad place. I just wish I'd tried harder to reach her, you know? She deserved better.

CHAPTER 46

Rachel

Amanda has the clip file in front of her. She lifts it from the coffee table as if it's an ancient bible, precious, fragile, liable to disintegrate.

'I want us to revisit your folder. Is that all right?'

This is a different day. I'm wearing new jogging bottoms and a clean white T-shirt. I can remember having a shower this morning. There was a woman standing outside the cubicle, big bunch of keys on her belt. They gave me some breakfast: cereal and some rehydrated prunes, toast, tea. They brought me along the corridor and Blue Eyes was here. Her name is Amanda. Amanda Frost, which is a good name for someone with bleached hair and blue eyes. Ice Queen. Except she's not icy, she's kind. I don't know why she's so kind to me.

I don't want to talk about the file.

'I'm not going to go through every single clipping,' she says, obviously not picking up on my reluctance. 'But now that you've told me your story, I think it might be useful to look at some of the things you've mentioned. You see, the mind can be a cloudy place and sometimes we have to try and bring it back from abstract feelings of anxiety or fear or guilt and make sense of those feelings. My job is to listen to the way people talk about themselves and their experience, what matters to them, and try and somehow get underneath that. And a very good way to do this is to get them to tell me their story, because the interesting thing about stories is that they help us to process what has happened to us. Most often if that something is bad.

'For instance, if the bus is late, you don't arrive for coffee with a friend and say, *The bus service in this borough is unreliable*, do you?' A smile itches at the edges of her mouth but it doesn't take. 'What you do is set the scene: you were at the bus stop, perhaps you add the weather conditions – it was raining or terribly cold; perhaps you'd run there so as not to miss the bus. The bus doesn't come, the minutes tick by, the time of your appointment approaches. You run through your mounting frustrations moment by moment, building to a kind of climax – at last the bus arrives! You complain to the driver or whatever. You tell that story and you shake your head and say something along the lines of *I'm here now, thank goodness*, and the tension falls away on a kind of slope at the end, do you see?' She steeples her hands. 'All of this to say that the stories we tell each other and ourselves are how we process life. Mishaps, disasters. And in your case, tragedy.'

I nod. There's a feeling in my gut that I can't name. Anticipation, possibly, something like that. Dread, maybe.

'I have your statement here.' She looks down at her notes. 'But what I've been listening for in these sessions, Rachel, is what you included and what you left out of your story. The event that started it, the feeling of not being seen by one's family or by the world, is common for many women, particularly women your age. If, given your childhood, your recent history and also your medical history, you experienced this as trauma, then that's valid. The trauma belongs to you and is meaningful to you. You matter, Rachel. What you feel matters.'

She holds my gaze. Embarrassed, it's me that breaks it.

Amanda lifts a sheet of paper and glances down at it. 'I'd like to start with your first experiences of your ability to "read" other people. The man in the park and the GP near the canal. I agree with your friend Lisa that an ability to intuit others quickly comes with age. We have more experience, quite simply. We can make educated judgements based on that experience. What's more interesting is what you surmised.' She glances again at her notes, back to me. 'You said the man in the park was lonely. That he was yearning for something lost. Grieving, perhaps, you said. You *felt* it. The GP, you said, was divorced, afraid of losing his girlfriend and his children. What do those emotional details make you feel now, Rachel?'

'How do you mean?'

'I suppose I'm asking you if they resonate at all. Loneliness, grief, loss of children, marital breakdown, romantic insecurity…'

The tissue box has been replaced with a new one. She pulls out a handful of tissues and passes them to me. I press them to my eyes and nose. My nose is sore, my face is sore. She is leaning down to a soft leather bag on the floor by her chair. She rummages in it, pulls out a small blue and white tin.

'Here,' she says, giving it to me. 'I never go anywhere without this.'

It's Vaseline. I open the tin and rub some over my lips, under my nose. It smells vaguely of petrol.

'I must look a sight,' I say.

'A little shiny, but it will soothe the skin.' Her smile reaches further than I've seen it in all the time we've been here. 'You can keep that; I have another. I'll bring you some Sudocrem tomorrow. I've got a miniature pot at home.'

'Isn't that for nappy rash?'

'Yes. But when my girls were small, someone told me it's great for zits and chapped skin, and it is.'

I laugh – I can't help it. I would never have expected her to say zits, for a start, and for the first time I wonder what she's like when she relaxes. I suspect she likes a laugh as much as Lisa and I do. But she's at work now, of course. And I'm in custody for murder.

'I had you down for more expensive potions,' I say.

'Oh, I have those too,' she says. 'But sometimes the most basic products are better.'

'It's to do with me, isn't it?'

'The potions?'

'No. What I was picking up from that chap and the GP. It's *my* loneliness. My grief. My marriage.'

She nods. 'It's called projection. Your feelings are being projected onto others like film onto a cinema screen. Does that make sense?'

'It does. It does, yes.'

'It doesn't mean you were wrong about those people. It's down to what you notice and how you interpret it. You mentioned a customer who is addicted to gambling and comes to celebrate or drown his sorrows at your pub.'

'Phil.'

'Yes. Of all the customers you might have mentioned, you chose to tell me about him. A broken man from a troubled domestic background seeking solace where he shouldn't, or rather where he won't, ultimately, find it.' She pauses. 'Have you any thoughts on that?'

I nod. I have the same sensation I do sometimes when I put my reading glasses on, except it's my mind that's sharpening, coming into focus. 'That's what I was doing, wasn't it? Escaping? Not from trouble exactly, but yes, I suppose you could say my home life was troubled and I suppose you could say that talking to strangers wasn't ultimately going to help me solve the problems at home. I was putting my… I suppose I was putting my love elsewhere.'

She mirrors my nod, adds the trace of a smile. 'Good. That's great. Keeping that in mind, let's talk, if you think you can, about the evening you met Joanna Weatherall.'

'OK.' The Vaseline on my face has calmed the sting but my face feels strange and greasy.

'There were a couple of things you mentioned in your account that, in the light of knowing about how we project our emotions sometimes, you might now be able to look at a little differently.

You expressed a connection with this young girl that was maternal, would you agree with that?'

'Yes. Definitely. I didn't mean her any harm. If anything, I felt protective of her.'

'And despite revisiting that moment in our sessions, you still can't remember doing her any harm. You've left that out of your story. You believe that your mind has blocked out those details because the idea of them is so horrific to you. What you do include is how she, Joanna, made you feel. Can you remember how she made you feel?'

'Protective,' I say. 'I said that.'

'What else?'

'Maternal.'

'Yes…'

I think back, put myself there.

'Appreciated,' I say. 'Seen. Funny. I made her laugh.'

Amanda glances at her notes and back to me. 'You said she reminded you of how you used to make your daughter laugh. Katie. You said you last laughed together with Katie over a year ago. Do you have any thoughts on that?'

'It was when me and Katie were close. Now she's shut herself in her room, started painting her face all day long, living online instead of in the world. She's always cross with me. Seems to be anyway.'

'And Joanna?'

'She was my daughter?'

Amanda raises her eyebrows.

'Jo was Katie,' I continue, encouraged. 'That's what you mean, isn't it? She was the relationship I'd lost. With Katie. That's what you want me to say, isn't it?'

'I don't want you to say anything you don't feel. We're working together to try and understand what happened – does that make sense?'

'No, but it's obvious, isn't it? I was desperate for my daughter but I couldn't reach her. Everything I said was wrong. We just couldn't get on. She was always so furious with me. And I suppose Katie was doing the same as me and Phil, in a way. I never thought about that. She's been looking for solace, as you put it, online. Looking for love – likes, followers. And going out too much, getting drunk, well, that's not unusual at her age, but maybe she was doing it too much, I don't know. And Mark, I suppose, out with Roy... well, with Lisa. And then, I guess, when I was thinking about pushing Jo under the water, well, that was me wanting to push myself under the water, wasn't it?' A sob comes from deep in my chest, an unlocking at the very heart of me, a slow opening. 'I've been suicidal. I have. But I've been too ashamed to admit it.'

'Take your time,' Amanda says softly, and yet again I'm struck by her compassion, given all that I've done. 'Have some water. We don't have to talk about Jo anymore if you don't feel able.'

'Oh, don't mind me. I've been crying for a year. I don't mind it if you don't. I'll just crack on, I think. There've been times this last year when I've felt like killing someone but I never thought I had it in me to actually do it. I imagined stabbing her. Afterwards, I mean. How it would feel. But at the same time, the me I know – me, Rachel, the person I think I am, or thought I was, anyway – would never do that to another mother, let alone a kid. Never. I'd never take another woman's child. But I've been so cross. Cross with everyone. With Mark, with Katie.'

'OK. Tell me about that.'

'I was cross at Katie for leaving me alone, for us not being close anymore. And I'm cross at myself. I've been rubbish. A rubbish mother.'

'What makes you say that?'

There's a moment of silence. I can't speak. She doesn't speak. Until she does.

'Let's look at the man in the cemetery. It's not in your statement because it was never recorded as a crime. But I think it can take us somewhere because it's in your story.'

'Henry.'

'Henry Parker. It was important to you to give him a name. You were adamant that he should have an identity. Why do you think that was?'

'I… I think everyone should have an identity. We're all human beings, aren't we? I suppose… was it because I felt like I'd lost my identity? Yes, I suppose that's it.'

'Good.' She gives me a brief smile of encouragement. 'Henry Parker was never stabbed. I checked the incident report, and as far as anyone's aware, he was never strangled either. Does—'

'But it said in the news report that he was.'

'It didn't. Again, it's down to what we notice, what we read into things. The report said he'd partially asphyxiated. His alcohol levels were toxic. He'd passed out and vomited and almost choked. There was no strangling. And there was no information as to when exactly he had collapsed, so it could have been much later. You say you woke up with pain in your head, still behind the gravestone, the jump leads loose around your knuckles. What do you think really happened?'

'I must have… I must have fallen. Maybe I fainted and hit my head on the gravestone? Maybe I'd wound the leads tight because I was so cross. I was angry about having to go for chips, about having wet clothes on, about the car… about a lot of things. I mean, they say the menopause causes rage, but to be honest, sometimes I think what women have to put up with at this age is enough to make anyone furious.'

She chews her cheek, stops herself, lips pressing together tight. 'It was a little earlier in your story that you mentioned that your husband didn't want you physically anymore. Can you see any connection between that and your experience of the man in the churchyard? I know this is delicate, but it will help if you can talk about it.'

'Mark? Do you think Henry was Mark? The pervert? In my mind?'

'Not exactly. In our sessions, you mentioned that Mark no longer wanted you sexually. He turned his back on you, figuratively and literally, leaving you feeling very alone.' She looks up, meets my eye. Her eyebrows rise a fraction.

'You're saying I was angry at Mark for not wanting… not wanting me in that way?' I can feel myself blushing. I can't say it like she can, just come out with it like that. 'You're saying it was that type of connection I was looking for?'

'The mind and how it processes trauma is a complicated thing, Rachel. I'm not saying it was exactly like that, and it may well be oversimplifying, but thinking in these rather simplistic terms might help you to solve the puzzle of yourself and these attacks. You've mentioned carrying a surplus of love. Everyone who has given a statement is at pains to say that you're incredibly loving. When Kieron was born, you suffered postpartum psychosis. You chose to share that with me and you included the very phrase that your psychotherapist gave you at the time. You remembered this phrase. It meant a great deal to you.'

'Love on steroids.'

She almost smiles. 'Eighty-five per cent in the "Are You an Empath?" quiz. That has come up more than once.'

'When you explain it like that,' I say, 'it's like you're telling me what I already know. It clicks, if you know what I mean. It's like my brain conjured up this grubby scenario for me to make me feel even worse than I already did.'

She is nodding. 'If it makes sense to you, then that's helpful. I have no doubt that you really did stumble across this man doing what you said he was doing, just as I'm sure you went to the pond with Joanna Weatherall. It's what you did with your perception, or your memory of how it played out, that might help us unravel your version of events. We might never find out exactly which parts were true and which parts were… as you say, conjured up, but we might find other things.'

'I've told you the truth.'

'I don't doubt it. But we have to try and figure out what this truth means.'

CHAPTER 47

Mark

Transcript of recorded interview with Mark Edwards (excerpt)
Also present: DI Heather Scott, PC Marilyn Button

HS: Mr Edwards, your wife seemed to be under the impression that there might have been something more than a neighbourly relationship between you and Ingrid Taylor. Have you any comment to make on that?

ME: Yes, I have. (Becomes immediately agitated) There was nothing at all between Ingrid and myself. Nothing, have you got that? She was a bit full-on, I'd say, but I didn't take too much notice. I gave her a lift to work and she did call round on pretexts when Rachel was out – could I countersign the photos for her passport, could I help her read her gas meter, that type of thing – but that was it. She'd sometimes stop for a chat. She was lonely, I think. She was cut up about her divorce. But there was nothing else. I made it clear I wasn't interested and she took the hint in the end.

HS: Mr Edwards, on the night of Saturday the twenty-eighth of September, you said you were at the golf club with your friend Roy. I'm looking at a map, and I can't help but notice that the golf club appears to be very close, by car, to the town hall. No more than a few minutes. Would you agree?

ME: Where are you going with this? I went nowhere near the town hall on Saturday night. I had nothing to do with that lad. I had a beer with Roy and then I went home to bed. Rachel got in very late. I just thought maybe she'd stayed on at the Barley Mow or gone somewhere else for a late drink, maybe Lisa had persuaded her.

HS: You didn't ask her where she'd been?

ME: No. I… I pretended to be asleep. As I say, things were difficult. Especially that day.

HS: For the tape, can you tell me what these are?

ME: They're… they're cigarette ends.

HS: Anything else? Can you describe them?

ME: Well, they're brown, a bit of white… is that what you mean? A couple of them have lipstick on.

HS: Mr Edwards, these cigarette ends were found in the garage of your house. Do you have any light to shed on that?

ME: (Shakes head) I don't know anything about that.

HS: Are you saying you've never smoked a cigarette in your house?

ME: No, I… I have. I mean… I don't smoke as a rule, but sometimes if I'm offered… Ingrid always offered me a cigarette when she came round and… well, it was silly really, but I did have the odd one of hers.

HS: Only with Ingrid?

ME: Well, no. I had one with Lisa. On the Friday. She's like me, more of an occasional smoker. I didn't see the harm. We were both upset. Worried, I mean. About Rachel. I don't see what this has got to do with anything.

HS: Mr Edwards, your wife is currently convinced you are having an intimate relationship with Lisa Baxter. She's said she thought for a while that you were with Ingrid but believes she discovered on Friday afternoon that you were in fact with Lisa when she saw Lisa driving away from your home. Despite having spoken to your wife on the phone on Friday afternoon, Lisa did not say she had been with you at your home. When Rachel returned from a visit to her father, you made no mention of her best friend having been at the house, despite the evidence of the cigarettes. Indeed, you did a similar thing on another occasion with Ingrid. This is why Rachel collected first yours and Ingrid's cigarette stubs, then yours and Lisa's. She was planning to confront you about them but had not worked up the courage.

ME: What? What's all this? What are you talking about? I would never... Lisa's our closest friend. She's practically family. I didn't say anything to Rachel because Lisa had come to talk about Rachel's obvious... her obviously troubled state of mind. It's not nice to know that your friends have been talking about you, so we didn't tell her. I said I'd talk to her and convince her to seek help. I didn't want it to come as a shock. I was building up to it. I needed to ask her if she'd see the GP. But it's not an easy thing to say, is it? How do you say that to someone you love? And we've not been talking much, so that made it even harder. But there's nothing between Lisa and me, never has been, never will be. I mean, I love her as a friend, but that's it. Honestly. I would never do that to Rachel, never. Neither would Lisa. She's our oldest friend, do you know what I mean? And Rachel's my wife. She's the mother of my kids, for Christ's sake.

HS: (Pause) Mr Edwards, a cigarette end matching those found in your garage was discovered near the pond in the town-hall gardens. Another two matching cigarette ends were found in the car park of Brookvale Leisure Centre. We have taken DNA samples from all of these cigarette ends, the ones found in your home and those found at the crime scenes. In light of that information, do you have anything you wish to add?

CHAPTER 48

Ingrid

Transcript of recorded interview with Ingrid Taylor (excerpt)
Also present: DI Heather Scott, PC Marilyn Button

HS: Let's look at last Thursday, the twenty-sixth of September. Can you remember where you were that night? It's more recent, I suppose, so that might help.

IT: At home. Where else? Not like I can afford to go out, is it?

HS: Ms Taylor, we spoke to Pamela Bain, personnel manager of the records and accounts department of ICI.

IT: I see.

HS: She told us that after your trial period, she offered you a short-term contract, which you turned down. For the benefit of the tape, Ms Taylor is shrugging her shoulders.

IT: As I said, it paid a pittance.

HS: Can you explain why you accepted a lift each day from Mark Edwards, why you chose to give him the impression you were going into work in the same building as him?

IT: Look, he was lonely, all right? Poor guy needed somebody to talk to. He'd been kind enough to get me an interview; it would have been rude to tell him I hadn't taken the job. I'm a nice person. Unlike some, I actually care about people's feelings.

HS: Ms Taylor, can you explain how you meet your living expenses?

IT: Why are you asking me this when you clearly already know? I rent out my house in Helsby, so what? I don't see what this has got to do with anything.

HS: Is there any reason you would choose to move opposite Mrs Edwards?

IT: I didn't even know her then! Why on earth would I try and move near to her?

HS: Ms Taylor, going back to the evening of Thursday the twenty-sixth, the night Anne-Marie Golightly was murdered, Rachel Edwards says she asked you to come to an exercise class. Is that right?

IT: She asked me, but – and I mean this in a nice way – it's fine for people who are overweight or stressed or whatever, and Rachel was definitely… Suffice to say, it's not for me. Like I say, it's fine if you like getting sweaty in unflattering Lycra trousers for no good reason, but honestly? I prefer to emulate the French. Eat less, smoke in moderation and leave the jumping about to people who… you know, people who join things.

HS: Ms Tay—

IT: She looks a lot better now, by the way. Rachel. Murder obviously agrees with her. Sorry, that was… I'm a bit nervous. I mean, I came here of my own free will and it's Rachel who's confessed, and before I knew what she was capable of, obviously, I suppose I'd become a little resentful of her and her whole poor-me thing. I mean, you have to take responsibility for yourself at some point, don't you? I suppose I wanted to shake her by those slumped shoulders of hers and say, wake up! Do you have any idea what you've got there? A kind, decent man who isn't pissing all your money up the wall like mine did. A man who can actually father a child and provide, OK, nothing to set you flicking through yacht catalogues, but a steady income. A man who actually comes *home* after work. A man who doesn't set light to your life savings and your annual all-inclusive holiday in the Seychelles, who doesn't arrive home stinking of alcohol having sold the Discovery to pay for his stupid, selfish habit. Mark would never do that. And I know I'd have to adjust, but I would *appreciate* him. He's going to need someone now that Rachel's not going to be around. I'm still young enough to have a child. I mean, it breaks my heart to see him work so hard, and he's so sweet, and when he comes home expecting a little comfort, some company in front of the television, where's she? Out walking the dog! Or not, as we now know.

HS: Ms Taylor—

IT: When I think of all the times I was alone with her, in her house. I mean, it could have been me next.

HS: Ms Taylor. Ms Taylor? If we can stick to the evening in question. For the benefit of the tape, Ms Taylor is taking a drink of water. (Pause) All right. Ms Taylor, we have two witnesses who say they saw a woman matching your description near the entrance to Brookvale Leisure Centre at around eight forty-five on the evening of the twenty-sixth. How do you respond to that? (Pause) For the benefit of the tape, Ms Taylor is shrugging.

IT: I can't imagine you have a *precise* description of me, Detective. I wasn't there.

HS: You're sure about that?

IT: Of course I'm sure. No offence, but it's not me who's lost their marbles and gone off knifing innocent people. I was at home.

HS: You've told us that you knew where Rachel was going that night. Mr Edwards… Mark… has told us he dropped you off to see a friend in Juniper Way before going on to the Norton Arms. I don't know if you know, but Juniper Way is a cul-de-sac off Barnfield Avenue. Which is where the Brookvale Leisure Centre is located. So it would appear you were in that part of town even though you've said you were at home. And for whatever reason, you didn't want to use your car. For the benefit of the tape, Ms Taylor has closed her eyes and is shaking her head. Ms Taylor?

IT: I forgot, OK? I thought that was the Wednesday. I'm sorry. And I'm sorry for being flippant earlier – it's just nerves and I'm still so upset by what's happened. I went to see my friend on the Thursday, that's right. But I had no idea it was anywhere near the leisure centre.

HS: Could you clarify what you mean by 'friend'?

IT: My ex-husband has a flat there. Not quite a friend, I suppose.

HS: So it's fair to say you were in the immediate vicinity of Brookvale Leisure Centre and that the witnesses who saw someone matching your description that evening could conceivably have seen you?

IT: It's conceivable. But I had no idea where Rachel was that night other than at some class. I needed to see my ex about something.

HS: Conceivable. You had, as you say, no idea where she was going for her class. However, after a cursory check of leisure facilities in Halton borough, I discovered that there are three places where she could – conceivably – have gone. One, Runcorn Baths, but that has only a gym and pool, no hall or dance studio. Two, Widnes Leisure Centre—

IT: I know what you're getting at. Widnes was closed for refurbishment. I could have researched it easily. Just a matter of finding out where the spinning class was. But I didn't. It wasn't like that. I was chatting to Mark and—

HS: Would it be fair to say you called at the Edwards home immediately Rachel had left for the class you knew she was going to?

IT: The way you say it makes it sound wrong, but he's my friend! He said he was heading out, so on the off-chance I ended up having something to drink, I grabbed a lift. I don't drink and drive. I would never do that.

HS: You appear to be clearer now on which class Rachel Edwards attended, Ms Taylor.

IT: I'm sorry?

HS: Earlier you said 'some class'. Just now you said 'the spinning class', which is indeed accurate. You seem to have recovered your memory.

IT: I know what you're trying to do. But I hadn't forgotten – I was being flippant, for which I've apologised. I didn't realise I was under suspicion. I came here voluntarily to help with your enquiries. I mean, she confessed, didn't she? She turned herself in? You've recovered the knife, I presume, from her house? The file?

HS: Ms Taylor, can you tell us where you were on the night of Saturday the twenty-eighth of September?

IT: At the risk of repeating myself, I was at home. I really was. I live alone. It's very difficult to provide an alibi when you live alone, but that's hardly my fault.

HS: For the benefit of the tape, PC Button is showing Ms Taylor four images. Ms Taylor, if you'd like to look at these images. The first two are taken from the CCTV camera at Brookvale Leisure Centre. The second two… I'm not sure if you're aware, but shortly after the attack on Joanna Weatherall, the CCTV cameras operating on Boston Avenue, which had been out of order, were serviced. If you'd like to take a look and tell me who you think that is near the town-hall gardens?

IT: This is outrageous. I know what you're trying to do. Well, let me tell you something, I did see Rachel with that girl. Joanna. I did. I saw her go into the gardens!

HS: And why didn't you tell us that earlier?

IT: Because I didn't want anything to do with it! But I saw her. I was out walking and I saw her talking to that girl and I saw her take her over the fence and away into the dark. I'm telling you, it's Rachel Edwards you want, not me. I want a lawyer. Get me a lawyer now. I'm not saying another word until I have a lawyer.

CHAPTER 49

Rachel

'Rachel, are you familiar with the term somnambulism?'

'I'm not, no, sorry.'

'Sleepwalking.'

'OK… but I don't sleepwalk.'

'Not in the sense of going for walks while you're asleep. But you've described waking up in strange places with no memory of falling asleep, hot flashes, night sweats et cetera.'

'Yes, but most women my age have to put up with all that.'

'Agreed. And many other symptoms besides. You've described falling into deep sleeps during the day, sleeps that you described as being pulled into the underworld by Hades himself.'

'Oh God, aye. Like being sucked into the sofa by a big Hoover attachment – I suppose that's less poetic.'

'Another common symptom of menopause is the occurrence of these… attacks, almost, of tiredness. This is obviously exacerbated by difficulty sleeping at night, night terrors or nightmares. You've told me about dreams concerning invisibility, yourself wielding a knife, and these nightmares are all part of the storytelling I mentioned, the stories our mind tells us, the processing of things we find difficult or stressful, and in your case, traumatic. I think it might be possible that you've been experiencing catatonic episodes, where you simply fall asleep and wake up later wondering how long you've been there.'

'That might've happened in the graveyard, mightn't it? Well, it could've done. I was never sure whether I'd strangled him or not, though you're saying I didn't.'

'There were no marks on his neck, Rachel. In your story, you describe yourself waking up still behind the gravestone. Which leads us to your encounter with Anne-Marie Golightly and her subsequent murder.'

My throat thickens. 'Anne-Marie.' Her name sets me off again. 'She was a nice, nice woman.'

'You've told me a lot about your friend Lisa. You love her. She's a huge point of reference for you. Your best friend.'

'She was until I realised she was shagging my husband. That sort of thing'll come between you. Sorry for saying shagging. It's vulgar. Sorry.'

'That's all right. Do you know for certain she was… involved with your husband?'

'Why else would she not mention where she was, only for me to see her heading away from our house in her car? Why else would Mark make no mention of her having been there? And the two cigarette stubs in a saucer in the kitchen. You could say that was perfectly innocent, and it would be if either of them had said something. But they didn't, did they? She's always had a soft spot for him, and now her husband's gone, she wants mine.'

'Can you think of any other reason why Lisa might have been seeing Mark and not telling you?'

'No.' I fold my arms. 'What's this got to do with me killing people?'

'Nothing. It has to do with how we read events. In their statements, both Mark and Lisa have expressed concern for your well-being.'

'Oh yes, I know all about that. Power of suggestion, isn't it? That's all it is. Tell someone they look green around the gills enough times and they'll be down the doctor's wanting a prescription. I know what her game was. Trying to make me think I was losing it, get me shipped off to the nuthouse so she could move in with Mark. I wouldn't be surprised if it was her that put the knife in my bag, trying to send me round the…'

'What is it? What is it, Rachel?'

I shake my head. I have no memories of putting that knife in my bag.

'Nothing,' I say. 'Did they match the knife to the… to the killings?'

'They never found the knife.'

'Right, well there you go.'

'Rachel, is it possible that you might have underestimated how much your friend and your husband care about you? A huge loss of self-worth, often accompanied by paranoid thoughts, is common in moments of anxiety and trauma. Both of them have said that they met up without your knowledge to discuss how worried they were about your state of mind. They kept this secret because they didn't want to frighten you. The time you saw Lisa driving away, she and Mark had made the decision to call a doctor and both felt conflicted by that. They didn't know how to handle the situation. Lisa has said that she hasn't known how to stay close to you. Mark has expressed this too. They wanted to alert a medical professional not so they could continue an affair but because they love you. They love you, Rachel, and they know your history. They're both devastated that you've turned yourself in.'

'So you're telling me there's nothing between them?'

'Nothing. Other than decades of love for you.' Amanda stands, goes to the door, opens it. I hear her murmuring to someone in the corridor. She comes back and picks up her pad, sits and writes something down. Outside, traffic passes, the sky darkens shade by shade, inching towards another night. I can hear what she's told me as if she's still saying it; the words are still falling in the air. Like blossom. Like snow. I don't know how long I've been in this place. Blue Eyes Frost is not a policewoman, she's a forensic psychiatrist. Her kindness is a tool of her trade, that's all.

The door handle rattles. A woman comes in with two cups of what smells like coffee and puts them on the table.

'There you go,' she says and leaves. She closes the door with painstaking care, like a burglar in reverse.

'You met Anne-Marie,' Blue Eyes says, 'at a time when you were troubled about your relationship with Lisa. You were drifting apart. You were fearful of having committed acts of violence, couldn't talk about your fears, and this secrecy was coming between the two of you. You felt that you no longer had a close friend, someone you felt safe with. And then you met Anne-Marie and saw in her someone you felt you could become friends with, is that right?'

'She was so nice. She was a good egg.'

'Good.' Amanda reaches for her coffee, takes a sip.

'I was missing Lisa, wasn't I?'

'Possibly.' She slides a sheet of paper from the bottom of her notes and hands it to me. 'Rachel, I want to return again to the clip file. This is the first entry you put in there, as I'm sure you know. I want you to read it aloud to me, if you can.'

I recognise the clipping straight away. I knew what it said, every word, before she placed it into my trembling hands.

I shake my head, my belly heating with anxiety. 'I can't.'

'Do you recognise it?'

'I can't.'

And despite telling her I can't, I do. I read it.

CHAPTER 50

Rachel

Third knife attack in capital this year

Police have released details about a stabbing that took place last night in Hoxton. Officers were called to Bar Go at about 11.45 p.m. after a report of a knife attack outside the popular nightspot.

'When officers arrived on scene, they located a 20-year-old male who had been stabbed on the pavement immediately outside the bar,' police spokesperson Rania Hanif said. 'The man was transported to the Royal London Hospital and is said to be in a critical condition.'

After an anonymous tip-off from a customer, the police traced a 28-year-old man to a flat in Blackhorse Lane and have taken him into custody.

This story will be updated as more information is released.

Another sheet of paper shushes across the table.

'I know this is difficult.' Amanda's voice comes to me as if through water. 'I want you to read this article too if you can.'

I pick up the sheet of paper. I know it off by heart. But I read it.

Stabbing victim loses fight for life

The man attacked late on Thursday evening outside Bar Go, Hoxton, has died of his injuries. He has been named as Kieron Edwards, an art student at Goldsmiths, University of London.

A 28-year-old man, who has not been named, was held for questioning but has been released. Police are appealing for witnesses to come forward.

'We offer our deepest sympathy to the victim's family,' police spokesperson Rania Hanif told reporters in today's press conference. 'And we will stop at nothing until the perpetrators are arrested and charged.'

'In the six years I've been here,' said landlord Sid Black, 'I've seen fights break out but I've never witnessed anything like this. We welcome anyone into this pub and anyone who objects to the lifestyles of others should find somewhere else to drink. This was an unprovoked hate crime as far as I'm concerned. The police need to step up their efforts to protect the public and stop the scourge of hate and prejudice in our cities.'

'London remains committed to a zero-tolerance attitude towards knife crime,' Mayor Sadiq Khan later commented. 'Anyone caught carrying a knife will be arrested and charged. Parents would be wise to remind their children that the penalty for possession of a knife is four years.'

The papers fall from my hands. I hear them slide to the floor.

'Rachel. In the story you told me, you mentioned a couple of times texting your son, Kieron, at university.'

'I did.'

'You told Anne-Marie you had two children.'

'I… I did.'

'You told Ingrid that your son was at university.'

'I did.'

'Can you tell me what these newspaper clippings relate to?'

The breath stills in my chest, shudders out of me in a heavy rush.

'My son,' I manage. 'I can't. I can't.'

'I understand. It's a difficult thing to say, Rachel. You've found it impossible. As have Mark and Katie. The three of you haven't spoken about Kieron at all, have you? About his death. Is it possible you haven't been able to believe it?'

'I don't know. I just… can't talk about it. I don't want to.'

'Can you tell me? Can you tell me now, do you think?'

I close my eyes. Time stills in the silent room. I think of Kieron's bedroom door at home. I think of my hand on the door handle, the breath caught in my chest. I haven't been into that room for a year. I can't go into that room. I cannot.

'Rachel? I know this is harder than you can bear, but if you can articulate it, it will help, I promise.'

'It won't bring him back, though, will it?'

'No. No, it won't. But it will help you to grieve. It'll help you to get to the bottom of all of this.'

'He was murdered.'

'Who was? Can you tell me who?'

'My son. Kieron. He was stabbed outside a bar in London.'

'Yes. Yes, he was, Rachel.'

Outside the silent room, the intermittent hum of traffic. I glance at the window, hoping to see the fly. But it isn't there.

'He'd only been away from home four days,' I hear myself whisper. 'It was freshers' week. He'd gone on a date with this lad he'd met. He texted me. He sounded happy. Like he was making friends, having a good time. As he came out of the bar, him and his friend were set upon. His friend managed to get away, but

Kieron… he didn't. He didn't get away. They rushed him to hospital but… he didn't make it.'

The room is silent. Outside, the droning of the cars. Life continuing as if nothing has happened. How can life continue as if nothing has happened?

'You've been incredibly brave, Rachel. You've found words you never thought you'd find and you've said them out loud. There are other things you can't imagine you'll ever do, but you will. I think this is the heart of all of it. Kieron. Your son. Your son is at the heart of this.'

I am nodding. My jogging bottoms are spotting with tear drops.

'The attack on Ian Brown,' she says. 'It's the only one you remember clearly, is that still the case?'

'Yes. The others are just… they're just… images.'

'And you remembered that attack after you'd read about it in the news.'

'Yes. That's when it all came flooding back.'

'You remembered being in the pub, and taking the boy to the pond where you took Joanna. You said he reminded you of your son, even though physically they were not alike.'

'Something about him. And he was gay as well, like our Kieron.'

She shifts in her chair, leans forward with her hands clasped together in front of her.

'And the date, Rachel. The twenty-eighth of September. The day you decided to raise your passing acquaintance with a homeless boy to something more. A friendship, with yourself in a maternal role. You wanted to adopt him, in a sense. You wanted to give him a fresh start. You chose the twenty-eighth of September to do that, but you didn't mention the significance of the date in your story. Do you think you can now?' She pulls out some tissues. 'I know it's hard, but you're doing so well.'

'It's the anniversary,' I say.

'Of what, Rachel?'

'Of Kieron. Of him… of his… I can't say it. If I say it then… I don't… I don't… I don't want…' I grasp a tissue, another, another. There aren't enough tissues in the world. I will cry for the rest of my life and still he won't come back. He will never come back. My boy. My son.

'Knifed,' I manage. 'Hate crime. How can I say that? How can any mother say that?'

A moment. Two.

I look her straight in the eye. 'I just wanted to comfort him, that's all. I wanted to hold him to me so that he wouldn't have to die alone. Kieron died alone. We got the call and went straight there. We drove all the way without stopping, straight to the hospital, but he… he'd gone. He died afraid and lonely and I wasn't with him. I wasn't with him. Do you see?' I plunge my face into my hands. 'I wasn't there for my boy. I wasn't there.'

CHAPTER 51

Katie

Transcript of recorded interview with Katie Edwards (excerpt)
Also present: DI Heather Scott, PC Marilyn Button

HS: And the final date, this Saturday just gone, can you confirm your whereabouts? (Pause) For the tape, Ms Edwards is composing herself.

KE: I was in Warrington with my mates. I wanted to be with my mates. Get wasted, like. It was the anniversary and I just couldn't take it. I was in a state. I thought Mum would be doing something but she left for work without saying anything to anyone. My dad didn't say anything to me that morning either, apart from asking if I was all right, which I wasn't, obviously, and neither was he. None of us were. Dad said he was going out with Roy so I thought Mum must be going out with Lisa. I didn't realise she wasn't seeing Lisa anymore. I couldn't believe she hadn't asked me what I was doing, but now, with everything that's happened, I suppose I hadn't asked her either, had I? I mean, she was ill. She is ill. And that's what that means, people not behaving like themselves. I mean, you see it on Facebook and Insta and everything but it's just, like, slogans? When it's real, when it's someone you love, it's actually really hard. After our Kieron died, my mum set the table with four places for weeks. We couldn't get her to stop. I mean, we say we understand if someone's depressed or whatever, but then we expect them to behave normally and get pissed off if they don't. And I was pissed off at her for not taking any notice of me, I suppose. I was grieving too! But I should have got it, you know? Before. We were all in such a bad place. Kieron was so cool. He DJ'd at my eighteenth – all my mates loved him. I loved him. I loved him so much and he was taken. Liam's mum said that grief is selfish and I was really offended when she said that, but I know what she means now. Grief is selfish. It is.

HS: So did you speak to your mum that evening? For the benefit of the tape, Ms Edwards is nodding.

KE: She rang me. I could tell she wanted to talk. She might even have wanted to talk about Kieron, she might have been ready, but I'll never know that now, will I? She asked if I wanted to do a late night with pizza and wine. We hadn't done that since before Kieron died. She was lonely. I could hear it in her voice. I knew I should go to her, get in a cab and go. I told her I loved her but I went back into the club. I wish I hadn't. If I'd gone to her, this would never have happened. I should have gone to her. She was lonely and I left her alone and now this has all happened and it's too late. (Breaks down)

CHAPTER 52

Lisa

Transcript of recorded interview with Lisa Baxter (excerpt)
Also present: DI Heather Scott, PC Marilyn Button

LB: I saw her walking down her road. I was coming from her house but I kept my eyes dead straight. She looked like she was in a world of her own, to be honest. And then I texted her the next day, the Saturday, because it was the anniversary, you know? I asked if she was OK. I tried to get her out for a drink or just to come round, but she didn't even reply. I should have rung her. I feel terrible, but at the same time, she wouldn't have answered, and if someone won't talk, won't come out and won't reply, what else can you do? I should have gone and got her from work and forced her to come to mine or something, anything. I shouldn't have left her on her own that day. No one should. But you have to be brave to keep chipping away at someone. Brave or stupid. I didn't know what to do, how to be a friend. Which is weird, because we've been friends our whole lives.

HS: And you're saying you were at home that night, the night Ian Brown was knifed?

LB: Yes.

HS: For the benefit of the tape, can you describe what's in front of you?

LB: Cigarette ends.

HS: These four cigarette ends were found in a plastic bag hidden in the garage at Rachel Edwards' house. Can you tell us anything about that?

LB: No. I don't know why anyone would keep dog ends in the garage. But as I say, Rachel wasn't herself. I realise now that I didn't know the half of what she was doing. I only found out about the clip file when Mark showed it to me.

HS: Mrs Edwards says she found evidence of you and Mr Edwards having smoked in her absence. Could the cigarette ends be yours?

LB: Possibly. We did have a sneaky fag because we were both stressed. But why would she keep my dog ends?

HS: Rachel did see you driving past her last Friday, clearly on your way from her house. When she got in, she found the cigarette ends in the kitchen. She kept them, planning to confront you about it later. She believes you and Mr Edwards were having an affair.

LB: An affair? What do you mean, an affair?

HS: A love affair.

LB: Me and her Mark? Are you yanking my chain? (Laughs) Oh my God. You're actually serious? Sorry, but that's ridiculous. I'd never do that to a friend, and certainly not to Rachel; that'd be like doing it to my own sister! Really, you can forget that one. Strike it right off your list. Besides which, Mark's not my type at all. He's too nice, for a start. I seem to prefer total bastards, if you'll excuse my *français*.

HS: Ms Baxter, cigarette ends were found near the town-hall pond on Sunday the twenty-ninth of September and in the bushes near the car park of Brookvale Leisure Centre late in the evening of Thursday the twenty-sixth. Following forensic examination, a DNA match has been found with the sample found at Rachel Edwards' property. Can you shed any light on that? Ms Baxter? Ms Baxter?

CHAPTER 53

Rachel

Amanda sips her coffee. I hear the soft gulp as it goes down her neck. This is a new day. Yesterday she held my hand, told me that I was brave.

'Rachel,' she says after a minute or so. 'I want to ask you now about David King.'

'Dave? As in my manager Dave? Why? What's he got to do with it?'

Slowly she picks up my statement. 'You confessed to the murders of Joanna Weatherall and Anne-Marie Golightly, and the strangulation of Henry Parker. You claim to have killed Ian Brown. But there's nothing in here about the murder of David King.'

I wipe my eyes, blow my nose, warmth flashing through the length of me. 'David King? Dave?'

'Your manager, yes. He was found dead in his flat in Duke Street, about ten minutes' walk from your place of work.'

'When?'

'Two days after you made the call. But he'd been dead for over forty-eight hours. Which means he was killed sometime on Saturday afternoon or evening.'

'What?' Heat bursts in my head; my hair is damp.

'He was murdered. Stabbed twice in the ribs with the same knife. You haven't mentioned him other than to say he popped in around midday, that he made you a cup of tea. Do you remember anything at all?'

'No, I… I didn't know.'

'Rachel, I'd like to try something with you, if you're agreeable. I'd like to try hypnosis. Would you be willing to do that?'

It's a strange kind of laugh that escapes us in moments where we can't imagine ever doing anything of the sort, and it's that kind of laugh that breaks from me now.

Amanda smiles, her blue eyes half closing. 'It's not… I'm not going to perform any tricks.'

'Not going to make me stand on one leg and cluck like a chicken?'

'I was hoping to take you back to the pond. I was hoping that now that you've been able to voice what happened to Kieron, we might be able to dig a little deeper into that memory. All right?'

'All right.'

'So you're happy for me to use hypnosis?'

'Yes.'

'All right. All right, Rachel.' She shifts her bottom to the edge of her chair. 'Close your eyes.'

CHAPTER 54

Rachel

'You'll hear my voice, Rachel, and my voice reminds you that you're safe and calm and relaxed, really relaxed and warm in your safe place. Now I want you to know that all information that you have ever seen, heard or felt since the day you were born is stored in your subconscious mind, and that's where we're going to go. That information is available to you at will if you want it. All you need to do is to relax and let go… It has always been there, and will always be, for your easy access, just like taking something from a shelf. I want you to go back to the park that night. I'm here and you will hear my voice and my voice will remind you that you're safe and calm and relaxed.

'You and Ian are walking through the town-hall park towards the pond… Reach in now and remove any block to your memory that you may have had. Any time you feel a block coming back, take a deep breath, and as you exhale, you can command that block to leave you. It is your mind, your cache of information… you own it. And you control it. I'm here beside you, Rachel, and you will hear my voice, and my voice will remind you that you are safe and calm and relaxed, relaxed and warm in your safe space.

'You now have total recall at will. Remembering is a priority for you. It is easy and natural for you to remember. As you receive new information, you have total recall of this information at will. You now have the ability to retrieve that information and I am here beside you… You're in the park and you're walking towards the bench by the pond…'

I hear her voice in the sky. I'm walking through the park and I'm telling her I'm walking through the park and I hear myself tell her I'm walking through the park. My voice is mine and someone else's. My voice is a radio. The radio is broadcasting my voice and my voice is calm. I am calm. There is a breeze on my face and the air is cool and smells of night. Blue Eyes is in the sky; the sky is dark blue and calm. The boy is with me. He feels like Kieron beside me, the way he walks, his energy, his smell. He's young and he's telling me his troubles like Kieron used to do. I tell him it's going to be all right. I tell him being gay isn't wrong. He's going to be OK and one day he'll find someone who loves him for all the reasons he thinks he's unlovable. There'll be heartbreak along the way but there's heartbreak for everyone and the important thing in this life is to love, to get out there and love, love your head off and take the knocks as they come because living without love isn't living at all, not really.

'We get to the bench and he sits down,' I hear myself say from the sky. 'I put my arm around him. With my other hand I feel the knife in my bag. And he's talking to me and I'm comforting him and telling him everything's going to be OK. And then he says he needs to go and I say OK, all right, I'll walk you back to the road, and there's… there's a smell. And he says he has to go. And I say I'll walk with him but he says he's changed his mind, he wants to stay awhile. I say OK. OK, love, I say, and I say goodbye and I wish him well and I tell him not to worry about things and I smell smoke. I can smell cigarette smoke. It's strong, wafting over on the breeze. But there's no one there. There's no one… there's no one there…'

'Rachel?' Blue Eyes, blue skies, calling my name my name my name. 'Can you look in your bag, Rachel. Look inside your bag.'

'I can,' I say to the sky. I am calm and the air is cool. I am opening my bag and my bag is dark.

'Can you tell me what's in the bag, Rachel?'

'My purse. My cloth bags for the supermarket.'

'What else?'

'My umbrella. Glasses case. Tissues.'

'Can you find the knife, Rachel?'

I am looking into my bag and my bag is dark. I am rummaging around in my bag, rummaging around around around.

'Can you find the knife, Rachel?'

'It's not in my… I can't… but I can smell smoke.' My breath comes shallow and fast. I am not calm. The air is cold.'

'Can you find the knife, Rachel?'

'The bench is cold. I can smell… I can smell cigarettes.'

'Rachel, can you find the knife?'

'Cigarette smoke. I can smell… Oh God. Oh God help me.'

'Rachel.' Amanda's voice in the sky. 'Rachel, it's OK, we're going to come out in one, two, three… out.'

I open my eyes. I am panting. There is sweat on my forehead and my mouth is dry.

Blue Eyes is looking at me with concern. 'Are you all right?'

'I said goodbye to him,' I say. 'I left him there on the bench. He was alive. There was an umbrella in my bag. Not a knife. I smelled cigarettes. But neither of us smoked.'

And at last she smiles, a proper smile with all her teeth. And I was right. It was worth the wait.

'That's very good,' she says. 'Good work.'

'I comforted him.'

'All right.'

'I comforted him. I told him it was all going to be OK. We said goodbye. We had a little hug and I went on my way. I didn't take the knife out of my bag – the knife wasn't there. I could smell cigarettes even though there was no one else there. I don't smoke. And he didn't smoke. I didn't put the knife in him. I just imagined it. I just imagined it. I didn't kill him, did I? I didn't kill that beautiful boy.' My eyes fill.

'Rachel, look at me.'

I look at Blue Eyes. Amanda, that's her name. She is called Amanda Frost and she can see me.

'Rachel, are you listening to me?'

'Yes.'

'You didn't kill that boy.'

'I didn't?' I stifle the sob in my throat.

Her clear blue eyes are on mine. 'You didn't kill anyone.'

CHAPTER 55

Rachel

My head is throbbing. There's a pain behind my eyes. I know what she's said is true. I've always known it somewhere because it fits with the perfect click of a missing piece.

'The tissues,' I say. 'The tissues in my rucksack. I've just remembered, I didn't have a hot flash outside the leisure centre, I had a nosebleed. That's why I leaned against the wall. I stuffed the tissues in the front pocket of my rucksack, and by the time I came out of the class, I'd completely forgotten about the nosebleed.'

Blue Eyes takes a deep breath. 'One thing at a time, but that's good, that's great.'

'The knife. Oh my God, I did put it in my bag. After Jo, I woke up in the middle of the night and I went downstairs and it was in the cutlery drawer so I... I put it in my bag and I must've forgotten it the moment I'd done it, must've been half asleep, though when I brought it in from the garage is anyone's guess. I'd felt scared walking home that night. I saw two lads vaping and I can remember thinking, what if they're wrong 'uns, what if they come at me? But I must've been half asleep when I did that because what the heck is a knife going to do to protect me? I'd never be able to use it on anyone. I'd never have time to get it out of my bag let alone... But hang on, if I didn't kill anyone, who did?'

She holds up her hand. *Patience, woman.*

'The police found the clip file in your kitchen,' she says. 'And Ian's clothes in the washing machine and the cigarette butts in the garage. Cigarette butts were found near the scene of the attacks on Anne-Marie, Ian Brown and David King, along with fabric fibres and hairs. The DNA from the cigarette butts matched with DNA from other cigarette ends found near the car park of Brookvale Leisure Centre. These also matched one of the cigarette butts that you kept and hid in the garage.' She meets my eye, holds my gaze. 'Hair strands found in Anne-Marie's car matched hair found in your house.'

'What are you saying? It wasn't Mark, was it? I know it's always the husband, but it's not, is it? It's not my Mark – please tell me it's not.'

'No, Rachel, it isn't.'

'It's not Lisa. Oh God, please tell me it's not her. Please, Amanda.' I meet her eye, see the almost imperceptible shake of her head. 'Oh,' I say, and suddenly everything is obvious. 'Ingrid.'

'Matching cigarette stubs, hair and garment fibres left at the town-hall crime scene were found in Ingrid Taylor's flat along with calendar entries in her iPhone detailing your movements over the past eight months.'

'Eight? But she only moved in in the summer.'

'The police arrested Ingrid Taylor almost a month ago, Rachel. In questioning, she revealed a worrying fascination with your whereabouts as well as an inappropriate interest in your husband, Mark. She had apparently taken a selfie in her underwear and sent it to him. Your husband revealed that she had been pestering him. Not his choice of words, but it seems she was calling at your house whenever you were out. We did some digging, spoke to people she knew in Helsby. There was an… incident. A woman accused Ingrid of sleeping with her husband. Ingrid attacked this woman, held a knife to her throat apparently… it all happened at a cocktail party. It seems they struck a deal: Ingrid was to move away and no charges would be brought.'

My chin is on the floor, manner of speaking.

'Blimey,' I say, breathless.

'She was watching you, Rachel. And she was following you. Sometimes she would simply follow you, sometimes she would double back and call in at your home, knowing you to be out. She knew you were at a spinning class and called at your home moments after you'd left, eventually persuading Mark to give her a lift to the leisure centre so that her car wouldn't be picked up on CCTV. We have captures of Ingrid following you into St Michael's cemetery and on the road near the leisure centre. Fibres matching her clothing were found under David King's fingernails. Footage of her was also taken from the CCTV outside the Red Admiral pub late on Saturday evening, the night Ian Brown was attacked.'

'I can't… I can't take it in.' The information hovers. I have heard it, I know I have, but it's not made its way into my brain yet.

'In interview, Ms Taylor exhibited several traits of narcissistic personality disorder.' Amanda leans forward. 'Arrogance is one of those traits, Rachel. She offered herself as a witness, convinced she'd been one hundred per cent successful in framing you for the murders. She didn't request a lawyer until very late in the questioning, by which time she'd tied herself in knots. She's not as bright as she believes herself to be – it's completely in keeping with her personality disorder, the belief that others are less intelligent than herself. It appears that while other traits manifested strongly – a refusal to take responsibility for her actions, a strong desire for status, particularly through material goods, and a failure to acknowledge boundaries – it was arrogance that did for her in the end. She simply could not imagine that her story would not be believed. And so she did not get her house in order, so to speak.'

'I can't take it in.' But my body knows it. My shoulders have lowered. There's an ease in my spine, a looseness in my jaw.

'If you remember, Mark helped her with a passport form.'

'Yes.'

'Well, it seems she'd booked herself a little holiday to the Seychelles, which she fully intended to take. She's been charged with stalking with malicious intent, and with the murders of Joanna Weatherall, Anne-Marie Golightly and David King, and the vicious attack on Ian Brown. She claims she is innocent, which is textbook – the failure to take responsibility for one's actions and the consequences of those actions. We tried to tell you, to explain it to you, but you were too ill.'

'How d'you mean?'

'Everything I've told you in the last two sessions is information you'd already been given. But you were convinced you were responsible for the attacks. Nothing could dissuade you, nothing.'

'But I was there. For all the attacks I was there. How do you know it was Ingrid?'

'Because she was there too. That's what I'm telling you. There was CCTV footage, there were blood traces on her clothes and shoes matching three of the victims, mud samples taken from the soles… I could go on. There were notes in her phone, including the date of your spinning class, and the date of the anniversary of Kieron's death, which she claimed not to know about even though your husband said he told her. But it appears she followed you regularly and often. She followed you the night you crossed the churchyard. It's possible she knocked your head against the gravestone or hit you with something, but she hasn't confessed to that and we have no proof.'

'And you've told me all this before?'

She nods. 'When you gave your statement you were suffering from delusions caused by overwhelming levels of stress, but also, I believe, from a form of menopausal psychosis, which took us longer to diagnose but which ties in with the postpartum psychosis you suffered when Kieron was born. There is also the great weight of grief.'

I nod. Tears fall down my face as usual, but they're different tears somehow.

'Rachel, are you clear that I'm not a detective and I'm not a lawyer but a forensic psychiatrist?'

'Yes. But I thought you were building a case. Studying a murderer for insight or something. I didn't care. I just wanted someone to listen to me. To see me.'

'Of course. I understand completely. But once it became clear that reasoning with you would not work, my chosen course of therapy was to let you tell your story from beginning to end according to your truth, without interruptions or corrections. I wanted to listen to it as you lived it and see if I could gain insight into the roots of these strongly held delusions and how I might help you overcome them. We've discussed how every attack tied into elements of your life that troubled you, have we not?'

I nod, reach for the tissues.

'And how you were working through these things, but that what lay at the base of all of it was your son's death, your feelings of loss and guilt relating to that and the subsequent loneliness you felt at the further loss, as you saw it, of your family – your husband and daughter – who were struggling to cope in their own ways, and your best friend, who couldn't figure out how to be close to you.

'Your empathic nature made this very difficult, Rachel. Empathy without boundaries is dangerous. It can make us ill. It made you very ill indeed. Quite simply, from the moment Kieron died, you felt the pain of every victim whose story you read and printed out. You felt their pain and the pain of their families as if it were your own, because in a way it was your own. On top of that you felt guilt for every one of them, which was your own terrifying guilt at not being there for your son in his last moments. And as if that wasn't enough, you made yourself responsible for all those deaths because you felt on some deep level responsible for your son's death, do you see? Your own failure, as you saw it, to protect him. When the attacks and deaths happened close to home, that responsibility you felt, coupled with Ingrid Taylor's campaign of hate against you… well, eventually it became a reality. You took full responsibility. You turned yourself in.'

I press the wad of tissues to my eyes. 'We drove straight to the hospital, but Kieron was…'

'It was too late. I know. And that has been more than you or your family could bear. It's more than anyone should ever have to bear. It broke you into pieces, but you were not aware that it had done so. You carried on as if you were whole because your family were relying on you to be whole. You wanted to take your own life but you felt trapped by the responsibility of staying alive for those you love and who love you. All three of you carried on, your husband, Katie and you; you carried on with no real idea how or why or what you were doing or how to talk about it to one another, and so, quite simply, you didn't.'

I hear her chair creak. She slides my notes onto the coffee table. I can see her hands clasped on her knees. 'Emotions are like water, Rachel. Didn't you tell me that? Anger is the leak in the bathroom and hate is the water that escapes through the kitchen wall? You have described yourself as water more than once. All feelings are water. They can be and often are misdirected.'

'I did say that.'

'Yes. You had the answers all along. The hate of the world, hate for others, prejudice, bigotry is often no more than misdirected anger for something altogether different. Our own pain. Our own dissatisfaction. Our own failure. We can't control our pain and often we can't identify where it's coming from. We drink it or gamble it away, find comfort where we can. Whether it's true or not, your reflection on David King having tattoos done because it was a pain he could at least control was very perceptive. The same with Phil, your customer. He gambled for the stress of it because it was a stress he understood. So when you believed that no one could even see you, you were alone with your pain, with all of it, do you understand? And when you picked up loneliness in everyone you met—'

'It was my own loneliness.'

'Precisely. So you see, I had to let you tell me what you thought had happened in its entirety, almost as a story, and together we've had a think about what that story means. And it occurred to me that the only attack you never claimed was David King and the reason for that was simple. You didn't know about it.'

'Meaning?'

'Meaning that you, or your mind, only claimed your victims *after* you'd read about them. You can't take responsibility for something you know nothing about. If you'd killed David King, you would have known about it. The others you read about. And because you'd read about these people, and met them and spoken to them, your empathy for them and sense of responsibility towards them, which had been raised to harmful levels since your son's death, combined with a difficult hormonal mix, not to mention a dangerous woman who had misdirected her anger towards you and attempted to ruin your life, well, all that was enough to create chaos.' She sits back, an expression almost of satisfaction on her face.

'Wow.' I shake my head. If it's possible to blow a mind into repair, well, that's what this feels like, like an explosion in reverse. 'I can't take it in, but at the same time it makes perfect sense.'

'It's quite a load. Your mind created memories that would support your idea that you were to blame for the injuries and deaths because you felt that you were to blame for your son's death. But they weren't memories, they were horror. The horror you felt at what happened to your son. You weren't to blame for your son's death and you weren't to blame for the deaths in the newspapers and you weren't to blame for Joanna's or Anne-Marie's or David King's deaths either. That glass globe you were carrying on your back? It's no wonder it was too heavy. You were quite simply trying to bear the weight of the entire world, which you felt was being destroyed by hate. Single-handedly and in a very fragile state, you were trying to stop hate from breeding hate by using love.'

'Love on steroids.'

'Exactly.' She smiles. 'Love on steroids. And meanwhile, Ingrid Taylor had made you responsible for all her woes. She was disgraced, ostracised. Her husband had left her. She was looking for somewhere to put her pain and humiliation. Do you see the difference? You took on responsibility for the world; she made you responsible for hers. Her unhappiness, her divorce, her childlessness...'

'But she said she didn't want children.'

'She lied. People like Ingrid Taylor lie with no problem whatsoever. They rewrite history, they reinvent the world so that it fits with their very problematic subjectivity.'

'My subjectivity was hardly a walk in the park, though, was it?'

She laughs. 'Well, no. But hers was devoid of empathy, the principal trait of the narcissist. They simply cannot conceive of how their behaviour causes pain to others, or rather, they know it does but they don't care, not really, not in any depth. To Ingrid, you were a thing. A thing to be moved out of the way.'

'Moved?'

'Well, yes. It seems that in her hate campaign against you, she... how can I put this... realised that there might be some spoils for the taking.'

'Spoils?'

'Your husband. Mark.'

'So I was right?'

'Mark was an unforeseen bonus of her hate campaign. In trying to frame you, she realised she would have Mark to herself.'

'Why not just kill me? That would've got me out of the way much quicker.'

Blue Eyes pauses, bouncing the tips of her fingers together.

'She was already cultivating her relationship with Mark,' she says after a moment. 'She knew she'd be a suspect, possibly the main suspect. She knew the neighbours would have seen her in Mark's car, seen her calling at your home while you were out. She's been a victim, she claims, of gossip before. I'm sure she realised Katie had her eyes on her, that Katie didn't trust her. If she played the sympathetic friend, if she made sure to report back to Mark on your evening wanderings, she could build up a picture of you as unstable and sinister – mad, if you like – making sure that those close to you would have no choice but to believe you'd committed these crimes, even making *you* believe it, ultimately.'

'Wow.'

'Indeed. Not that she admitted to any of this. Narcissists reinvent the world and find evidence where none exists, often despite evidence to the contrary.'

I shake my head. 'I suppose I'm guilty of reinventing the world to fit my delusions.'

'I guess. But the truth was there underneath. You knew it was there, that's why you didn't turn yourself in until… until you didn't know it. The moment you truly believed you'd committed a crime, you called the police.'

'You said Ingrid had been charged with the murders of Joanna, Anne-Marie and David. What about Ian?'

'Ah.' She leans back in her chair and crosses her legs before meeting my eye once again. 'What the news report actually said was that he was "fighting for his life". Like Kieron was. The exact same phrase. You jumped ahead, could see no other outcome for him but death. But Ian didn't die, Rachel. He survived.'

'Oh God.' My eyes fill. I press my hands to them, a great sigh escaping me. 'Oh, that's wonderful. That lovely boy. Oh, that's so…'

I look up, meet her eye. A cloud passes over the sun.

'Wait a second,' I say. 'You said Ingrid waged a hate campaign against me. Why the heck would anyone single me out for a hate campaign? What did I ever do to her?'

CHAPTER 56

Ingrid

Transcript of recorded interview with Ingrid Taylor (excerpt)
Also present: DI Heather Scott, PC Marilyn Button, Ms Janice James (solicitor)

IT: Before you charge me, I just want to say something. You're doing a lot of talking and you're making it sound like I had it all worked out, but I didn't. I'm a nice person. I've been suffering from… from undiagnosed depression after a traumatic divorce. I'm a really nice person. It was all just a horrible series of coincidences. If my ex had spent enough time in bed and less time pouring our savings down the toilet, I would never have ended up in this mess. That was him all over: selfish. I thought he was having an affair – that's the only reason I followed him. Any woman would have done the same. I mean, I thought he was on drugs, don't you see? I even checked his arms for tracks.

That I actually followed him makes me laugh now. It makes me sick, to be honest. It's been terrible for me, really hard. No one understands, absolutely no one. The humiliation has been unbearable at times. The shame. To see him go into a *bookmaker's*, a bloody *gambling* shop, and suddenly everything becoming clear. The money draining from the bank account, the weight loss, the dark circles under his eyes. Money, our money, haemorrhaged on bloody horses of all things, drip-fed over hours into slot machines, funnelled into football results. And when the chips were down, as they invariably were, there was the inevitable self-pitying drowning of sorrows at the pub, weeping into the bosom of Rachel bloody Edwards. Every day, when he said he had to work late, off he went, until there was no money left to piss away.

So I watched. So what? I've become a great watcher. Any woman would have done the same. And when he filed for divorce and all that business in Helsby… I was bullied. I've been bullied. What you're using against me is gossip. I was *hounded* out of that town, as if none of them had ever put a foot wrong. I didn't touch that woman's husband and what happened at the party is my word against theirs. The knife was on the worktop; I just held it for two seconds, literally two. I only went out for a couple of lunches with the stupid cow's husband and that was only because I was bored to death at home. But sleep with him? No way, I would never do that.

All I ever did was focus on my health. (Laughs) Sorry, if I'm laughing it's only at the irony of giving up work, taking folic acid, devoting time to my flute when all the time the main task at hand, for which I needed his *input*, was the one task left undone. That man took me through my entire thirties and now look at me. Darling, you had one job, as they say.

And so, yes, I watched. You can't charge me for that. And yes, I watched Rachel Edwards. With her fallen features and fried hair, her palpable apathy and rounded shoulders. No one called her a Jezebel, did they? Well,

I'll just say for the record that the other woman doesn't always wear a tight red dress. There she was with a friendly hand on his shoulder, a pint pulled ready to greet him after a day flushing my money down the drain, always welcoming, always with the *How are you, Phil? All right, Phil?* Chat, chat, chat. Chat, chat, chat, chat, chat, while he ruined my life, my life not hers, with his filthy habit.

Enabler.

Home wrecker.

And his name is *Philip*, by the way, not Phil.

When the flat came up for sale on Rachel's road – sorry, *close* – it was the perfect opportunity to start again. I was being hounded out of Helsby like a *witch* – have you any idea how that feels? No one understands. You can't prove I knew where Rachel Edwards lived. I'd had a change in circumstances and needed to downsize, that's all. I couldn't have stalked her even if I'd wanted to; she didn't even exist online.

And this idea that I was somehow after her husband? That's because of what happened in Helsby, isn't it? That underwear shot you seem intent on using against me was only because Mark had texted me one morning to ask if I was ready and I'd answered with that picture with the caption *Not quite, lol*, for a joke! A joke! You've taken it completely out of context. Mark and I used to make each other laugh all the time, this is what I mean by you twisting everything against me. He only deleted it because he said his weirdo wife might not understand my sense of humour. She might get the wrong idea. I mean, not being funny, but if she couldn't trust him to be *friends* with someone, it's obvious they were at the end of the road. I'm certainly not to blame for the shitty state of their marriage.

And as for the people who have come forward with stories of how she helped them talk through their problems, how they'd come to think of her as a friend, I can see what you're doing, pitting her profile against mine, but, well, they're weirdos too. Dog walkers are strange, end of. They buy an animal so that they can stick it on the end of a rope and walk around the neighbourhood in endless circles picking up poo and making small talk with people they don't know, never will know and will never invite into their homes. Weird. I wasn't doing that, was I? All I did was go for a couple of walks and that's enough to put me in the frame for brutal murders? Rachel Edwards could easily have broken into my flat, smeared the victims' blood over my clothes, nicked my silk jacket, my shoes and secretly put them at the back of the wardrobe when I wasn't in the house, stolen some cigarette ends and placed them at the scene, somehow got my fingerprints on that car. And how anyone could tell it was me from those CCTV captures I don't know. What a joke. My own mother wouldn't have known me. (Pause)

HS: For the tape, Ms Taylor is composing herself.

IT: OK, so you've got evidence for that Golightly woman, that David guy and the tramp kid. OK. Happy? I have no chance, I get that. I mean, who can compete with the mother of a murdered child? No one. In the Top Trumps of Victimhood, she holds the winning card, even if she did keep a file of death in her kitchen and go around chatting up strangers in the dark. People always prefer the underdog, the down-at-heel middle-aged woman, over the younger model when it comes down to who to believe. That's just sexism, pure and simple.

All the blame cast on me for no other reason than that I'm more attractive. Well, I'll tell you something. As far as I'm concerned:

Rachel Edwards steals husbands, not me.

Rachel Edwards ruins lives, not me.

Rachel Edwards is a murderer, and I'll tell you how I know.

I should have said it straight away. I should have told you, but I could tell you were trying to pin all this on me. But I saw Rachel Edwards go into the park with that girl. I saw her but I said I didn't because only a fool would put themselves at the scene of the crime. I said I wasn't there but I *was*. I was, OK? I *saw* her. I know you don't have the CCTV, but I was there, I did see her, I swear. And the next day, when I read about that girl in the paper, I knew it was her, Rachel, Rachel Edwards. I couldn't believe it when you didn't trace it to her. Middle-aged woman, little black dog, walks the streets, talks to strangers, keeps a file of death? Just how much evidence do you need? It was exhausting. I would never have killed so many if you'd done your fucking job. Two more deaths and one near miss… and even then she had to do your job for you, turn herself in. I know you're under-resourced, but honestly, you're as stupid as her blind, trusting husband, to whom I dropped enough hints to sink a battleship. I'm telling you, Rachel Edwards killed Jo Weatherall. Rachel Edwards, do you hear me? I might be a murderer but she's a murderer too.

CHAPTER 57

Rachel

One year later

Amanda Frost recrosses her legs and fixes me with that blue gaze. It's almost a year since I turned myself in. I'm off the antipsychotics now and this third type of HRT suits me a lot better than the other two, thank heavens. Sometimes the drugs do work.

'Like we've said,' Amanda says, with the air of a lawyer summing up, 'sometimes it's not one thing that can result in such extreme outcomes, but a number of things. And often it's something relatively small that tips us over an edge we've been teetering on for some time.'

'Like *Crackerjack*.'

'Like *Crackerjack*.' She smiles. 'You have a wonderful support network. You have people who love you. How do you feel about Katie leaving? Liverpool, isn't it?'

'I'm OK. I'm all right. I mean, she's a lot less angry since the counselling and I know I might have thought I couldn't bear for her to leave, but I saw what her not leaving meant, not following her path, and it was terrible. And I know she's academic, but it's stage make-up she loves and that's what she should do. You've got to follow your heart, haven't you? Do something you're passionate about. And I'll be glad to get shut of all her props, to be honest – they're taking over! I just want her to be happy. I'm following her now, by the way. On Instagram, I mean. Me and 4,000 others. She's an influencer, did I tell you? Whatever that is.'

'And Liverpool isn't too far away.'

'Not too far away, no. Half an hour on the train, not even that. She can still be independent but she's near enough if she needs us after… after everything. And she can still be here for Kieron's anniversary.'

'Which is next week. Are you doing anything specific?'

'We're going to scatter his ashes and play his favourite song.'

Her eyebrows go up. 'Where?'

'Town hall.' I smile. 'The pond.'

Her eyebrows, which had barely landed, are up again. 'What's your thinking?'

'I'm thinking that hate is going to eat this world up if we're not careful. And what we need is love. The town hall is where Mark and I got married. It's where we registered our children's births. It's where I took them to feed the ducks when they were little, watched them play. That place was always love for me and I'll not have it ruined. I'll not have it ruined by hate.'

'You're reclaiming it.'

'I suppose I am, yes.'

When she says goodbye, there are tears in her eyes, as there have been at other moments when we've spoken. She is in her late thirties, as I thought, and she has two kids, two little girls. This last year, as I've got better, I have managed to make her laugh more and more. I know she's here if I feel things getting on top of me again, and I know I'll see her for my follow-ups, but now it's time for me to go.

'Thanks for everything,' I say. There are tears in my eyes too, but I'm sure you'd guessed that.

'Good luck, Rachel. I wish you every possible happiness. You deserve it.'

'I'll miss you.'

'And I you.'

We hug each other like old friends. When we part, I give her a little wave, then I go out of her office and close the door. As I step out onto the street, I burst into tears so violent that I have to sit on the kerb for a few minutes to compose myself.

'You all right, love?' someone says.

I look up. There's a middle-aged woman with two carrier bags full of groceries. She looks tired, a bit frazzled. She digs in her handbag and pulls out a packet of tissues. She's trying to wrestle one out of the packet, but after a moment she gives up and hands me the whole lot.

'Here,' she says. 'You going to be OK?' I wonder whether they see her at home, whether they hear her when she says something, laugh when she tells a joke. I want to tell her that I see her. But I don't, obviously; that would be nuts.

'Yes, thanks,' is all I say. 'I'm going to be OK.'

'All right, love, mind how you go.'

I watch her go on her way until someone else appears, coming towards me. At the sight of me, he lifts his hand in a wave. He said he might be able to meet me out of today's session on his way home from college, and here he is, how lovely. Ian didn't die, did I say that? He pulled through. He was only sixteen, as it turns out – cheeky monkey, telling me he was nineteen – so the attack alerted the local authority to his situation. They found him some temporary sheltered accommodation and he's seeing his mother once a week. He's started a plumbing course at Widnes FE College. I vouched for him. He and Katie get on very well, so if he gets his diploma, I've told him he can have Kieron's room for a year while he gets himself sorted.

'Rachel,' he says. 'What're you doing sitting on the kerb?' He holds out his hand and pulls me up.

CHAPTER 58

Rachel

A week later, on the second anniversary of Kieron's death, Mark, Katie, Lisa and I walk to the town-hall gardens at dawn. At the pond we stand together and say goodbye and scatter my son's ashes on the water, listening to 'Into My Arms' on Katie's iPhone. When I ask her if it's Rick Cave, she rolls her eyes, but before she can say, *Mum, it's Nick, not Rick*, I tell her I'm only joking and she laughs and throws an arm around my waist.

Later, before we go out for dinner to celebrate our son's too-short life, Mark and I are sorting through his remaining things. This last year I have come into his room often to sit and be quiet and remember. I have listened to his favourite vinyl records, and if I close my eyes, I can tell you every poster and scrap of paper and photo he has Blu-Tacked to the wall.

'Shall I take this stuff to the car then?' Mark is standing at the door, nodding at the totem pole of cardboard boxes by his feet.

'I'll come with you. Just let me sit here another minute.'

On my lap is a box. In it are Kieron's dancing and football medals and shields, his bolt and hoop earrings in a smaller, velvet-lined box, his soft ripped jeans and his Antony and the Johnsons T-shirt, which still smells of him, and which has the words *I Am a Bird Now* on the front. Yes, I think. You are a bird now, my love.

I'm keeping his art folders and English books from every year of his school life – some of his ink drawings and paintings I have put into frames and hung in the hall and the kitchen, where I can see them every day. His childish compositions I will read and reread, and no matter how much it hurts. I will try not to look away from the memory of him at eight years old reaching for the right way to say something. There is no right way. That much I know. Sometimes there is no way at all, because saying it will make it true. If you're lucky, someone will help you find maybe not the right words but the words you need in that moment. Amanda was that person for me. She was able to help me swim down to a truth I had no heart, no stomach, no lungs for. The last compassionate act of my grief-addled mind was to trick me into saying the words I needed to say to my beloved boy in his dying moments to another boy in a memory entirely of my own making. What would any of us say? *I love you. You'll be all right. Sleep now, my angel.*

Anger gets trapped inside us, becomes hate. If we're not careful, hate becomes a force often too hard to control and which solves nothing. A father punishes a son for damage done by his own father. A child beats up a weaker child to avenge violence done to him at home. A grown man stabs another for fear of what lurks in his own chaotic nature, perhaps – who knows? We punish the wrong people, too hard, for the sins of others, for our own frustrations, our own failures. Ingrid found me in her sights and, humiliated and rejected, decided I would be the one she punished for all that had gone wrong in her life. In the end, the only person she hurt was herself. That's the thing about revenge. It's an act of hate and not the satisfying finale everyone believes it is, the action-movie climax where the villain dies a horrible death in a plume of flames and everyone cheers. Revenge is not a dish best served cold. It is a dish best served not at all.

When I turned myself in, they saw a woman made mad by grief and believed me until the evidence and testimonies didn't add up. All I wanted was connection. I wanted Mark and Katie to be able to look at me and me at them and for us all to see the memory of Kieron and be able to keep looking. I wanted to live in a world where love wins out over hate.

Mark is still standing at the door.

'Are you hovering?' I ask, folding up Kieron's T-shirt to put in the 'keep' box.

'I thought…' He seems to lose his train of thought a moment before starting again. 'I thought after this we could walk down to the canal and maybe call at the Wilsons for a half, just the two of us, before we meet Katie at the restaurant.'

'OK.'

He pushes his bottom lip up against the top one and shakes his head. He's looking at me. His eyes are greeny-brown and they change according to the weather. I'd forgotten.

'What?' I say. 'What are you looking at me like that for?'

'I'm not looking at you like anything. I'm just looking at you.'

My eyes prick but I don't take them from his. 'And what do you see?'

'I see the girl at Tanya Hodgkins' eighteenth at the Mersey View wearing the tightest black minidress I'd ever seen and big black DMs, dancing like she was on something. I see the girl I asked out for a walk that first time when I had no money to take her out for a drink.'

'You nicked flowers from that garden.'

He smirks. 'You were worth stealing for. And you bought us a packet of Hula Hoops and a can of Bass shandy and we shared them on the bench by the pavilion. I thought, *I'd better get a job if I'm going to have any chance of getting her to be my girlfriend.*'

'An apprenticeship, no less. There's flash, I thought. I thought, he's going places. And—'

He holds up his hand, biting his lip now against the stuff on his mind, and I realise he's been waiting to say his piece, that he's probably rehearsed it, knowing that words are not his strong suit, that he's been waiting for the right moment, which has never come, and so now, surrounded by our beloved son's things packed into all these cardboard boxes, he's saying it anyway.

'Go on,' I almost whisper.

He comes nearer, slowly, like a child. 'And then, well, I see the woman I kept out till midnight so it would be her birthday before I asked her to marry me. And I didn't really think she would but she said, *All right then, you're on.*' His eyes have started to shine; mine too, I can feel them – how hopeless we both are.

He sits next to me on our son's bed. I feel the weight of him, the warmth of him. He's not looking at me anymore, he's looking at the knot of our hands on my lap.

'I see the woman who hurt my fingers squeezing them when she brought my beautiful boy into the world, who did it again when she gave me my crackpot daughter. I see a woman with her nose covered in flour when I came in from work, making biscuits with the kids and no dinner for me.' He stops. We are both crying now – we can't help it. He is telling us the story of our life so that we can look at what we've lost and be thankful for all that we still have.

'Don't say any more,' I manage.

'I want to.'

'I know. Just sit here with me for a minute. Let's sit.'

I lean my head on his shoulder. He puts his arm around me. Simple things.

'I see the woman on the phone that terrible night,' he whispers. 'I see her break into tiny pieces and I know in that moment that I can never put her back together.'

'You see all that?'

'Every time I look at you. Every time I look at you, you're everything you've ever been in every moment we've been together, and I see that, I do – I see all of it and it's just that for a time there I didn't want to. I couldn't cope with seeing it, Rach. And I'm so sorry.'

'There's no need to say sorry to me, love. I didn't see you either, did I? Not really.' I kiss his cheek and we cry fat tears together because at last we can, and it's tough, the toughest, but it's better than crying alone.

'Let's go for that drink now,' I say. 'I'll finish my essay tomorrow.'

It's for my bereavement counselling course. If it continues to go as well as it has been, I should qualify next year. As I said to Amanda, I'm pretty good at making connections. I've had a lot of practice. And it wasn't just me who felt invisible. There are many people who live their lives thinking no one sees them: the homeless, the elderly, the poor, the lonely, the heartbroken, the grieving, the mentally ill, the disabled, those who haven't found their voice, those who haven't discovered what they're good at, those who shun praise and attention, those who work quietly with love and patience. I could go on. I want to connect to all of them. I want to connect to you. I want to tell you that whoever you are, I care about you. I am interested in the troubled tickings of your heart; I want to know what makes your soul ache, what makes it sing. I want to tell you that all our souls ache sometimes, sometimes sing. I want to tell you that love helps. I want to tell you that love heals. I want to take your hand in mine. I want to tell you that I see you.

EPILOGUE

Saturday night. A middle-aged couple cuddle up in front of a film, takeaway boxes stacked on a tray at their feet. Their daughter is away at university. The house feels empty without her, but they are making plans for their first holiday alone together in over twenty years. If you saw them from the street, you would see a peaceful, happy couple, warm and safe in their home. Lucky them, you might think, so close after all these years. You would have no idea what they have been through, how strong they have to be every day just to keep going. But no one sees them. No one is watching them. Not anymore. On the street, all is still. It is October, cold, no night to be out.

But people *are* out, despite the chill, the hint of mizzle in the autumn air. Down in the town, a homeless man shuffles along the bank of the canal. It is shadowy here. From the bridge above, the reflection of a street light elongates, yellow and shimmering in the water, the amber glow of the moored-up gas-lit barges. He sleeps beneath the bridge these days, in a dirty Oxfam suit and a sleeping bag he found behind the pub where he used to drink. He doesn't go there or to the betting shop anymore. Even if he had any coins left to feed into the machines or buy himself a pint of bitter, they would drop through the holes in his tattered trouser pockets.

He is hungry. He is so hungry that, there on the towpath, he digs into the rubbish bin in the hope of finding some food. There are a few plastic bottles, fast-food containers, a half-eaten pasty, which he devours in three animal bites. The meat and pastry are cold and soggy with rain, but it tastes all right. Further in, an apple core, which he slips into his pocket. The rubbish piles up on the wet gravel. Almost at the bottom of the trash, a supermarket bag ignites a spark of hope. But in it are only writhing maggots, left by the fishermen who come here at weekends. In disgust, he throws it into the canal, where it floats, then fills, then sinks. If he were to dive in after that bag, those maggots, he might see the glint of a blade in the dark depths of the water, a knife lying flat on the canal bed. A Spanish hunting knife, the type you'd find in a tourist shop, unsheathed from its brown patterned leather case, washed clean of blood. But he doesn't dive in; why on earth would he? Instead, he carries on pulling out the litter, finding nothing more.

Leaving the scattered rubbish on the path, he shuffles back to his makeshift home and sits on the decrepit foldable picnic chair he salvaged from a skip and repaired with a coat hanger. Here under the bridge, at least it is dry. He lights the gas lamp one of the barge dwellers gave him for light and warmth, takes a fiery swig from his hip flask. From his breast pocket he plucks the front page of an old edition of the local newspaper, whose headline he reads most days, the name he knows as well as his own bones in bold black capitals above the picture of the woman whose almost daily cruelty crushed him up so tightly he has never been able to unfurl.

Ingrid Taylor given three life sentences.

He felt shock, yes, but not surprise when he first read that headline. What was a surprise was that Ingrid appeared to have had his friend Rachel, the barmaid from the Barley Mow, in her sights, had waged a hate campaign against her and driven her to a breakdown. He has no idea why she would do this, but he knows that she could – that she is capable. He knows that this was what she did to him. People like her leave bodies behind them on the road, literally and figuratively.

He folds the page back into its pre-made creases, returns it to his inside pocket and pats the neat square it makes over his heart.

Along the canal path, a couple of young lovers are taking a stroll, pointing out the group of coloured barges, there, where the canal breaks into a fork. They don't say hello. They don't see him. No one sees him.

At the other end of the canal, the sandstone railway bridge, black with soot, shudders under the beat of the train that speeds away towards Liverpool Lime Street. It is the same train a young woman catches on her way back to university after a visit home. She too is outside on this cold autumn night. She has taken a bus from her student lodgings to Sefton Park and now stands on the grass, surrounded by trees in the near pitch darkness. In her numb, gloveless fingers is a white sheet of A4: a typed letter, signed in biro. Her therapist told her to write letters during her anger-management counselling. Anger is common in grief – the girl knows this now. She knows too how it can inhabit a person, how it can turn to hate, how that hate will find a way out, no matter what. She and her mum have spoken about this. But she is not the girl she was back then. She doesn't know who that girl was, but it wasn't her.

There is no one about. No late-night walkers on the path that runs around the lake. But even so, she feels self-conscious at what she is about to do. It is time to fulfil a promise, her promise to a dead girl. She kneels on the damp grass and clears her throat.

'Dear Jo,' she whispers aloud, her throat already closing with tears. 'I am so, so sorry for what I did to you. If I could turn back time, I would. I was in a terrible place. My brother was everything to me, and when he was killed, my world fell apart. My family exploded and there was nothing left. My mum wouldn't speak to me, my dad was never there. I was so lonely, Jo, and I was so angry, but I know that doesn't excuse what I did. I only took the knife from the garage because I wanted to protect myself. After what happened to Kieron, I thought it would keep me safe. I was stupid, I was wrong. The thought of my beautiful brother on the wrong end of a knife that night and me using one on someone else, some other innocent person, is too horrible to think about. I can't stop thinking about it. I'm not saying I'm a victim. All I know is, every single day I think about how, if I hadn't taken that knife out with me, what happened would never have happened. I was so angry. And when I saw you talking to my mum, linking arms with her, laughing, I just freaked. I was jealous, raging. I was mad. I should never have come after you. I was only going to have a go at you for talking to my mum; I swear I never meant to hurt you. I only wanted to scare you and I don't even know why. I'd been drinking and I know I did scare you. I scared myself. But when I read that you'd died, I couldn't believe it. I still can't believe it. I know others were killed but I had nothing to do with those, I swear. But I'm so sorry for you. I'm sorry for your parents and everyone you loved and who loved you. Please forgive me, Jo. I am truly better now and I will never, ever carry a weapon with me as long as I live. I'd rather die than kill. I wish I could go back and change what I did, but I can't.

'Rest in peace, Jo.

'Yours, Katie.'

Crying violently now, she stands and digs out the cigarette lighter from her jeans pocket. A flick of the cog, and the flame licks at the corner of the paper, spreads quickly. At the last, she drops it to the wet grass, where it flashes, consumes itself and dies. A gust of wind sends it rolling, then dancing away in black, flaking wisps.

'Goodbye, Jo.'

She turns and walks slowly back to the pathway, her boots sucking at the soaked lawn. There is no one about. No one would see her if there were. She is lost in the darkness. Invisible.

A LETTER FROM
S.E. LYNES

Dear Reader,

Thank you so much for taking the time to read *Can You See Her?* My next book is well under way, and I hope you will want to read that one too. If you'd like to be the first to hear about my new releases, you can sign up using the link below. You can unsubscribe at any time and your email address will never be shared:

www.bookouture.com/se-lynes

This is my seventh novel, so if you are new to my work, hello, I hope you enjoyed this so much that you now want to read my back catalogue! If you have been reading me since my debut, *Valentina*, thank you for sticking with me – you're a trouper.

Many disparate elements go into the making of a book. The seed of *Can You See Her?* was found in an article on the invisibility of the older woman. Among other works of fiction quoted in the piece, *Mrs Dalloway* was mentioned. I had read this Virginia Woolf novel years ago, and on closer inspection, I found all sorts of relevant passages, not only on the invisibility of the older woman but on her intuitive power, the intimate embrace of death, time and the torture of hours passing, the 'thousand pities' of never saying what one feels, the deep need for communication… all sorts of ideas that related to what I was trying to do with Rachel. Principally I wanted to look at the menopausal years and ask whether or not it's really *all* about the hormonal shift or whether much of women's mental load could be made lighter. I certainly wanted to play my part in getting this subject into the open in a way that women could relate to and men could read about while being entertained.

I also wanted to put an empath at the heart of a psychological thriller for a change. The relationship between the predatory narcissist and the empath is well documented and a central trope of psychological thrillers; the challenge was to give credence to the idea that too much empathy, the erosion of personal boundaries, could, in extreme circumstances, become something obsessive and much, much darker. Whilst the reader is in no doubt that Ingrid is a 'wrong 'un', I wanted the reader to at least accept the possibility that Rachel could have become ill enough to be seeking the ultimate connection in the shared experience of death. In this story, the whodunnit was not the real mystery. The mystery was Rachel and how she could be brought to an understanding of herself, her grief and despair, which is where the sad and shocking twist lay.

As a parent of two grown-up kids who are always out and about in the city, I worry a lot about knife crime. I tend not to have a high body count in my books, but in this one it was unavoidable. Knife crime is an ongoing tragedy of our time and the sheer number of deaths, particularly among the young, is part of that tragedy. The double tragedy of the murdered/murderer siblings provided the last twist as well as a moment of dark symmetry. The real-life tragedy begins perhaps in the fact that our young people feel the need to arm themselves in the first place. But what emerged through the crafting of this story was what was really troubling me most deeply: namely the atmosphere of anger and hate that seems so pronounced at the time of writing. The idea of anger becoming hate and hate always being misdirected and never solving anything became a very important theme, and again there was a pleasing symmetry in a story about a woman misdirecting her love towards strangers when she could not find it at home. In a book full of water images, I liked the idea of the leak in the bathroom finding its outlet in the kitchen wall.

For *Can You See Her?* I have returned again to my home town, Runcorn, where I lived until I was eighteen and which formed much of who I am. I was married in the town hall featured in this book, spent much of my youth in the Red Admiral pub and the Cherry Tree disco, and if we ever got fish and chips, it was from the Langdale Road chippy, where we would run to catch it before it closed. I took some geographical liberties with St Michael's graveyard – coming from the Grange area of town, Rachel would have gone to a nearer chippy and she would not have had to park so far away and cross the cemetery to reach Langdale Road, but hey, I needed that scene.

I could go on and on, but if you enjoyed *Can You See Her?* I would be so grateful if you could spare a couple of minutes to write a review. It only needs to be a line or two and I would really appreciate it! I am always happy to chat via my Twitter account and Facebook author page if you wish to get in touch. I am happiest when answering questions about my work or hearing that what I have written has resonated with someone. Any writer knows that writing can sometimes be a lonely business, so when a reader reaches out and tells me my work has stayed with them or that they loved it, I am utterly delighted. I have loved making new friends online through my novels and hope to make more with *Can You See Her?*

Best wishes,
Susie

@selynesauthor
SE LynesAuthor

ACKNOWLEDGEMENTS

First thanks go, as ever, to my editor, Jenny Geras, who when I first proposed this idea said something along the lines of *yes, that – but not that*. Thanks for helping me transform a study of deterioration that broke my heart into a proper psychological thriller. Rachel was so fascinating to me that I'd quite forgotten to do that! Thanks to my agent, Veronique Baxter, for your enthusiasm for this character and her story and how it all came together and turned itself on its head at the end.

Thank you to my friend, talented photographer and supporter of all things artistic, Richard Kipping. Thank you for having the patience to take my author photo, the imagination to find that great location under the arches at Richmond and for getting me to stop goofing around for entire minutes while you made me look every inch the crime writer.

Thank you to the team at Bookouture, particularly Kim Nash and Noelle Holten, the amazing publicity duo, two phenomenally supportive women, friends, and fabulous authors in their own right. Kim is also my fellow champion cheese snaffler #1; it feels important to acknowledge this. Thanks to my copy-editor, Jane Selley, and my proofreader, Laura Kincaid.

Thanks to psychotherapist, Augusta Annesley, for advising on what kind of process a person suffering from menopausal psychosis would undergo. I used artistic licence to reduce the timings of Rachel's treatment in order to keep the narrative moving. Thanks also to Heather Geddes for psychological insight into why Rachel might be so triggered by her experience of invisibility.

Last time I wrote my acknowledgements it was for *The Lies We Hide*, a book I'd started over ten years ago and I barely knew where to start. I don't keep lists, have no filing system, but this time, I'd like to try and give a shout-out to some of my online supporters even though I usually avoid this because I know I will inevitably miss someone out and cause offence without meaning to.

Firstly, thanks to the not-so-secret secret Facebook book club TBC, run by the one and only Tracy Fenton. This club was my first online home when I published my debut, *Valentina*, in 2016, and was where I first realised, to my enduring wonder, that writing stories would connect me to people I had never even met. Thanks to the team: Helen Boyce, Claire Mawdesley (who *might* have a cameo role in this book), Juliet Butler, Charlie Pearson, Charlie Fenton, Kel Mason and Laurel Stewart. Thanks to Wendy Clarke and her team at Facebook's Fiction Café, Laura Pearson at Facebook's Motherload Book Club, Anne Cater at Book Connectors, Dee Groocock and the team at Book on the Positive Side and Mark Fearn at Book Mark! Thank you to all the online book clubs and the people who gather there to share their love of reading. If I've missed you out, I'm sorry, that's a mistake; I'm stressed about it even before I've realised I've done it, so do message me and I'll make sure to give you a wave in the next book, which I'm already writing as you read this.

At yet further risk of missing someone, and in no particular order, thanks to flag-waving readers Teresa Nikolic, Philippa McKenna, Karen Royle-Cross, Ellen Devonport, Frances Pearson, Jodi Rilot, CeeCee, Isobel Henkelmann, Sumaira Wilson, Audrey Gibson, Joan Hill, Bridget McCann, Moyra Irving, Alessandra Nolli, Anne Burchett, Audrey Cowie, Alison Turpin, Theresa Hetherington, Donna Young, Mary Petit, Donna Moran, Ophelia

Sings (whoever you are, your reviews make me cry), Gail Shaw, Lizzie Patience, Fiona McCormick, Alison Lysons and many more not named here. Thank you. I read every single review, good or bad.

Every now and again, someone seems to want to have a pop at bloggers, but bloggers are unpaid and work very hard spreading the word about the books they enjoy on account of their passion for reading, and I for one am very grateful for them. I would like to thank the following bloggers, using their blogging names in case you wish to check out their reviews: Chapter in my Life (hen!), By the Letter Book Reviews, Ginger Book Geek, Shalini's Books and Reviews, Fictionophile, Book Mark!, Biblophile Book Club, Random Things Through my Letterbox, B for Book Review, Nicki's Book Blog, Fireflies and Free Kicks, Bookinggoodread, My Chestnut Reading Tree, Donna's Book Blog, Emma's Biblio Treasures, Suidi's Book Reviews, Books from Dusk till Dawn, Audio Killed the Bookmark, Compulsive Readers, LoopyLouLaura, Once Upon a Time Book Blog, Literature Chick, Jan's Book Buzz, and Giascribes. If I have missed anyone, please let me know and I'll include you in my next book.

Thanks to my friends and family who have continued to read and review my books even though they don't need to: Elaine Binder, Sam Johnson, Laura Budd, Fiona Kelly, Alison Gaskins, Claire Gowers, Paul Gowers, Warwick Hampton-Woodfall, Jackie West, Katie West, Tracy May, Rachel McDowell, Hannah Droy, Fiona Audibert, Katie Lawrence, Nicky Dyer, Susie Donaldson, Elizabeth Bazalgette, Sue O Dea, Susy Smith, Helen stealer of fudge Barnett, Barbara Matthews, Nicky Andrews, Tara Munday, Louise Oliver, Mike Oliver, Gwen Lynes, Andrea Frost, Andrea Robinson, Sue Thornett, Madeleine Black, and my sister Jackie Ball.

Thank you to the tremendously supportive writing community, particularly Zoe Antoniades, Judith Baker, Anna Mansell, Barbara Copperthwaite, Pam Howes, Patricia Gibney, Jennie Ensor, Carla Buckley, Joel Hames-Clarke, Angela Marsons (Queen), Emma

Robinson (fellow champion cheese snaffler #2), Sue Watson (fellow champion cheese snaffler #3), Eva Jordan, Vikki Patis, Marilyn Messik, Heide Goody, Louise Mullins, Julie Cohen, Kate Simants, Louise Beech, Becca Mascull, Isabella May, Rona Halsall, Fiona Mitchell, Claire McGlasson, Callie Langridge, Tara (Cagney!) Lyons, Paul Burston, Lisa Timoney (whose witty reflections on the menopause in @lisatimoneywrites.com provided inspiration and after whom the character of Lisa Baxter is named), Catherine Morris, Hope Caton, Robin Bell, Adam Woods, Sam Hanson, Colette Lewis, Jayne Farnworth, and my friend and first-ever writing tutor, who always gets a special shout, Sara Bailey. I will definitely have missed someone out and I am already sorry, but please let me know and I'll shout you next time. I don't have a spreadsheet, I'm not made that way. This is a running theme, isn't it?

Finally, thanks to my first reader, my mum Catherine Ball, artist in her own right; Stephen Ball, who told me after reading my last book that one aerates the soil, one does not ventilate it – got it, Dad; my kids, Alistair, Maddie and Franci Lynes, whom I love more than my own life despite their inability to change a loo roll, and finally and as always, himself, Mr Susie, Paul Lynes. I'm sorry for living with make-believe people for a good portion of the time, and for having poor concentration when it comes to numbers and indie bands, but at least I'm always up for a pint and a packet of crisps, so every cloud…